DATE DUE

PRINTED IN U.S.A

The Summer's End

Center Point
Large Print

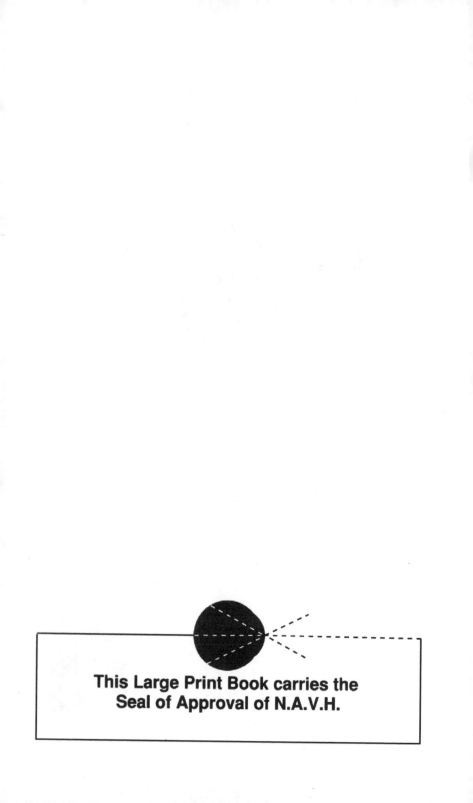

**This Large Print Book carries the
Seal of Approval of N.A.V.H.**

The Summer's End

MARY ALICE MONROE

CENTER POINT LARGE PRINT
THORNDIKE, MAINE

This Center Point Large Print edition is published in the year 2015 by arrangement with Gallery Books, a division of Simon & Schuster, Inc.

The text of this Large Print edition is unabridged. In other aspects, this book may vary from the original edition. Printed in the United States of America on permanent paper. Set in 16-point Times New Roman type.

ISBN: 978-1-62899-678-4

Library of Congress Cataloging-in-Publication Data

Monroe, Mary Alice.
  The summer's end / Mary Alice Monroe. —
    Center Point Large Print edition.
      pages cm
  Summary: "Three sisters bound by love for their grandmother and the timeless beauty and traditions of the lowcountry find the courage to face the future and decide the course of their lives as summer comes to an end"—Provided by publisher.
  ISBN 978-1-62899-678-4 (library binding : alk. paper)
  1. Large type books.
    2. Domestic fiction.
    3. Psychological fiction.
    I. Title.
PS3563.O529S89 2015b
813'.54—dc23
                                          2015020447

Dedicated to my daughters—
Claire Dwyer, Gretta Kruesi,
and Caitlin Kruesi.
You are my heroines.

ISLAND TIME
By Marjory Wentworth

Piercing the layers of night with flames
that melt the long hours before dawn,
the sun gently peels a shroud of fog
from the misted island. She embraces
the ripening surface of the earth,

where houses wrapped in sleep emerge from
    darkness
like hundreds of seeds scattered along roadsides.
Streetlights are still burning. Beneath them,
cars pass. Weary ships with passengers
given time to rearrange the memories of night,
as the day spreads itself before them
like an unwanted offering.
Each unfilled hour, ticking
ahead on the clock in their minds.

A woman rises from bed to sit
at her window and wait for daylight
to take hold of the world
spinning into place. She is
searching for a child, the ghost
of a child, a scrap, his small voice
in the wind, a carved smile
on the face of the moon—

just any familiar sign
from one of a billion stars.

And while shrimp boats glide out to sea
on the rows of first light, she watches
a dolphin caught in the marsh
swimming an endless circle

Excerpt from *Noticing Eden*,
Hub City Writers Project, 2003.
Printed with permission.

Chapter One

The dawn of another summer day. Mamaw tightened the soft cashmere throw around her thin shoulders. Slivers of light pierced the velvety blackness over the Cove, and pewter-colored shadows danced on the spiky marsh grass like ethereal ghosts.

Mamaw sat huddled on an oversize, black wicker chair on her back porch, her legs tucked beneath her. The fog was moist on her face and the predawn chill seemed to penetrate straight to her bones. She couldn't seem to get warm with Lucille gone. Since her dear friend's death, many nights she'd awakened from a fitful sleep and come outdoors hoping the fresh air would settle her. She'd found scant warmth or peace in the chill of predawn. In the distance, the Atlantic Ocean, her mercurial friend, roared like a hungry beast. The waves were devouring the dunes in a relentless rhythm. Echoes reverberated over Sullivan's Island.

Over a week had passed since Lucille's death. Yet she still felt her old friend's presence around her, hovering in death as she had in life. Dear Lucille. Death came to us all. She knew that. Mamaw was no stranger to death. At eighty years of age, she could hardly have been spared the loss of loved ones. She'd buried her parents, and, too early, her son and husband. Tonight she felt the past was more alive than the present. Memories of her loved ones played vividly in her mind.

Mamaw drew a long, ragged breath. From far away, she heard the mournful bellowing of a ship's foghorn. From a nearby tree, a bird began calling out his strident dawn whistles . . . a cardinal, she thought.

She listened, stirred from her lethargy by the dawn song. She watched as the morning light, in degrees, brightened the skyline, revealing the ragged tips of green sea grass, palm trees clustered on a hammock, and the towering Ravenel Bridge, appearing as two great sailing vessels, in the distance. Slowly, the rising sun illuminated the darkness, peeling away the shroud from her heart. She felt her despair dissipate with the mist. Mamaw said a prayer of thanks to the rising sun and took a deep breath of the cool, mud-scented air.

Another day was dawning. The worst was over.

Foolish old woman, she chided herself as the gray sky shifted to blue. *Look at yourself, sitting in the dark, mourning your friend. Wouldn't Lucille give you what for if she spied you moping like this outdoors in the damp chill, still in your nightclothes?* Who had time to lollygag? Their plan for the summer was not finished! She'd invited her three nearly estranged granddaughters to Sea Breeze in May—and they'd come. The first time they'd been together in over a decade. True, it had so far been a tumultuous summer of change and growth, ups and downs, joys and heartaches. But it was her triumph that they'd weathered the vicissitudes *together.* Eudora, Carson, and Harper had rediscovered the sisterly love they'd shared as children when they played together during the summers here on Sullivan's Island. Howling at the moon? She should be crowing like a rooster!

Yet, much was still to be done and she was running out of time. It was already August. The sea turtles were finishing another season, the children would be heading back to school, the ospreys would soon head south with the other migrating birds and butterflies. Summer's end was fast approaching. Soon, too, her Summer Girls would be leaving.

Mamaw felt a twinge of loss at just the thought. She would miss them—their sweet faces, their chatter, tears, laughter. The footfalls in the house, the drama, the hugs and kisses liberally offered. What a summer it had been!

Her smile slipped. Not only would her granddaughters leave in the fall. She, too, would be leaving Sea Breeze. Moving to a retirement home when Sea Breeze was sold. With her granddaughters and Lucille gone, she would, she thought with a shudder, be utterly alone.

Mamaw lowered her cheek to her palm. She at

least knew where she would go at summer's end, but where would her girls go? Each of the women was unsure of what her next step would be when she left the safe embrace of Sea Breeze. Dora's divorce was pending, Carson was pregnant, and Harper was, for lack of a better term, completely adrift.

"Ah, Lucille," she said aloud to the presence she felt hovering in the pearly light. "You were the one who always rallied me in my dark moments. We lured them here. And there is still much yet to do to finish our plan." She sighed. "I don't know if I can do it alone. But I must try."

Mamaw's eyes rose to the sky, where great shafts of pink and blue continued to break through the horizon. A smile eased across her face. The moon might be gone, she thought. But the sun was rising on another day.

In another room of Sea Breeze, Harper lay on her bed in the steely light, her hands tucked beneath her head, listening to the mighty roar of the ocean. How loud the sound of the waves was this morning, she thought. The echoes reverberated in the still night. She thrilled to the sound, so different from what she was accustomed to in the city.

In New York, Harper awoke to the blare of police sirens, honking horns, and banging garbage trucks. So much was different here. *She* was different here. Over the past few months since she'd arrived on Sullivan's Island, her body had slowly acclimated from the fast pace and sense of urgency she experienced in the city to the slower, quieter rhythm of the lowcountry. She no longer went out to parties or bars until late at night, nor did she charge out of bed in the morning at the sound of an alarm. At Sea Breeze her days were ruled by the sun. Early to bed, early to rise.

Harper smiled, wondering if she'd ever foreseen how much she'd enjoy this lifestyle. No, she didn't think she had. In fact, initially she had quite dreaded the prospect of spending time at Sea Breeze this summer. She recalled her outrage when, only a few days after her and her sisters' arrival, Mamaw had announced her true intentions: that the women stay the entire summer. Harper stretched languidly while the light brightened to give the room a pearly glow. As she turned to her side to look out the window, her hand brushed against something. Surprised, she sat up to investigate. Sheets of paper lay strewn across her bed and scattered on the floor.

She rubbed her eyes as understanding took hold. Her book . . .

She must've fallen asleep while reading her manuscript, she realized, yawning. She rose from her bed and gathered the two-hundred-some sheets into a pile, taking her time to put the pages in order. As she did, her eyes reread a sentence here and there. Not bad, she thought to herself. The emotions in the words felt true. Then again, she was a biased judge. Her mother had made it brutally clear when she was just a girl that she didn't have talent. Just like her father, her mother had said dismissively, waving away Harper's fledgling attempts at short stories and poems. Her mother was a renowned editor, so Harper had taken her words as fact. Those fateful words still stung, even after decades.

Since then, Harper hadn't shown her writing to anyone. She'd pursued a career as an editor, discovering she had a talent in assisting others with their stories, with taking their innermost thoughts and putting them onto the page.

Yet she'd found editing others' words didn't bring her the same satisfaction as writing her own. So she'd continued writing—in her room, in coffee shops, on trains—in secret. Like a sinful pleasure she could indulge in when she wanted to dish out her anger or amusement. Not until this summer, this block of time she'd given herself without interruption—or rather, the time that Mamaw had thrust upon her, not taking no for an answer—had Harper decided to write a book. A whole body of work with a beginning, a middle, and an end. She would never know whether she could actually write a book until she'd finished one. And, she thought, picking up the papers in her hands, she was nearly done.

Harper rose and placed the manuscript on her desk, resting her hands on the pile of papers, overcome with a sense of ownership and pride.

Her book.

Her sisters thought she'd been taking the summer off, shamelessly idle while they scrambled to find jobs and apartments. True, she'd been enjoying her break at Sea Breeze, gardening, swimming, talking with her sisters, and roaming the far ends of the island. But she'd been privately working, too. She didn't dare tell anyone about it, because if she did, she knew they'd want to read it.

No, she thought, slipping the manuscript into the desk drawer. She would keep her manuscript all to herself. She wasn't as outgoing as her sister Carson, who was quick-witted and clever. Nor was she as bold as her eldest sister, Dora, who had strong opinions on every subject, even when unasked. Harper expressed herself best on paper.

And, she thought with a rueful smile, her sisters wouldn't be pleased to learn that she was writing about them.

Outside her window she heard the strident dawn whistles of a bird singing in a nearby tree. She paused to listen, wondering what kind of bird it was that awakened her most mornings. She vowed to find out. She wanted to learn the names of the birds and the trees and the plants of this island that she'd come to love. She'd spent all of her twenty-eight years in beautiful places—her mother's fashionable apartment overlooking Central Park in New York City, the house in the Hamptons, and her grandparents' manor house in England. Not to mention the exclusive boarding schools and Ivy League college she'd attended. But nowhere did she feel so at home or content, or as much herself, as she did here in the lowcountry, by the ocean, at Sea Breeze.

She'd be leaving soon.

The thought came unbidden and struck a chord of sadness in the morning's sweet music. Harper went to the window and opened the wooden slats of the plantation shutter to peer out. Pale gray light illuminated the shadows. Carson was always nattering on about how glorious it was to be out on the water when the dawn exploded over the ocean. How it was her favorite time of the day. Carson could be so passionate about anything connected to water.

Harper suddenly felt a stirring to witness that sight for herself. Why not now? she asked herself. Before it was too late. What was she waiting for?

She quickly slipped into a swimsuit and denim shorts. Laced up her running shoes. As quietly as the mouse she was nicknamed after, she slipped open the sliding door that separated her bedroom from her grandmother's. It rattled on the track, and grimacing, she paused. She didn't hear Mamaw stir in her dark bedroom. Harper tiptoed quickly across the carpet, closing the door behind her.

The house was quiet, everyone still asleep in the wee morning hour. Even Carson, who, for all her talk, had begun sleeping in after announcing her pregnancy. Making good her escape, Harper flew out the front door, aware that the sun waited for no man or woman. She was met with cool and sweet-tasting morning air. The wind that had roiled the ocean all night had chased away the humidity and heat, leaving the morning air unusually refreshing for August. In the quiet, all sounds were amplified. Above her, the leaves of the great oak tree rustled in the breeze and the palm fronds rattled. Beneath her feet the gravel crunched loudly as she hurried across the drive-way to the garage. The rusty, trusty old bicycle leaned against the wall. She pulled it out from the garage, swung her leg over the seat, and took off.

Despite her twenty-eight years, Harper felt no older than thirteen as she pedaled furiously along the streets. The neighboring houses appeared blanketed in the shadows, their occupants still asleep in the hush over the island. Only a few feral cats darted soundlessly across the roads. She hadn't seen as many of them clustering on the island this summer as she remembered from her girlhood summers spent at Sea Breeze. People said it was the coyotes. She kept her eyes peeled as she pushed on along the muted street. Past Stella Maris Catholic Church, with its hallowed steeple. Past the ominous, giant molelike burrows of Fort Moultrie. Past the tight cluster of restaurants, shuttered now and deserted. Only a few joggers and an occasional automobile shared the road with her.

At last she reached the northern tip of the island, where Carson had told her the surfers gathered. She turned off Middle Street toward the sea. Several cars, all with roof racks for surfboards, crowded the narrow side streets. Harper pushed the wheels of her bike through the soft sand of the path past the tall barrier of shrubs. The surf was unusually loud this morning. When at last the path opened up to the beach, she stopped to catch her breath.

The dusky blue sky and gray sea came together to form one infinite horizon line. The sun did not rush to her glory. She rose at her own pace, imperious, radiant, bursting in her display of achingly beautiful pastels that were reflected on the water. Harper felt small in the presence of a view so profound. Yet at the same time, she felt connected to it. Empowered to be part of this godlike perpetuity. In that dazzling moment she felt the glistening light enter her soul to fill her with hope. Harper understood at last why Carson so loved this moment, had risen early to catch it day after day. It truly was spiritual.

Harper clutched the handlebars of her beach

cruiser tight. The new day was spread out before her like a blank page, ready for her to fill with her words, thoughts, feelings. She'd given herself this one summer to discover—at long last—what *she* wanted to do with her life. No longer would she continue meekly following what *her mother* had planned.

She didn't know what her future would bring. Standing in the glow of the rising sun, Harper was filled with a tingling sensation that her future was only just beginning.

The sea was calling her. Carson lay in the dim light of her bedroom listening to the incessant roar of her old friend the ocean. It was rare for the waves to come in hard, as they were now. When they did, Carson had always grabbed her board and gone to the water. It was in her nature to do so. Salt water ran in her veins.

Carson didn't jump from her bed this morning, however. She continued to lie still, her palms resting on her abdomen. She no longer was free to follow her whims. No longer the fearless surfer or world traveler, able to pick up and leave when she wished.

She let her fingers gently stroke her belly, still flat despite the life growing beneath the taut skin. So much for her womanly intuition. It had taken the echolocation of one very intuitive dolphin to tell her she was pregnant.

"Oh, baby," she crooned. "What am I going to do with you? I'm not married, I don't have a job, I don't even have my own place to live. How am I going to take care of you?"

She brought to mind her last conversation with Lucille, the night she'd died. Carson had been struggling with what to do about the pregnancy and went to Lucille to sit at her knee, as she had so many times growing up, and once more ask for advice. Lucille hadn't told her what to do. That wasn't her style. Instead, the old woman guided Carson's thoughts to find her own answer. Carson would never forget her words.

You've got good instincts. Listen to them. Trust them. You'll know what to do.

Carson knew Lucille was right. When she was surfing, Carson had to trust her instincts on the wave, to know when to step left or right. It was all a matter of balance.

She had to listen to her instincts now. It didn't make sense for her to have a baby now. All her rational arguments were against it. But over the rational thoughts her instincts spoke loud and clear. That and her raging hormones, she thought with a snort. Lying on the bed, listening to the echoing sound of the waves rolling to the shore, Carson knew she had to ride this wave home.

"Well, baby," she said, patting her tummy, "it's me and you now. I'm not running away."

● ● ●

Dora's arm shot out to silence the alarm clock. She groggily opened one eyelid: 7:00 a.m.

"Rise and shine," she mumbled.

Dora moved in a stupor, accustomed to the routine. She dressed quickly in running clothes, splashed cool water on her face, applied SPF moisturizer, then did a few stretches. This past summer she'd learned that she had to get her exercise done first thing in the morning, because if she waited, she'd slip into a thousand lame excuses why she didn't have time. She'd learned to make time for the things that mattered to her.

And nothing mattered more to her than her son.

Dora swiftly walked down the hall and gingerly pushed open the door to Nate's room. She wrinkled her nose at the stuffy, closed-in smell. Nate, unlike the rest of the inhabitants of Sea Breeze, did not like to sleep with his windows open. He was adamant about his likes and dislikes, quick to let you know if something was right or, more often, wrong. She went to the side of his bed and stood for a moment, staring into her nine-year-old son's face.

Her heart bloomed with love for him. Did a child ever look more angelic than when asleep? she wondered. Nate's long, pale lashes fluttered against his cheeks. His lips were slightly parted as he breathed heavily. He was small for his age, but his thin frame had filled out this summer at Sea Breeze and his skin glowed with a tan. Sea Breeze had been so good for Nate, on many levels. He loved the water now. Dora smiled. She called him her little fish. As her eyes hungrily roamed his face, she noted that his shaggy blond hair needed a trim, and she made a mental note to take him to the barber. It would be a fight, she thought with a sigh. Nate hated to have his hair cut.

Poor little guy, she thought as she reached out to gently stroke hair from his forehead. She felt the perspiration at his brow. Cutting his hair was the least of the changes he'd be facing soon. Her obstinate, fretful son who hated any change would soon transition from homeschooling to a classroom. It was a big decision, long and hard in coming. She'd found a private school that specialized in bright children with special needs, like his Asperger's. The school offered highly individualized instruction and schoolwide positive behavioral support. Dora had to face the reality that Nate was older and needed more than she could offer. He needed to learn to communicate and socialize with his peers.

Dora sighed. They both did. Isolation had not been good for either of them.

On the heels of this decision was her intention to move to Mt. Pleasant, closer to the school. A new school . . . a new home . . .

She bent to gently kiss Nate's cheek, breathing

in the scent of him. When he was awake, he didn't like to be kissed.

"We'll be fine," she whispered close to his ear. "Mama's here. I won't let you down."

As Harper pedaled back to Sea Breeze, her mind filled with words that could capture that glorious sunrise: *iridescent, shimmering, glittering, ethereal, inspiring* . . . Harper parked the bike in the garage and hurried toward the house, eager to slip quietly back into her bedroom and begin writing. She wanted to describe what she'd seen and her feelings that had swirled like brilliant colors. As she made her way across the back porch, a cough drew her attention. Harper turned her head to the back corner of the porch and was surprised to see her grandmother sitting tall and straight-backed in one of the large, black wicker chairs. In the dim light, wearing her long, white cotton nightgown, Mamaw appeared almost ghostly.

"Mamaw!" Harper exclaimed. "What are you doing out here?"

Mamaw smiled as Harper approached, but it was a tired smile. Her pale blue eyes were sunken and her arms were wrapped around her slender body as though she were chilled.

"I couldn't sleep. I woke very early and my mind kept wandering." Mamaw shook her head. "It's so exhausting when that happens. A curse of old age. I just gave up and came out here to sit a spell. I thought the fresh air might help."

On the glass-topped table Harper saw a line of playing cards. Her heart pinged. Mamaw was playing solitaire. The image of Mamaw and Lucille playing endless games of gin rummy together on the porch at all hours of the day and night flashed in Harper's mind.

Harper hurried to put her arms around her grandmother's shoulders. "How long have you been out here?" she asked, alarmed. "You're chilled to the bone." She rubbed Mamaw's arms briskly with her hands, trying to warm her.

"Mmm . . . that's nice. Thank you, dear."

Harper pulled up a chair and dropped into it. She leaned forward, elbows resting on her knees. "What's got your mind wandering?"

"Oh . . . I was thinking of Lucille," Mamaw said wistfully.

Of course, Harper thought.

"It was a nice funeral, wasn't it?" Mamaw asked.

"It was. I'd never been to a Gullah funeral before. So much song, tears, and rejoicing."

"And *amens*," Mamaw added wryly.

Harper smiled in agreement. She'd been moved by the unrestrained calling out at the service, the passion, the strong sense of community.

Mamaw looked back out over the water. "I was sitting here, looking across the Cove, and it brought to mind what the preacher talked about at Lucille's service. How their ancestral spirits who came to the lowcountry—those by force and those who came after—lived, thrived, and died here. They worked hard, cooked rice, cast nets for shrimp, raised children, and now they've all moved on to the bounty of the afterlife. That's what Lucille believed, you know. She was tired at the end, I daresay looking forward to crossing the water." Mamaw sighed, remembering. "I confess, lately I might be ready, too."

Harper leaned forward to grasp Mamaw's hand. "Don't go yet. We still need you."

Mamaw's lips slipped into a wobbly smile, briefly, then fell again. "I'm having a hard time believing she's really gone."

"It all happened so fast." Harper also felt deep sorrow at Lucille's swift battle with cancer.

Mamaw looked at Harper. "Do you believe in an afterlife?" she asked pointedly.

Harper released Mamaw's hand, leaned back, and scratched her head, thinking this was a heavy conversation to have before a first cup of coffee. She'd never warmed to the idea of a God that rewarded the good with heaven and the others with an eternity of brimstone and fire. It seemed so unforgiving. Still, after much soul-searching, she'd come to believe there was a higher being. She'd felt a connection to that infinite power this morning while staring out at the sunrise.

"I guess so," she said with hesitancy. "I don't think much about it."

Mamaw smiled ruefully. "You're young. You think you're immortal. When you get to my age, you'll think about it . . . a lot."

"I don't like to see you out here alone, playing solitaire and thinking of death. It's a tad morbid."

"I'm not feeling the least bit morbid. Quite the opposite." Mamaw patted Harper's hand with a weary smile. "Death is becoming an old friend."

Harper rose and tugged gently on Mamaw's arm. "Come inside and I'll make you a nice breakfast. Something warm."

Mamaw resisted, leaning back in her chair. "I'm not hungry. I've just got the dwindles."

"How about I bring you a nice hot cup of coffee?"

Mamaw perked up at the suggestion. "Well, I wouldn't say no to that."

"Coming right up." Harper paused. Mamaw was always an elegant woman who took great care with her appearance. She had been a leading Charleston socialite known for her extravagant parties as much as her polished beauty. To see Mamaw sitting on the porch still in her night-clothes, her white hair flowing unbrushed, wrapped up in a coverlet like a bag lady, shook Harper to the core. This was an outward sign of the state of Mamaw's mind.

Harper made a bold suggestion: "Mamaw, while I make coffee, why don't you get dressed?"

Mamaw turned her head to deliver a stern face with a brow raised. "I beg your pardon?"

Harper rushed on, "Don't you remember, you used to tell us how Thomas Jefferson wrote his eleven-year-old daughter letters on deportment from France? He admonished her to always rise and dress promptly. Neat and clean and tidy." Harper paused, pleased to see her grandmother was listening. "You told us your mother read you his letters, and you read them to us. Why, if you caught us lying about in our jammies, you sent us straight to our rooms to get dressed."

"I'm delighted to learn you paid attention." Mamaw offered her hand in a regal manner. Harper took it and helped Mamaw to her feet. "Very well. The sun is up and so I should rise with it. It is, to paraphrase Scarlett O'Hara, another day."

Chapter Two

The kitchen was as quiet as a tomb.

Here, in the kitchen, Lucille's absence was most felt. Every morning during Harper's childhood summers spent on the island, she'd wander sleepyheaded into the kitchen to be greeted by the clanging of pots, the smell of coffee, biscuits in the oven, bacon sizzling on the stove, and a hearty hello from Lucille. The comparative silence now caused an ache deep in her chest.

Harper stood at the threshold and looked at the dimly lit, empty room through her pragmatist eyes, not clouded by the blur of nostalgia. It was the classic kitchen found in a house that once held a staff. It had what people in real estate called good bones. The room was big, with windows that overlooked the Cove. A butler's pantry with glass-front cabinets separated the kitchen from the dining room. It was all charming, if outdated. To her, the room was like a vintage dress that needed a good cleaning and maybe a new zipper.

The once-butter-colored walls now appeared rancid, and the appliances were terribly out-of-date. Harper frowned to see dirty dishes in the sink and, on the long wood table, an empty package of fig cookies, crumbs scattered. Wouldn't Lucille claim she was going to "look for a switch" if she saw the state of her normally spotless kitchen?

Harper entered the empty room, wrinkling her nose at the smell of bitter coffee grinds and day-old garbage. She tossed the cold filter, then went to the sink for water to make a fresh pot of coffee. As she lifted the sponge in the sink, out from under it skittered an enormous brown cockroach. Harper screamed, dropped the coffeepot into the sink, and leaped back. The commotion sent the enormous bug flying past her head.

Dora came running into the room, her eyes wide and searching. "Harper? Are you all right?"

"Yes," Harper said breathlessly, her hand over her pounding heart.

"You screamed bloody murder!"

"I just saw the biggest cockroach. At least I . . . I think it was a cockroach. I swear . . . it *flew* past me!"

Dora's face shifted as she burst out laughing.

"It's not funny," Harper fired back, sourly eyeing Dora in her perky running outfit with her blond hair pulled back in a ponytail. Ironically, Harper had been the runner out of the three sisters at the beginning of the summer, but since Dora had taken up regular exercise, she'd been—literally—on Harper's heels.

Her older sister only leaned against the doorframe and laughed harder.

Carson rushed into the room looking as if she'd leaped from her bed. She was in her pajamas and her long, dark hair was loose down her back. "What happened?" Her eyes were wide with alarm. "Is anyone hurt?"

Dora muffled her laugh and waved her arm in a calming gesture. "No cause for alarm." She caught Carson's eye and added with a smirk, "Harper saw a palmetto bug."

"Not *just* a bug," Harper said in self-defense. "It was as big as a rat."

A smile of genuine amusement spread across

Carson's face. "Ah, so our little sister's met our state bird?"

The laughter erupted again.

Harper didn't enjoy being the butt of their lowcountry jokes. Though the three half sisters shared the same father, each had a different mother and they'd thus grown up in different parts of the country. Carson was raised in California, Dora in the Carolinas; and Harper in New York. They loved to tease their Yankee sister about her city ways and her unfamiliarity with all things southern.

"If you're so familiar with them, go catch it," she challenged sullenly.

"I'm not going after that thing." Dora shook her head. "I always send a man after that. They're the hunters, right? My job is to jump on a chair and scream."

"Don't look at me," Carson said.

"I thought you were nature girl," Harper said.

"I'll take a shark any day over one of those critters. But I think Mamaw has one of Papa Edward's hunting guns. You could shoot the thing."

Dora joined Carson in a renewed bout of laughter.

Over the past months working in the garden, Harper had become all too familiar with the wildlife that teemed in the lowcountry—insects, anoles, frogs, snakes. She'd learned to deal with them, but she didn't think she'd ever get used to their jumping out at her. Once, she was pulling weeds from the grasses in her garden when a snake shot straight out from the grass. Lucille had told her the grasses were a favorite hiding place for snakes, which is why the basket weavers always had their men go fetch the sweetgrass for them.

"I think I'd rather face a poisonous snake than a palmetto bug," Harper said. "But I'm not about to be made a laughingstock by no friggin' roach." She grabbed a thick wad of paper towels, set her jaw, and marched with purpose to the sink, where she thought she'd seen the bug land.

"What are you doing?" Dora asked.

"What do you think I'm doing?"

Her sisters watched as she went to the sink and, with an outstretched arm, poised to leap back, nudged the dirty pot. Then the sponge. Suddenly the bug bolted. But not fast enough. Harper pounced and heard a gross pop that had her stomach reeling. In a rush she dispatched the bug to the trash. When she turned back to her sisters, she saw with great satisfaction the look of shock mixed with awe on their faces.

"Don't throw it out," Carson said. "You should cut off its head and wings and stake them around the perimeter of the house as a warning to all the other bugs out there to what happens if they come inside."

Dora laughed. "Good one."

"I'll tell you what's *not* funny"—Harper frowned—"the state of this kitchen." She waved her arm, indicating the dishes and food scraps on the table, then the sink overflowing with dishes. "Dirty dishes left in the sink, crumbs on the table. No wonder we have bugs." She shook her head. "Lucille must be rolling over in her grave."

Dora and Carson were immediately chastened. They gazed around the kitchen with somber expressions.

"It's not only the kitchen," Harper said. "There's a film of dust on all the furniture. Dust bunnies on the floor."

"Mamaw had to cancel the cleaning crew," Dora said. "She said she had to cut back. All of us living here, eating her food, using her hot water, has really upped her monthly expenses."

"Not to mention the bedrooms she created for us," Harper added.

Dora shook her head. "We're still acting like those little girls who used to come here in the summer. All we did was play and eat and fight and think of ourselves. We didn't do a lick of work, not really. And here we are, doing the same thing. Only we aren't little girls anymore, are we?"

Harper walked to the table and lifted the nearly empty carton of cookies. "Okay, who ate all the cookies and just left the package out, crumbs and all?"

With her long hair flying Carson looked like an

Amazon princess on the warpath as she stomped to Harper to snatch the carton from her hands. She took out the final fig cookie and popped it into her mouth. "I'm sorry," Carson snapped. "I was hungry. Hey, I'm pregnant. Didn't you ever hear of midnight cravings? It happens."

Harper looked at Carson's abdomen and wondered again how a baby could be growing inside that flat, taut belly.

Dora said, "We don't care about you eating the cookies. Eat as many as you want. Just clean up after yourself! We're not your maids. Besides, it's not just Carson making a mess. It's all of us."

Carson looked at her older sister. "You're right, of course. We can't expect Mamaw to take care of us. Nor should she. We should be taking care of her."

"Amen," Dora said.

"I wanted to talk to you about that," Harper said, warming to the topic. "I'm worried about her. Want to guess where I found her this morning?" She paused, watching them shake their heads with curiosity. "Sitting on the porch. Playing solitaire."

Dora's mouth opened in a silent gasp.

Carson looked stricken. "Playing solitaire? That's just too sad."

"She even asked me if I believed in an afterlife."

"No . . . ," Carson breathed.

"Bless her heart," Dora said with a sorry shake of her head.

Harper continued, "She's having a hard time with Lucille being gone."

"Lucille doted on Mamaw," Dora said. "And when Lucille got sick, Mamaw doted on her. I 'spect she's lonelier than God right now."

"She shouldn't sit around all alone," said Carson. "Maybe we can think of things to do with her. Get her out of the house."

"We can go on a shopping trip to Charleston," suggested Dora. "Then have tea at Charleston Place. Maybe a little champagne. Girl stuff. She'd like that."

"We can play gin rummy with her, like Lucille did," said Carson. "Mamaw loves to play cards."

"I don't know how to play gin rummy," said Harper.

"It's easy. I can teach you." Carson's voice quickened with excitement. "How about we all play cards together, like we used to in the summers when we were little? I loved that. What was the name of the game we played . . . ?"

"Canasta!" said Dora, her eyes gleaming.

"Yes, that's it!" Carson said.

"I don't remember how to play that, either," said Harper. "Anyone know bridge?"

Carson shook her head. "It's got to be canasta . . ."

"Or hearts. We played that, too," Dora added with authority.

"Hold on," Harper interjected. "Before we start

playing, can we talk about working? We have to divvy up the chores."

"Right." Carson gave a military salute and smirked as she walked to the small desk. "Since when did you become the little general?" She rummaged through the drawers. "We can make a schedule, like I made for Nate in Florida."

Dora called after her, "I don't think we need drawings of stick figures, suns, and moons."

"Ha-ha," Carson quipped, returning to the table, hands filled with supplies. "Okay, I've got some paper, markers, pens." She pulled out a chair and sat, spreading the materials in front of her with enthusiasm. "You two muddle about who does what. I'll make the chart."

Dora caught Harper's eye and they smiled. It was amusing to see the freewheeling Carson get behind something as orderly and routine as a schedule.

"I'll make coffee." Harper headed to the sink with renewed purpose. "I'm no good making any decisions without my caffeine jolt." Harper approached the sink hesitantly and plucked up the sponge with two fingers. She looked over her shoulder to see her sisters watching.

They burst out with renewed laughing.

"It's not funny!" But this time Harper laughed as well.

"I'll pass on the coffee," said Carson, patting her abdomen. "Makes me nauseous."

"Would you bring a cup up to Mamaw?" Harper asked. "I sent her to her room to get dressed. Poor thing was just lying about in her night-clothes."

Carson's face registered shock. "Really? Damn, she must be seriously out of sorts. Let's do this."

After Harper made coffee, Dora cleared the long wood table and wiped away the crumbs. Soon, steaming mugs were on the table, and a stack of raisin toast. The scent of coffee and cinnamon filled the air as the three women sat together and began making plans. First they created a formal schedule of chores to be done daily and those to be done weekly. Allocating the workload took a little more time as they argued about who did what chore best. Finally they set up a schedule for cooking meals and shopping. In the end, no one complained. Harper felt buoyed by the sisterly cooperation.

As they worked, they reminisced about the meals Lucille had prepared, the homespun advice she'd offered, and laughed at the shared anecdotes. Harper thought to herself how talking about Lucille kept her memory alive in their hearts and memories. When the schedule was finished, they posted it on the fridge with magnets and stood back to admire it.

"I don't think there's anything on that schedule that will help organize my life," Carson said with a rueful grin. "But at least the house will be clean."

"I hear you," Harper added, and the two women clinked mugs.

"Speaking of schedules." Dora carried her mug to the sink. "I hate to throw a wrench in our newly laid plans, but I don't know how much longer I'll be on your work team."

"Why not?" Carson swung her head around.

Dora set her coffee mug on the counter and took a deep breath. "Well, I've made some decisions."

Her sisters sat staring at her silently with rapt attention.

"I'm not moving back to Summerville. I've decided to stay close by. Mt. Pleasant probably."

"Nate will be happy," Carson said. "He loves the water."

"Nate's the main reason I'm staying."

"And Devlin . . . ," added Carson mischievously.

Dora laughed in acknowledgment. "Him, too. But . . . the main reason is that I've found a school for Nate. It starts next week."

The announcement was met with surprised silence.

Harper was delighted with the news but had to ask, "You're not homeschooling anymore?"

Dora shook her head and turned to the sink. She squirted soap into it and turned on the hot water. Water gushed through the faucet as the sink filled.

"No. I've decided to send Nate to the Trident Academy. It's a private school that has a wonderful program for children with Asperger's syndrome." Dora turned off the tap and turned to face her sisters. "I've given this a lot of thought. It's time for Nate to mingle with other children. And it's time for me to get out more, too." Dora picked up the sponge and studied it. "So I've begun looking for a place in Mt. Pleasant, and let me tell you, it's hard to find a rental I can afford."

"Aren't you worried about all these changes for Nate? All at once?" asked Harper.

"Of course I am." Dora's face was troubled. "Leaving Sea Breeze, a place he loves, to move into a strange place will be tough for Nate. But on top of that, he'll be starting a new school, a whole new program." Dora turned back to the sink and began to wash dishes with vigor. "That's why I need to get him settled in a permanent place as soon as possible. We all know how difficult transitions are for him."

Harper rose to collect the dishes from the table and carry them to the sink. "How can we help?"

Dora returned a grateful look. "Just asking him about it, bringing the school up in conversation, reminding him how many days till school begins. That kind of thing. We just have to get him used to the idea so it's not a sudden shock. He'll have a tour of the school at the end of the week. I'm hoping Cal will join us for that."

"Cal supports your decision?" Carson opened a drawer to grab a towel. "That's a switch."

"You know Cal. He's got to feel in control."

"What does control mean in this scenario?"

"He put up a fuss initially about the cost of tuition." Dora handed Carson a wet dish. "It's high. There's no sugarcoating that. But when I told him that I was getting a job to pay for half the tuition, he quieted down. Now he can tell everyone how he's such a good father, putting his son through private school." Dora made a face. "That wasn't very nice, was it?"

"Just honest," Carson quipped. "Are you looking to buy or rent?"

"Lord, I can't afford to buy a birdhouse until my divorce is settled and the house in Summerville sells. It's all kind of scary, but also exciting." Dora laughed shortly. "I'm thirty-eight, and for the first time in my life I'm getting my own place." Dora pulled the plug in the sink and, turning, grabbed the towel from Carson.

Harper saw a new confidence in Dora's face. "You sound happy."

Dora snorted and dried her hands briskly. "I think that's hysteria you're seeing." Her arm dropped and the towel hung limp from her hands. "It's not a happy thing to go through a divorce. Ten years of marriage . . ." She snapped her fingers. "Over. There's a world of hurt mixed up in all of this. But," she said with an optimistic tone, "it's a new start. The end of a long period of unhappiness."

"I'm proud of you, Sis," Carson said.

"I've a lot to do in a hurry. Seems to be my mantra lately. At least I can carpool to the school from here without trouble till I find a place." Dora looked around the room. "Thank God for Mamaw and Sea Breeze. It's been all of our saving grace. But the sale of this house is imminent. We all have to face the fact we've got to move."

There followed a long silence.

Dora tossed the towel on the counter and turned to Harper. "What about you? Where are you headed at summer's end?"

"Don't know yet," Harper answered evasively, leaning back against the counter. Inside, her thoughts were roiling. She'd been searching the Internet for possible editorial positions, writing, all the while keeping physically busy in the garden. Nothing she could report. Certainly nothing as life changing as Carson's baby or Dora's moving forward in her life, full steam ahead. "Still figuring things out."

"Everything okay?"

"Everything is copacetic." Harper forced a noncommittal grin.

Dora turned her questioning gaze to Carson.

Carson held up her hands like a shield. "It's free rent. I'm staying here for as long as I can."

Harper thought that sounded defeatist. "Any luck on the job front?"

"There's not a big demand for a stills photographer in Charleston," Carson added sarcastically. Then more seriously: "I'm knocking on everyone's door in LA but nothing's turned up yet. I've called everyone I know, and I mean everyone. It's embarrassing. But I need to get *something*. I'm not kidding when I say the coffers are empty."

"I could lend you some money," Harper hesitantly offered. She averted her gaze. The subjects of her wealthy family and her trust fund were touchy between her and Carson.

"Thanks, Sis, but no. I don't want to feel beholden to you. Our relationship is too important to me to risk."

Harper could appreciate that. She glanced back at Carson with a sly smile. "How about I pay you for a job?"

Carson cocked her head. "Like what?"

Harper considered. "Like surfing. I've always wanted to learn. I could pay you up front for a series of lessons. How does that sound?"

"I'd love to," Carson replied soberly. "But surfing isn't exactly recommended for pregnant women. In case you forgot . . ." She motioned toward her belly.

"But I thought—" Dora blurted.

Carson sent Dora a level gaze. "You thought what?"

Harper heard the cold challenge and tensed, fearing the abortion argument between conserva-

41

tive Dora and liberal Carson would erupt again.

Harper jumped in the fray. "She thought, as I did, that you'd decided not to have the baby."

Carson's face was difficult to read. "I wasn't aware that I'd decided anything."

"Oh." Harper picked up her mug and took a quick sip.

An awkward silence followed, a sharp contrast to the easy banter of only moments earlier.

Carson's face changed, seeing her sisters' confusion. "I went to talk with Lucille, the night she died."

"You did?" Dora tilted her head to catch every word. "What did you talk about?"

"Oh, we talked about a lot of things. Mamaw, Blake, the baby . . ." Carson looked at her sisters. "You two."

They chuckled and muttered comments about what might have been said.

Carson added, "It seems like it was just last night."

Dora sighed in commiseration. "I know. I miss her terribly. So does Nate." She turned to Carson, truly interested. "So what did Lucille tell you?"

"She didn't tell me what to do. That wouldn't be her style. It was an emotional evening. I was teary and she was consoling." Carson shook her head in disbelief. "She was the one dying, and she was consoling me."

"That was Lucille," said Dora.

"Lucille told me how she used to watch me surf." Carson picked at her nail, trying to keep her voice level. "All these years and I never knew that."

"Sounds like something she'd do," said Dora.

"She and Mamaw both. We talked about the waves, and how when she watched me, she could tell that I knew instinctively how to move, where to place my feet to keep balance. She told me to remember that I had good instincts. And that I had to trust them. Now more than ever."

"What are your instincts telling you now?" Harper asked softly.

Carson rested her hands over her belly. "My instincts are telling me to stop obsessing over this decision and to just *be*. To live and let live. This baby is here." She patted her belly softly. "I'll just have to work out the details as they come along."

There followed a moment's stunned silence.

"You mean . . . you're keeping the baby?" Dora asked.

Carson nodded.

Dora's eyes widened as comprehension sank in. "We're having a baby!" she hooted, clapping and practically bouncing in her chair.

Carson put up her hand to still the explosion. "Let's not start all that again. I'm trying to get used to the idea. You know me. Just the thought of being tied down to anything, anyone, makes me panic." She put her hand to her heart. "Oh, God, my heart's pounding at the thought. I'm not sure I'm ready. If I'll ever be ready. I worry if somehow I'll lose myself. Become invisible."

Dora grabbed her hand. "You won't disappear. We won't let you."

"You'll shine," added Harper.

"Promise me you'll keep reminding me of that," Carson entreated.

Dora put her hands to her cheeks in wonderment. "We're having a baby!"

"Slow down, sister mine," Carson admonished. "Let's take it one day at a time, like you said."

Dora asked, "Does Blake know?"

Carson shook her head. "And you're not going to tell him. Or Devlin."

Dora opened her mouth to argue but, on second thought, snapped it shut.

Dora's come a long way, Harper thought, pleased to see her eldest sister showing some restraint where, only a short time earlier, she would have plowed full steam ahead with her unwanted advice.

"Okay," Harper said to Carson. "I guess I'll pay you for the surfing lessons *in advance.*"

Carson laughed with resignation and relief. "Yeah, okay. And thanks."

"If you really want to thank me, you can start vacuuming." Harper pushed off from the counter. "Don't think being pregnant gets you off easy.

Dora, you've got garbage duty. FYI, it's recycling day tomorrow. I'm going to start in the kitchen. Come on, girls." Harper clapped her hands. "We're wastin' daylight."

Dora looked at Carson, her arms spread out in a gesture of incredulousness. "Who *is* that girl?"

Hours later Mamaw walked into the kitchen to prepare lunch. She was arrested at the threshold by a vision of utter chaos. The entire contents of the cabinets—boxes of food, tins, spices, and all the dishes—had been emptied out and grouped into piles on the kitchen table and counters.

Mamaw put one hand on the doorframe and stared in mute shock at the pots and pans littering the floor. "What on earth . . . ?"

Harper was scrubbing the inside of a cabinet. Hearing her grandmother's voice, she crawled out from deep inside and raised her head. The sponge in her hand dripped water to the floor.

"Hi, Mamaw," she called in a cheery tone.

"Child, what in heaven's name are you doing?"

"I'm cleaning the kitchen."

Of course, Mamaw thought ruefully, it wasn't enough for Harper to simply tidy the kitchen. She had to disassemble it, scour it, then reorganize it. Where did she get her energy? Mamaw wondered. She couldn't ever remember having that kind of energy. It seemed as if all Harper's domestic talents, dormant all these years, were bubbling out at Sea Breeze.

Mamaw stuck out her hands toward the table. "I came in to fix some lunch, but there's no room to make a cup of tea, much less a meal. Everything is everywhere!"

"Is it lunchtime already?" Harper looked around at the mess. "I guess I lost track of time. I started cleaning the drawers and . . ." She made a face. "Oh, Mamaw, they were so dirty and dusty. That led to the cabinets. Do you even know how long it's been since anyone scrubbed those out? And there's no rhyme or reason to where things are put. Everything is helter-skelter. And"—Harper shivered in disgust—"I'm putting roach traps everywhere. It's war."

Mamaw felt a twinge of guilt that Lucille's kitchen was being criticized, as if she should defend Lucille somehow. Yet, truth was, Lucille had been so ill before she'd passed on that she hadn't even had the energy much of the time to leave her little cottage, let alone march into the house and whip things into shape. Even before that, she'd lost her zeal for cleaning and projects. Not that Mamaw could find fault in that. She felt the same way. Old age had a way of taking the starch out of one's sails.

She pointed to a specific trash bag. "Why are the pots and pans in the trash?"

Harper had the grace to look sheepish. "Yeah,

about that." She sat back on her heels. "Honestly, Mamaw, some of these have to be tossed."

"No! You can't throw them away. Lucille used these for fifty years."

"My point exactly. They're no good any longer. Take this iron skillet, for example." Harper dug it out from the trash bag and held up a rusted iron skillet with a long wooden handle, distaste skittering across her features.

Mamaw, her face reflecting her horror, rushed to grab the skillet from Harper's hands. "This was my mother's skillet! Her mother gave it to her when she was married, and she gave it to me. I was saving it to give to one of you girls. It's an heirloom!"

"Oh." Harper looked slightly ashamed. "But, I mean, who'd use it? It's all rusty."

"It simply needs to be reseasoned with oil," Mamaw said with a hint of scold. "Any good southern housewife appreciates the sentiment of an iron skillet that's been passed down. Knows how to maintain it. I tell you, this skillet is perfectly good. I'll show you how to season it. You should know."

Harper looked at the rusty skillet with an expression of doubt, but didn't want to fight Mamaw on it. "Thank you," Harper had the manners to reply. "Okay, the skillet is a treasure. But these aluminum pots," she continued, not to be deterred, "they're hopelessly battered, and frankly, they're not safe to use anymore."

"Lucille cooked some very good meals in those pots."

"This is no comment on Lucille's cooking, Mamaw. I know you have an emotional attachment to them, but look at them. They've worn down to nearly nothing. I've gone online and learned that not only are these old aluminum pots and pans leaching dangerous metal, but research has linked aluminum cookware to Alzheimer's."

"Oh," Mamaw said, her complaints suddenly silenced.

"I'm going out today to buy some stainless steel pots and pans."

"You mustn't spend your money—"

Harper put up her hand to stop Mamaw's objections. "I'll need them anyway if I'm going to set up my own place."

Mamaw's attention sharpened. "You're making plans, are you? Going back to New York soon?"

Harper shrugged. "I suppose so." She looked at her grandmother. "I better start firming up those plans, I know. But till then," she said in a more upbeat tone, "Dora, Carson, and I huddled together this morning like a bunch of old crones. We had a good heart-to-heart."

Mamaw brightened. "Really? I'm so glad."

"There was a method to the madness. We know you've let go the cleaning service and we haven't done our part. So we put on our big-girl panties and divvied up chores. We've organized the cooking, too."

"Mercy!"

"Brace yourself, Mamaw. It's time to get a food processor."

"Whatever for? I won't cook in the old-folks home I'm heading to."

Harper scoffed at the term *old-folks home*. The place Mamaw was intending to go to was lovely and up-to-date. "Like I said, I have to buy this stuff anyway for wherever I'll set up a kitchen."

Mamaw's attention riveted on that comment. "You're not going back to your mother's apartment?"

Harper shook her head firmly. "No way. I won't go back there. Looking forward, Mamaw." She gave Mamaw a kiss.

Mamaw put her hands to her cheek where Harper's lips had been. "Well, if you think so . . ."

Harper seized the moment. "While the cabinets are empty, wouldn't it be a good time to give everything a fresh coat of paint? What do you say?"

"Paint?" Mamaw said feebly against the onslaught of energy and ideas.

"Absolutely. A clean white. Let's do the walls, too, while we're at it. They're dreary."

Mamaw looked around at the dingy walls. "I've always wanted to freshen things up a bit, but Lucille chased me out every time I suggested it. It was *her* kitchen, you know."

"Let's do it now. There's no hope for the appliances, but it's probably not worth replacing those if you're moving." Then Harper's voice changed, softening. "Other than that fabulous old Viking oven. It's built like a tank. Anyone who buys the house will probably gut the room and build a kitchen around the oven." She sighed and let her gaze lovingly linger on the mammoth appliance. "I know I would."

Mamaw felt suddenly as ancient as the oven. "But the cost . . . I'm afraid I have to be, shall we say, conservative now."

"It's my idea, thus my expense." Seeing Mamaw open her mouth to object, Harper pushed on, "No arguments. Consider it rent. And tuition for the cooking classes that I'll be getting from you and Dora."

Harper noticed the confused look on Mamaw's face and changed the subject. "Enough about the kitchen. Let's do something fun today. What would you like to do?"

"Oh, I feel a bit tired. I might lie down after lunch."

Harper came closer and her eyes sparkled with enthusiasm. "Perhaps after dinner we could play cards."

"We?"

"All of us. You, me, Dora, and Carson. Like we used to."

Mamaw rallied. "Oh, that would be nice. All

right, dear. But"—she looked around the disarray in the kitchen—"what should I do about fixing our lunch?"

"You don't have to do a thing." Harper hugged her. "I'll order something. You just relax and I'll get this mess all tidied up in no time."

Mamaw cast a final glance at the trash bag filled with the old and worn aluminum pots. Useless. Outdated, and ready to be tossed out.

Like her. She turned and walked slowly from the room.

Chapter Three

By midafternoon, Harper had finally finished scrubbing the kitchen. All she had to do now was put all the dishes in boxes and store them until after the paint job. She pushed back a wayward lock of red hair from her brow as she surveyed the room. Her back ached from bending, her manicure was ruined, and she was covered from head to toe with dirt and spills. Hard work, yes, but she was enjoying herself. In an odd way, by cleaning Sea Breeze she was developing an even deeper bond with the old house. As though each scrub were a caress. Each stroke of the broom on the floor made the house somehow hers. It didn't make sense, but it was how she felt.

She leaned against the counter and thought back to when she was twenty-two and spending the summer in England with her grandparents before entering Cambridge's postgraduate program. Greenfields Park was an imposing house in the countryside with a manicured lawn in front, expansive flower gardens in the back, and a kitchen garden close to the house. Farther out on the property was the orchard. She remembered the cherry and apple trees heavy with fruit and how raspberries ripened in profusion. The gardens were a delight.

Inside, however, the house was somber. Large rooms with fine plaster and wood rococo decoration were filled with well-formed antique furniture that had been passed down in the James family for generations. There wasn't a comfortable chair to be found where one could curl up and read a book. Harper wanted to feel an attachment to the house, knowing full well that it was her grandmother's dream that she marry an Englishman and settle down at Greenfields Park.

That same summer Granny James had initiated her campaign to introduce Harper to eligible young men from good families. Knowing that Granny James liked to prettify her house with bunches of fresh flowers in every room, Harper had gone out to the garden to pick some and make a surprise bouquet for her. Harper had been enjoying herself when she was chased away by the head gardener, politely of course. Later, in her bed-room, she'd moved the furniture to her liking, only to return from an outing to find the furniture put back in its original locations. Much like the household staff, her grandmother had also disapproved whenever Harper tried to cook or do some simple house-work. "Best to leave that be," Granny James had advised. "Betty gets quite upset if we mess her kitchen." Harper found the house more a museum than a home, and though she appreciated its beauty, she never felt comfortable there. It was the same in her mother's house in the Hamptons, and even their apartment in New York. Though Harper lived in the gorgeous postwar apartment overlooking Central Park, she never thought of it as hers. It was always—clearly—Georgiana's property.

Sea Breeze, for all that it was elegant, surrounded by the giant oak in front and graced with a series of decks in the back, was an island home built for comfort. The antiques might not be as old as Granny James's, or the paintings and portraits as historic, but Mamaw had developed a relation-ship with many of the local artists. She liked to say how each painting on her walls felt like a friend. At Sea Breeze, Harper's help around the house was not only welcome, but needed.

She was ruminating on all these thoughts, finishing mopping the kitchen floor, when the front doorbell rang. Exhausted, she paused, put her hand on her aching back, and listened to hear if anyone else would answer the door.

The doorbell rang a second time.

"Can someone get the door?" she called out.

The house was silent.

Cursing, Harper set the mop back into the soapy bucket, splashing water on the floor. She hastily crossed her clean floor toward the entryway, dripping a trail of water from her gloves. Where were her lazy sisters? she wondered. Here she was, slaving away in the kitchen, and they were probably out lying in the sun reading a book. So much for the chore chart, she harrumphed inwardly.

The doorbell rang a third time, followed by an impatient rap on the door. Harper felt her temper rise. She opened the door with a frustrated swing.

The man at the door was tall, over six feet, with shoulders so broad and straight they stretched the blue chambray shirt. The shirttails hung out over sun-bleached jeans, and the sleeves were rolled back, exposing muscled, tanned forearms. His brown hair was cut short, but she couldn't make out his expression because he was wearing aviator-style sunglasses. The military bearing in everything about him shouted, *Back off.*

Then he reached up and took off his sunglasses.

Her breath caught in her throat.

She *knew* him. She didn't know how, but she felt it with the tingling in every fiber of her body.

He was handsome with a broad forehead, a straight nose, and full lips. The muscled, athletic type that she'd always fancied but rarely dated. But it was his eyes that captured her. They were a pale green—the turbulent, changing color of the sea. Their gazes met, and once held, all the words of polite greeting that she'd formed in her mind fled. Instead, she heard herself thinking, *Oh, it's you.*

She felt as if she were standing still in time, staring at this green-eyed stranger with the overwhelming sensation that she knew him, would always know him. Yet another part of her brain told her she was being ridiculous. She didn't really recognize him. She'd not met him before. At least not in this lifetime.

The long silence grew awkward and the man shifted his gaze.

Harper gathered her wits and offered a weak "Hello?"

He smiled, so quickly she almost missed it, seemingly embarrassed for his own lapse of staring. Then he looked at his feet. "Hello," he said with a strained smile. "I'm looking for Carson. We met in Florida and, uh, I'm in town and I thought I'd look her up. Is she in?"

Carson? He was here to see Carson?

Harper's heart fell as she looked down at her damp and dirt-stained shirt and torn jeans, the yellow rubber gloves dripping soap water, her flyaway hair falling out of its elastic. She inwardly groaned, imagining the picture she made. *Of course* it would be the beautiful Carson he was here for.

"Carson Muir," he elaborated. When she still didn't reply, his brows furrowed. "Do I have the wrong house? Hey, I'm sorry." He turned to leave.

"Wait! You have the right house," Harper rushed to say. "Carson lives here."

Relief softened his face. "Is she in?"

Now that she'd set aside her romantic vision, caution intervened. "How did you say you knew her?"

"We were friends at the Dolphin Research Center. I was learning to train dolphins and she was there with Nate. Hey, is that little guy here, too?"

"Yes, they're both here." Now that she was satisfied that he knew Carson, years of breeding kicked in. "Won't you come in?" She ushered him into the foyer.

He dwarfed her as he stood beside her in the foyer. He held his hands behind his back in a military stance while his gaze scanned the hall and living room with such intensity she thought it was as if he were sweeping the house for mines.

The intensity was a bit intimidating, and again her guard went up. "I'm sorry, but I didn't catch your name."

"Oh, sorry. My name is Taylor. Taylor McClellan. From Florida."

"Well, if you'll wait here a moment, Taylor McClellan from Florida, I'll go get Carson." She turned to walk away.

"Wait," he called after her.

Harper stopped and looked over her shoulder, their eyes meeting for a second time.

The man exuded confidence as a teasing half smile eased across his face. "And who are you?"

Was that flirtation she saw in his eyes? she wondered. Or was he merely offering tit for tat? "I'm Harper." She did her best impression of her mother's haughty, self-assured tone. "Harper Muir-James. From New York."

Taylor put out his hand. His smile bloomed, softening the harsh edges of his face. She took her rubber glove off, wiped her sudsy palm on her jeans, and reached out to take his hand, returning the smile. His skin was rough and callused, accustomed to physical work. She felt her neurons tingle when his big hand tightened around hers. He held it longer than politeness required.

"Nice to meet you, Harper Muir-James from New York."

Harper felt her face flush and tried to hide it by taking her hand back and turning her head. "Be right back." She walked away down the hall in as ladylike a fashion as she could while dripping soapy water with her shoes squeaking. She could feel those green eyes on her back. Her head felt as if it were spinning as she hurried to Carson's room. This man had unnerved her, shaken her to the core. She felt an undeniable attraction to him, as though, in some crazy, unexplainable way, he was supposed to be here to meet her.

But instead, he was here for Carson.

She knocked briskly on Carson's bedroom door, then pushed it open. The room was shuttered and dim.

"Carson?"

No answer.

"Carson?" she called louder, closing the door behind her.

Carson jerked her head up from the pillow as one interrupted from a deep sleep. "What?"

"There's someone here to see you."

"Blake?" she asked with alacrity.

"No, not Blake."

"Who?"

"It's some guy. Taylor McClellan from Florida."

After a pause, Carson sat up and mopped her face with her hands. "Taylor? Are you sure?"

"Yes, I'm sure. Big guy. Good-looking. Military haircut."

She sighed heavily. "Yeah, that sounds like Taylor."

"You met him in Florida?"

"Yeah." Carson groaned. "Shit. What's he doing here? I told him I had a boyfriend."

Just hearing those words made Harper's spirits sink further. So he was interested in Carson and had come to see if there could be anything between them. Of course.

Harper made her tone neutral. "Only one way to find out. He's waiting in the foyer."

"Do me a solid. Can you stall him? Talk to him. Something." Carson flopped back on her pillows with a sigh of resignation. "I need time to get dressed." She shook her head in her hand. "Ugh. I feel sick. The last thing I want to do is entertain."

"I could tell him to come back."

"No." She sighed again. "Be nice to him. He's pretty closed, but once he lets his guard down, he's a nice guy." Carson reached over to take a sip of water from a straw. She groaned softly, then turned to Harper. "I'll be there, but it might take a while."

"Okay," Harper replied as nonchalantly as she could. Inside, her heart did a cartwheel. "I just need a second to wipe the soap and grime off. I'm a mess."

She rushed into Carson's bathroom, slipping off the rubber gloves en route. She tossed them and the filthy shirt to the floor. Her heart beat the tempo as she gave herself what Granny James called a French bath, a quick once-over with soap on a washcloth at the sink. She yanked out her elastic, raked her tangled hair with a brush till it had the luster of burnished gold, then redid her ponytail. There was no time for makeup.

Once she felt refreshed, she hurried to Carson's dresser to open a drawer. She was appalled as usual by the hoard of crumpled clothes she found crammed inside. When they were roommates, she'd been the neat freak Felix Unger to Carson's Oscar Madison.

"God, Carson, don't you ever fold your clothes?"

"Hey, do I prowl in your drawers?" Carson called back with a dismissive wave. She was slumped at the side of the bed nibbling a saltine cracker.

Harper decided not to let clothes come between them. Mumbling to herself, she pulled out the least wrinkled top she could find. "Need to borrow this," she called out as she slipped it over her head. Like most of Carson's clothes, the aqua-colored, stretchy camisole top was snug, revealing Harper's slender figure and small, rounded breasts.

Carson waved her hand again. "Don't leave him out there alone."

Harper ran to the door, then paused to take a deep, calming breath before exiting. She usually couldn't care less about a stranger's interest. Yet for this man, she was as nervous now as she was when at her coming out to society she was presented to the queen of England.

She opened the door and, fixing a smile, walked

with studied grace back to the foyer. She found Taylor standing in the front hall, slightly bent at the waist, his hands behind his back, peering at a painting of a dock scene somewhere in the lowcountry. Shrimp boats lined the dock, their great green nets high.

"Do you like it?" she asked, drawing near. "It's by a local artist. West Fraser."

"I like it very much," he replied, eyes still on the art. "It's McClellanville."

Harper took a step closer to study the painting, searching for details. To her, the scene could have been one of many docks in the lowcountry. "How can you tell?"

He looked over his shoulder and his eyes twinkled with amusement. "Because that's my dad's boat. The *Miss Jenny*."

"Really?" Surprised, she stepped closer to look at the large shrimp boat with the green and white colors, huge nets hanging. "Your father is a shrimp-boat captain?"

"Was. He left the business. He couldn't afford to operate the boat anymore."

"Oh, I'm sorry to hear that. What happened?"

A sigh rumbled in Taylor's chest as he put his hands on his hips in thought. "It's been coming on for years. The local shrimpers have been hit hard by the deluge of imported shrimp, the high cost of diesel fuel, and small yields. It's been a perfect storm. My daddy hung on as long as he could. Like the others. But . . ." Taylor lifted his shoulders as though to say *What could he do?*

"Is he still in the fishing business?"

"No." Taylor looked away.

Standing so close, Harper could see the texture of his deeply tanned skin, the tiny crow's-feet at his eyes. "Were you ever a shrimper?"

"Me?" His smile was quick and fleeting. "Sure. You can't be the son of a shrimper without working on your daddy's boat. I helped him from the day I could walk. So did my mother and brother. It was a family business. But I always knew I'd do something else to make a living someday. Doesn't mean I don't love the boat. And the water. It's in my blood."

"I've always been intrigued by the shrimp boats. As a tourist, that is. They're such a staple of the southern waters. When I was young, I remember seeing a lot of them docked at Shem Creek. One after the other. Whenever I cross Shem Creek, I look out hoping to see one, but there don't seem to be many now."

Taylor crossed his arms and shook his head. "Nope. The boats are mostly all docked. For sale. It's all restaurants and bars now. A few kayakers in the water. It's the state of things out there."

"I find that sad."

"Yeah."

Harper didn't want to see Shem Creek become a museum of days gone by. She loved the vibrancy of the working dock. "I'll have to see one soon, before they're all gone."

"If I can, I'll take you to see one sometime."

Her surprise at his invitation lit up her face.

He must've noticed because he suddenly averted his gaze and peered down the hall as though looking for Carson.

Harper felt like a schoolgirl who'd forgotten to deliver the headmistress's message. And worse, she was acting like a schoolgirl, mooning over him. She felt a blush burn her cheeks. "Oh, I'm to tell you Carson's on her way. She was taking a nap and she asked if you could wait. She has to get dressed. . . . It might take a while."

Taylor let his palm slide against his pelt of hair as he considered this. "Sure, but if it'll be a while, I need to check on my dog. I left him out by the car."

"Your dog?"

"Yeah. Come on. I'll introduce you to Thor."

Harper followed Taylor out the front door and across the gravel drive to where a black pickup truck sat parked in the deep shade of the giant oak tree. Rounding the fender, she spied a large black dog sitting in the shade. He lifted his head at their approach and, seeing Taylor, stood and looked at his master adoringly.

Taylor reached down to deliver several strong pats on the dog's broad head. Turning, he waved Harper closer.

Harper moved tentatively forward, intimidated by the immense black dog with his deep chest and floppy ears. The dog turned to look at her as she drew near, eyeing her with curiosity.

"Is it a Great Dane?"

"Mostly. He's a rescue dog. Great Dane and part Lab. He looks more Great Dane, but he's all Lab at heart. Loves being in the water. That dog is one swimming machine."

She noticed that the dog was not tied down. "He doesn't need a leash?"

"No."

Harper was impressed. She wasn't familiar with dogs, never having had one growing up. No pets whatsoever. Not even a parakeet, though she'd wept and begged for years for one as a child. Her mother simply wouldn't tolerate any "foul, disease-ridden animal" to mess up her meticulously decorated apartment.

"He's awfully big," she said feebly.

"He is that. Thor's a big guy, but he's gentle."

Harper glanced at the man standing beside her and wondered if that description didn't fit him, as well.

"Go ahead, you can pet him."

There was no point trying to explain to a man like Taylor how someone could be afraid of even a seemingly gentle animal as large as Thor. The only animals she was accustomed to growing up were the horses at Greenfields Park. They terrified her. She'd had bad experiences with them.

Harper was compelled as a child to ride the big animals that towered over her, pawed the earth with their big hooves, and snorted when she timidly approached dressed in her riding outfit and carrying a crop. Her mother, of course, was a superb rider. When Harper was six and balked at getting on a horse, Georgiana told her to "stop being so weak willed and get on that bloody horse." Harper was more afraid of her mother than the horse and complied. After all, learning to ride was considered mandatory for a James. Yet, even after years of lessons, whenever she mounted, Harper never lost the feeling that she would throw up. The horse instinctively knew that Harper was afraid. Once she was on its back, the horse would turn its head to look at her, then promptly fart and disregard her commands. Harper couldn't imagine any horse anywhere daring to ignore a command given by her mother.

Perhaps, she thought, staring into the big brown eyes of Thor, that was what frightened her so much about Taylor's dog. He was as big as a horse.

"Come on. He won't bite." Taylor gently took her wrist, encircling it with his thumb and forefinger. "You're a little thing, aren't you?"

She wasn't so afraid with his hand over hers as he guided it toward the dog's enormous block head. She felt the smooth pelt of Thor's shiny black fur under her fingertips. To her relief, Thor took it all in stride. She had the sense he was accustomed to tolerating fools.

Taylor released her wrist, and she withdrew her hand swiftly and took a step back.

"Could I trouble you to guide me to a place I can fill his water dish?"

She led the way around the house to the back porch, Thor trotting happily behind his master. She helped Taylor find the water spigot and fill the dog's bowl. Thor lapped up the water noisily, drinking his fill.

"Okay, boy, settle," Taylor commanded with a discreet hand signal.

Thor trotted to a shady corner of the porch and, after circling a few times, lay down, resting his head on his giant paws.

"Is he always so obedient?"

Taylor nodded. "I trained him myself. He's the smartest dog I've ever known. He wants to do his job. If he makes a mistake, I swear it hurts his pride. Gotta love that about him. He'll stay there until I tell him to get up. Or, unless he feels I'm in danger."

"He doesn't think I'm going to hurt you, does he?" She eyed the enormous dog. "I don't want to upset Cujo."

Taylor laughed shortly and shook his head. "I hardly think he sees you as a threat."

Another awkward silence fell between them as they waited for Carson to appear. Taylor put his hands on his hips and took a long look at the property. She followed his gaze, seeing Sea Breeze as she imagined he or any other stranger would see the historic island house for the first time.

Sea Breeze showed her best side to the water. The back of the house was lined by three tiers of long porches from one side to the other that overlooked the water. At the top, the left side of the porch was covered by a sleek black-and-white awning that sheltered several glossy black wicker chairs. Here the women of the house congregated in the morning for coffee, and in the evenings for tea and gossip. Below, a second porch surrounded the swimming pool. The third was more a wide step to the grounds that sloped down to the Cove and the wooden dock that stretched over the racing water.

"It's quite a place," Taylor said, the awe in his voice informing her that he appreciated the house's unique qualities. Taylor pointed to the dock. "That where Carson's dolphin came to visit?"

"Delphine, yes."

"Carson told me about her. Sad story." He turned to look at the house again. "Do you live here?"

She shook her head. "No. New York."

"What part of New York are you from?"

"Manhattan." She refrained from telling him that she still lived with her mother. "And you?"

"Juno Beach."

"But you said your family is here? You're visiting them?"

"That's right. McClellanville's not too far from here. Thought I'd swing by and see Carson while I was in town. We became friendly at the Dolphin Research Center. She isn't the type to remain a stranger," he added with a short laugh.

"No." Harper wished she had that talent. Carson had it, as did Mamaw. Harper was more reserved, like her Granny James. But Harper's stomach fizzed a bit at what Taylor had just said about himself and Carson. So perhaps they hadn't been romantically involved, after all?

"What college did you go to?" she asked, going for a change of subject. Then held her breath, not knowing if he *did* go to college, not meaning to insult.

"The Citadel."

"Here in Charleston?"

"Is there another?"

"Isn't that a military college?"

"Yes."

"Was it hard? I mean, I heard about the hazing and things they did to the freshmen."

"The knobs. That's what they call the fresh-men. And, yes, it was hard."

"Did you miss out on the regular college life?"

"No. Fraternities were not my thing."

"Mine, neither."

"Where did you go?"

"Radcliffe. There weren't any sororities. But that didn't stop them from having cliques."

"Radcliffe is an Ivy League, right?"

"Yup." She saw he was impressed and cocked her head. "I went to good schools, got good grades. But getting into those schools is often a matter of who you know and how much your family will donate even more than how smart you are. My mother's family has lots of connections. And deep pockets."

"So you're saying you're rich?"

"I'm saying my family is."

"Where's your family located? New York?"

"Yes and no." She wondered whether to give him the long or short version of her history. She decided on the short. "My mother is English and her family, my grandparents, live in England. At Greenfields Park."

"Is that some kind of gated community?"

She laughed. "No, the name of their property is Greenfields Park. We often call large estates *parks* in England."

Taylor looked amused. "Your family has a large estate in England?"

Harper didn't like where this conversation was going. "Just a great big house and, oh, some hundred or so acres."

He snorted with surprise. "Just a few hundred?"

So, the long version, Harper thought to herself. "It's a farm. Trees and great gardens and barns with cows and sheep . . . lots of sheep."

"A farm. Cool."

Taylor seemed at a momentary loss for anything else to say, and having exhausted basic introductory chitchat, Harper fell back on good manners. "Can I offer you something to drink? Coffee? Iced tea?"

"Tea sounds good. A beer would be better."

"Sorry, but Sea Breeze is a dry house."

"Tea it is."

When they entered the kitchen, she cringed at the state of the room. Dishes and pots and pans were stacked on the table, counters, any bare surface. The entire pantry was loaded in boxes on the floor. But the kitchen gleamed and smelled of pine soap.

"I've been cleaning the cabinets," she said in way of apology.

"Big job."

"Just beginning, I'm afraid. After I finish organizing, I'd like to fix it up a little. Paint, at least."

"Now's a good time, since you've already got the cabinets cleared." He put his hands on his hips and took a sweeping assessment of the room. "It's a great room. Lots of charm." He walked toward the back windows, put his hands on his hips, and stared out. "And look at that view."

"Yes." She drew closer to join him at the window.

Taylor turned and looked around the room again, his eyes gleaming. "There's something about old architecture. They don't build 'em like they used to."

Harper warmed to the subject. "Exactly. I've always loved old houses. This one in particular. It's got good bones but it needs some freshening up. I'd really love some new appliances, but those have to wait."

Taylor paced the room, measuring it. He reached out to check the wood of the cabinets. "Solid wood. That's good." He rubbed his jaw in thought. "Wouldn't take much. You should call my father. He's good. And honest."

Harper was taken aback. "Your father?"

"He's an independent contractor. He paints, does carpentry, a little electrical work. A good boat captain has to know a little bit about everything, and after the shrimping business dried up, he turned to that sort of work." Taylor put his hands on his hips and thought a moment, then looked at Harper again. "My dad's doing a job on the island now. I could ask him to swing by on his way home to give you an estimate. If you like," Taylor hedged.

"Yes. Please."

He half smiled and pulled out his phone. Walking to the windows, he conducted a brief phone conversation. Harper waited, wringing her hands, hoping she wasn't overstepping bounds. Mamaw had tentatively agreed to her plan, but this was moving quickly.

Taylor tucked his phone back in his pocket and crossed the room back to her side.

"Says he'll swing by later this afternoon."

"Great. I'll be waiting." Again, their eyes met and Harper felt that fleeting sense of something important about to happen.

Just then, a voice shouted from the door, "Taylor!"

Harper blinked with surprise when she saw Carson stride into the room. The woman was transformed. Radiant in a long, white caftan, her dark hair slicked back in a braid, she walked in holding her arms out in welcome to Taylor. Gone was the sleepy, nauseated woman Harper had encountered in the bedroom. Carson's California, beachy look, her glowing tan and brilliant blue eyes, all exuded sex appeal and confidence. Taylor walked directly to her, a wide grin on his face, and hugged her.

Harper turned away and busied herself getting Taylor's glass of iced tea, all the while keeping a hooded gaze on the couple as they chatted. Looking down at herself, she suddenly felt dowdy in her torn denim shorts and tank top. Of course it was her luck to be caught playing

Cinderella for the day. But if he'd come yesterday, would it have made much difference? Not really, she realized. Yesterday she was in jeans, sweating in the garden. Clothes used to matter to her. She was accustomed to New York chic designer outfits and shoes. Polished nails. Hair and makeup styled to perfection. Not a hem hanging, a button loose. Her mother had trained her to always look her best. A safety pin on clothing drove Georgiana to distraction.

Harper brought her hand up to push back a wayward lock. She couldn't remember the last time she'd been to the hairdresser. Or put on a sleek dress, spiky heels, and smoky eye makeup. She glanced at her nails. She desperately needed a manicure. She shrank into herself, wondering again who she was. It seemed the more she discovered herself on the inside, the less she recognized herself on the outside.

Carson said something that made Taylor laugh. Harper glanced over quickly, surprised at how the taciturn man appeared more relaxed now. With Carson. Harper turned back to add ice to the glass. The high hum and clinking of ice from the fridge set her teeth on edge.

Nate strolled into the kitchen, an electronic game in his hand. He wore his usual T-shirt and soft, baggy shorts, skinny legs sticking out from them like toothpicks. He casually looked up, then stopped short to stare at the mess, momentarily confused by the state of the room. Then he saw Taylor, and his scowl lifted to a bright smile.

"It's you!" he called out, pointing to Taylor.

Taylor turned and grinned at seeing the boy. "It's me!"

Nate hurried to his side but stopped a few feet in front of him, his arms at his side, eyes wide and appealing. "Did you bring your games?"

"Sorry, pal. Not this time."

Nate scrunched up his face in disappointment.

"How are you?" Taylor asked.

"Good."

"Me, too."

Nate tilted his head, curious. "So what are you doing here?"

"I'm here to see Carson."

Nate considered this. "Are you going to marry Aunt Carson?"

Carson barked out a laugh.

Harper swung her head around.

Taylor took the question in his stride. "Why would you think that?"

"On account of she's going to have a baby and I was wondering if you're here to be the daddy."

Taylor's gaze slid to Carson.

Carson slipped her palm on her cheek, speechless.

"You're having a baby?"

Carson dropped her hand and shrugged. "Yep."

Harper watched Taylor digest this news and

was relieved to see him smile in genuine pleasure. "Congratulations."

"Thanks. I'm just getting used to the idea," Carson said breezily. Then she launched into the story of how she'd been in the pool with Delphine and how the dolphin had been persistently echolocating on her belly.

"You were diagnosed by a dolphin?" Taylor summed up with a short laugh. "Classic."

"I know, right? Gotta admit it's a great story. I can use it at parties for decades."

Nate tugged Taylor's shirt. "Is Thor here?"

"Sure is. He's out on the porch."

"Can I go see him?"

"He'd like that."

"Will he remember me?"

"Sure. He'll be glad to see you again. Go on out and keep him company."

"Okay." Nate took off like a shot.

Carson smiled. "A boy and a dog. Another classic."

"Iced tea's ready," Harper called out. She set out a tray with two tall glasses of sweet tea, lemons, and sugar cookies.

"Thanks," Taylor said, trying to catch her gaze.

Carson said, "Let's go out to the porch. There's no place to sit in here."

Taylor turned to Harper. "Are you coming?"

Harper smiled, pleased at his invitation. "If I'm not interrupting . . ."

"You're not interrupting!" Carson exclaimed. "The more the merrier."

They were just leaving when Mamaw entered the room.

"Girls!" she sang out in a high voice reserved for guests. "Look who's come by for a visit."

Mamaw stepped aside and everyone fell silent as a smiling—and then suddenly very confused-looking—Blake followed Mamaw into the kitchen.

Chapter Four

"Blake!" Carson sounded astonished. Harper could understand her sister's surprise: Blake had not been to Sea Breeze in weeks, though he lived on the same island. Their breakup had not been amicable. Glancing furtively at Taylor, Harper thought this couldn't be more awkward.

"Hey, Carson." Blake stepped hesitantly into the room filled with people. He was wearing a NOAA polo shirt and carried a computer bag. He glanced around, spotted Harper, and nodded with a quick smile of recognition. "Harper."

"Hey, Blake." Harper glanced quickly to Carson, who stood still and silent, her eyes haunted.

Mamaw instinctively moved in to smooth the awkwardness. "My, but there's a party in here!"

she exclaimed, arms outstretched. "How wonderful." She zeroed in on Taylor. "Harper, dear, you have a friend." She walked toward Taylor. "We haven't been introduced."

Harper stepped forward as years of training clicked in. "Mamaw, I'd like to present Taylor McClellan. Taylor, this is my grandmother Mrs. Muir."

"McClellan," Mamaw repeated, rolling the name over in thought. "Are you related to the McClellan family in McClellanville? I know Sarah McClellan. But, wait, she married so her last name would be different. What was it . . . ?"

"McDaniel," Taylor replied. "Yes, ma'am, I am. She's my aunt. She married Stuart McDaniel."

Mamaw's face brightened with the connection. "Of course. What a lovely couple. It's been far too long since I've seen either of them. So you're their nephew. It's a pleasure to meet you, Taylor."

Taylor stood straighter and took Mamaw's offered hand with a particularly warm smile. "The pleasure is all mine, Mrs. Muir."

Harper saw Mamaw cock her head in approval of the young man's manners. Harper stifled a smile, thinking maybe all they needed to bring Mamaw out of her funk was a handsome young man to pay her some attention.

"I'm Blake." He shifted his computer bag to the other hand and stepped toward Taylor for a handshake.

Taylor shook Blake's hand firmly. "Taylor."

Blake and Taylor were close in height and both deeply tanned from the summer sun, but there the similarity ended. Blake was as lean as bacon, his face long and narrow. He stood in the relaxed stance of an islander with his hands in his well-worn pockets. His dark brown hair was longer than usual and fell in salt-stiff curls around his head.

In contrast, Taylor was broad and muscled. His shirt was ironed, his face clean shaven. He stood straight and alert in a military stance.

"What brings you to our neck of the woods?" Blake asked Taylor. "You a friend of Harper's?"

"Yes, I hope so." Taylor smiled briefly at Harper. "But I actually came by to see Carson."

Blake skipped a beat and his expression grew more guarded. "How do you know Carson?"

Taylor, hearing the hint of an interrogation in the question, stiffened perceptibly.

"Taylor and I got to know each other in Florida," Carson offered, seeming to find her voice. "At the Dolphin Research Center. He's in town and looked me up. Mamaw, you remember me talking about him."

"I do, indeed," Mamaw replied graciously.

Carson walked to Blake, her caftan swooshing against her legs. Harper sensed the tension between them and was sorry for it. Harper had always liked the marine biologist who'd claimed

Carson's heart—and the hearts of all the Muir family with his steadfast love for Carson. His rescue of Delphine earlier in the summer had been nothing short of heroic.

"Blake, what brings you here?" Carson asked, an edge to her voice, her tone unwelcoming.

Blake's eyes flashed briefly, then he took a step back. "I had some news about Delphine," he said coolly. "But we can talk later."

"Delphine?" Carson went for the hook. "What about her?"

"I don't want to interfere with your . . . reunion. I should've called first."

"Is she all right?"

Blake paused to meet Carson's gaze. "Yeah." His lips suppressed a smile as he offered her a loaded glance. "She's more than all right."

Harper watched as the two shared a long look that spoke volumes and made the rest of them feel like voyeurs to witness it.

Carson turned to Taylor. "I'm sorry, Taylor, but this is important. It's about Delphine, the dolphin I told you about. Can I be terribly rude and ask you to wait a bit longer?"

Taylor inclined his head toward the porch. "No problem. I just came by to say hey. I've got to run. The dog and all." He glanced at Blake, then turned to leave.

"I'll walk you out." Carson walked to Taylor and slipped her arm in his. She offered him a brilliant smile that melted the awkwardness. "Seems the least I can do."

Harper stood by the door, still holding the tray of iced teas and feeling very much the fool for it.

Passing her at the door, Taylor offered a smile. "Nice to meet you, Harper."

She looked in his eyes, pulsing with warmth. She wanted to say something . . . anything . . . but couldn't.

When Carson drew near, she heard Taylor say to her in a low voice, "I didn't mean to cause any trouble."

"You didn't." Carson patted his arm. "The trouble was there before you arrived. It's a long story."

Harper stood stock-still after the door had slammed behind Taylor and Carson. She squeezed her eyes shut, embarrassed for the gush of romantic feelings that had been roiling inside her since she'd met Taylor McClellan. Enough, she told herself. No more dreaming. It was time to put away childish thoughts and focus on tasks at hand. She had a job to get, an apartment. She had to make plans to return to New York.

She turned and walked resolutely across the kitchen. Mamaw and Blake were struggling to keep up some semblance of polite conversation while Carson was out.

"Care for some tea?" Harper asked Blake and Mamaw.

They each took a glass with thanks. Harper heard her phone ding and, setting the empty tray on the counter, quickly checked it.

It was a message from her mother.

After making her excuses and retreating to her bedroom, Harper closed the sliding doors and sat on the four-poster bed. Her mother's terse query asked why Harper hadn't responded to her mother's e-mail from the previous week, checking in on Harper and where she stood with her return plans. Harper groaned inwardly, knowing she couldn't keep putting her mother off. She hadn't spoken to her since their blowout on the phone back in May. She was sure her mother had been waiting for her to come crawling back to New York. As the days flew by, however, and Harper remained on Sullivan's Island, it brought Harper a smug pleasure that her mother had reached out first.

But it wasn't smugness that had kept Harper from responding to her mother's e-mail. Georgiana had been pleasant enough in the e-mail, but Harper could imagine the foot tapping in her mind. Rather, Harper didn't know what she'd say to her mother. She hadn't made up her mind what to do or where to go come fall. She'd been hoping the answer would become clear to her. It seemed instead she was going to rely on her default program and return to New York for lack of other options.

Staring at her phone, she summoned her courage. Sitting on the edge of her bed, she dialed a number she hadn't called since Memorial Day.

On the second ring she heard the familiar clipped British accent. "Georgiana James here."

"Mummy?"

"Harper!"

"Yes, hello. It's me."

"I was just thinking of you."

"Were you really?"

"Yes. I've just returned from the Hamptons and the apartment is so quiet with you gone." Georgiana released a dramatic sigh. "I'm exhausted. It was a madhouse. Everybody was there. I had to come back to New York to get some rest before the next onslaught at Labor Day. But it's always so beautiful there, and I'm expected. We do what we must. You should have been there. Everyone asked where you were."

Harper doubted that but she heard the thinly veiled criticism. No one even knew she was there most of the time. Harper wondered why her mother insisted on filling the house with tiresome guests only to complain about it later. There was never respite from the loud, slightly inebriated conversations, the raucous laughter, and the long string of parties. Her mother's packed social calendar was her life's blood. In contrast, Harper couldn't bear constantly being "on." Usually she retreated with a book to the beach or with her laptop to her room, much to her mother's annoyance.

"It's quite peaceful here," Harper said.

"I'm sure it is, darling." Georgiana skipped a beat. "There's no *there* there."

"Well, I'm quite content." Harper could already feel herself growing petulant and contrary in the face of her mother's disapproval.

"About *that*." Harper tensed at the tone that signaled a lecture. "When are you coming back from your summer vacation? I mean, really, darling, aren't you going stir-crazy lost in the swamps?"

"Not at all. They're called the wetlands, by the way."

"Is that so," Georgiana said in a bored tone. Then, getting back to her point: "Summer holiday is over. It's time to come home. We have a very exciting fall lineup. I need you back at work."

"I didn't think I had a job to come home to," Harper rejoined pointedly.

Harper heard the sound of her mother inhaling from her cigarette. "I vaguely recall that you quit."

"I suppose I did."

"It was a heated moment."

"Yes, it was." Harper recalled the bitter phone call the previous May when her mother made clear, in terse words, that Harper worked for her and had to do as she was told, not only for her job but in her personal life. That moment had crystallized for Harper the true nature of her relationship with her mother. With the veil of sentimentality ripped off, she was able to stand up to her mother for the first time and declare her independence. Or, a first step toward it. She'd found the strength to quit her job, which freed her up to spend the summer at Sea Breeze. Something she'd not planned on doing, but had turned out to be a blessing.

"Actually, Mummy, that's why I called. I wanted to talk to you about a job."

"Good. You must come back as soon as possible. You were quite right about that girl," Georgiana pushed on in a confidential tone. "Absolute nightmare. She can barely spell, much less punctuate a sentence. And entitled?" She exhaled. "Can you believe the twit wanted to be promoted to editor? Already? Imagine. I sent her packing." Another exhalation.

"Nina? You were singing her praises last time we talked. You were quite clear that you thought she'd be a better editor than I. How I wasn't ready." Harper's cheeks flushed at the memory.

"You're imagining things. You've always been oversensitive, Harper. The salient point is that I need you back. All is forgiven."

Forgiven? Harper's fingers clutched the phone in a fistlike grip. Her mother always had the ability to twist things around so that in the end she was the victor. "I'm not coming back to—"

"Not coming back? Where would you go? Wait a minute . . . Has Mummy been talking to you again about moving to Greenfields Park?" Georgiana laughed, a high trill sound. "Typical. Now you know where I get my wheedling and conniving side from. Well, I can't blame you if you choose to move to England. I've been a disappointment to them, so I suppose there's some satisfaction in knowing that at least my progeny can fulfill their dream."

"But I haven't—"

"Haven't what?"

"Mother, will you let me finish a sentence?" Harper said with heat. There was a silence. She continued in a calmer voice, "I haven't chosen to move to Greenfields Park. I haven't chosen anything. What I began to say was I'm not coming back to being your editorial assistant. Though I appreciate the opportunity," she hurried to add, "I've grown beyond that position." She thought that more politic than declaring she no longer wanted to be her mother's lackey. Over the past two years she'd given more of the editorial jobs to the other employees and her personal agenda to Harper.

"Not be my assistant?" Georgiana sounded affronted. "But who else can do the job?"

Harper prayed for patience. Why was it her job to ensure her mother had a satisfactory assistant?

"Mummy, you can hire someone new to be your personal assistant. I'll train her, if you like. But I'm qualified to be an editor. More than qualified."

Harper waited. She knew her mother would often make whoever was on the other end of the conversation wait in silence for long periods while she thought things through.

"I'm going to start sending out my résumé," Harper said flatly, ending the standoff. "I wanted you to know first. I'd appreciate a letter of recommendation."

"When did you become so heartless?"

"I beg your pardon? How am I heartless?"

"Who do you think nurtured your career in publishing all your life? Sent you to the best schools, mentored you, introduced you to every important publishing house? Me. You never could have made the connections and have the opportunities you've had were it not for me. And this is how you repay me? You threaten me that you're going to another house? That's like turning down my option clause."

"I'm not turning anything down," Harper said with exasperation. "Other than the job as your assistant. You haven't offered me anything else yet."

There was a pause and she heard her mother puffing away like a locomotive. At length Georgiana spoke again, this time in her business tone of voice—clipped, heavy on the British accent, impersonal. "You always were hard to reason with when you're at that place. I'd hoped you'd outgrown your grandmother's influence."

"Which grandmother are you referring to? Not that it matters. Mother, I've not discussed this with either Mamaw or Granny James. I'm not talking to you as your daughter but as your former editorial assistant who wishes to apply for a position as editor."

There was another long pause. This time, Harper waited her out.

"Very well. If you're serious about applying for a job as an editor, I'll be happy to discuss it with you. In my office, like any other applicant. Call me when you get back to New York to set up an appointment. Must go now. Cheers."

Harper heard the click of disconnection. She fell back on the mattress to stare at the ceiling, momentarily stunned and confused. When she'd called her mother, she'd been filled with determination to make decisions, to return to New York. Yet once again her mother had shown her that her hopes were naive.

Working for her mother in any capacity was a bad idea. Harper realized that now. Georgiana James would turn on her. Tell her she wouldn't succeed. But what else was new? The logical, pragmatic side of Harper knew she had to stop stalling and apply to other houses.

But the emotional part of her was feeling belittled and hurt. Harper brought her hands in to cover her face, then turned on her side and curled up in a ball. Rejection hurt. Even after all these years. She thought she'd get used to it. But she kept this childish hope that someday her mother would, if not love her, at least appreciate her qualities. Not Georgiana James. She excelled at letting Harper know, in every manner possible, that she didn't matter. Or if she did, it was only in how Harper could fill her mother's needs and wants.

Any attempt at autonomy, even typical teenage experimenting with clothing and makeup, was strongly opposed. Harper wondered if her mother had any idea how crazy Harper could have gone at the boarding schools. Or what a good girl she'd been all those years when her friends were sneaking out at night, trying drugs, sex, and booze. Then Harper snorted a very unladylike laugh. Georgiana was too self-absorbed to have even noticed, let alone cared.

Harper wiped her eyes, feeling the spark of anger. She was twenty-eight now. Why did she still allow that woman to hurt her?

Harper rose and walked to the small wood desk. She had discovered the only way to release her pent-up hurt and emotions was to write. She sat and flipped open her laptop, placed her fingers on the keys, and started tapping furiously. She felt the tension ease the moment the words began to flow. Even the effort of writing a book, something her father had done, would be an affront to her mother. She hated anything in Harper that hinted at her DNA connection to Parker Muir.

Harper lost herself in the world of her characters. In Harper's book, she'd created an alter-ego character. Hadley was an empowered woman, intelligent, and not easily swayed. One who didn't let anyone demean her or stand in her way of achieving her dreams.

When Harper was a young girl, she often wrote stories where she embodied a heroine who faced obstacles similar to the adventures of her favorite storybook characters. She journeyed through a wonderland like clever Alice, traveled through time and space like Meg Murry. As she grew older, Harper sat in coffee shops, in airports, train stations, places where people clustered, and eavesdropped on conversations. She enjoyed finishing their conversations or story lines in her writing, adding flourishes to the tales with an improvisational twist. Most of all, Harper had discovered that her journaling provided her with an outlet for her pent-up frustrations and hurt.

Harper sat at her desk and rewrote the recent telephone exchange, firing off the words to her mother that she wished she had said. The character Hadley was fiery tongued.

"Every word out of your mouth is a put-down!"

Hadley shouted. "This is the end of your lifelong campaign of control over me." "You violate my boundaries, undermine, demean, and criticize me." "You are a destructive narcissist!"

Harper didn't realize that she was smiling as she wrote. When she finished, an hour had passed. She leaned back in her chair and let her hands rest on the keys, feeling the cathartic relief she always did after writing.

As she closed her laptop, her smile wavered and she wondered if she'd ever find the courage to confront her mother in the real world, not just in her stories.

Blake didn't smile when Carson reentered the kitchen. "New friend?"

"Yes," she replied in a deliberately breezy manner, ignoring his probing stare. "Grab your drink and let's go outside. It's hot, but not too bad in the shade. This room is a disaster, thanks to Hurricane Harper." She took a sweep of the room and shook her head, muttering, "I don't know what that crazy girl was thinking."

She led him to the shaded portion of the porch where the offshore breezes stirred the humid air. Carson loved hot weather—couldn't abide the cold. She was like any other fish that absorbed the sun and tolerated the heat. One of the things she liked about Blake was that he was equally at home outdoors. They both preferred to sit in fresh air than in air-conditioning. Carson pulled out one of the large wicker chairs, then slunk gracefully into it, tucking one leg beneath her.

Blake set his glass beside hers but hesitated before sitting. He stood before her, concern on his face. "How are you feeling?" he asked cautiously.

Carson tapped her fingers along the chair, knowing full well that he was fishing for whether she'd had the abortion. She knew he had the right to ask, and at some point she planned to tell him her decision. But she'd only just made it.

She looked directly into his eyes. "Queasy." She slipped on her sunglasses.

Blake went still, appearing momentarily blindsided. "As in sick?"

"That's usually what *queasy* means. Nauseous. Also known as morning sickness."

"You mean . . . you're still pregnant?"

"Seems so."

She saw hope spring into his eyes, and a quick smile of relief flashed across his face as he digested this information.

Carson removed her sunglasses to meet his gaze. "I've decided to have the baby."

Blake's emotions shot from zero to sixty. He dropped his computer bag and stepped forward, arms out to hold her. "Carson, I—"

Carson shrank back and put up her hand to ward him off. "Stop!" When he dropped his hands, she said, flustered, "I don't want to get into this with you right now. Okay?" As he stepped back again, she took a moment to calm her nerves. Glancing up, she saw confusion on his face, and gripping as tightly to her independence as to the chair arm, she pushed on, "I didn't do it for you. Or for *us*."

Blake's smile slipped but the relief still shone in his eyes. "Okay." He nodded in affirmation. "Got it. But I can still care, right? I can't *not* care."

Carson's shoulders lowered, grateful for his understanding and not pushing her into a commitment. She nodded, allowing a half smile to escape. She felt a bit sheepish for being so churlish. "Of course you can." She looked into his eyes, so dark and appealing. Suddenly she smiled. She had not offered him a smile before, but she smiled now, and in that instant the old affection bloomed. "I don't mean to be a bitch about this, but I get nervous when you come on strong. I'm just getting used to the idea myself. I need time, okay?"

"Okay."

Her smile grew wry. "And I don't want you begging me to marry you."

When she'd first told Blake about the tiny life growing inside her, he'd tried to push her into moving in together and marriage. Carson had promptly fled, completely overwhelmed and unable to stomach the idea of all that commitment. They'd broken up then and there.

Blake crossed his arms across his chest, eyeing

her narrowly. "Who said I wanted to marry you?"

Carson looked askance and smirked.

He dropped his arms. "Okay, I want you back." Blake shrugged insolently. "I love you. So sue me."

She laughed, accepting his humor, and his determination, with equanimity. "I love you, too. You know that. But that doesn't mean I want to get married, at least not right now. Let's start with being friends again, and see where things go from there."

Blake's dark eyes pulsed. "I can do that. Friends." He smiled again, carving deep dimples into his cheeks. "It's a good place to *start*."

"Blake . . ."

He laughed, clearly so happy with the turn of events that he couldn't be discouraged.

"So what's this about Delphine?" she said, dragging them back to the subject at hand. "Or was that just a ploy to get rid of Taylor? Because if it was, it worked."

"I'd like to think I was that clever. But I should've known anything about Delphine would trump whatever else was on the table."

"You're right about that. Sit down"—she indicated the chair beside her—"and tell me what's going on."

Blake took the wicker chair beside her. He leaned forward in his chair, holding his hands together between his knees. When he spoke, it was in the way of announcement. His eyes sparkled with excitement. "I've received word that Delphine has improved to the point that Mote is recommending release."

Carson sucked in her breath. "That's great!" she exclaimed, slipping her leg out from under her to sit straighter in her chair. They sat knee to knee and she leaned forward with anticipation.

Blake nodded in agreement. "Her progress has been nothing short of amazing. And, more than one person has commented on how your visit turned things around for her."

Carson felt her heart lurch at that news. Her visit to Delphine at the hospital had been emotional and had confirmed the bond between them.

"It's also your relationship with Delphine that has us worried, though."

Carson shifted her weight.

"We've begun assessing her for release to the wild. It's a complex procedure. I came to ask you a few questions. It won't take long."

"Sure." She thought it was strange that NOAA would need her to answer questions. Still, she noted that Blake had lost his authoritarian tone from earlier when he'd been furious with her for attracting the dolphin to the dock in the first place. Blake had seen that as a betrayal to all he'd believed in, and his forgiveness had been hard-won. "I'm willing to cooperate in any way I can."

"Good. Let's get started." He pulled papers out

of his bag. "Prior to the release of any cetacean, the National Marine Fisheries Service requires that a thorough evaluation be done. This includes all historical, developmental, behavioral, and of course medical records. So far, they've completed her medical evaluation, and as I said, all checks out. That's good. Her behavior was approved insofar as she has retained the skills necessary to find and capture food in the wild. We also know she can identify predators in the wild, given how she battled the shark to save your life."

Earlier in the summer, Carson had been at the mercy of a shark when Delphine swooped in and saved her, which had been the start of Delphine and Carson's special bond. Carson felt, as she always did, the weight of her gratitude to the dolphin.

"This is where it gets tricky," he continued. "Ideally, after rehabilitation the cetacean is released into its home range with the same genetic stock and social unit. Unfortunately, we still don't have proof that Delphine is part of the Cove's resident dolphin community. We haven't found a photo ID of Delphine in my computer database. And believe me, we looked."

Carson felt her stomach tighten.

"The hospital couldn't find any freeze branding or dorsal-fin tags, either." Blake sighed and leaned back in his chair, letting the papers in his hands fall. The movement suggested defeat.

"Bottom line, without some form of identification, it's unlikely Delphine will be approved for release to the Cove."

Carson's heart sank. Neither of them could do anything. She felt the day's heat and wiped perspiration from her brow.

In contrast, Blake didn't seem bothered by the heat. "I'm not ready to give up on this." She saw again the spark of determination in the eyes of the dedicated marine biologist she'd fallen in love with.

"Me neither. What can I do to help?"

"My gut tells me that she *is* part of the community. Despite her bond with you—and we'll get into that in a minute—she stayed in the community longer than she would have if she were merely migrating through."

"But she was injured."

"True, but not seriously. At least not at that point. Only a small part of her tail fluke was bitten off. She could still hunt and forage. Lots of dolphins do fine out there with those minimal injuries." He shifted his weight, getting to the heart of the matter. "I need to find any physical characteristics, such as scars that were present before the accident, that I can use to run against my computer data and identify her. We're down to the wire on this. Can you think of any?"

Carson considered this as she folded a sheet of the newspaper from the table into a fan. Fanning herself, she blew out a plume of air. "Rather than trust my memory, I have a lot of photos that I took of her in the Cove over the summer."

Blake chortled. "Like baby photos?"

"Hey, I'm a photographer. It's what I do." She gave a short laugh. "Do you want to search those?"

"Absolutely."

"They're on my computer. Come on." Carson rose to her feet. She led the way back into the kitchen, aware of Blake's eyes on her as he followed.

Once inside Carson's room Blake made a beeline for the computer on Carson's desk. "So where are these photographs?" Blake was already opening his manila folder, intent on work.

A half hour later, Blake was leaning against the desk, his body so close beside hers that they often grazed each other when he pointed to something on the screen. As the minutes ticked by, she was finding it harder to concentrate on the photographs and not on the chemistry simmering between them. There had always been a visceral physical connection.

"This is the best one I can find," Carson said with finality, showing a close-up of Delphine staring up at the camera. "See the scar at the bottom of the rostrum? It's not something I thought about before, but it's in every photo. It's a defining scar. Will that work?"

"It's something." Blake stepped back and straightened. He put his hands on his back and stretched. "I just don't know how many close-up photos we have of dolphins that would show a small scar on the rostrum."

Carson sighed with frustration. "Where else on the body should we look?"

"That's the problem. The notches in the dorsal fin are like a fingerprint. We primarily use those for photo ID. Unfortunately, the dorsal-fin photos of Delphine that you already showed us are not in our database. And now, her dorsal fin was compromised by the fishing line. Lopped off the tip. The damage there is small, but it's like cutting off part of your fingerprint."

"What about the tail fluke?"

"We already documented the shark bite." He shook his head. "We'd need some mark that was there before the shark bite."

Carson rose to her feet as a memory surfaced. "Wait a minute! I just might have something." On her camera, she scrolled through countless photos. "I took more photos of Delphine when I was in Florida."

"Those won't help. I need pictures documenting scars before you met her."

"I know, I know. Hold on . . ." Carson knew what she was looking for. Suddenly she stopped. "Found it!"

Blake leaned over to take a closer look at the

photograph showing Delphine diving under the water, her fluke high in the air.

"I've seen her injured fluke."

"Don't look at her left fluke. Zoom in on her right tail fluke." Carson waited while Blake did so, aware that his chest pressed against her back. "There!" She pointed. "See that small hole?"

Blake zoomed again. "That small one? The size of a dime?"

"Right. During the summer when I took those other photos of Delphine in the Cove, I was focusing on her eyes, her expression. Like a mother taking photos of her baby. But these"— Carson indicated the photos on the camera—"I took these to document her scars. I thought it was important to follow up her healing. That's when I noticed that small hole on her right tail fluke. I thought it was odd how it's perfectly round, like it was punched with a paper hole puncher. She had this hole *before* she went to the hospital. It's not a normal scar, right?"

"Right," he said slowly, studying the photograph. "A round hole isn't normal, like notches or rake marks from other dolphins. It certainly would be unidentifiable."

She chewed her lip. "Do you have photos of tail flukes in your database?"

Blake lowered the camera and met her gaze, only inches away. He was smiling. "We do."

Carson released a heavy sigh of relief and beamed. "Thank God."

Blake straightened and crossed his arms. "We still have one other concern to cover."

Carson stared back at him. "What's that?"

"You."

Carson heard the word like a blow to the midsection. "What do you mean, *me?*"

Blake shifted his weight, then looked directly into her eyes. "One of the key conditions for clearance is the dolphin's behavior. Knowing that the dolphin did not take food from humans while in the wild." His expression was implacable. "We both know the answer to that one."

Carson stared back.

Blake shifted as though uncomfortable, clearly reluctant to say anything that would cause Carson pain. His tone softened. "Simply put, Delphine's ability to survive in the wild is considered compromised by your actions."

Carson felt awash with a wave of guilt, and her chin wobbled as she tried not to cry. Not only was she responsible for Delphine's injuries, but that she might be the reason the dolphin was not released back into the wild was a crushing blow.

"But," Blake continued, and Carson felt a flash of hope, "there is something we call a conditional release."

"What are the conditions?"

Blake paused to open the folder again and

shift through the papers. Finding the passage he searched for, he read aloud, " 'Attraction to humans in the wild has been extinguished.' " Blake closed the folder.

Carson stared back at Blake. In her eyes she saw a NOAA official determined to follow the rules and to do what was best for the dolphin. But she also saw compassion.

"Can you assure me—promise me—that you will no longer have interaction with the dolphin known as Case Number 1107?"

She nodded. "Yes."

Blake held her gaze and lifted his hand to count off his fingers. "You will not attract her to your dock. You will not feed her. You will not whistle or call to her. You will not do anything to draw her to you in any way, shape, or form. And you promise to let her be wild in the full sense of the word." Blake dropped his hand.

"Yes."

"Then it's possible Case Number 1107 will be cleared for a conditional release." Blake's expression grew serious. "But you should know me well enough by now that I will not play favorites. If Delphine persists in hanging around your dock or does anything else that exhibits her inability to let go of her attachment to you, I will recommend recapture."

"What happens then?"

"That would depend on the dolphin's health at

that point. If Delphine doesn't thrive after release, if she doesn't hunt or become a social member of her community, she'll go back to rehabilitation. The choice then would be to release her to a facility or euthanize."

Just the possibility of euthanasia had Carson's knees weak.

"The bond is two-sided. We have to see if Delphine will be able to leave *you* alone, too."

Carson averted her gaze, remembering how Delphine had whistled with joy at seeing her again at the Mote hospital. "Maybe we shouldn't take that chance. Maybe we shouldn't release her here in the Cove. At least if she goes to the Dolphin Research Center, she'll be safe."

"It doesn't work like that. The first goal is to release the dolphin to the wild. Delphine is still young and reproductively in her prime." Blake released a reluctant smile. "I have to tell you, after what you've just said, I believe that you'll do whatever you have to do for Delphine's best interests." He smiled at her. "My recommendation will be for release to the Cove."

Carson gave in to impulse and leaped to her feet and wrapped her arms around him. "Thank you, Blake."

Neither one of them made a move to pull away, each enjoying the contact again after so long. It was always this way between them. Sparks flew when they touched. Carson finally, reluctantly loosened her hold and slid slowly away. She teetered, feeling dizzy.

Blake's arm shot out to steady her. "You okay?"

"Fine. Just lost my balance." She snorted. "Hormones."

"Have you seen a doctor yet?"

"I made an appointment. Next week."

"Can I . . . I mean, is it okay if I take you?"

Carson hesitated. This was a big step. A first in their being partners in her pregnancy. She looked into his eyes, felt his arm holding hers, steadying her.

"Yes. I'd like that."

Chapter Five

The following morning Dora stood in front of an ironing board, pressing one of the two dresses she was considering wearing for her first job interview in almost fifteen years. She stood dressed only in her fancy new lacy bra and panties in front of the glass sliding doors to Devlin's bedroom porch. The large room was graced with a patio that offered a sweeping view of the ocean. The doors were wide-open to the onshore breezes.

"Now that's what I call a view," Devlin said from behind her.

Dora threw Devlin a saucy look over her shoulder, knowing full well which view he was referring to. Devlin was lying on his enormous, king-size bed that they'd just made love upon, one knee up, one leg hanging off the side of the mattress, as naked as a jaybird. He didn't care that he had a paunch growing, and that at forty he wasn't as trim as he'd been at seventeen when they dated all those years ago, only to end up with other people and ultimately find their way back to each other. Unlike Dora, Devlin had no modesty issues and was completely at ease with his body.

In contrast, Dora had always struggled with her weight, especially the tire around her middle. She had her mother's figure and cursed that she'd not inherited the long, lean frame of the Muir clan, like Carson and Harper. She also resented the biological burden that women carried, those damned extra fat cells on their hips for reasons of reproduction. Since she'd started her walking regimen, however, she'd whittled down that tire, and her body not only looked better, but she *felt* better. Exposing even some of her body was, for her, a measure of confidence.

She turned back to her ironing, shaking her head. "You're such a man."

Devlin chuckled low in his chest. She smiled. Even his laugh had a lowcountry accent. "Darlin', I just spent the last hour trying to prove that very point to you."

Dora blushed, remembering the details of the past hour.

"The only sight prettier than a woman ironing is a woman cooking a meal."

Dora pressed the steam button on the iron. "I can't believe you just said that."

"Why? It's the truth. Put on an apron and I'll show you."

"Hush now, you're being ridiculous." She huffed in feigned annoyance. "You know I've got to get going. I'm running late, thanks to a certain distraction." She pulled the pale blue cotton dress with white-stitched embroidery off the ironing board and held it up in front of her. "Which do you like best for the interview? This one?" She gave him a minute to observe, then set the blue dress down and held up a chocolate-brown shift. "Or this one?"

"I like you with neither on the best."

Dora rolled her eyes. "Try to be serious, Dev. I need to look good. Real good. I need this job."

He sighed with resignation, giving up the tease. "What job is that?"

Dora took a breath, trying to be patient. She'd told him about her job interview at a local dress shop earlier, but to be fair, he'd begun kissing her neck at the time. "Don't you recall? I told you that I had a job interview at a dress shop in Towne Center. The location would be so convenient. I don't want to have to go to the city to find work."

"A dress shop? What do they pay?"

She shrugged. "Fair wages." When he gave her

a doubtful look, she conceded, "Minimum wage. But I get a discount on my clothes."

"Uh-huh." Devlin rose and walked to the end of the bed to slip on a waffle-weave robe. "Why don't you come work for me?"

Devlin owned his own real estate firm on the barrier islands. He'd done extremely well during the boom of the past twenty years, but like most Realtors was hurting during the downtrend in the real estate market. The market was just beginning to pick up.

"What would I do?"

"Be my assistant."

"I don't have any secretarial skills. I can barely find my way around a computer, much less a fax machine. And you've already got a receptionist."

"I need help scouting out houses to flip. You'd be my right-hand gal. You have a great eye for real estate. You're a natural. You can study for your real estate license."

The idea of getting her real estate license was tempting. She and Devlin had been working together shaping up a darling cottage on Sullivan's Island. But working with him as a couple and working for him as an employer were not the same thing.

"No."

"Hear me out." Devlin laid his palm out in the air. "Look how well you and I do together working on that cottage. It's turning out real well.

And don't we enjoy working together?" When she nodded, he grinned. "I think so, too. You've got good instincts with houses, Dora. That's something you can't learn in school. You're born with it."

"No."

"I'd pay you well. Hell, a sight better than minimum wage."

Dora walked to him and placed a chaste kiss on his cheek. "Thank you. You are a prince among men and I appreciate the offer. I really do. But, no."

"Why the hell not? You like real estate."

"I do."

"Why accept a minimum-wage job when I'm offering you something better?"

"Because you don't really need me. *And*"—she emphasized to discourage his objection—"I want to get a job on my own, without someone handing it to me. Not this time. This is important to me. Try to understand."

With his tousled blond hair and baby-blue eyes, he looked like a pouting child. "I never heard you talk about wanting to be in retail."

"I don't particularly."

"Then why?"

"Because, frankly, I don't have a college diploma, secretarial skills, computer skills, or training in any particular area, for that matter. I've done volunteer work most of my life. What can I say? I saw the ad in the newspaper. It's either this or asking the customer if she wants fries with that."

"So go back to school. What's your hurry?"

"Nate has to go to school, not me. He starts private school in a few weeks. You know my house hasn't sold. We haven't gotten so much as a single offer, not even a lowball, so money is tight. I'll get child support and alimony, but it won't be enough to handle this expense. If I want Nate to start at the private school, I have to contribute. It's as simple as that. And that's okay. I'm looking forward to working again. Earning a paycheck. Putting something toward my Social Security. It'll make me feel . . . independent."

Devlin scratched his jaw but didn't reply.

Dora picked up the brown shift, held it up, and asked again, "So which looks better?"

He pointed to the blue. "Matches your eyes."

"You don't think it will make my butt look fat?"

"Honey, I ain't stupid enough to try and answer that one."

Dora sucked in her belly, wishing she'd had the discipline to skip the grits the night before. She stepped into the dress, wriggling as she tugged it over her hips. It was snug around the caboose, but it fit. "Harper picked these out. She always goes for that sleek, severe look. Don't you think it's a bit plain? I wish it had a bit of ruffle, or some bling on it." She sighed and walked to Devlin's side. "Zip me up?"

Devlin obliged. It was like being a married couple, she thought contentedly as he worked the tiny clasp at the top. Only better. She was free to come and go from his house as she pleased, though she supposed that would come to an end once she and Nate moved out of Sea Breeze and he didn't have his aunts or great-grandmother to keep an eye on him at a moment's notice. Devlin wanted to tie the knot, but after a lifetime of being at her mother's or her husband's beck and call, she was enjoying her newfound freedom—though she didn't dare tell him that.

"How's Carson doing?" Devlin asked.

She'd already told him that Carson was keeping the baby. It was typical of Dev to be concerned about her. He and Carson had been surfing buddies since they were kids. Dora was secretly convinced that Carson once had a crush on Dev back when he was a dashing blond surfer and a leader in her surfing crowd. Though, of course, Carson denied it.

"Good. Real good."

"Saw her with Blake. They on again?"

"You mean Rhett and Scarlett?" She chuckled. "The jury's still out on that. They're seeing each other ostensibly to make plans for Delphine." Dora smirked. "But they're not fooling anyone." She thought of the knowing smiles, the cuddling, and other indicators. "But you know Carson. When things get too close, she bolts."

"I always said that was one fish that was hard to catch."

Dora chuckled as she began to set her blond waves, knowing it was true. Carson's history of running from relationships was legendary. "I think the only reason she hasn't run back to Los Angeles yet is because she can't afford to." Dora sighed. "She's jumpier than a driver who's got to pee looking for exits."

Devlin chuckled, a low rumbling sound. "You get like that whenever I mention marriage, too."

Dora scoffed and waved her hand dismissively. "Not the same thing at all. I figure her being stuck here is a good thing. She's forced to stay and deal with her problems rather than run from them. Or from a guy."

"Blake's a good guy." Devlin went to the bar and poured himself a glass of seltzer water over ice. Dora noticed, pleased that he was cutting back on his drinking. "Speaking of guys, what was that you were mentioning about some guy coming from Florida to see Carson and getting our boy all riled?"

Dora put down her brush, her eyes gleaming with news. "Mamaw told me all about it. It was a big misunderstanding. Anyway, this Taylor fella . . . Mamaw say's he's quite the looker . . . is just a friend of Carson's. From when she was in

Florida. But"—Dora's eyes sparkled—"as it happens, he turns out to be a person of interest for Harper."

"Harper?" Devlin said with doubt. "Our Harper? I didn't figure she got her nose out of her computer long enough to be attracted to any guy. Thought she'd have hooked up with one of those online things . . . what you call those, anima icons?"

"Avatar." Dora knew such things because of Nate. "What you talkin' about, boy?" she teased. "Our Harper's got plenty of interest from real flesh-and-blood fellas. Except she's not interested in them. According to her, she's waiting for true love to hit. Thinks it'll happen at first sight. And, she thinks it hit with this Taylor fella."

Dev appeared amused by this notion as he walked closer. "She doesn't strike me as the *love at first sight* type. More like she'd be analyzing any guy for his pros and cons."

"Our sweet academic turns out to be a closet romantic. Don't you just love it? And I'll have you know that she's not on the computer nearly as much now as she was when she first arrived. In fact, she's outdoors a lot now. In that garden she's mad for. And she's been asking me to teach her how to cook. Bless her heart. She barely knows how to boil water." Dora poked Devlin in the ribs with her elbow. "Yep, I'll bet she's standing there in front of the stove right now, wearing an apron, stirring a pot, or cutting up vegetables." Dora wiggled her eyebrows. "Should I be jealous?"

Devlin laughed again and moved to slip his arms around her and rest his hands on her ample bottom. He gave a gentle squeeze. "You might be if she had a little more meat on her bones."

Dora laughed out loud, then kissed him full on the lips, amazed at how this man could always make her feel beautiful.

"You know," he said in a low voice by her ear, "I fell in love with you at first sight."

"I was thirteen," she said as a rebuff. "What did you know about true love back then?"

"Hell, woman, I'm not talking about when you were thirteen. I'm talking about last June, when I spotted you walking down Middle Street. All red in the face, sweat soaking that USC T-shirt."

Dora barked out a laugh and slapped away his roving hand. "You dog! I was trying so hard not to look winded." She laughed harder. "I thought I was going to die either from the heat or from you seeing me like that after fifteen years."

"I never saw anyone more beautiful. Like I said, I fell in love with you on the spot. Again."

Dora softened and, reaching up, tenderly brushed his shaggy blond hair from his forehead. "You do turn a girl's head."

Devlin slipped his arms around her again. "Shame you put that dress on," he murmured in her ear.

Dora glanced at the clock on the wall, then smiled at the sound of her dress zipper humming down the track.

Mamaw stood on the dock, staring out moodily as she did so often lately. It was early in the morning, but warm, hinting at the heat that was surely coming as the sun rose higher. Normally she wasn't one to sulk and let days slip away without notice. She had interests, hobbies, friends. Still, here she was, wandering about aimlessly, feeling pitifully lost without Lucille.

Lucille had come into her employ when Mamaw was a young bride in her new home on East Bay in Charleston. They'd grown old together. While always a treasured employee, Lucille had evolved over the years into Mamaw's companion, her confidante—her dearest friend. Lucille had held Mamaw up during the dark days following her son's death, then her husband's. She'd stood by her side, made sure she ate, encouraged her to get outdoors and walk. Day by day they had created a routine that altered the nature of their relationship. Marietta had no secrets from Lucille. They'd been like two peas in a pod.

Unlike Edward or Parker, Lucille had been a part of Mamaw's everyday life. Every question—concerning her granddaughters, the house, meals, the garden—was discussed between them. Every decision—from major issues such as finagling a way to get her granddaughters to agree to come to Sea Breeze for the summer, to minor ones such as what to watch on television—was negotiated with Lucille. Usually over a game of gin rummy.

Now Lucille was gone. The wheel that turned Mamaw's daily life was missing a cog. She'd known that she would grieve, yet she hadn't anticipated how Lucille's absence would be felt countless times a day, in all the small details Mamaw had come to take for granted. Being with Lucille had been as natural as breathing. Without her, she couldn't seem to take an easy breath. She knew her granddaughters were worried about her. The dears, they'd all gathered the night before to play a game of canasta with her after dinner. She stroked her arms. It was fun, she supposed. She just couldn't seem to muster excitement about anything these days. Was this what they called depression? she wondered.

"Marietta!" a voice called, drawing her from her reverie.

She turned her head toward the voice. Across the water, standing on the neighboring dock, was her neighbor Girard Bellows—Gerry, his friends called him. He was precariously bent over a small johnboat as he loaded gear. When he straightened, he lifted his hand in a neighborly wave. His long, lean frame could make even his nylon fishing pants and patched shirt look elegant.

Marietta smiled, remembering how Girard

Bellows had always been a handsome man, especially back in the days when his hair was as black as an eagle's wing and her hair was as golden as sunlight.

Marietta returned the wave.

Girard shouted, "How've you been?"

"Fine, thank you," she called back, trying to be neighborly.

Girard raised his finger in the universal signal to wait one minute. She nodded, then watched, curious, as he climbed into his small johnboat, fired the outboard motor, and came cruising the short distance over to her lower dock. Mamaw, perched on the upper dock, leaned over the railing and watched him jump to her dock and tie up with the grace of a man half his age. When finished, he looked up at her with a wide, white-toothed grin. He wore a Harvard baseball cap over his shock of white hair that contrasted handsomely with his tanned face. Girard had a vigor about him that was as youthful today as it had been back when she fished with him almost fifty years earlier on this very dock.

"Couldn't see making a lady shout," Girard called out as he drew near. He pulled off his sunglasses, revealing his pale blue eyes.

My, but Girard Bellows has aged well, Mamaw thought to herself. She'd always found him attractive. Even fancied him a bit, though it was all innocent enough. Girard came from an old moneyed family in the Northeast somewhere. He had that grace of movement that she thought was a gift of one's DNA. He always liked to tease her that his folk, who had come over on the *Mayflower*, were on the eastern coast long before hers in Charleston. That's when she claimed her pirate ancestry as her trump card. Who knew when and where the Gentleman Pirate first arrived on these shores? It had been a running joke between them for years, and she smiled now, remembering it.

When they were younger, neither of them lived on the island full-time. Local couples shared occasional drinks on weekends when families returned to Sullivan's Island for the season. The Bellowses were never invited to the Muirs' Charleston house, nor were the Muirs invited to the Bellowses' home . . . it was in Connecticut, she remembered. Later, both families retired to Sullivan's Island. Then Edward had died, followed soon after by Girard's wife, Evelyn. Mamaw hadn't seen much of Girard at all since Evelyn's funeral.

Nate had connected them again earlier this summer when he'd wanted to learn more about fishing. Nate had spotted the older man fishing on his dock and somehow found his way next door to ask Girard for help. Girard loved few things more than fishing and had taken immediately to teaching the boy, who proved to be an apt pupil.

Nate called him Old Mr. Bellows, Mamaw recalled with a light laugh.

Then there had been the accident with Delphine, and all fishing stopped.

"Haven't seen you out here for a while," Girard said.

Marietta shook her head. "I've been busy. Lucille passed."

Girard's smile immediately fell and he offered sincerely, "My condolences."

"Thank you."

"And your great-grandson, Nate. Nice boy. He sure loves his fishing."

"It was nice of you to take the time to teach him."

"Did he go home?"

"No, he's still here."

"Really? I haven't seen him out on the dock. He hasn't come asking for fishing advice." Girard shook his head. "That's one determined little guy."

"Nate hasn't touched his fishing rod since, well, not since the dolphin was hurt."

"Oh, right." Girard's face grew solemn at the memory. "Sorry business, that."

"Yes."

"Did the dolphin survive?"

"She did. Delphine went to the Mote Marine Cetacean Hospital. Nicholas Johannes flew the dolphin to Florida in his plane, otherwise I don't think the dolphin would have lived."

"Good man to do that."

Marietta nodded.

"Well, tell that rascal Nate he's welcome to come over anytime."

"That's very kind of you."

Girard looked down at his boat bobbing at the lower dock. "I seem to recall you were a pretty good fisherman in your day."

"Fisher*woman*. I still am," she replied, taking umbrage. "Fishing is like riding a bicycle. Once you learn you never forget."

He looked at her, smiling. "Is that so?" Girard crossed his arms. "In that case, why don't you and I go fishing together sometime?"

Mamaw was startled by this invitation that seemed to come out of nowhere. Flustered, she felt her heart beat faster. Fishing, indeed . . . What a thought! She was busy. She had things to do. She couldn't just jump into a boat and take off on a lark.

As she opened her mouth to decline, she heard the high-pitched cry of an osprey. She could never refuse the call of an osprey, and looking up, she spied the beautiful, black-winged raptor circling the Cove.

Beside her, Girard paused to take in the sight. "The great fish hawk at work," he said with awe, bringing his hand up to his brow to shield his eyes. "No better fishers in the world."

"I've always loved ospreys. They're site loyal

and mate for life. I think that makes them rather noble, don't you?"

"I do, indeed." He pointed to a small island to the right. "I built a platform on that hammock right over there. The same couple have returned to the nest, year after year, for about ten years. They've got fledglings now."

Mamaw turned to study Girard with new eyes. "That was you?"

"It was."

"I've wondered for years who did that. I've enjoyed watching that nest, the couple returning every February, checking for hatchlings, enjoying the fledglings. They're getting ready to leave again." She turned to cast him an assessing look. "And I have you to thank."

" 'Fraid so."

She remembered then Girard's love of nature, which she had appreciated when she was on the board of the land trust and had helped Girard arrange to put his family's considerable land holdings in South Carolina into a conservation easement. Like other wealthy northern families, his family had owned a large plantation upland that they'd used for hunting parties. South Carolina was richer today for the thousands of acres now in conservation across the state. That deal had been the feather in her cap at the land trust.

Marietta turned to study the handsome profile

of the man beside her. She reconsidered his invitation. "I might could go fishing," she said, slipping into vernacular. "When do you have in mind?"

"Why not right now? No time like the present."

She scoffed. "Now? How could I? I'd need to get my fishing rod, sunscreen . . ."

"Excuses. I have all that."

She closed her mouth, flustered. It was true. No one at the house needed her help. She was moping about aimlessly. In truth, she needed nothing but a little gumption. Marietta felt a lightening in her chest, the first since Lucille's death. Wouldn't that old marsh hen cackle to see her and Girard Bellows out fishing together again?

Marietta took a deep breath. Then she released it with a laugh that was carried out on a breeze like an echo to the osprey's call. "Why not, indeed?"

Chapter Six

August was bearing down hard. The entire weekend the beaches were packed with colorful towels and sunburned bodies. Even on Sunday morning it appeared folks were skipping church and praying on the beach. Everyone was trying to beat the heat and cram every last beach day in before the school season began.

By Monday morning, it was hotter than a sauna, even early morning on the beach while Harper attempted her daily run. The sand felt baked beneath her feet and radiated the heat. Harper considered herself lucky that she seldom perspired. Today, however, sweat was dripping down her face. That summer storm the forecasters predicted for the end of the week couldn't come fast enough, she thought.

Harper swiped her hand in front of her face, shooing away a swarm of pesky gnats. Cursing, she gave up the fight and cut her run short, slowing to a walk on the way home. By the time she reached Sea Breeze she was sweaty and as splattered with bugs as a windshield. She staggered along the tilting slate walkway to the back of the house, past the overgrown gardenia shrubs to the outdoor shower. A huge banana spider sat in its gorgeous web under the eaves. She jolted to a stop. She saw more of them out now in late summer as the humidity rose. She used to be spooked by them, mostly because of their size. But once she learned that the brilliantly colored spiders with tarantula-like legs were in fact not only harmless, but helpful because they ate mosquitoes, she'd reached a truce. She'd give the spiders their space if they didn't invade hers.

She carefully stepped around the intricate web and under the flow of water. It was bliss even as it sputtered warm from the old, miserly faucet to cascade down her body. She lathered up with the lavender shampoo and soap that Mamaw kept in supply, the sweet, calming scent filling the small space. When finished, she slicked back her hair, wrapped herself in a towel, and walked, refreshed, into the kitchen, dripping a small trail of water. All she wanted now was a cool glass of water.

The kitchen screen door slammed behind her, alerting the tall young man standing in the kitchen. He swung his head around to face her.

Harper stopped short, mouth agape.

Taylor's gaze took in Harper dressed only in a towel, and a slow grin spread across his face. "Good morning."

Harper tightened her towel around her, her face coloring. "Good morning. I, uh, didn't expect to see anyone." She looked around the room. "Where's Carson?"

"This isn't a social call. I'm here to work on your kitchen. You talked to my dad and set us up for beginning of the week, remember?"

"*You're* doing the work?"

His genial expression shifted to reflect his worry. "I know what I'm doing. Is that a problem?"

"No," Harper hurried to reply. "I'm just surprised, is all. I was expecting your dad."

"He's still working on another job. I offered to help out. It's the only way he could've gotten the project done right away." Taylor shifted his weight and added offhandedly, "To be honest, we pushed your job in front of another project."

"Oh." Harper felt instantly grateful. "That's great." She tightened her towel around herself, even as she wanted to sink right into the floor.

When his father had stopped by the day before, he'd taken a quick look at the kitchen and offered a reasonable estimate for the job. When she'd asked if he could begin right away, he'd replied that she was in luck. He had some extra help now. She didn't imagine that the "extra help" would be Taylor.

Dora burst into the room, returning from her run. She was drenched in sweat, her face as pink as her soaked T-shirt. Wiping her brow with the back of her arm, she hollered, "I'm sweating like a two-dollar whore on nickel night!"

Harper stifled a laugh. She glanced at Taylor and saw his lips twitch in a smile.

"Oh." Dora's eyes went wide when she spotted Harper in a towel standing beside a strange man. "I didn't know you had a guest."

Harper nodded her head in Taylor's direction. "This is Taylor. The man who befriended Nate and Carson at the Dolphin Research Center?"

Recognition dawned on Dora's face and she hurried over to his side, her grin widening. "You're *that* Taylor? Well, I'll be. It's a pleasure to meet you. Lord, as far as my son is concerned, you walk on water. He doesn't make friends easily, so high marks to you." Dora wiped her palm on her running shorts and offered it to Taylor.

While they began talking, Harper muttered, "I'm going to run off and get dressed." She hurried to the bathroom she shared with Mamaw and stared at herself in the large Venetian mirror that hung over the sink. She saw a slender woman in a towel with red hair slicked back and freckles from the sun popping out across her nose. What were the odds she'd again meet up with Taylor looking a mess?

She hurried to dress but took some time to apply a touch of makeup, leaning forward closer to the mirror. A few new lines bordered her eyes, too. She cursed, hearing her mother's voice in her ear: *Stay out of the sun. You have milky-white James skin.* Harper gently added more moisturizer over the offending lines with her fingertip. Turning from the mirror, she went directly to the armoire in her bedroom and pulled out a soft green summer shift, simple and cool for a hot day. She slipped it over her head and smiled, pleased with how the vibrant hue complemented her peachy coloring.

When she returned to the kitchen, she found Dora and Taylor huddled over the kitchen table studying paint samples. Harper approached slowly, eager to join in. She cleared her throat. "What do you have there?"

Taylor immediately turned to face her. "You have to pick out your colors."

"Oh. Of course." She moved closer to look at the samples spread over the table.

Dora stepped toward her, the challenge of a new decorating project shining in her eyes. She was still in her running clothes but her face was no longer flushed. "Mmm, you smell good. I, on the other hand, must smell like Patty's pig. Anyway, come take a look. I found some paint colors I used for the cottage. I think they'd look beautiful here. They're soft and beachy."

Harper drew close to the table, feeling a clenching in her gut. She appreciated Dora's help, but she was also aware that Dora might take over the kitchen project as she had done with the garden. This was *her* project and Dora tended to be a general, making Harper the private. "I have a few ideas." Harper had spent hours searching online for kitchen decor over the past few days and even had a file of printed pictures.

"Of course you do," Dora replied reassuringly. "Taylor told me you wanted white cabinets. That's what I painted the kitchen cabinets at the cottage. So I thought I'd show you the sample colors I selected. If you like them, fine. If not, fine." Dora glanced up at the clock. "Here." She handed the color chart to Harper. "I've got to scoot. Devlin is taking Nate and I for a final fishing trip before school starts. I'll be back in a few hours, if you have any questions." She winked at Harper. "Have fun."

Harper flushed, hoping Taylor didn't notice the wink. While she'd been anxious for her sister to leave them only a moment before, now she keenly felt Dora's absence. It was just she and Taylor again. She suddenly felt awkward.

Taylor turned back to the table. "I've painted both of these whites before in other houses I've worked on. This one is very bright, the kind you see on all the prefab cabinets. This one"—he lifted a creamier white—"is softer. I think you'll like it better in this older house, especially with all the natural light you'll be getting from the windows. You don't want it too bright in here. Hold on. I'll paint a swatch on the cabinets so you can judge for yourself. You have to see the paint on the walls. It's always different than the swatch or in the can."

She watched, curious, as he pulled out his pocketknife, then lowered to his haunches to pry open the sample cans of paint that Dora had provided. Harper noticed his hands had a few scratches, the kind one got from outdoor work.

After stirring the paint with a few swirls of the paint stick, he rose and fetched a paintbrush from his supplies. "You'll want to stand back. Wouldn't want to get paint on that pretty dress."

She was pleased he'd noticed. For her part, she couldn't help but notice how his white T-shirt, thin and torn, stretched across his back and the muscles of his forearms flexed as he painted one large square of paint on one cabinet door, then a second color on another. She usually dated the more slender, intellectual type of man, whom she met through work, family, or friends. But secretly she'd always been physically attracted to a well-muscled man. A workingman. She stepped back as he'd suggested, as much for a distraction from staring at him as to keep her dress paint-free.

When he finished, he came to her side, and they stood almost shoulder to shoulder and together studied the colors.

"You're right," she told him at length. "The creamy white is better."

"The other is too Home Depot."

"I wouldn't know. I've never been to a Home Depot."

He swung his head. "You're kidding. It's a hardware store. Like Lowe's or Menards?"

"Never been there, either. Not even Sears."

His gaze was disbelieving. "That's almost un-American," he teased.

"Have you ever been in a Saks? Or a Neiman Marcus?"

He laughed, conceding. "Point taken. Well, you're in for a treat. You should hightail it to the hardware store of your choice and pick out the color you want for the walls." He picked up one of Dora's papers. "Or, here's the address of a paint store that's close. It'll be easier for you to deal with than a hardware store. It's smaller and the guy will help you out." Holding out the sheet, he added, "I'm guessing this'll be a first for you, too?"

She nodded with a sheepish grin as he shook his head in disbelief. The difference in their worlds was clear. And she was intrigued.

He released the paper with a wiseacre grin, then turned to cross the room to the sink. As he rinsed the paintbrush, he looked at her over his shoulder. "Tell them you want samples of paint. Don't buy gallons."

"Okay, boss." She was sure she would have brought the gallon buckets if he hadn't warned her. "I'll be right back."

She was beginning to feel a camaraderie between them. Being friends was good, she resolved. No preening or positioning. No clever repartee. Just comfortable honesty. Before leaving, she glanced over her shoulder to see Taylor stretching his arms out to remove a cabinet door. Sighing, she turned away, her fluttering heart betraying her resolve.

Dora showered and changed into clean clothes, her eye on the clock. Devlin would be pulling up at the dock shortly with his boat. He was so excited about the day, had made all the plans, eager to bond with Nate. Dora had permitted Devlin to meet Nate a few weeks back, but this would be the first time they'd be spending any significant amount of time together, and Dora's heart squeezed as she realized how much Devlin wanted everything to go perfectly.

She slipped a broad-brimmed hat on her head, then hurried to Nate's room down the hall, feeling the tension that accompanied an appointment scheduled with Nate. Always in the back of her mind was the fear of a meltdown. She knew the next week would be a big challenge for her son as he started a new school. She so very much wanted this day to be fun for him.

Outside his bedroom door she said a quick prayer, then gently pushed it open. Nate was sitting on the floor, fully dressed in his soft shorts and a T-shirt, playing with his Legos. His head was bent and his blond bangs covered his eyes. Her expression softened and her heart surged with love.

"Ready to go fishing?"

Nate's head swung around at the sound of her voice. He nodded and leaped to his feet. "I'm ready!" He went to collect the cherry-red fishing rod Mamaw had given him in May, the one that had once been his great-grandfather Edward's.

Dora's gaze devoured her son, noting how he'd filled out this summer and how his usually pale skin glowed from time in the sun.

Since he'd returned from Florida, Dora had made a point of trying to be more a fun mother than a strict one. She took him on outings, whereas before she had always talked herself out of it for fear of one of Nate's meltdowns. Their favorite thing was to kayak in the Cove. Together they'd explored the local parks, walked the beach in search of turtle tracks. Best of all, her little boy had let go of his guilt about Delphine's accident and picked up his fishing rod again.

"Can we go now?" he asked in the tone of someone who'd already waited far too long.

"Aye, aye, Captain."

About an hour later, Devlin guided the Boston Whaler through the winding waterway with the peacock pride of the captain of a beautiful boat. He grandly gestured as he pointed out new and expensive houses or spotted a great blue heron or some other shorebird searching out a meal. It was lovely out on the water that mirrored the blue sky, though they were one of only a few boats out today as summer wound down. Dora leaned back against the cushion, sipping her fizzy water, and felt as if she were the queen of the Nile. On this hot day she enjoyed the occasional splash of water when the boat bounced on a wave.

As lovely as the scenery was, Dora much more enjoyed the sight of Dev and Nate at the wheel. Dev stood a few paces behind Nate as the boy took a turn to steer. She could tell by Nate's rigid stance that he was taking his task seriously. And having the time of his life. It was an easy thing to offer, yet something Cal never allowed his son. Her heart expanded with gratitude to Devlin.

He was a fine figure of a man, she thought, sprinkling drops of cool water on her face. She thought back to when she and Dev were young and rode along these same waters. They'd drop anchor and jump without a thought into the water for a swim. Ah, youth, she thought with chagrin. No way she'd do that today. Age brought reason, and she knew how fast a boat could come speeding out of nowhere.

Devlin pointed to a small creek ahead. "That's where we turn off. It's my secret spot, and, man, oh, man, we're gonna catch us some fish!"

"When school starts, does that mean I can't go fishing no more?" Nate asked.

"Anymore," Dora corrected automatically. "Of course not. You can go fishing all year round, if you can bear the cold."

"Then I'm gonna," he replied, picking up Devlin's speech. "I don't mind the cold. Fishing is my most favorite thing in the world."

Devlin met Dora's eye and smiled before he called back to Nate, "That makes two of us." Then Devlin turned the engine low. "Okay, son, I best take over here. You keep an eye out on the edges. Call if I get too close."

Devlin veered off into a narrow creek that looked to Dora like all the other small creeks they'd passed. She always marveled at how Devlin could navigate these backwater creeks and never get lost. She'd heard stories of less confident captains getting lost and then stuck in the mudflats when the fickle tide turned. Once stuck, they'd have to wait hours until the tide returned.

A soft wind swayed the spartina. Dora listened to the rhythmic scraping of the salt-grass stems and in the distance heard the loud hyena cackle of an unseen bird.

"Look!" Nate exclaimed.

Dora turned to see Nate leaning over the edge of the boat, pointing.

"Someone's found out your secret spot!" Nate exclaimed, offended. "Can they do that?"

A small johnboat sat anchored along a mudflat with fishing rods already in the water.

"It's a free country." Devlin steered the boat to the opposite side of the creek so as not to cause a wake for the other fishermen. "Plenty to go around. We'll just mosey on a little farther up the creek."

Dora turned her head to view a gray-haired man and woman sitting side by side in the boat. Their backs were to Dora, but something about them was familiar. Dora turned her body to lean over the boat's railing, squinting to get a better look.

"Oh, my word!" she exclaimed. "That's Mamaw!"

"What?" Devlin slowed the engine to a growl, then moved to the side of the boat for a better look. "Well, I'll be damned, it is. Who's she with?"

"I don't know."

Nate exclaimed, "It's Old Mr. Bellows."

"Are you sure?" Dora squinted.

"Oh, yes." Nate gave a confident nod. "They're friends. I saw them talking at the dock."

A small smile played at Dora's lips. "Really?"

"Yes, really," Nate replied matter-of-factly.

As they drew nearer, Dora cupped her hands over her mouth and called out, "Hey, Mamaw! Ahoy there!"

Mamaw swung her head around, following the call. Her mouth opened in a silent gasp at recognizing them. Dora laughed at her grandmother's startled expression and waved her arm in a wide arc, gleefully thinking, *Aha, caught in the act!* Nate and Devlin called out greetings as well. Mamaw waved back with a feeble gesture, obviously flustered. They were traveling farther away from the couple, but Dora could still see them sitting, shoulders touching.

"Mamaw, what are you up to?" Dora murmured to herself. She couldn't wait until the card game that night.

Mamaw was well aware that she and Girard were sitting so close that their shoulders were touching. She'd not only allowed it, she enjoyed it. It had been a long time since her stomach had fluttered at the touch of a man. And it was harmless enough. They were two old acquaintances, even friends, fishing together on a summer morning. It was all perfectly innocent.

Then why did it feel like anything but when Dora had caught them together? It was downright disconcerting, she thought as her hands tightened on the rod.

Girard chuckled at her side, lost in his own thoughts.

"What's so funny?" she asked, slightly annoyed.

"Oh, just feeling a bit like two teenagers caught sneaking out."

Mamaw glanced at him, saw his amused expression, and couldn't help but laugh. "It's true," she said ruefully. She'd wanted to keep this to herself. The outing was above suspicion, yet she knew the thoughts racing through her mind were far from dewy innocent.

She'd been remembering the crush she'd had on Girard Bellows some fifty years ago. She'd met Girard at a welcome party thrown for the Bellowses by their good friend Bitsy. Sullivan's Island was a small community and, in those days, close-knit. Many of the families in their group had connections that spanned generations in Charleston. They'd grown up together, went to the same churches, their children and their children's children went to the same schools. The Bellowses, however, were considered "from off" by the local families. This created a powerful curiosity factor that had the island gossips eager to learn more about them.

The party had been at Bitsy's shore house. On this balmy night the katydids were singing. Cars were parked along the narrow streets for blocks and Bitsy had the cottage lit up. A group played soft jazz, and tables creaked under the weight of food. Marietta had stepped out onto the back porch to escape the smoke-filled rooms. She remembered the heavy scent of jasmine lingering in the air. The sun was setting and candles were flickering in the hurricane lamps like fireflies.

Across the porch a tall, lean man was standing in a cluster of men drinking scotch or bourbon and talking about guns or money or business. Although most of them were tan, his was darker— that of a man who spent time on the water. His blue eyes shone brilliantly against the ruddy color, and when he laughed, which he did freely, his teeth shone white. Bitsy had thought he was dreamy, like Cary Grant. And, she'd added meaningfully, his family was very old money. His wife, Eleanor, was exceedingly beautiful and well-bred, yet Marietta had always found her dull and even dim.

Marietta had walked up to the cluster of men. Bitsy's husband, Bob, was in his cups and grandly introduced her as "our resident nature lover."

Girard had immediately turned an interested gaze upon her and began asking a series of questions, surprisingly well informed, on the local wildlife. His upper-crust New England accent fell sweet on her ears, though, she recalled, it had grated against Edward's.

That initial conversation was the beginning of a longtime friendship. Though there might have been a slight undertone of flirtation to it, the only passion they'd shared concerned wildlife and the local landscape.

"Do you remember the first night we met?" she asked him.

Girard turned and smiled. His blue eyes, paler now with age, still had the ability to capture her attention and hold it. "I most certainly do. I remember thinking you were the most interesting woman I'd met that night."

"Only that night?"

"The most interesting woman I'd met in my life."

Marietta scoffed at that. He always was a charmer. Though it was his intelligence that had attracted her the most. He had eclectic tastes and she found his opinions challenging. Girard could discuss finance, science, art, and politics with equal ease and distinction.

"Why do you ask?"

"No reason. I was just remembering how, even from the first, you and I could talk on and on and I'd lose track of time. Like right now. I have no idea whatsoever what time it is." She laughed. "And I couldn't care less."

That first evening at Bitsy's party they'd stood together on the porch and talked while the night darkened around them and the candles sputtered in the lamps. It was terribly rude not to mingle, but she despised idle gossip and was having such a good time talking about environmental issues with someone who cared.

"I remember being annoyed when your husband came to draw you away," Girard said.

"Later, he admonished me for sparking gossip. We had quite a row about it."

"I can't imagine you being silenced by a bunch of gossips."

"Hardly. We were doing nothing wrong."

"A bit, perhaps. Evelyn was jealous."

"Of what?" she asked, shocked.

"Of our shared interests and projects."

"I never meant not to include her."

"Precisely. Conservation never interested her." He looked out over the water.

Marietta cast him a furtive glance. "You know, Edward was always jealous of you, as well. A little."

Girard swung his head around again. "Was he?" His eyes sparkled.

"Oh, yes. Especially the time you took me sailing."

Girard laughed then, a soft chuckle. "He's lucky I didn't sail off with you."

"Really . . . ," she said with feigned scorn, and looked away feeling a slight blush coloring her cheeks. "Just as well I didn't know you had such fanciful thoughts," she said, enjoying the flirtatious banter. "After that land-trust deal you were my hero."

"So you're saying I missed my chance to steal you away?"

She turned and raised her brow. "You just might have succeeded . . . that one time."

They both laughed.

"I think," Girard said with finality, pulling in his fishing rod. "The fish aren't biting today."

"Doesn't appear so." She was grateful for the distraction of pulling in her own rod. "We gave it the old college try."

"I owe you another shot. What do you say, Marietta? Are you up to try again?"

"I owe it to myself to catch at least one."

"Good!" His white teeth shone against his tan. "We'll try again tomorrow. For today, let's shove off."

The boat's motor ignited and churned the water with a great growl. Mamaw clutched her hat with one hand and the side of the johnboat with the other as Girard sped up. The small boat bounced as it cut through the water, spraying water in her face. She laughed out loud at the giddy experience. She looked up at the sun shining above, feeling its light warm her, reminding her of the spring of her youth, bringing her back to life.

The midafternoon sky was cloudy, hinting at rain. Harper leaned against the back of the dock bench with her legs up and her computer in her lap. She was glad for the clouds that kept the pounding sun at bay and promised much-needed rain for her garden. She'd been out here for hours, her fingers flying on the keyboard as her story flowed. She was so caught up in her story that she startled when she heard a voice.

"Want some lemonade?"

She swung her head up to see Taylor standing beside her carrying two glasses of lemonade. Flustered, she hurriedly closed her computer and moved her legs to sit up.

"Thanks." She took the cool glass dripping with condensation. She took a sip and found it perfectly tart. "It's delicious."

"My mother made it. She makes me a thermos every day." He laughed lightly. "She hovers."

"Sit down." She indicated the empty bench with her hand.

"Are you sure I'm not bothering you."

"Not at all. I could use the break."

He seemed pleased by the invitation and sat beside her, letting his arm stretch out over the back of the bench. Taking a long drink from his glass, he looked out over the Cove.

Harper turned her head as well. She'd been sitting here all afternoon and had stared only at her laptop. The sky was startling in its contrasts. Shafts of pearly light shot out from steely-gray storm clouds in sharp angles, looking like an art deco painting. The light cast translucent shadows on the murky water.

"It's beautiful here," Taylor said.

"I look out at this same view every day, and every time I see it differently. It's always changing. Never boring."

"How long are you here for?"

"Till the end of summer."

"Not long."

"No." She let her finger trace the condensation on the glass. "Longer than I've ever spent before, though. When I was a child I only spent a few weeks. Had to be home in August for school."

"This is a pretty great place to spend the summer."

She smiled hearing the truth of it. "It was a magical time for me and my sisters. A real Huck Finn existence. Carson and I used to run wild over the island." She leaned forward as though telling a secret. "My grandmother tells us that we are descended from a pirate." She made a shocked face. "Imagine."

"Is it true?"

"I honestly don't know. But I like to think so. The Muirs have a long line of sea captains."

Taylor lifted his brow. "Really?"

She laughed, not surprised that he'd found that tidbit interesting, given that his father was a captain. "Yep. Anyway, there's this story, a legend really, that the Gentleman Pirate—that's our ancestor—buried his gold somewhere on Sullivan's Island. So naturally, Carson and I dressed up as pirates and searched for the buried treasure."

"Ever find it?"

She chortled and shook her head. "Nope. But we had the best time looking. Mamaw didn't allow television during the day and scooted us out of the house to play. Carson and I . . ." Harper smiled. "What a pair we made. We both loved adventure. I was . . . am . . . a big reader. I loved to come up with plots for our make-believe, mostly from books I'd read." She looked out over the water as memories played in her mind. "Our imaginations knew no bounds. Day after day we went out, absorbed in our made-up worlds." When she turned back, she found him studying her face. She blushed and looked at her hands. "You must think that's silly."

Taylor shook his head. "Actually, I think that's pretty great."

She flushed with pleasure and turned her head. The shimmering water was racing with the current. "This summer is the first time I've been here in years. Since I was ten or eleven. The first time all of us have been together since Dora's wedding. It's both strange and really nice to be living under the same roof with Mamaw and my sisters again."

"I get that. I'm staying with my parents. For a few weeks, anyway. It's nice to visit, but I wouldn't want to stay longer than that. I don't think any of us could stand it."

She thought about that comment. "A few months ago I would've agreed with you. Back in May I didn't think I'd be able to stand a whole summer with these women I hardly knew. Sure, we're related, but did we *like* each other? Or would we tear each other's hair out?"

"And . . . ?"

"And it turned out we did like each other." She smiled. "Though we've had our moments of hair pulling, too."

"Where do you fit in the lineup? Who's the eldest?"

"Eudora's the eldest. Then Carson. Then me."

"So you're the baby."

She rolled her eyes. "Please . . . That's a name I've been trying to outgrow most of my life."

Taylor gave a low whistle. "Hold on. Eudora, Carson, Harper. I see a pattern."

Harper shook her head. "Yes, right. That's my father. He was a writer and had the idea to name his daughters after great southern authors."

Taylor leaned back, looking at the sky in thought. "That's Eudora Welty. Harper Lee. Carson . . ."

"McCullers. *The Heart Is a Lonely Hunter.*"

"Oh, yeah." He nodded his head with approval. "That's cool."

Harper took a sip of lemonade and shrugged. To this day her mother rued the day she'd agreed to call her only child after a southern author rather than a British one.

"Are you close?"

"Me and my sisters?" Harper pursed her lips. "We couldn't be more different. We each were raised in different parts of the country. Carson in California, me in New York, Dora in the Carolinas. We have different lifestyles, beliefs, style of dress. Mothers. But somehow, when we're together, we all fit, like pieces of a puzzle made whole. Take this summer," Harper said, warming to the subject. "We've all been in varying states of transition, and it's been like Sea Breeze is our lifeboat and we're all in it together, paddling for shore. We've helped each other along, and in the process, we've become more than sisters." She looked back at the water. "So yes. We're close. We've become best friends."

Below, the water slapped the wooden dock, and the wood moaned. After a moment, Taylor said, "Sounds like you've found your treasure."

Harper turned her head back to look at him, pleased at his perspicacity.

Taylor swallowed the last of his lemonade in a gulp. "I best get back to work. Nice talking with you, Harper." He touched her shoulder, briefly, then turned and walked away.

Harper put her hand on her shoulder and watched his long, purposeful stride back up the dock to the house.

Chapter Seven

Canasta was a card game in the gin rummy family, so Mamaw felt her blood stirring when she pulled out the decks of cards. It was another steamy afternoon in the lowcountry, and feeling particularly thirsty, she poured two liberal fingers of rum over ice. It was almost five o'clock, wasn't it?

She met her granddaughters in the living room. They were abandoning the porch due to the continuing heat wave. The room was more formal than the rest of the house, filled with what Mamaw referred to as "good" family antiques, which meant museum quality, all early American, with pale blue silk upholstery. Not the usual room for playing cards. The air was festive as they opened the folding card table and chairs, turned on music, and gathered around.

"Girls," Mamaw called out when they clustered around the table, "before you sit, we have to choose partners."

The girls eyed each other nervously.

"I hate choosing teams." Harper frowned petulantly. "It always reminds me of when I was young and in physical education at school. No one ever picked me for their team because I was too little." She looked at Carson. "You were probably the first one picked."

"As a matter of fact, I was," Carson said with a wry grin.

"No fears, my dear." Mamaw fanned out a deck of cards across the table. "Pick a card. The closest numbers will be partners."

Relieved, they all drew a card. Mamaw and Dora were paired against Carson and Harper.

"The South shall rise again!" Dora warned them.

"Here we go . . . ," groaned Carson with a roll of the eyes.

"It feels weird to play cards in the living room," Dora said, arranging four glasses of iced tea and a bowl of mixed nuts on the table. "I always felt this was the room we all had to be proper in. Well behaved."

"A lady?" Carson asked teasingly.

Harper silently mouthed, *Death to the ladies!*

Carson chuckled at their childhood mantra. Then her smile fell as her gaze swept the room.

"The last time we were all in here was during the storm. In July, remember?"

"Of course we remember, sugar," Dora said. "It was her last night with us."

Mamaw was shuffling the cards but paused to look around the room. Frank Sinatra was crooning "Summer Wind" and candles flickered. Mamaw closed her eyes and said softly, "Lucille still is with us."

Harper smiled then, a sad smile.

Mamaw opened her eyes and, with determination, briskly shuffled the two decks of cards. They snapped in her hands with a croupier's precise movements. "It's better indoors today. I swanny, the weather is positively wilting. We'll expire if we play outdoors. I'm old enough to tell you that I've suffered through plenty of years without air-conditioning—sleeping outdoors on porches, fanning ourselves relentlessly, drinking cool drinks. I might not be a big fan of air-con out here on the island, but on days like this I bless the birth of Willis Carrier."

"Amen," added Dora, raising her iced tea in a salute.

"I'm a convert," said Carson, lifting the long braid from her back. "I used to hate it. Coming in from the water, air-conditioning always made me too cold. But ever since I got pregnant, I can't take the heat like I used to."

"It's your body heat, dear," Mamaw told

146

her. "It's warmer now. You're working harder."

Carson eyed Mamaw skeptically.

Mamaw's eyes widened. "It's a fact! Look it up." She began dealing the cards.

"It's not the heat that bothers me. It's the humidity," said Harper. Lifting her hair like Carson, she twisted her shoulder-length hair up into a French twist and secured it with a clip. Then she rubbed her arms, dotted with angry bites. "And the bugs. I got sucked dry yesterday during my run."

"Summer in the South . . . ," mumbled Dora.

"The heat riles the skeeters up," Mamaw said, picking up her cards.

Harper scratched her leg and groaned. "Well, they love me."

"It's your red hair," Dora said with authority as she picked up her cards, one by one. Her blond hair was neatly pulled back in a ponytail with a pink ribbon. "The color red attracts bees and mosquitoes."

"That's an old wives' tale," Carson said dismissively.

"It is not," Dora argued, looking up from her hand. Dora didn't like to be corrected.

Carson skewered her with a look. "It is."

"Hold on." Harper grabbed her phone and bent over it for a moment.

Dora wagged her foot with frustration. "I know I'm right."

"Here it is." Harper glanced up to smile conspiratorially. "You're both right. Bees don't see color."

"Told you," said Carson with a gloating smile.

"But"—Harper pointed her finger in an arresting motion in the air—"it's true mosquitoes tend to go for clothing in black, dark blue, and red. *And*"—she giggled as she pointed to Carson—"pregnant women." Then with a laugh: "*And* drinkers of beer."

Dora and Harper burst out laughing. Mamaw held her cards up to cover her smile.

"Well, damn," Carson said, in typical self-derisive fashion. "In either case, I lose. I stopped drinking, but now I'm pregnant." She rolled her eyes. "Figures."

Harper eyed Mamaw's rum drink skeptically. "Speaking of drinking, when did we relax the rules about alcohol around here?"

Mamaw raised her glass to her lips and took a prim sip. "Since I discussed it with Carson."

Carson shrugged. "Why shouldn't Mamaw have her nip of rum at night? The smell of alcohol makes me sick, so no temptation. Seems wrong to punish her. It's her house, after all."

"You mean, I can have a glass of wine?" Dora asked eagerly.

"Be my guest," Carson said.

Dora smiled like a Cheshire cat. "For medicinal purposes only, of course."

"Enough chatter," Mamaw announced. "Let's play cards."

Time flew by as they played canasta and the relaxed chatter floated in the air. "Mamaw, your color is back," Harper said as she looked over her cards. "You look, I don't know, happier."

"Why, thank you, dear." Mamaw arranged her cards. "I was just thinking how I feel better."

Dora looked at her cards and asked nonchalantly, "Been outdoors much? Say, on the water?"

Mamaw knew this was coming. She discreetly looked over her cards to deliver a squinted-eyes warning at Dora.

Dora ignored her and blithely continued as she picked a card from the pile, "You know, when I was out on the boat with Devlin and Nate earlier today, we passed this small johnboat with two people fishing together. A man and a woman. They were just as cozy as could be. Why, Mamaw, I could have sworn the woman was you. Didn't you hear me call out to you?" Dora's voice sounded innocent but she held her cards over her mouth to conceal her grin.

Mamaw simmered as Harper and Carson first looked with astonishment at Dora, then at Mamaw.

"Okay." Carson lowered her cards. "What's going on?"

Mamaw sniffed and took a sip of drink. She then sighed as if a long-suffering soul who had to put up with the antics of a child. "Tempest in a teapot. Girard Bellows and I went fishing," she declared as if it were the most natural thing in the world. "We've been friends forever. He saw me sitting on the dock and no doubt took pity and invited me out on his boat. I had a very nice time, thank you very much. End of story." She tapped her cards on the table. She made a show of arranging them. "By the way, Dora," she said archly, "you should use more sunscreen. You're burned as red as a boiled lobster."

"You went out with Old Man Bellows?" asked Carson incredulously.

Mamaw lay her cards on the table. "First of all, we didn't go *out*. We went fishing. Secondly, he's not Old Man Bellows. He's *Mr.* Bellows to you." She gave Carson a no-nonsense glare. "And we most certainly were not being cozy." Mamaw picked up her cards. "It was a small boat."

Dora leaned over the table and said in a stage whisper, "They were shoulder to shoulder. Canoodling."

The girls started snickering.

Mamaw looked at her cards. "I'd say I've found the jokers in this deck."

Carson hooted. "And you're the wild card!"

Mamaw relented and joined their laughter, relishing the first sounds of merriment in Sea Breeze since Lucille's death. Even if it was at her own expense.

The late afternoon stretched on into evening as they played hand after hand of canasta. It was so hot no one was very hungry, and since the kitchen was out of order, they nibbled crackers and cheese, leftover quiche, and raw vegetables. While they played, the talk never ceased. They discussed ways that they could each help an anxious Nate prepare for his new school. They spent a long time coming up with possible names for Carson's baby, which ranged from family names to silly ones. Harper was leaning heavily toward Poseidon, but Carson only rolled her eyes. Eventually the conversation turned to the progress of the kitchen's makeover.

Carson, fanning her cards and smiling, asked Harper, "How's it going with Taylor McClellan?"

Harper shrugged noncommittally and peered at her cards. "He's doing a good job. Moving right along."

"Interesting that Taylor's doing the project. And not his father," Carson said.

"Not really," said Harper. "I suspect he's helping his father this summer."

Carson moved a few cards around in her hand. "Actually, that's not what I heard."

Harper's glance darted up from her cards.

Carson's eyes were gleaming. "I heard that he asked his father if he could do the job."

"That's not unusual. He's doing jobs and picked this one. He's your friend."

"Except he's not working for his dad. He's in town for job interviews."

Harper looked up from her cards. "Then why did he ask for this job?"

Carson tapped her cheek in feigned wonder. "I can't imagine."

Harper sat back in her chair. "Really?"

"And"—Carson laid down a discard—"he asked me if you were seeing anybody."

Harper's grin widened.

Dora narrowed her eyes. "Are you sure *you* aren't canoodling?"

The women burst out laughing again.

"I just love that word," Harper said, her mood shooting skyward. "But I'm not even sure what it means." She discarded.

Mamaw picked up the card. "It means to fondle and kiss."

Harper balked. "No, ma'am, we are definitely not canoodling. Unfortunately."

"Yet," added Carson.

"Well, I just love the blue you chose for the walls." Dora discarded. "It's just the right shade. Kind of a haint blue. It will be gorgeous against the creamy-white cabinets."

Harper basked in the compliment. "Thank you, partner." She picked up a card. "What is haint blue?"

"That's the blue the Gullah-Geechee paint on their porch ceilings to protect it and chase away negativity," replied Dora. "It's meant to keep the evil spirits out."

"Amen to that," muttered Carson.

"More lowcountry lore to learn," Harper said.

"Why bother doing the kitchen now?" asked Carson.

Mamaw spoke up. "Because this house deserves it."

"And it'll improve resale," Dora added.

"Mamaw, that reminds me." Harper forced her tone light after Carson's comment. "I'd like to get some new knobs and pulls for the cabinets. Do you mind if I change them?"

"Not at all, dear. But before you go shopping, take a look-see up in the attic. I have a bunch of old knobs and door handles and all kinds of whatnots up there. All collected from family houses over the years. God only knows all what's up there." Mamaw smiled wryly. "Help yourself to whatever you find. I don't know if they're any good, but—" She was interrupted by the sound of tires skidding to a halt in the gravel driveway, followed by a car door slamming. "What in heaven's name . . . ?"

Mamaw, who sat closest to the window, pushed back the curtain and peered out. "Lord, Carson, here comes Blake. And he's barreling in like a hurricane!"

Carson dropped her cards on the table and stood up, eyes wide.

The doorbell rang, followed by three impatient knocks. While Mamaw and the other two women straightened in their chairs, Carson hurried to the front hall. She opened the door and Blake rushed in, swooping up Carson in his arms. He swung her around a few times, grinning like a fool. Mamaw, Harper, and Dora set down their cards, the game forgotten.

"Blake!" Carson laughed into his face as he swirled her. "Put me down!"

Blake gently set her feet on the floor but kept his hold on her arms. He was grinning from ear to ear in triumph. "We found her!"

Carson stared back, uncomprehending. "Found who?"

"Delphine!"

"What?"

"I found her in the database."

Carson's heart leaped to her throat. "Oh, Blake!" Impulsively she leaned forward to plant a kiss on his lips.

Blake leaned back but kept his arms around Carson. "It was that little hole you found in the tail fluke." He rushed his words. "I spent the last two days poring over thousands of photographs and I found it. I couldn't believe it. When I blew the photo up, I saw the scar on her rostrum, too. It's a match. Delphine is definitely from our community. Baby, she's one of ours!"

Carson's voice was choked. "I knew it. So

Delphine can be released into the Cove?"

He nodded and lowered his forehead to hers. "Yes."

Carson wrapped her arms around Blake and buried her face in his neck. Inside, her heart was spinning with joy. She wanted to shout out, dance, jump up and down. But all she could do was weep.

Delphine was coming home.

Chapter Eight

The following morning, Harper sipped coffee in the kitchen and prayed to the gods of caffeine that the liquid she was pouring into her system would soon take hold. She'd spent another long night up writing and was feeling utterly spent. Musing over a chapter she had pounded out at a particularly late hour the night before, Harper didn't even hear Taylor come in. She jumped as he shut the door behind him. A gust of wind sent the papers and droplets of rain flying.

"It's a day for ducks," she told him as he removed his rain jacket. He wore shorts and a white T-shirt splattered with different colors of paint. The short sleeves were frayed and so worn he'd rolled up the edges over his biceps. She took his jacket, shaking raindrops onto the floor.

"Yep. I don't mind bad weather." He slipped out

of his shoes. "Out on the boat, you learn to deal."

He looked up and Harper's heart skipped a beat. Rivulets of water dripped from his hair down his face, making his green eyes shine even brighter against his tan.

Harper rushed to a drawer, pulled out a kitchen towel, and handed it to him. Their fingers brushed when he took it and she felt a rush.

"Thanks." Taylor wiped his face, then tossed the towel on the counter.

Harper glanced around, as much to take her eyes off him as to take the room's measure. The cabinets had been primed, and the cabinet doors were neatly stacked against the walls. Blue painter's tape bordered the cabinets on the walls and floor. Here and there, sample swatches of different shades of blue paint splattered the walls.

"Everything's so organized."

"I'm a Marine. We're trained to run a tight ship," he said, half-serious, half in jest.

Harper was glad they'd broached the subject she was curious about. "When did you leave the Marines?"

"You never leave the Marines. Once a Marine, always a Marine."

"Oh." She'd heard the pride in his voice. "So, you're still in the Marine Corps?"

"I got out four years ago."

"Were you in Afghanistan?"

"Yes."

"Is the war the reason you joined the Marines?"

"That's not so simple to answer. I graduated from the Citadel and the war was escalating. It was a no-brainer to go in with my classmates. I wore the ring."

"And now you're back."

"Yes." His face went still. "Not all my classmates were so lucky."

Words fell away and his stillness gave away nothing.

"Okay, then," he said with finality, prying off the lid of his Styrofoam cup. Steam rose from his coffee. He took a sip, then set the cup on the counter. "Best get started. Can't open the windows with all this rain, but at least this part goes faster."

"Before you do, I wonder if you'd come with me to the attic?"

"The attic?"

"Uh, yes. I want to change the knobs and pulls on the cabinets. They deserve something better, once they're all freshly painted. Don't you think?"

He shrugged. "I guess that'd be nice. Yeah."

"Mamaw said there were some vintage ones stored up there that we could use. I want to give them a look first to decide. If we like them, I don't know if I could carry them. I don't know how heavy they'll be." She looked out the window, indicating the weather. "I thought if we did it now, while it's early, it might be cooler up there. Especially with this cold front in." She took a breath. God help her, she was rambling.

He gifted her with one of his rare smiles. "Sure."

"Okay." She squeezed her hands, then turned. "It's this way."

She was aware of him walking behind her as she led the way through the living room to the west wing of the house where the girls' bedrooms were. Midway through the hall a trapdoor led to the attic. She reached for the rope handle, but Taylor reached up to grab it first. After a yank he had the wooden stairs pulled down.

"You can go first," Harper told him, then followed him up the narrow stairs. "There's a light switch at the top."

In the center of the large attic the steep roof was tall enough for even Taylor to stand up, but it sloped sharply on either side. Two dormers cut through the roof on the front side of the house, and each had a functional window, though they were filthy, and the room smelled musty. She sniffed, then sneezed.

Rain pattered on the roof like a drumbeat, slow and steady.

Taylor stood with his hands on his hips, his gaze traveling the attic with an appreciative expression. "What a great space."

Harper had only been in the attic once, when she was very young. She and Carson were exploring the forbidden territory one afternoon when

Mamaw and Lucille had gone off shopping. She'd found the space dingy and dusty and filled with boxes and furniture, boring to two young girls searching for pirate's booty.

She looked around now with a woman's eyes and saw a treasure trove of vintage furniture and knickknacks. There were old trunks and suitcases and paintings in heavy frames, mostly landscapes, some with cracked glass fronts. In the corner sat a dusty old gramophone. Wrought-iron and brass bed frames were lined against the walls. She recognized the two twin beds that she'd slept on earlier that summer. She smiled when she spied her old wooden dollhouse. Boxes were every-where, stacked high, tilting, dust laden and spotted with mold.

Her hands itched to open the boxes and discover what lay inside. Who knew what she'd find? Linens, vintage clothing, shawls, jewelry. Letters. Her heart leaped. Maybe even her father's book. She couldn't wait to begin searching. Then, glancing at Taylor, she calmed her excitement. She couldn't keep him tied up here all day searching through boxes.

She stooped to pick up a brown velvet hat with a feather trim. "I can only imagine what's in all those boxes." She dusted off the hat. It was actually quite pretty. "I feel like I'm on a treasure hunt." She put the hat on. "How do I look?"

Taylor scrunched his face.

She laughed. The sound seemed to float in the closed room.

Taylor, it seemed, was interested only in the architecture. "Whoever designed this house intended that this space should be built up. Look"—he pointed—"that roof could easily be raised, making a whole new floor up here." He walked a few feet, peering at the roof. "In fact, you're due for a new one. Overdue, I'd say." He pointed to where the roof showed alarming signs of sagging, and where water stains showed on some of the boxes.

"I'll tell Mamaw. She won't be pleased."

Taylor's eyes gleamed as he studied the roof-line. "You could add more dormers in the back. Or"—he was getting caught up in his idea—"what I would do is put doors there with a deck over-looking the Cove." He crossed the floor to a small window. Bending low, he peered out. "Man, it's a great view from up here."

Harper walked closer. "Mamaw already has a widow's walk up on the roof."

"But here you can create two new bedrooms. And a bath. It'd be no problem."

"Have you done that kind of work?"

"Sure. With my father. Expanding old family houses is steady business in these parts. People don't like to sell. Memories are part of the houses."

"Well"—Harper began winding her way through the narrow path between boxes to the rear of the attic—"that will be a project for the new owners."

"You're selling the place?"

"My grandmother is."

"That's too bad. Hasn't Sea Breeze been in the family for generations?"

"Yes." She wasn't sure she wanted to get into this subject but she stopped to turn and face him. "Mamaw held on to it as long as she could. It's too much for her now. Plus she's all alone now. She's moving into a retirement community at the end of summer. Putting the house on the market."

"And no one in the family wants it?"

Harper knew he meant the three sisters. "It's not a question of wanting it. It's being able to afford it."

"It's a common enough story. Lots of my family members are selling, or have already long sold off, family property. Their kids don't want the burden, the taxes are high, or they've moved off. It's happening all over."

"What about your parents?"

"My parents never had a big house. They were lucky and got their house on the water back in the day when they could afford it. But," he added with pride, "my mother's great-grandfather once had a plantation along the Santee River. It'd been in the family since before the War. That property's been divided up so many times now there's nothing left but a memory." He shrugged.

"Doesn't matter. I like the house they have in McClellanville. It's right on the water. Suits a shrimper."

Harper put the hat on a high box. "Mamaw said the knobs were in the boxes in the back right. Next to the rocking chair."

He reached her side. "I see a rocking chair."

The space was so narrow between the boxes that he couldn't pass her. The air suddenly felt close between them.

"This way," she said awkwardly, then turned and led the way single file. The floor under the rafters was nothing more than wooden planks, which wobbled as they crossed the attic. Moving around a table that jutted into the walkway, she stumbled. She flailed her arms, trying to catch herself. Suddenly Taylor's hand shot out and grabbed her arm just in time.

"Whoa." He pulled her back.

She fell back against his chest, aware that he held her arms while she steadied herself. "Sorry. Clumsy me."

"Watch out for land mines."

Her heart was pounding as she brushed away hair from her face. He was still holding her, longer than necessary. Self-conscious, she looked at his hands, so large he could wrap his fingers around her forearms. "Thank you," she said in a hushed voice.

He immediately released her.

She rubbed her arms nervously. "I would've fallen facedown in that pile of . . ." She paused when she looked to where she'd have fallen.

She squinted and stepped closer to the small, leather-bound trunk. It was so old patches of the dark brown leather had dried and chipped off like bits of paint, exposing the wood. The initials *MC* were carved in a brass plate on the top. *Marietta Colson.* Mamaw's maiden name.

"I know that trunk." Harper reached for it. Her fingers could just touch it but she couldn't lift it.

"Here, let me get it." Taylor moved around her as they changed places in the narrow walkway. Their bodies pressed against each other, and the neurons of her body traced each touching point. His shirt was still damp from the rain, and she caught the scent of something musky lingering in the fabric.

"Cozy," he said to break the tension between them.

"Yes." She laughed lightly, glad he'd named what they both were feeling.

Taylor easily lifted the small trunk and carried it to an open space in the center of the attic. Harper knelt before it, her long pants collecting a layer of dust. Taylor went to the nearest window and, grabbing hold of the handles, pushed to open it. The swollen wood wouldn't budge. He pounded the frame several times with the palm of his hand and tried again. This time the old window rattled up the frame, but only halfway. Immediately a cooler breeze blew in that smelled of sweet rain.

"The rain's stopped. At least for a few minutes." He slapped his hands on his shorts.

"The breeze is nice." Harper felt the cool breeze cut through the musty air. "This was my grandmother's trunk," she told him when he returned to her side. He lowered to his haunches beside her. "She gave it to my sisters and me to store our treasures at the end of the summers." Her expression softened as the memory came alive in her mind. "It was always a special moment when we returned the next year. Mamaw would gather us together and she'd open the trunk in a grand manner." Harper smiled. "Mamaw can be quite dramatic. She has a gift for making even the simplest thing seem extraordinary." Harper ran her fingers gently over the top of the trunk. "I haven't seen this since I was, oh, ten or twelve. I can't imagine what's still in it."

Taylor moved to sit on an old footstool. His legs were so long, his knees nearly touched his chin. "Aren't you going to open it?"

"Okay." Harper pried open the lid. Bits more of the leather flaked off in the effort. She gasped in wonder when she discovered the trunk was filled with items from the sisters' childhoods. "To think she kept all this all these years."

Harper pulled out a yellowed handmade

collection of papers filled with cutout letters and clippings of fashion models and teenaged movie stars glued to them. It was all tied together with colored string through the punch holes. On the cover, in big letters, was *Southern Stars*.

Harper remembered, "It's Dora's magazine! She created lots of these magazines every summer. She spent hours working on them. Whenever Carson and I tried to help, she'd shoo us out of the room. She was the older sister, you see. She saw us as pesty girls and made a show of not wanting to play with us. We were mad at the time, but in retrospect it was a blessing. Carson and I bonded and we created games of our own." Harper smiled wickedly. "One of which was to spy on Dora." Harper opened the magazine. "She was so proud of these things. She boasted that someday her magazine would be a national hit."

"Creative."

Harper refrained from replying as she began leafing through the pages while Taylor bent low to look over her shoulder. The carefully cut out photos of teenaged stars of the nineties included Winona Ryder, Marky Mark, the cast of *90210*, and others, mostly country-music stars. When they saw Dora's head shot superimposed on the bodies of blond teen stars, they both howled. Harper leaned against Taylor's legs, laughing till her sides hurt.

"She never let me see that part." Harper wiped

her eyes. "This is priceless. I've got ammunition for years. No wonder Mamaw kept them."

As the laughter subsided, Harper became aware that her hand was resting on Taylor's knee and his hand was on her shoulder. When she turned to look at Taylor, he was still smiling, totally relaxed. Laughter had broken the ice between them at last, she thought, looking at his sparkling eyes.

Reluctantly she set aside the other four *Southern Stars* magazines, vowing to share them with her sisters later. Returning to the trunk, she next pulled out several swimming trophies and award ribbons. "These were Carson's. Of course. She was really proud of them. That girl is more fish than human." Harper handed them to Taylor, then looked back into the trunk.

She spied a black bandanna and two eye patches. "Oh. My. God."

"What are they?"

"Carson's and my pirate patches! I can't believe it."

"Maybe there's some of the lost pirate gold in that trunk?"

"Fingers crossed."

Harper rummaged through the remaining contents, pulling out a few old shells that had broken over time, a troll doll with neon-green hair, a pale blue My Little Pony. She handed them to Taylor, who chuckled at each one. Then her hand went still and she felt a sudden chill. Four small square booklets made of cardboard fronts and paper were stacked on the bottom of the trunk. Like Dora's magazines, these had holes punched into the edge and were bound by yarn.

"What are those?"

She wanted to cover the box from Taylor's view. To hide them. "Books I wrote. When I was a little girl," she said softly. She reached in and pulled one out. The square of cardboard had been painted blue and had faded over the years. On this was a child's drawing of a whale, smiling and spouting water. Written in a child's script was *Willy the Wishful Whale.*

In a flash, Harper was eight years old again, sitting across the desk from her mother in her elegant apartment in Manhattan. Harper had thought she'd been called in to be complimented for creating her first book. Something she was sure her mother, who worked with books, would be proud of. She'd preened with excitement, her heart fluttered with anticipation. Pleasing her mother was paramount to her.

Instead, her mother had been furious. Her anger was visceral, and though she never lashed out at Harper with physical abuse, her words could sting far worse. The scars, though not seen, were carved on Harper's soul. That afternoon Georgiana accused Harper of copying the idea from something she'd read in other books. Worse, she compared her lack of talent to her father's. To be like her father in any way was the worst insult her mother could bestow.

"Your father wasn't a writer," Georgiana had spat out, her eyes glittering with anger. "He didn't have talent. And"—she'd dropped Harper's book from her fingers as if it were trash—"neither do you."

That day Harper had felt all her pride and enthusiasm for writing wither in her chest. Her mother had extinguished Harper's dreams at eight years of age as brutally as she did the cigarette in her hand. It was months before Harper ventured to write again, and then only at Sea Breeze, far from her mother. Where she felt safe.

Then one day the following summer Mamaw had called Harper into her sitting room. She found Mamaw with her feet resting on the chintz ottoman. Sunlight poured into the room, lending Mamaw's soft, white curls a golden glow. Harper had entered smiling until she spotted the ill-fated book in Mamaw's hand. Harper shrank back, sure she was again in trouble.

"I found this under your pillow." Mamaw lifted the small, cardboard-covered booklet in her hand. "Harper, did you write this little book?"

Harper was so nervous, she couldn't speak. She hovered near the chair and could only nod, eyes wide.

Mamaw gestured for her to come closer.

Harper took reluctant steps to Mamaw's side,

where she reached out an arm to hold Harper close.

"What a wonderful book!" Mamaw gave her a squeeze. "Absolutely charming. Tell me, dear, did you make it up? All by yourself?"

Harper couldn't believe what she was hearing. Was it a trap, like the one her mother had sprung? She simply shrugged noncommittally.

"You did, didn't you?" Mamaw's eyes shone with pride. "Clever girl. It's wonderful. So creative. Imagine, a whale wishing to find his family, searching the sea. You have a real talent, do you know that? And you drew the pictures so well. You might be a writer when you grow up."

Harper could only stare back in awe and wonder, confused.

Mamaw's face shifted and her smile became bittersweet. "Your father wanted to be a writer, you know."

"I know."

Mamaw reached out and with her fingertip gently lifted Harper's chin so that she looked deeply into her eyes. "I am very, very proud of you."

Harper had felt her chest swell with relief and pride and love for her grandmother. Uttering a soft cry, she reached out to wrap her thin arms around Mamaw's neck. She couldn't help the tears that began to flow.

"Why, whatever is the matter, child?" Mamaw

pulled Harper up into her lap and held her against her breast while stroking her hair until the tears subsided.

"Mummy told me that it was bad for me to write the book."

"Rubbish."

"She said that I was a bad writer. Like Daddy."

Mamaw's hand stopped moving. "Did she?"

Harper, ashamed, buried her face in Mamaw's breast.

Mamaw said in a huff, "I've never agreed with your mother on any other topic before, and it is no surprise that I do not agree with her now."

"Mamaw, was Daddy a bad writer?"

Mamaw began stroking her hair again. "Oh, child, honestly? We'll never know for sure. Parker never finished his book. He tried, you see, but he just couldn't manage it. And here you are, his daughter and only eight years old, and you finished a book! That in itself is very important. A triumph! Talent is only a part of writing a book. An important part, true. But the other part is putting in the hard work. That's the part your father had a difficult time with, I'm afraid."

Mamaw gently shook Harper in her arms. "But you listen to your Mamaw now. You *do* have talent. This is a wonderful story. Your mother is wrong, hear? So keep writing, Harper. Write your little heart out. And I'll happily read anything you write."

So Harper had started writing again. Story after story all that summer, and the summers after.

Harper looked at the four small cardboard-bound books in her hand. "She kept them."

"From the little I know about your grandmother, I'm not surprised. Can I see them?"

Harper shook her head no. She couldn't bear to hear him laugh at her books, the way he had at Dora's magazines. "They aren't very good."

"Says who?"

"I know I'm not a good writer." She retracted the books.

He dropped his hand, not pushing her. "Does it matter?"

"Of course it matters."

"I don't know that I agree. Not if you enjoy writing. It's a way of communicating. Of sharing a part of your soul with the world. Maybe you won't get published, but that's not the end all of writing. Writing is a process. When I write, I do it for myself."

"You write?" she asked, surprised by this admission.

He nodded and looked at her askance. "You didn't expect it from me, did you?"

"Well . . . ," Harper stumbled.

"It's okay. Most people don't." He snorted. "They expect to see the long hair, the turtleneck, and the pained expression. A Marine? Not so much."

Harper met his glance and felt a blush rise. "When you put it like that, I'm embarrassed. Of course there's no one kind of writer."

He didn't seem the least perturbed.

"I'd think you'd have a lot to write about," she said.

He nodded.

"What do you write? Memoir? Novel?"

"Poetry."

The man never failed to amaze her. "Really?" she asked, more a comment of being impressed. "I've always thought that poetry was the highest form of writing."

"I don't know if it's any good. Don't care. But I know it's good *for* me." He looked at his hands. "Writing poetry helps give me clarity. Life can be pretty confusing sometimes."

"Yes." Intrigued, she leaned forward. "That's why I write, too."

He looked up. "You still write?"

She nodded.

"Poetry?"

She had not intended to tell anyone this most private secret, but she wanted to share this with Taylor. "Actually, I'm writing a novel."

"A book." She found him looking at her as though with fresh eyes.

"I know everyone is writing a book these days," she said self-consciously.

"Even still. This is your book."

"I've written for as long as I can remember. Wrote little stories. But I've never finished a novel. My father spent a lifetime writing a novel he never finished. It's kind of a family joke."

"Not a very funny one."

"I'll always bear the onus of his reputation until I finish it. Beginning, middle, and end. It's kind of like proving a point."

"To whom?"

"My mother," she answered with alacrity. "And myself." She shook her head. "But even if I do, that won't stop my mother from mocking and degrading him every chance she gets. She despises my father and anything to do with him, his family, or his writing."

"That must make it hard for you."

Harper nodded. "It hasn't been easy. She's furious that I'm spending the summer here. Behind enemy lines."

"Is she furious you're writing a novel?"

"God, I'd never tell her I was writing. She's the one who told me I couldn't write. I believe her exact words were I *didn't have talent.*"

"Harsh."

"Yeah." She felt the pain anew.

"And you believed her?"

"Well, I was eight." Harper smirked, then said more seriously, "And she's a big-time New York editor and publisher at a major publishing house. So, yeah."

"But of course she'd tell you that you can't write. She doesn't want you to be like him. Your dad. Not if she despised him. It wouldn't matter if you wrote like Charles Dickens, she'd have told you that you had no talent."

In the silence that followed, Harper's mind went over and over that scenario. It would be just like her mother to lie for her own advantage. Georgiana James was, after all, a consummate liar.

Although Harper could hear the rain beginning again, tap-tap-tapping on the rooftop, it felt as though the sun had just come out and she could see for miles. The hope of possibility, the kind she'd felt as a young girl before her faith was quashed in her chest, sprang to life again. In a leap of faith, Harper picked up her worn and faded booklet *Willy the Wishful Whale*. She turned to the man beside her and was filled with gratitude because he had brought back her belief in herself. She handed the book to Taylor.

He took it into his hands carefully, as though he was afraid he might tear it. "Are you sure?"

"Remember, it was written and illustrated by an eight-year-old."

Taylor nodded and offered a reassuring smile. "I wish I could have seen you then. I'll bet you had pigtails and freckles."

"Please . . ."

They laughed, easing the tension.

"Thanks."

Harper sat back on her haunches and watched his face as he opened the book, catching any change of expression. She leaned forward against his legs. He tilted the booklet at an angle so she could read it along with him. One by one he flipped the pages, revealing neatly printed words and drawings of a whale and other sea life. As she read it aloud, it felt to her as though someone else had written the words. So many years had passed, she felt no claim to them.

Taylor closed the book. He tilted his head and stared into her eyes. "Harper, that was really good."

She searched his eyes, not wanting to be patronized. In the pale green she saw sincerity and beamed at the compliment, believing it. "Yeah, it was kinda cute, wasn't it?"

"Can I read the others?"

She looked at the other three booklets, reached into the trunk, and pulled them out. "You have to promise you won't show them to anyone else."

"I promise. What about your other book? Your adult book? Can I read that?"

She cringed. "Yes. But not yet." She wasn't ready to go that far. "It's not done."

He accepted that with equanimity. "I can wait. And it's okay if you don't want me to read it. I remember when I started writing poetry, I was terrified to show it to anyone. It's scary to show your underbelly. I had a lot of anger inside of me. And pain." He shook his head in a self-deprecating manner. "A lot. Poetry helped me get it off my chest. So, sure, it was tough to let someone see it. One of the scariest things I've ever done. And I've done a lot of life-and-death things. But it helped, you know? The more I wrote, the more I got critiqued, the better my poetry got."

"Can I read some of your poetry?"

"Sure. I've self-published my first collection. I have a huge sales record of about ten. I bought eight of them. My mama bought the other two."

"Aw, it can't be that bad." She laughed.

"It is." He grinned. "Hell, I didn't do it for sales. Mostly so I could have my poems collected in one place so I can give them to someone." He skipped a beat. "Like you."

She felt her breath hitch. "Thank you. I'd love a book. Be honored."

"The way I see it, writing is a gift. Offering someone the chance to read your writing is akin to giving a bit of your soul to someone else." Taylor lifted Harper's children's books in his hands a bit higher. "It's a gift you're letting me read these. Thank you."

"You're welcome." She sounded so terribly formal.

Lightning flashed at the windows, followed by a renewed burst of rain. It pounded the roof with a clap of thunder that felt as if it exploded right overhead. Startled, Harper leaped from the floor into Taylor's arms. For a moment she clung to him as the storm wailed outside and a deluge of rain blew sideways against the house, into the open window. The attic echoed with vibration.

She closed her eyes, feeling the warmth, the strength of his arms around her. Smelled the lingering scent of soap on his skin. He didn't release her. She felt her breathing quicken to match his, in and out, aware that he was counting their breaths, too.

Taylor moved to look down at her. He framed her head with his hand and gently tilted it so that she would look at him.

When she looked in his eyes, all the noise around them ceased in her mind. Her whole world was focused on those two green eyes, pulsing with emotion.

"Harper . . . ," he whispered.

Suddenly all the doubts in her mind fled. She saw only herself reflected in his eyes. She read desire and something more . . . something that felt very much like déjà vu. She took his hand from her face and brought it to her lips and gently kissed each finger. She heard his breath suck in.

In a sudden swoop he pulled her higher in his arms and his mouth came down on her open one. The storm roared outside as they kissed hungrily, like lost lovers who had found each other again. Kisses that meant to go on forever.

Until thunder clapped again, shaking the house.

They both pulled back. Taylor tightened his hold on her. Then, in a burst as sudden as the thunder, they both started to laugh at the deafening roar.

She looked into his eyes and he smiled back. They both knew that the other had felt it. They both knew that this kiss was as earth-shattering as the thunder.

"Will you go out with me?"

"Love to," she said.

He put his hand to his ear in mock deafness against the din. "What?"

"Love to," she shouted at him.

He grinned. "I'd like to take you to Monday Night Poetry and Music."

"Okay. . . . What's that?"

"It's one of the poetry readings that takes place in Charleston. Locals read their stuff, but we also get visiting poets sometimes. Poet laureates. It's very cool." He had to lower his head and talk by her ear to be heard.

"Sounds perfect."

He bent to place another kiss on her lips, this one gentle. Then, reluctantly, he lifted his wrist to check his watch. "It's getting late."

"I don't care."

"We'd better get those knobs." He moved out from her arms to stand, pulling her up beside him. He had to talk close to her ear to be heard over the noise of the rain pounding the roof. "I'll close the window and meet you back there."

She nodded. Taylor helped her to her feet, then wound his way to the window. Harper walked foot over foot, in the opposite direction to the back of the attic. Luckily, she spotted in the forefront the two boxes marked in large letters KNOBS. Beneath them was another, larger box labeled DOOR HANDLES. The tape was so old the glue had dried off. Pulling back the bubble wrap, she was thrilled to discover dozens of glass knobs, wooden ball knobs, and old brass and ceramic pulls. Sorting through them, she saw that most of them were in good condition.

By the time Taylor came beside her the thunderous rain had subsided to a steady patter. He slipped an arm around her waist possessively. "Find anything?"

"A treasure trove! There are so many. Mamaw must've taken off every knob and pull in the house."

"You did say you had pirate's blood in you."

Harper laughed at that, imagining her proper grandmother going from door to door removing the door handles. He laughed again, and she knew he was imagining the same thing. She hadn't laughed with a man as openly or freely in a long time. Taylor was slowly opening up to her, and she to him.

"These are perfect. Can you carry these boxes?"

"I think I can manage it." Taylor smirked and stepped forward and picked up all three boxes as easily as if they were filled with feathers. "If you can grab the small trunk. It's not heavy."

She picked up the trunk.

Taylor turned and cast her a hooded glance. "Careful. I can't catch you this time."

As she followed Taylor down the stairs, leaving the dust and rising heat, she was sorry to leave the attic.

Very sorry, indeed.

Chapter Nine

For the next several days as the rain pattered the roof and Taylor painted the kitchen, Harper's fingers tapped at her keyboard. Taylor's words had sparked her enthusiasm anew. She couldn't stop the flow.

"But of course she'd tell you that you can't write. She doesn't want you to be like him. Your dad. It wouldn't matter if you wrote like Charles Dickens, she'd have told you that you had no talent." The more she thought about it, the more true Taylor's words rang.

It had been a good week. She was making progress on her novel. In some ways it was more memoir than pure fiction, rather what she imagined Louisa May Alcott must have thought while writing the first draft of *Little Women.* Harper wasn't putting any pressure on herself to make it one thing or another. She was simply intent on getting the words down on paper, and she'd edit it all later. She didn't yet know how the story would end.

By one o'clock her stomach growled. She'd risen early and dived right into her work. She hadn't eaten yet that day, though she'd drunk coffee like a camel. She rubbed her eyes, then closed her laptop.

Looking out the window, she saw that the rain had finally blown off, leaving in its wake a clear, fresh day with an azure sky that stretched to forever. The birds were out in force, calling out songs of joy in the sunlight. Harper rose and stretched. After so much rain, it was too beautiful a day to be cooped up indoors.

She'd been working at the desk in Lucille's cottage because it was the only place that didn't smell of paint. Nothing in the cottage had changed since Lucille's death. The girls had talked about sorting through her things, but Mamaw had promptly put a stop to anything of the sort, declaring that she wanted everything left untouched until she had time to go through it herself. Harper looked around at the cottage, as crammed full as the attic. Clearly Mamaw wasn't ready to tackle that emotional hurdle yet. But the house had to go on the market. Sooner rather than later, she and her sisters would have to confront Mamaw with the reality that time was running out.

Harper went to the cottage kitchen, which they'd been using during the painting in the main house. She made herself a cream-cheese, tomato, and sprouts sandwich, then carried it out with a glass of almond milk to the front porch of the cottage. She found Mamaw sitting on one of the rockers, reading.

"There you are. Hungry?"

"I already ate. Thank you," Mamaw replied distractedly.

"What about Dora and Nate? And Carson? Did they eat?"

Mamaw looked up from her reading and pulled off her glasses. "It's just us chickens, I'm afraid. Dora's gone out to visit the new school with Nate, and I don't know where Carson is. She left without a word."

Harper looked off to the garage. The door was open and inside it was empty. "So Carson took the Blue Bomber?"

"She did."

"And Dora took her car?"

"Of course."

"Rats. I need to pick up the lighting fixture I ordered for the kitchen. I guess I'm stuck here."

"There's a bicycle in there somewhere."

"Oh, Mamaw, I can't very well pick anything up with that old thing."

"I suppose not." Mamaw put her glasses back on and returned to her book.

"I can't be cooped up at the mercy of whether Dora or Carson are home to let me borrow a car. I should just rent one. Where's the closest place?"

"Mt. Pleasant, I'm sure."

"I don't know why I didn't do this before. I'll call a cab to take me to the rental office."

Mamaw lowered her book. "Won't renting a car for a month or longer cost a small fortune?"

"What choice do I have if I want wheels?"

Mamaw's expression turned crafty. "You could buy a car."

"Buy one? What would I do with a car once I leave? I live in Manhattan. The only people who have cars there are commuters, the very rich, or crazy."

"I suppose your mother would fit into all three categories," Mamaw said archly. "Doesn't Georgiana need a car to go to the Hamptons?"

"Mummy has a driver take her everywhere she goes."

"Of course she does," Mamaw remarked snippily.

Harper ignored Mamaw's tone, not wanting her to go off on a Georgiana rant, which she was apt to do with little prompting. "I had a car when I was in college. To get back and forth. But I sold it when I started working in the city. It was expensive to keep up and traffic in the city is beyond ridiculous. I catch the subway or a cab."

"Well, you can't do that here." Mamaw removed her eyeglasses. "As luck would have it," she began in a tone that usually meant she had something up her sleeve, "I happen to have a friend who is selling a sweet little car. Very sporty. A Jeep, I believe it's called. I wonder if you didn't see it? It's parked on Middle Street with a FOR SALE sign on the windshield."

"You mean the one close to the fire station? The cream-colored one?"

"The same."

"It is cute." Harper remembered the Jeep Wrangler, which looked in good condition. "But it can't be cheaper than renting."

"It might be."

"How much does she want for it?"

Mamaw rose to her feet, a woman on a mission. "I can call and find out. Follow me."

They went straight inside the cottage to the phone sitting beside the sofa. The cottage still carried the barely perceptible smell of vanilla.

"Mamaw, we should really tackle the cottage. There's a lot to sort through," Harper suggested gently.

"Not yet. We have plenty of other things to do."

"I know. Like the attic. I was up there getting those knobs for the kitchen, and it's chock-full of stuff. Mamaw, when did you think you were going to sort through all this?"

Mamaw waved her hand, dismissing the subject as one would a pesty gnat. "Later, dear. Later."

"Procrastination," Harper muttered softly as she

followed Mamaw. She knew full well that when *later* came, it'd be tinged with panic.

Mamaw sat by the phone and dialed a number. Her eyes sparkled with excitement when she glanced up at Harper. "Hello, Paula?" Mamaw said with a cheery voice. "It's Marietta." They exchanged pleasantries for a few minutes before Mamaw cupped the phone and got down to business. "I'm calling about that sweet little car you're selling. . . . The Jeep, yes. Is it still for sale? . . . It is?" Mamaw winked at Harper. "Can I ask how much you want for it? . . . Uh-huh." Mamaw made a face. "That much? You've had the car for quite a while, haven't you?"

Looking for clues, Harper watched Mamaw's animated eyes as she listened.

"Well, thank you for sharing all that, Paula. My granddaughter Harper is in need of a car, nothing too expensive. This might be just the thing if you have a little wiggle room in the price. . . . Why, yes, I think she could come by and take a look at it right now. . . . What was that? You will?" Mamaw nodded at Harper. "Very good, then. We'll be right over. It may take a few minutes. We're walking!" She laughed.

"Mamaw, ask her if I can write a check," Harper whispered at her side.

"Oh, Paula, one more thing. Harper is visiting for the summer, which is why she doesn't have a car. If things progress, could she write you a personal check? I will personally guarantee it. . . . Oh, thank you, Paula. You're a good friend. . . . What's that?" Mamaw's eyes widened and she gave Harper a thumbs-up. "Why, that's very generous of you. . . . Yes, it would be nice to clear it off the grass. . . . Yes, it can be an eyesore." Mamaw hung up and smiled at Harper.

"Well?"

"Let's hightail it right over. She bought the Jeep years ago on a whim. Bless her heart, she thought her family might have fun driving it. Thing is, no one ever did, and a Jeep is not the style of car that, shall we say, suits a woman of her age and station. So it's just been sitting in the garage all this time, collecting dust and taxes. She's eager to get rid of it. She said if you buy it today and take it off her front lawn, she'll give you the friends-and-family discount!"

Harper and Mamaw walked the six blocks to where the cream-colored Jeep sat parked on the grass on Middle Street. When they drew near, they stopped talking to walk around the car, peer into the windows, and check it out for bumps or rust.

As promised, the Jeep appeared pristine, obviously having been kept in a garage for the majority of its life. Harper didn't spot any wear and tear on the removable top, either. "This is the proverbial car that was never driven and kept in the garage by an old lady."

"We should just thank our lucky stars that it's still here. Like it?"

Harper nodded. She did like it. Very much.

"Then let's not dally. Paula is expecting us."

Mrs. Randolph's house was one of the many historic cottages on Sullivan's Island. Most of the early houses were built by Charlestonians as summerhouses to escape the heat and humidity in the city. Smaller, filled with individuality and charm, these cottages held the two-hundred-year history of the island. Newer, grander houses now peppered the island, but to Harper's mind, the cottages gave Sullivan's Island its appeal. Harper especially admired Mrs. Randolph's long, white porch and the line of white rockers and robust planters spilling over with annuals.

The front door swung open and Mrs. Randolph stepped out, crooning her hello to Mamaw with a friendly hug. She was a full-figured woman of Mamaw's vintage. Her face was plump and coursed with lines but her eyes were bright with warmth and vitality.

"It's such a beautiful day," Paula exclaimed. "Why don't you and I have a chat and sip our tea on the porch while Harper gives a look-see to the Jeep?" Paula handed Harper the keys. "Take your time, dear."

Harper strolled across the scrubby island grass to the car. She didn't know much about cars. She made a show of looking under it and climbing into the driver's seat. Once inside, she felt the excitement of possibility. It was adorable. Fun. A perfect island car. And it looked almost new and had the bonus of having only twelve thousand miles on it. She thought of her bank account and knew she should be prudent. After all, she had to go back to New York, pay a security deposit on an apartment, rent, utilities. And she still had to find a job.

A half smile crossed her face. But she'd be getting a check from her trust fund soon. Enough to tide her over for a little while. Harper ran her hands over the steering wheel, feeling a desperate desire to own it. Maybe she was right about love at first sight. She giggled. Only for her it was a car.

She walked with an easy gait to the porch. Mamaw and Mrs. Randolph were sitting on rockers, their heads bent, deep in conversation. When she drew near, they turned their heads and stared back like two contented cats.

"I'll take it!" Harper exclaimed.

"Wonderful." Mrs. Randolph clapped her hands.

After the paperwork was signed, Harper took hold of the keys of the first car she'd owned since college.

"How do you feel?" Mamaw asked as they walked back to the Jeep.

Harper squeezed the keys in her hand. "As free as a bird able to take off and go anywhere at whim."

"That kind of freedom doesn't last long. Enjoy it."

"You know, for the first few weeks at Sea Breeze I didn't want to go anywhere. I was perfectly content to live a hermit's life. I enjoyed the lack of pressure. Not having someone"—she looked meaningfully at Mamaw—"my mother . . . always calling my name. But"—Harper sighed— "now I want to get out and explore."

"Like you did as a child."

"Exactly! Only now I have wheels."

" 'Oh, the places you'll go!' " Mamaw said, quoting the title of a Dr. Seuss book she'd read to Harper as a child.

They laughed together, and Harper found it good to see her grandmother having a good time. She went around to help Mamaw climb up into the Jeep.

"Goodness," Mamaw exclaimed, settling into the seat, "I can understand why Paula didn't drive around in it herself. It's a workout just getting in and out."

"That's what makes it fun. And I need a little fun in my life."

She climbed into the driver's seat, put the key in the ignition, reached for the clutch, and suddenly her excitement dropped like a lead balloon. "Oh, no." Harper stared at the transmission, stunned.

"What's the matter?"

"It's manual transmission."

"Yes, dear. So?"

"So . . . I don't know how to drive stick." Harper put her palm to her forehead.

"Didn't you ever learn?" asked Mamaw, surprised.

"No. I had to learn the basics of how a clutch worked when I learned how to drive. But I always drove automatic. I mean, really. Who drives stick anymore?" Harper shook her head in dismay. "I didn't even think to ask. I just assumed the car was automatic." Harper unbuckled her belt and grabbed her purse. "I hope Mrs. Randolph won't get upset. I have to return it."

Mamaw grabbed Harper's arm. "Now don't get your knickers in a twist. The deed is done," Mamaw admonished. She set her pocketbook on the car floor. "You won't find another deal like this one, I promise you. Paula practically gave you the car. You're a smart girl. You can learn how to drive a stick. In my day, all the cars were manual."

"But who's going to teach me? I don't know anyone who drives manual transmission."

"I do."

"You?"

"Yes. I could teach you."

Harper just stared back.

"Don't look so surprised. I'm old but I'm not senile. I'll have you know I'm a very good driver. Never had a ticket."

Harper remembered her grandmother's turtle-like driving. "I don't think they give tickets for going too *slow.*"

"Maybe not, but I've gotten my quota of honks," Mamaw quipped. "Now, buckle up, sweetie. We're going for a ride."

Mamaw turned out to be an excellent, if demanding, teacher. For the next half hour Harper jerked, stalled, and shifted gears along the side streets of Sullivan's Island. Mamaw was patient but firm, not allowing Harper to quit until she could go from first to second to third gear and reverse without stalling. With few other cars and even fewer people walking, she could start and stop often without drawing someone's ire.

By the time they returned to Sea Breeze, both the Blue Bomber and Dora's silver Lexus were back in the driveway. Taylor was loading paint cans into the back of his truck. Harper slowly maneuvered the Jeep into the space beside his. When she put on the parking brake and pulled out her keys, her shoulders slumped in relief.

"Very good, dear," Mamaw exclaimed. "You should take it out every day and just drive around the neighborhood until you get the hang of it." She paused. "Before you venture into traffic." Mamaw climbed down from the car.

"Thanks, Mamaw," Harper called out. "I couldn't have done it without you."

Mamaw's smile was wobbly. She reached up to smooth her hair. "Yes, dear. I know."

Harper let her hands slide along the steering wheel with pride.

"New ride?"

Harper startled and put her hand to her chest. She swung her head to see Taylor bent low, looking in her driver's window, his face inches from her own.

"Didn't mean to creep up on you."

"I was just lost in my thoughts." She smiled. "I just bought it. What do you think?"

His gaze scanned the tan interior. "It's right pretty. Looks new but I'm guessing it's a '95, with those square headlights. I like the looks of those better, and it has a sweet spring leaf for a bouncier ride."

"But it's manual transmission."

"That's good."

"Not if you don't know how to drive manual. Mamaw just gave me my first lesson."

His eyes crinkled up as he tried not to laugh. "Is that why your grandmother was running like the cavalry up the stairs?"

"No doubt heading for her rum."

"Don't worry. You'll get used to it. Before you know it, shifting gears will be like water off a duck's back." He walked around the Jeep, appraising it.

Harper grabbed her purse and climbed out of the Jeep. Her knees still felt weak from her lesson with the clutch.

"Say," he said, returning to her, his eyes narrowed in mock suspicion, "is this the Jeep that was parked over on Middle Street?"

"The same."

A look of chagrin crossed his face as he shook his head remorsefully. "I thought I recognized this cream puff. I looked at it the other day when I drove by. I was thinking of buying it for my little brother. He's turning fifteen and this would be a sweet ride for a high school boy."

"Well, you might still have your chance at the end of summer."

"You're selling it? So soon?"

"I won't need a car in New York."

Maybe it was her imagination, or the glare of the setting sun in his eyes, but he blinked hard and she thought he looked disappointed.

"When you planning on heading back?"

"At the end of summer sometime."

He shifted his weight, and for a moment neither spoke. A crow cawed loudly from the neighbor's tree.

"I got the cabinets done today," he said, shifting to a businesslike tone, looking toward the house.

She got the sense he wanted to look anywhere but at her.

"Next I'll start on the walls. I should be about finished tomorrow. You ladies will have your kitchen back in no time."

"I thought it would take a little longer."

"Nope. I got the trim done today. The walls go fast. I'll put the knobs and pulls on last. Best let the paint dry for twenty-four hours."

"You're doing a wonderful job. You know, I've been meaning to ask. You said your father does some electrical work. Can he hang a light fixture?"

"He can. So can I."

She held back her smile. "Oh, good. I bought a new one. I have to go pick it up, but I can have it for you by tomorrow. Do you have time to hang it?"

He rubbed his jaw in thought. "If you're doing that, the ceiling will need to be patched. Then painted. It'll be extra, but not too bad. And it'll take another day."

Harper dismissed her inner voice telling her not to spend the money. After all, she had just promised the next installment from her trust fund to Mrs. Randolph and the new Jeep. But she wanted to do the job right for Mamaw. And . . . it meant another day with Taylor.

"Let's do it."

He looked at her and seemed to relax. "All right, then." He glanced over his shoulder to make sure they were alone, then he lowered his head to kiss her. The moment she felt his lips, her blood raced and she leaned into him, slipping her hand around his neck. He made a soft sound in his throat and brought his arms around her, pressing her against him.

He released her with a reluctant smile, then tapped the roof of the car twice. "See you Monday." He turned and walked to his truck. Whistling.

Dora was discouraged.

She was sitting outside a house in Mt. Pleasant beside Devlin in his truck. Devlin had accompanied her as she toured three potential houses to rent. This was the last of a week's effort in rain and shine and not one could she see herself bringing Nate to live in. They were either in deplorable condition, in a sketchy neighborhood, or something was simply weirdly off, such as this one's being smack-dab next to a power line.

"I don't think I'm going to find a decent house that I can afford to rent. Not even a small one. I guess it's time to chuck hopes for a house. The only option in my price range seems to be to rent an apartment."

"Will that no-count husband of yours give you any more for rent?"

She shook her head. "He says he doesn't have it. Not with all the work going on at the house. And still no offers."

Devlin grunted and tightened his hand on the wheel but didn't reply.

"I've got some good news, though. I think I may have got the job at the dress shop!" she exclaimed, interjecting a note of cheer.

"That's real good, honey." Devlin reached out to squeeze her hand. "If you have a minute to spare, can I stop at that cottage on Sullivan's? I have to check a few things before it goes on the market."

"Of course. You gave up your afternoon for me." When he fired up the engine and drove off, Dora asked the question niggling at her. "The cottage is finished?" She had helped Devlin refurbish the quaint little structure over the summer. "Why didn't you tell me you were ready to put it on the market?"

"I just did. Thought you'd like to see it now that it's all spruced up. Seems only fair, seeing as how you saw it at its worst."

"Never at its worst," she said with a twinge of sadness. "That house always had its sweet side."

A short time later he pulled into the newly created tabby driveway. Dora peered out the window, taking in all the landscaping that had been done since she'd last seen the house, only a few weeks ago.

"You used my landscaping ideas," she exclaimed.

"Course I did. I told you that you were good. Your design really opened up the place, especially that pergola over the garage. Real classy. I never would've thought of that."

His words were like salve on a wound. Still, it broke her heart to see the cottage going on the market, even though it had been her job to ready it for sale. Seeing the pretty cottage all decked out and with new landscaping was like giving away a puppy after whelping and raising it for a full eight weeks.

"Come on inside." Devlin fiddled with the key. "I have to put this lockbox on the front door for the Realtors. You go on and take a look around."

Dora walked from room to room of the cottage, her head turning from left to right as she took in the freshly painted walls in colors she'd chosen, the molding, the refinished hardwood floors, the spanking-new lighting fixtures that she'd selected. Out back, Devlin had created the patio area that she'd designed to complete the larger pergola that matched the one out front. A stone pathway wound its way to Hamlin Creek. Dora stood on the patio with her fingertips to her lips and tears forming in her eyes when she saw the new wooden dock stretching out over the racing water.

Every color choice, every light fixture in the cottage, she'd selected. Each paver, each plant, each tree outdoors, was directly from her design. It was as if she had been decorating the house for herself.

She heard a crunching of the gravel behind her, then felt Devlin's arms around her waist.

"What'ya think?" he asked in a slow drawl by her ear.

"It's beautiful. Perfect."

"I told you that you were good at this house stuff."

"Uh-huh."

"Could you see you and Nate living here?"

Dora's breath stilled. She turned in his arms to face him. "What are you saying?"

Devlin's blue eyes shone in the lowering sunlight, and in their light she read his love, so sincere that her heart opened.

"I have a proposal."

"Oh, Devlin . . ."

"I'm not asking you to marry me," Devlin said with mock frustration. "Woman, you do tire a man out. I'm talking about a plan I have."

Dora had the grace to blush. "Oh. Sorry." Her lips twitched.

"You've seen what your measly allowance could get you in a rental. Now, I could dance around this, but I won't play with your intelligence. I know your antennas are wiggling, so I'm going to put it right out there. You love this cottage. You put your heart and soul and sweat into fixing it up, right by my side. Don't think that didn't endear this place to me, too? I think we created some-thing really fine here. Don't you?"

Dora nodded, listening intently.

"I could put it on the market. I'd make a small profit if it sold today. But truth is, the market is slow and it might sit for a long while. That's never good. But if I hold on to the place awhile and let the market improve, which I'm betting it will, I'll increase my profit in a year, maybe two's time. After all, this little house is sitting on some deep water. It's got potential."

Dora didn't dare speak.

Devlin shifted his weight. "So I'm wondering if you'll do me the favor of living in it for a while. Look after it. Just for a year or so."

Dora drew back in his arms. "Absolutely not."

Devlin shook his head and let his arms drop. "Why the hell not, woman? Don't you like it?"

"I love it. And you know it."

"Then why . . ."

"Because if I accept this gift—because that's what it is—I'll be seen as a brazen hussy from this county to the next. I'm already dating you. Sleeping with you. They'll call me a kept woman." She shook her head with determination. "I can't let Nate live in a situation like that."

"A kept woman? What century are you living in?"

"You know what I mean. This is a conservative area."

"Then marry me!" he shouted.

"No!" she shouted back.

Devlin stepped back. He looked deeply hurt.

"I can't marry you," Dora explained, cajoling. Her fingers reached up to play with the buttons of his shirt. "I'm not divorced yet."

"I know that," he mumbled with dejection. "I meant later."

"Please, Devlin. Don't go there. Not yet. Not

tonight. I've told you already, I don't want to think about getting married again until I've signed my divorce papers. I want to take a deep breath as a single woman. To sign my name as Eudora Muir just once more before I change it again. Let's not confuse things between us. We'll still be together. A couple. Nothing's going to change between us but that piece of paper that means so little to you but is so very symbolic to me. It's who I am, Devlin. I'm a traditional girl and I'm already breaking a lot of rules here. I'll come around. And when I do"—she reached up to tenderly stroke the stubble on his cheek—"I promise, you'll be the first to know."

Devlin sighed and his chest rumbled with the effort. "Woman, you are one hell of a negotiator."

Dora smiled and kissed him. "That's the nicest thing anyone's ever said to me."

His hand patted her bottom with a proprietary air. "How about this? You rent the house from me. We'll make it legal."

"I can't afford—"

"I know what you can afford," he said, cutting her off. "And I'll rent it to you for that amount. You can tell the world you're renting the house, and that'll spare your reputation. Now, Dora," he said slowly, "think before you spout out another *no*."

Dora quieted and gave him his say.

"Nate will love living here. He loves the

island, knows it, thinks of it as home, and it'll keep him close to Mamaw. Living here won't be as big a change for him as moving into some condo a ways off." Devlin stretched out his arm, pointing to the dock. Her gaze followed his. "And look out there at that dock. Nate can fish out there anytime he wants. I built that special for him."

"Oh, Devlin . . ." Dora's eyes filled. He was hitting her in all her most vulnerable places.

"Hell, woman, I love you. You won't marry me. Won't even get engaged. Seems to me the least you can do is rent my cottage with no strings attached. To do less is just not kind."

Dora laughed then, a soft, trilling laugh that sounded to her ears like happiness. She leaned against him and wrapped her arms around his neck. "Yes, all right." She rolled her eyes in mock resignation. "I'll rent your cottage."

"That's good. Real good."

Chapter Ten

"Nooooo! I won't go!"

Harper and Taylor halted their discussion about where to place the light fixture, looking at each other in alarm.

It was mid-August in the lowcountry, which meant the children who lived here throughout the year—from frightened first-graders to seasoned high schoolers—were dressed in clean clothes, armed with new books, backpacks, supplies, and a haircut, and marching into schools at the sound of the bell.

Except Nate.

"I won't go! You can't make me!" Nate screamed again.

From down the hall they heard Dora's voice, cajoling and high-pitched, clash with Nate's insistent, angry refusals.

Harper set down her coffee cup and, leaning against the counter, crossed her arms to listen. She glanced at Taylor. He stood motionless, head cocked. "It's the first day of school for Nate," she explained. "He's been homeschooled all his life. So this is all new for him. With Asperger's, he doesn't take to change very well."

"Sounds like he's freaking out," Taylor said, concerned.

As if to confirm Taylor's statement, Nate began screaming again, shouting "No" over and over, each time sounding more hysterical.

"This could go on for a while," murmured Harper.

Taylor stood silently but his gaze was blank, as if his mind were somewhere else.

After several more minutes of screaming, Dora came into the kitchen looking disheveled, frustrated, and exhausted. She sighed and placed her hands on the counter, leaning against it with her head bowed. "God help me."

Harper came to her side and delicately placed her hand on Dora's shoulder.

"He's going into a total meltdown. I knew this morning would be tough for him, but I did everything I could to defuse the tension. We talked about the new school all last week, visited it several times. He even met his teachers. Last night we went over his new routine. We prepared. We really did!"

Harper saw the tears in Dora's eyes. "I know. We all know you did."

"He wouldn't get out of bed! He woke up and flatly said that he wasn't going to go to school. The more I tried to be encouraging, the more he freaked out."

"He bottled it all up. And this morning when the top popped off, he exploded."

Dora nodded. "I used to be able to hold him during one of his tantrums, but he's too big. I'm not strong enough anymore. Not when he gets this riled. I tried to soothe him but I'm at my wit's end." She put her hand to her face and said in a choked voice, "I don't know what to do."

In the background Nate was still screaming out of control. Harper didn't know what she could do to help.

"Do you mind if I go see him?" asked Taylor.

Harper swung her head around, surprised by

the offer. Taylor stepped closer, and his usually taciturn face was soft with concern.

Dora sniffed, wiped her eyes, and looked at Taylor with confusion. "Why?"

"I know something about meltdowns. I might be able to help."

Dora shrugged. "Go ahead. I'll try anything."

Taylor nodded. "Okay then." He turned and went to the porch door. Opening it, he whistled, sharp and short. In an instant, Thor was at the door. "He's a therapy dog. He knows how to behave in these situations." When Dora nodded, Taylor gave a discreet hand signal. Thor trotted to his side. "Come on, boy." Then Taylor said to Harper, "Which room is he in?"

"It's right down the hall."

"I'll show you." Dora led Harper and Taylor to the library room, where Nate slept. Though the door was closed, the boy's screams could be heard loud and clear. Taylor paused at the door, then turned to the two women.

"I should go in alone. With Thor. I'll leave the door open so he isn't scared. Is that okay with you?"

Dora looked at Harper questioningly. When Harper nodded in the affirmative, Dora said, "Yes."

Thor sniffed at the door and whined softly. Clearly he wanted in. Taylor patted the dog's huge head, then opened the door. Moving slowly,

Taylor entered the room. Thor followed, his nose to the ground sniffing. Harper and Dora stayed at the door, watching.

The curtains were open and sunshine poured in. Papers, books, toys, and clothes littered the floor, obviously tossed by an angry Nate, who was lying on the carpet, flapping his hands hysterically in the air and stomping his feet in a fury, shouting barely coherently through the screams, "No. You can't make me."

Taylor stood in the middle of the room a moment, hands on his hips, assessing. He walked to the television and browsed the video games. He selected one and started the game up. Then he attached two remotes and sat on the floor in front of the screen. He set one remote by his side and began playing the game with the other. To Harper's eyes it appeared as though he were totally ignoring the boy, but she knew better. When the game started, she recognized it as the one she'd purchased for Nate, a cooperative game that was meant for two players.

Meanwhile Thor circled the room, nose to the ground, eyes on Nate. As she watched, she noticed the big dog's circles getting tighter and smaller till he was circling the screaming boy, who was ignoring the dog. Thor finally stopped in front of Nate, whining with sympathy. He stepped closer and nudged Nate with his nose.

Nate sucked in his breath, startled, and

momentarily snapped out of his hysteria. He stared at the dog, then waved his hand. "Go away!"

Thor immediately lowered his head and began licking Nate's hand, which Nate allowed. Though he was still sobbing, great heaving sobs, the shouting stopped. Harper could see Nate was being soothed by the licking. Taylor glanced over his shoulder at the action but didn't move from his seat. He kept his focus on the video game, his back to Nate.

Nate made the first move. Still lying on the floor, he turned to his side and reached over with his free hand to begin petting Thor's chest. Thor responded by stepping closer and licking Nate's face.

Harper shared a look with Dora, who had tears in her eyes, watching the young boy being tenderly soothed by the big dog. Thor seemed to read Nate's emotions. No words were necessary. Nate, feeling the connection, kept inching closer, reaching higher up the dog's neck. Gradually the sobs subsided to a few ragged sighs. Thor lay down beside the boy with a grunt of comfort and let Nate continue to pet him, nuzzling his face against Thor's fur.

Harper lost track of time as she and Dora watched Thor soothe Nate. In time, after he'd settled, Nate realized that Taylor was in the room. Immediately he scowled. Nate didn't expect to see the man there and didn't like surprises. But as time passed and Taylor continued ignoring Nate, the boy sat up and with increasing curiosity watched Taylor play the game. Eventually, Nate rose and went to stand beside him. Taylor kept playing the game, eyes on the screen. Nate stood a few feet from Taylor for a few minutes, watching the game. Then, without speaking, he sat down beside Taylor and picked up the remote.

Taylor glanced at him, nodded noncommittally, and returned to his game.

Suddenly Nate was playing the game, too. All hysteria was gone. The silence in the room was broken now only by the beeps and noises from the game. Thor rose and padded over on thick paws to Nate's side, where, once again, he settled beside him, resting one of his huge paws on Nate's skinny thigh.

Dora nudged Harper and signaled that they should leave. Her final look in the room revealed the big man and the small boy playing the video game together. The boy had been calmed without a single word being spoken.

East Bay Street in Charleston is a historic road that travels beside the Cooper River along Charleston Harbor. From Market Street to Broad, some of the city's finest restaurants are clustered. From Broad Street south to the tip of the fabled Charleston Peninsula is a treasure trove of some of the finest colonial architecture in America.

Harper and Taylor walked down the crooked sidewalks, his hand closed over hers. The sun was setting and the streetlights were beginning to glow in the balmy night. Harper wore tight navy cotton pants and an icy-blue silk top that shimmered like water. Her coppery hair fell in a sleek sheath to her shoulders, where a chunky lapis and topaz necklace ringed her neck. She'd spent a long time dressing for tonight and wanted to look sexy. Special for her first date with Taylor. And it was the first time she'd worn spiky heels in months. She grimaced as she made her way along the pitfalls of the old, crooked sidewalks. Taylor's expression when she'd opened the front door that evening was worth the effort.

Taylor had made an effort, too. He wore a crisply ironed, gray, open-necked shirt that hung loose over dark jeans. The sleeves were rolled up his tanned forearms. On his feet he wore leather sandals, a switch from his usual work boots. He looked as fresh as if he'd just stepped out of the shower, and stepping closer, she caught the faint scent of aftershave.

They were one of scores of couples strolling along the popular street, peeking in the windows of art galleries, hurrying to dinner reservations, pausing to read menus posted. As she walked beside Taylor, Harper realized, pleased, that his mama had taught him to walk on the street side with a lady. He towered over her even in her highest heels. As she regarded his handsome profile, her heel twisted in a rut of a cracked sidewalk. With a yelp, she stumbled into Taylor's side. His reflexes were lightning fast. His arm shot out and he caught her, holding her steady.

Harper's cheeks flamed. This was the second time she'd stumbled. He probably thought she was a klutz. "Thank you," she gasped, regaining her footing.

"That's what happens when you walk in stilts." He grinned wryly. "Maybe you'd better keep a hold on me. It's just ahead."

She gratefully held on to his arm with two hands and took careful steps as they walked the half block to where a black sign over a door read EAST BAY MEETING HOUSE. The street-side folding doors were wide-open, and small bistro tables overflowed onto the sidewalk. Inside, it was very French. Bistro chairs and tables clustered between tall, drape-lined windows on the left and a classic wooden bar on the right. It was almost eight o'clock and the tables were nearly filled. Taylor grabbed the last table. Within minutes, it was standing room only.

Taylor raised his hand. A young, pretty waitress hurried over and took their order for drinks.

Harper looked around the cozy restaurant, let her hand run along the crisp cotton tablecloth, and thought, *I've missed this.* Going out, mingling with crowds, the excitement of a performance, sitting across the table from a handsome man. He turned his head and caught her looking at him. She blushed and tucked her hair behind her ear.

"Popular place," she said over the buzz of the crowded room.

"Lots of poets in Charleston." Taylor leaned closer to be heard. "But tonight's special. Marjory Wentworth, the South Carolina poet laureate, is reading from her new book of poems."

"Are you reading?"

"Sure am. We each get six minutes."

"Aren't you nervous?"

"Of course. But I don't scare easy." He shrugged. "Once I get up there, I lose the fear and get into the words."

Harper gazed at him, wondering what that kind of courage felt like. Her toes curled in her shoes at just the thought of someone reading her writing, much less standing up in front of strangers and reading it aloud to strangers.

The waitress delivered her white wine and his beer. Harper took a sip, tasted its sweetness, and almost purred. "This is the first glass of wine I've had since June."

Taylor swallowed his beer and looked at her with wonder. "You don't drink?"

"My sisters and I made a pact not to drink for a week, just to see if we could. At first it was torture, I confess. I like my glass of wine at night.

Then we just kept it up. After a while I stopped missing it." She sipped again, then smiled devilishly. "Until now."

"How's it taste?"

"Delicious." She set her glass on the table and her fingers idly stroked the chilled glass as she let her gaze wander out to the street. The night was deepening and the candles glowed on the tables. People walked past, chatting, laughing. "Charleston is so alive in the evening. I can count on one hand the number of times I've come to the city since I've been here. I wonder if that was wise. It's lovely."

"Don't you like cities?"

Harper let out a chuckle. "I love cities. I live in New York, remember? It's more that when I came to Sea Breeze early in the summer, I was in a quandary. Searching for something that required peace and introspection. I had to shut out the noise and distractions."

"Some people need that to write."

"Apparently I do. I've never written so much or so steadily."

He picked at the label on his bottle of beer. "Maybe you should stay here."

"You think?"

He looked directly at her and held her gaze. "I do."

The idea of not going back to New York had not seriously occurred to her.

"I'm an editor. I'll most likely find a job in New York."

He took another pull of his beer. "What about your writing?"

"I plan to finish the book before I leave. That's as far as I've gotten in my plans."

Their conversation was interrupted when the first poet approached the podium. The crowd hushed. Taylor gave Harper an encouraging smile. She returned the smile and, unwrapping her arms, leaned forward on the table to listen.

As one poet after another read a few poems, Harper felt surrounded by the music of words— the tempo, the cadence, the high-pitched tones and the low. Music that penetrated barriers, brought forth memories in bursts of color, images so real she saw them come alive right in front of her. She'd been to many prose readings before for her job in the publishing house, but never a poetry reading. It truly was performance art. Harper was mesmerized. It helped her understand the meaning and heightened the emotions kindled by each spare, carefully chosen phrase.

So lost was she in the readings that she almost forgot that Taylor was going to read. Then she heard his name called and he stood up. Her breath quickened as he walked to the podium, a slim volume in his hand. She felt anxious for him. She wanted him to be good. Her stomach tightened when he faced the crowd. The overhead light cast shadows on his face, highlighting his cheek-bones, his straight nose that flared slightly with nervousness.

He stood for a moment at the podium, his gaze sweeping the room. "I'm reading a poem I wrote when I returned from Afghanistan. It's called 'Wake Up. Keep Moving.' That's what they tell a guy with PTSD when he's having a nightmare."

Harper froze and her breath stilled in her throat. PTSD? She didn't know that he'd had post-traumatic stress disorder. Her mind raced. She knew he was a Marine. That he'd seen action. She recollected a photograph that Carson had shown her of Taylor and Thor at the Dolphin Research Center. Harper had been charmed seeing him—his beautiful body—directing two dolphins to leap in the air. Thor was on the dock. The dog had been wearing a black service-dog emblem.

I'm an idiot, she told herself. For all that she prided herself on being observant, she didn't put these obvious signs together. Suddenly all the small details of his behavior made sense. Taylor was more than reserved. He was alert. Hyper-vigilant. When he walked into a room, his gaze always scoped it out. He'd just checked for exits at the podium. Harper had done research on PTSD for Nate after the dolphin incident. She'd seen the symptoms. And been blind to them. Deliberately? she wondered.

Harper put her trembling hands in her lap and stared at the man she was falling in love with. Did this make a difference?

Taylor cleared his throat and raised his slim volume. She took a deep breath.

When he began to read, she didn't hear a hint of nervousness in his voice, and she remembered how he'd told her that once he started to read, his fear fled as he got into the words.

Don't thank me for the things I've done
Don't curse me for them either.
I've written suicide notes with blood
that say *Wake up. Keep moving.*

You don't know how you'll act under fire
Be the hero or frozen in fear?
Some say you fight for your comrade, your
    brother.
Others say *Wake up. Keep moving.*

Will I let you love me before it's too late?
Save me from a dishonorable fate?
Is there one more chance to be a hero?
You tell me *Wake up! Keep moving.*

I've killed more men than I can count
In the name of country and duty.
How does God take a man's measure?
The ghosts tell me *Wake up. Keep moving.*

His voice was strong and steady as he read his words in a marching cadence, bringing to life a hidden place of suffering. Harper's heart kept beat with the tempo while he read, completely immersed in his words. She leaned forward to catch every syllable, each nuance. Her heart went out to the pain he must've endured.

Since the first moment she'd seen Taylor, she'd been attracted to him. As the days passed, she came to admire his tenaciousness, his capacity for long hours of labor without a break, his neatness and unerring politeness. He was a Marine, after all. With animals he was gentle and firm. With Nate she'd seen his compassion and capacity for caring. She also grew aware of a restless energy simmering beneath his calm facade.

Tonight, listening to his poetry, Harper understood the misery he wrestled with, the guilt he carried, and the depth of feeling that he struggled to keep under wraps. He was intelligent, with an artistic soul. She listened in awe and with a new respect for the courage it took to share his feelings. For his battle to keep those raw emotions under restraint.

Tonight she was seeing Taylor with opened eyes.

When he finished, there was rousing applause. Everyone in the room knew that he'd spoken from the heart. As Taylor walked back to the table, many people stopped to talk to him, shake his hand. Harper saw how people liked him, how this was a group of his friends, a world of his that she'd not known about before tonight.

"You were incredible," she said excitedly when he sat down again at their table. "I understand now what you meant when you said sharing your writing is a gift. A giving of a part of yourself. I felt that when I listened to you tonight. That you were telling your story. It was so powerful."

He didn't respond right away. He doused his thirst with a long swallow of beer and set the bottle on the table. Then he reached out and took her hand. The gesture surprised her. It was so unexpected. So intimate. Suddenly it felt as though her whole being were captured in that one hand.

Taylor looked into her eyes. "I was reading to you."

She shut her eyes for a moment, then said in a soft whisper, "I know."

Another poet was announced, breaking the moment. An older woman with snow-white hair and black glasses approached the podium. Taylor glanced around the room, then rose to his feet, not letting go of her hand. He bent low to say in her ear, "There's a free table on the sidewalk. Let's go."

Quietly, so as not to disturb the reader, he led her to the outdoor table. She was sorry when Taylor dropped her hand to pull out her chair.

A different waitress, equally perky, promptly came to take their order. When she left, Taylor pulled a pack of cigarettes from his pocket. "Do you mind if I smoke?"

"Must you?"

He shrugged. "It puts me at ease." He put his hand up to arrest her argument. "I know it's not good for me and I'm going to quit." His gaze was resolute. "But not yet."

"Okay," Harper said, although in her heart it was anything but. She watched as he put a cigarette in his mouth, pulled out matches, and, cupping the cigarette in his hands, lit up. As a rule, Harper didn't date men who smoked. She thought it was a nasty habit that only brought misery in time. Looking away, she knew, too, that she had such bad associations with smoking because of her mother.

Taylor took a drag from his cigarette, then waved the smoke away from her direction.

She relinquished the battle. "I'm fine. My mother is a chain-smoker. I'm used to it."

"Just one. I promise."

The waitress returned with her wine and another beer for Taylor.

Taylor took a drink, as though summoning his resolve. He cleared his throat. "That poem," he said, referring to her earlier comment, "it *was* personal. I wrote it when I came back from Afghanistan."

"I figured that."

He paused to flick his ash. "You know I had PTSD?"

"No."

"Carson never mentioned it?"

"No. . . . How did *she* know?"

"That's what started me working with dolphins. It came up at the DRC."

"Of course."

He shifted in his chair. "Does it bother you?"

"No," she replied honestly, looking directly into his eyes. "Should it?"

He stared back, his eyes pulsing. Then he averted his gaze and shrugged. "It bothers some people. They don't want to get involved with someone who's crazy." He took a long smoke.

"You have PTSD. You're not crazy."

"No. I'm not." He looked up and she saw relief. Even gratitude. "I'm glad you know the difference. Not everyone does."

At that moment she wanted to be as eloquent with words as he had just been. To share all the feelings roiling inside her. To reassure him. To allay his fears. And her own.

There were no words. So instead she leaned toward him and cupped his chin in both of her hands. Then she kissed him. Sweetly, tenderly. A kiss filled with promise. When she drew away, she saw that he'd dropped his guard to reveal vulnerability.

Harper leaned back in her chair and picked up her glass. "Carson *did* tell me you were great with the dolphins." She smiled before she sipped the cool wine.

A smile filled with memories flitted across his face. He, too, leaned back in his chair and crossed his legs. "I went there as part of the Wounded Warrior Project. Dolphins are amazing animals. Honest. Funny. Wise. They have a very real presence. You look a dolphin directly in the eye and you know you're making contact with an intelligent being. You feel it in your gut. They see you. Really see you." He looked at his cigarette. "They helped me through tough times. So I just kept coming back."

"How did you get involved with poetry?"

He shrugged. "It was part of my therapy. When I came back from the war, I felt emotionally numb. I was hypervigilant. Terrified to go out in crowds. It's part of PTSD." He looked at his cigarette. "You want to die, and sadly, some guys do."

"I'm sorry."

"Yeah." He sipped from his beer. "I'm one of the luckier ones. My physical injuries healed. It took longer for the psychological wounds to heal. The wounds you don't see. I went through a lot of different therapy—art therapy, EMDR, the dolphins, video games. That's how I knew what to do with Nate this morning."

"I wondered about that. You were so good with him." Then she smiled. "And so was Thor."

"He's trained to bring me out of that dark place. He senses when I'm having a nightmare and licks my hand and my face to wake me up before I get to the red zone. You saw how it worked with Nate this morning. His job is to bring me back from the war raging in my head. We both knew what that little guy was going through this morning. When he's in a tantrum, it's like being stuck in a nightmare and you can't wake up. It tore me up to see him like that. Thor, too."

"I heard him whine."

He took a swallow of the beer.

Harper sipped from her wine, set the glass on the table. Waited, then asked, "What happened to you in Afghanistan? If you don't mind my asking."

"It's a long story."

"I have time, if you want to tell me about it."

Taylor took a drag from his cigarette and looked to the street, considering. When he turned back, he took a final swig from his bottle, then tossed his cigarette in. Looking up, she saw decision in his eyes.

"I was in Afghanistan," he began slowly. His voice sounded far away. "The days all seem to blur into each other in my mind, so I can't even say exactly when the accident happened. It sometimes feels like it was just the other day. It's all so different there—the smells, the sounds, the people. But we had our routines. Jobs to do. Sure it was tough, but we knew what we'd signed up for. And we had our friends. Our band of brothers."

He reached for his packet of cigarettes, paused as though remembering his promise, then let his hand drop.

"We were out riding in a caravan, on our way to a new location. Like we'd done dozens of days before. We were prepared for trouble. I was wearing body armor and a helmet." He laughed shortly. "Man, it was hot. Hotter than here, trust me. My buddy Dave took off his helmet to wipe his brow."

Taylor stopped speaking and rubbed his forehead. Harper went very still, knowing he was coming to the hard part of the story.

"I still can't wrap my mind around how one small, insignificant movement can mean the difference between life and death. He took off his helmet just long enough to wipe his brow . . ." Taylor paused to look off. "It wasn't our truck that got hit. If it was, I wouldn't be here now. No way." He shrugged, looking down at his feet. "One minute I was looking at his face, the next minute there was this loud bang and I went flying. Got knocked out. When I came to, I couldn't see anything. I mean, I was blind. Everything went white and my ears were ringing. Reaching up, I felt blood coming out of my ears. When my vision finally cleared, I saw I was lying in a ditch. I was in a kind of daze, not thinking clearly. I wasn't sure what had happened. When I could drag myself to stand, I wished I couldn't see. There was wreckage everywhere. Bodies . . . The head truck that caught the IED was shredded. My buddy Dave, he was dead. And three other brothers. Gone in an instant," Taylor said in a husky voice.

Harper didn't speak. She blinked back tears of sympathy trying to imagine that magnitude of loss and pain. And what it might do to a person.

"You know, I keep thinking how fate dealt the cards that day. If our truck was first in line, or if I was the one who'd removed my helmet, or if I was in Dave's seat, it'd have been me that died instead of him."

"But it wasn't."

He shook his head and said under his breath, "No."

Harper thought to herself, *Thank God,* but remained silent.

"They got me to the medic," he continued in a steady voice. "Compared to some of the other guys, I got off easy. I didn't lose my life, or my sight, or a limb. I told the doc I was fine and I could go back. I didn't have any wounds I could see. But I wasn't fine. It was the beginning of my second tour of duty and the third or fourth time I'd gotten blasted by some IED. This time, it was my ticket home. I hated being there and wanted to go home. But not like that."

"Did the doctor diagnose your PTSD?"

"Not right away. I'm a Marine and we like to think we can tough it out. But this time I couldn't."

Harper saw something in his expression that made her realize how he'd suffered during the time it took for him to reach the point to ask for help. Harper slid her hand across the table to put it over his. "How's your therapy been working out for you?"

He looked at their hands, then intertwined their fingers. "It's going good. I've been reaching out. Pushing myself. I had to once more muster up the courage and strength to make another plan. I decided it was time to come home again and get my life back on track. I have my college degree from the Citadel. I've applied at a few places for a job, and one here in Charleston called me for an interview. That's what prompted me to come back home sooner than later. So far, everything is moving on a trajectory."

"Any company would be lucky to have you."

He turned her hand in his, then gently rubbed his thumb across her palm.

She felt every neuron in her hand tingle.

He looked up from their hands and met her gaze. "Best of all, I met you."

They stared into each other's eyes, each aware that they were moving into new waters. Words, movements, emotions, all had to be navigated anew.

Around them came a smattering of applause and people began rising from their chairs. The noise level of the restaurant rose as good-byes were exchanged and congratulations offered. Taylor and Harper let go of their hands when a few of his friends stopped by the table to say good-bye and comment on his poems.

"Last call," the waitress said, coming up to their table. "We'll be closing soon."

Taylor turned to her. "Want to go?"

Harper nodded and Taylor settled the bill. He rose then without a word, reached over to take her hand, and linked arms, keeping his hand on hers. "Can't have you fall."

She wanted to say something like *I've already fallen,* but she couldn't bring herself to say anything so corny. So she only smiled, glad now for the silly shoes that kept her arm in his. Knowing with him she wouldn't be hurt.

They drove home along East Bay and over the Ravenel Bridge, which soared like a great bird over Charleston Harbor. Sitting high in the truck, Harper looked ahead at the trail of red brake lights. Most of the restaurants on Coleman Boulevard were closed. She and Taylor spoke about the poetry they'd heard, their favorite poems, and other readings they'd attended. By the time they began crossing the wetlands in single file on the long two-way road across the vast acres of marsh, they'd lapsed into a comfortable silence. The tires hummed beneath them and the moon shone bright, lighting up the black, ragged tips of oysters in the mud at low tide.

In the darkness Taylor slid his hand across the seat to capture hers. She sighed at the touch and smiled, moved by the simple gesture that was, she knew, a statement. The radio played country music, and though Harper wasn't a fan, she was attuned to the lyrics. Tonight had been a celebration of words, and these lyrical songs spoke of love and loss and life. While riding in a pickup truck with a lowcountry man, traveling over the moonlit marshes, Harper felt the music fill her.

Sea Breeze looked beautiful in the moonlight. Light dripped through the moss hanging on the heavy boughs of the old oak, bathing the gravel beneath in mystery. Taylor walked Harper to the front door. The fifteen steps felt like a mountain hike by the time they reached the porch. She stopped at the door and faced Taylor, her cheeks fevered. Desire pulsed between them. Mamaw had left the porch light on.

"I'd invite you in," she said softly, "but Mamaw . . ."

"No. And I don't have my own place."

He lowered his forehead to hers. She felt the heat of his breath on her lips. His green eyes were catlike, intense and seductive. Her breath came quick.

"You're driving me crazy, you know that . . . ," he said in a husky voice.

She laughed shortly. "Yeah."

Then he leaned back, creating a distance.

Harper's breath puffed out.

Taylor's lips slanted in a crooked grin. "I don't know if it's even proper for me to kiss you. I'm working for you and all."

Harper leaned forward to wrap her arms around his neck and pull his face close. "You're fired."

A wry grin crossed his lips. "Good." He wrapped his arms around her and lowered his head in a crushing kiss of passion and possession.

Harper fired and rehired Taylor several times in the following days.

Chapter Eleven

Mamaw walked into the kitchen, pleased to find it empty so she could take her time noting all the changes. Sunlight from the back windows poured into the freshly painted, bright room, filling the space with light. She reached up to touch the new roped chandelier over the table, then the gleaming, white-tiled backsplash. The room's outline was the same, but everything else was so warm and inviting. So youthful and vibrant.

Mamaw thought again how she wouldn't have done any of this without Harper's urging. Since Lucille's death she'd been stuck in a rut. Content with the way things were. Before that, even, if she was being honest. Young blood was good to stir the old pot once in a while, she thought.

Laughter and shouts from outdoors caught her attention. She hurried to the rear window, pushed the shutter wide-open, and peered out at the water. "Well, I'll be," she muttered, squinting.

A party was going on at the dock. Carson was on her paddleboard in the water, pushing close to the dock. Nate and Dora, still in life jackets, were climbing out from their kayak. Why, there was Taylor, too, she saw with surprise. Standing next to Harper. She watched Taylor as he bent to lift Nate's end of the kayak and hoist it to the upper dock.

Mamaw put her hand to her cheek. Bless their hearts, it must've been a coincidence that they all met up at the dock at the same time. "Thank you, Jesus," she muttered. Carson began calling everyone into the water from her board. She was laughing and waving her arm. Mamaw watched as Taylor tried to lure Harper into the water even as Harper was backstepping, trying to escape his grip. "Go on, Harper," Mamaw murmured aloud. "Don't be timid. Jump in! Get wet!" She couldn't remember seeing Harper swim in the Cove all summer. Harper preferred to swim in the pool, where the water was clean and there were no fish, no sharks.

Mamaw's eyes widened in surprise as Taylor lifted Harper up in his arms—to lots of clapping and hooting from her sisters. Nate was jumping up and down in excitement. "My, my, my." Mamaw smiled. Things must be progressing between those two.

She heard the girls count to three. Saw Harper kick her legs in Taylor's arms, watched her head duck on his shoulder as she clung tight and Taylor jumped into the Cove. Mamaw burst out laughing and clapped her hands together. Now Nate was jumping in! The first time he'd swum in the Cove since Delphine's accident. Dora ran down the dock and did a cannonball jump in after him. Carson dove off her board and emerged next to Nate. Everyone was laughing and splashing.

Mamaw laughed again and brought her clasped hands to her heart, overcome with joy. "We did it, Lucille," she said with a prayer to the heavens. "There's laughter at Sea Breeze again."

Mamaw turned from the window, feeling as though a heavy weight had fallen from her shoulders. She glanced at all the fresh changes that had been made in the kitchen. Mamaw knew what she had to do.

Without hesitation she went directly to Lucille's cottage. "No more procrastination. It's time for a fresh start."

• • •

Later that afternoon, Dora, Carson, and Harper gathered in the cottage at Mamaw's request, equipped with buckets, cleaning supplies, mops, boxes, and garbage bags. Mamaw had instructed the women to clean out and organize Lucille's cottage top to bottom, though in typical Mamaw fashion she had soon excused herself from the work, citing her need for a nap. Harper was delighted because Mamaw had asked Taylor to return in a few days to paint the cottage, too.

Sorting through Lucille's cottage proved more emotional than any of them had expected. Handling the personal items brought memories to sort through as well. They began in Lucille's bedroom. Medicine bottles were collected in a box to take to the pharmacy for disposal. Blake had told Carson how damaging it was to the local water quality for people to toss their unused medicines into the toilet. The medicine was not completely filtered out in the water filtration plant and ultimately ended up pumped back into the local water to be consumed by marine life. This pollution was one of the reasons dolphins were getting sick in the wild.

They packed away Lucille's personal items, took down the curtains, rolled up the carpet. Then they tackled the most intimate items—her clothing.

Carson opened the closet door and felt her

knees go weak as she caught the familiar scent that lingered on the clothes and saw the line of shirtwaist dresses in multiple colors. Carson pulled one out, in a soft blue, and brought it to her face. "It still smells like Lucille," she said, her voice muffled by the fabric.

"Vanilla," Dora said.

"When I think of Lucille, I always see her in one of those dresses," added Harper. "Even when I was little, it was always the same style."

"It was her uniform," Dora said.

"Don't call it a uniform," Carson warned. "Mamaw never liked that word. She didn't want Lucille to feel she had to wear one, but you know Lucille. She chose the shirtwaist because she liked it and wore it every day."

Carson set the dress gently down on the bed. "This is going to be harder than I thought." Her voice choked. "I'm feeling emotional these days."

They packed the dresses, shoes, and coats of all colors neatly into boxes to give to charity. Along the top shelf of the closet, in a neat line, was a row of hatboxes. Inside each was a magnificent hat, one showier than the next.

"Oh, Lord, these bring back memories." Dora held up a large-brimmed straw hat with bright coral-colored trim and enormous flowers. She hurried to the mirror and placed it on her head. "How do I look?"

Carson plucked the hat off Dora's head. "We

should be respectful. Lucille took such pride in her hats. Wore them to church every Sunday."

"I'm not laughing at Lucille. She could carry it off. I'm laughing at how *I* look in it."

"You'd look funny in any hat. You're not a hat kind of girl."

"What's a hat kind of girl? I'll have you know I love hats. Every woman looks good in a hat if it's the right hat."

Carson guffawed in exasperation. "I've never seen you wear a hat."

"I wear hats all the time."

Harper ignored the banter and instead opened another hatbox and gingerly pushed back the tissue. Slowly, reverently, she removed the magnificent hat—royal purple with a wide, sloping rim and a profusion of ribbons and feathers.

Harper remembered one Sunday in particular when she'd seen Lucille emerge from her cottage wearing a purple coat and this purple hat. Harper had been no older than ten. She'd stopped what she'd been doing to stare at the hat, completely agog. In England, showy hats and fascinators were common. Yet Harper had never seen such a hat in New York, and certainly not in the lowcountry. She'd walked over to the cottage porch to get a closer look. Lucille closed her pocketbook and, seeing the girl staring at her, tilted her head and eyed the child with suspicion.

"What you starin' at, child?"

"Your hat," Harper replied in her quiet voice.

"What about my hat?" Lucille's hands went to it. "Is it crooked?"

"It's so beautiful. Like a queen's crown."

Lucille smiled and preened a moment, adjusting the hat on her head. "Why, thank you, Harper. I do love this hat. Purple is my favorite color."

"Lucille, why do you wear such fancy hats to church?"

Lucille studied Harper's face a moment, then came down the steps, closer to Harper. "That question deserves a proper answer." Lucille reached out and cupped Harper's cheek in her hand and looked deeply into her eyes.

Harper could still feel how dry Lucille's skin was, and how strong her hand.

"I'm not surprised the question came from you. You might be a quiet little thing, but you never miss a trick, do you, girl? Well"—Lucille shifted her weight—"it goes way, way back. During the time of slavery, and after, many black women worked as maids and servants. We had to wear uniforms during the week. But on Sunday"—she lifted her hands for emphasis— "we broke from our uniforms and showed our individual flair with our hats."

She laughed then, her unique cackle that always made Harper laugh hearing it. "No matter what material the hat was made from, it was always

232

done up proud with ribbons and feathers and flowers. I reckon over the years the church hats have gotten bigger and bolder." She smirked. "Like the women who wear them." She reached up to lightly touch the hat on her head. "We consider our hat to be our crowning glory."

Harper remembered listening to Lucille and thinking she had never looked more like a queen than she did that day.

Eyes bright with unshed tears, Harper gently returned the elaborate purple hat to the box. "I'd like to keep this hat," she said to her sisters. "Would that be all right?"

"Mamaw said we could take mementos if we wanted," Dora replied. "Of course, if there's anything truly valuable, like her jewelry, we should give it to Mamaw to decide what to do," she clarified with typical authority.

"No, I don't want anything else. Just the hat."

"She left us each a painting, too, don't forget." Carson raised her hand. "Dibs on the Jonathan Green."

As the day wore on and they emptied the bureaus, drawers, closets, and bookshelves, each of the three women found some small personal item to keep that carried special memories. For Harper it was the hat. For Dora, an old fox stole, complete with eyes and a tail, which had been one of Lucille's prized possessions.

Carson kept the collection of Golden children's

books that Lucille had read to her back when she was young and had lived with Mamaw. She let her hand trace the titles: *The Poky Little Puppy*, *The Saggy Baggy Elephant*, *Hansel and Gretel*. "My favorite was *The Happy Family*," she told her sisters. "I remember reading this book over and over. See how worn the pages are? I loved the illustrations most. I used to pore over these drawings of the daddy, mommy, brother, and sister. They were all doing normal, everyday things together . . . working in the garden, saying prayers, eating dinner. I used to stare at the pictures and try to imagine what a normal life like that was like. I hardly had the stereotypical happy family."

"Neither did I," said Harper.

"No," Carson snorted with a roll of her eyes. "You only had to deal with which house you were going to live in." She held her finger up to tap her chin in mock display. "Let's see, where shall we go this week? The Hamptons? The Central Park apartment? Or the estate in England?"

"Shut up," Harper fired back, annoyed. This was far from the first time Carson had made a dig about Harper's family's money, and whereas before she had let the comments roll off her back, something about these past few weeks made her suddenly resentful of her older sister's critique. She'd had enough. "You always do that."

"Do what?"

"Bring my family's money into it, like it's the only thing that matters."

"It helps, that's for sure. You could've been stuck in my cheap apartment in a lousy section of LA, not knowing if your father was going to make rent or if you'd have to move again."

"I'm sorry you went through that. But you don't think being schlepped from one house to the next by a nanny was just as bad?"

Carson scoffed as she gathered scarves from the closet. "No."

Yanking the scarves from Carson's hands, Harper threw them onto the bed. "Well, it was!" she cried, eyes flashing.

Carson went still, shocked at Harper's anger. It was so unlike her to explode.

"Hey, time-out," Dora called out.

"No," Harper snapped, her hands in fists as she turned on Carson. "You've been needling me about my money all summer. All my life! Let's deal with it right now. What have you got against me?"

Carson appeared hunted, if not remorseful. "I don't have anything against you."

"Yes, you do. You're pissed that I have money."

"I'm not pissed that you have money. I'm pissed that I don't have any!"

"But why do you blame me for it?"

Carson ran her hands through her hair. "I don't."

"You do. All the time. Even when we were little

and hunting for pirate's gold, you used to say that if we found any, you'd get to keep it all because I didn't need any more."

"I was just teasing."

"It wasn't funny. And it still isn't."

"I guess I was jealous," Carson admitted.

"Jealous of my money?"

"Yes! I was jealous of your money," Carson shouted back. "You have so much! I was raised by a man who couldn't hold down a job. I never knew where the next dollar was coming from. Never knew from one month to the next if we'd be evicted or if the electricity would be cut off."

But Harper was past the point of feeling pity for Carson's upbringing. Who was to say that Harper had it any better just because the adults in her life had more money to throw around? "First, that man you're talking about was my father, too. I didn't know him. Dora barely knew him, either. I was raised by a sixty-two-year-old nanny who farted excessively and sucked peppermints to disguise the liquor on her breath. Want to talk about moving? I was shipped off to boarding schools since the age of six, to my grandparents' houses for holidays, and Mamaw's in the summer. Hardly the model family."

"At least you have money. There's a fear connected with not knowing if you have enough to eat that you don't have a clue about. And the worst of it is, no matter what I do, I always seem to end up back in that same place. How do you think I felt when you whipped out your checkbook and paid for the kitchen remodeling?"

"I was trying to make Mamaw feel better!"

"But you also made me feel like shit. Like I was a moocher. Which I am."

Dora said, "If you are, so am I."

Harper shook her head. "I can't win for losing. I try to be generous and you throw it in my face. Would you rather I didn't help Mamaw? Or you?"

The last point stung and Carson hung her head. "No. Of course not," she said in a lower tone. "I appreciate all the help you've given me. You know that."

Harper's voice cracked. "No, I don't." She felt her lips quiver and fought the hurt. "I don't want you to thank me," she said with despair. "I wanted to help you because I love you."

Carson's face contorted and she moved to put her arms around Harper. "I know. I'm sorry, Harpo. I never should have said those things. I didn't mean them. I can be such a bitch."

Harper hugged her sister back. "Yes, you did mean them, but I'm glad we cleared the air. I just want you to understand that I don't live a charmed life. What it's like to have a mother like mine who always makes me feel bad about myself. Sometimes I wish I didn't have a mother. That she'd have just given me to Daddy. Like your mother did. We could've been raised together. At least we'd have had each other."

Carson choked out a laugh and wiped her eyes. "Yeah. But I kinda wish my dad gave me to your mother. It'd have been easier. Trust me. Together we could've dealt with Georgiana."

Harper laughed at the idea of the two of them trashing her mother's elegantly appointed apartment. "I'd put you up against Georgiana any day."

"Bring it."

Dora wiped her hands with a towel and took a look around the cottage. "Before you begin the gladiator exhibit, let's finish up here. Other than the jewelry box, I don't think there's anything else that needs to be saved." She sighed. "I think we're done."

Harper looked around the small cottage readied for painting. The pine floors were covered with boxes each filled with items to be donated. The bookshelves were empty, the curtains taken down, the rugs rolled up to be cleaned or given away. The paintings were stacked neatly against the wall.

"A whole lifetime packed into these boxes," Dora said. "Seems so little."

"Does it?" asked Carson. "If I packed up everything I owned, I wouldn't have half this much."

"Seeing all these boxes makes me realize how unimportant all this stuff is," Dora said. "I felt this same way walking around my house in Summerville when I was there last. All my possessions were packed up, my furniture covered with tarp. You know, there was a time I'd have been frantic about leaving it all there, terrified someone would steal something. When I saw it all last week, it all kind of made me ill. I couldn't wait to get out. That house and all that stuff is an albatross around my neck. A battleground for the lawyers. They're dividing everything, even my furniture. I was upset about that at first, but now . . ." She shrugged. "Let Cal sell it. I can't take it to the cottage with me, and I don't want to spend money to store it. All this"—she spread out her arms—"it's all just stuff."

Carson opened the cottage door and strolled out to the porch. "It's going to be a good sunset," she called to her sisters. "Come join me."

Harper and Dora followed Carson to the porch. Carson moved a rocker to face the setting sun and slid into it. Dora took the second rocker, while Harper fetched a chair from the house. They sat together on the front porch in a collective silence as the western sky deepened to magenta.

"I was thinking," Harper said at length. "We packed up all Lucille's things and they won't be missed. What we'll miss is Lucille. The cottage feels so empty without her."

"What matters is what we remember," said Carson. "Our memories."

Dora smiled wistfully and her eyes took on the sparkle of memory. "When I remember Lucille, I won't think about her wearing the ol' fox stole or hat. I'll remember Lucille wearing her shirt-waist dress and standing in front of the stove, shaking her wooden spoon at me."

Carson smiled at the image. "She used that spoon on my behind more than once." They all laughed at the shared memory. "When I think of Lucille, I'll remember her sitting out on the porch with Mamaw, playing cards."

Harper and Dora murmured their agreement.

"How many times did we see them there?" asked Harper.

"I could kick myself for not once thinking of taking a picture of those two old hens together," added Carson.

"You have the picture." Dora tapped her forehead. "In your memory. We all do. That's what we're doing here now. This summer. Remembering the past. But we're also creating new memories that will keep us close in the years to come. After Sea Breeze is sold."

Dora reached out to take Carson's hand on her left and Harper's hand on her right. "We can't fade from each other's lives again. Not ever. We need to keep creating memories together."

Chapter Twelve

As a girl, Harper had often journeyed south with Mamaw and her sisters across the Grace Bridge to Charleston for shopping or an event. Only once in a blue moon, after much begging by the girls, did Mamaw head north to Myrtle Beach for the popular amusement-park rides, restaurants, and the occasional live show. But never had Harper been to McClellanville, the fabled shrimp-boat community, one of the few remaining on the southeastern coast.

Until now.

Taylor had reminded her of a promise he'd made when they'd first met to show her a shrimp boat.

Harper sat in Taylor's black truck and stared out the window at miles of passing pine trees of the magnificent Francis Marion National Forest and the Cape Romain National Wildlife Refuge. This was God's country, she thought, much of it the same today as it had been back in the eighteenth century when old rice plantations thrived. History breathed along the old King's Highway. Dotting the four-lane highway were the tilting wooden stands of the local women who filled the shelves with their hand-sewn sweet-grass baskets.

Harper cast a surreptitious glance at Taylor beside her, relieved to find his eyes steadfastly on the road ahead. She loved his strong profile, his thick brows, straight nose, and full lips. She idly wondered what he'd look like with his shorn hair grown out. He tapped his fingers against the steering wheel in time to the country music playing on the radio. The two hadn't done much chatting throughout the drive, oftentimes falling into a comfortable silence as Harper watched the magnificent scenery go by. She'd learned Taylor was the strong and silent type. Not shy but reserved. Even wary. She sensed she still had much more to learn about him. Then again, she thought with a self-deprecating chuckle, she had never been the chatty type.

Harper sat up and took notice when Taylor flicked on his signal. A blinking traffic light was the only marker for the turnoff.

"Not far now," Taylor said as he turned off the seemingly endless stretch of Highway 17 and headed eastward toward the sea. Pinckney Street meandered through a dense tunnel of oaks, pines, palmettos, and scrubby shrubs that offered welcome shade from the blistering August sun. Harper stared out the passenger window of Taylor's truck at the Eden-like wilderness and sparse houses they passed.

Before long Pinckney Street entered the heart of the small, picturesque fishing village—a few blocks of quaint, gingerbread-trimmed historic houses and shops nestled between majestic live oaks. Harper felt as if she'd stepped back in time. Children played on the green lawns, dogs slept on the porches, and adults strolled the narrow sidewalks that lined both sides of the narrow street. Her sharp eyes also took in the sobering effects of seaside living, evident in peeling paint, the wild growth of vines along clapboard houses, the streaks of rust. Empty storefronts where businesses had closed and FOR SALE signs on empty houses hinted at the hard times Taylor had spoken of. Still, the village had an ageless charm that brought her hand to the window glass with a sense of nameless yearning.

Taylor drove at a snail's pace through the historic district, allowing Harper time to gawk with a small, knowing smile playing at her lips. Pinckney Street came to an end at the glassy water of Jeremy Creek. He turned around and drove back up Pinckney Street, turning onto Oak Street, a smaller street that ran parallel to the water. This shaded street was bordered by an eclectic mix of larger, two-story Victorian houses and modest historic cottages. At the end of the winding road she spied the tips of shrimp boats.

Taylor stopped the truck at the wharf. Bright green marsh grass stretched out from shore to the sea, the tips waving when a breeze passed. Cutting through this, a jagged, fencelike line of pilings bordered the long stretch of docks splattered with gull droppings. Two pelicans perched there, staring in the water for their next meal. The boats were clustered together along the docks like shorebirds on a narrow strip of beach. The tips of the masts bore colored flags, and beneath them hung the great green nets that provided the fishermen's livelihood. The sound of gulls cawing pierced the air as they circled the sky, and beneath them Harper heard the creaks and moans of old wood and the gentle slapping of water.

From where she stood, it appeared the shrimping industry was in fine shape. She counted a dozen trawlers lining the main dock. Five more were moored at a second, all rocking gently against the creaking wood pier. Then she realized that these were not working boats. A number of the boats had a FOR SALE sign.

"There she is." Taylor pointed with pride to the last boat in the line of trawlers.

The *Miss Jenny* was one of the bigger trawlers. Sixty feet of white with dark green trim. She was not young, Harper thought as she noted the peeling paint and rust strips crusting the gear. But she was majestic. Looking at Taylor as he gazed at the trawler, she saw his love of the old boat shining in his sea-green eyes.

"The *Miss Jenny* may be an ol' rust bucket, but she's ours. There's a trick to getting aboard. I'll climb up and help you."

She watched, impressed, as Taylor deftly scaled the high wall of the boat. He turned and reached his arm out to her.

"I don't know . . ."

"What? Are you afraid I'll drop you?" he scoffed. "I've lifted coolers over this wall that weigh more than you."

Harper exhaled a plume of air, then took his hand. She tried to be as graceful as she could while being pulled up the side of the boat. At the railing she was hanging on her belly, one leg dangling. As graceful as a hippo, she thought as she righted herself on deck. Once she was on two feet again, Taylor hopped with practiced ease over the railing back to the dock.

"You leap about like Johnny Depp," she teased.

He laughed loudly at that. "You calling me a pirate?"

"You'd make a handsome pirate."

Taylor looked at her askance over his shoulder as he hoisted the supplies into her waiting arms as if they weighed nothing. Finished, he lifted the cooler and climbed back onto the boat.

"You know, we Muirs are attracted to pirates. We can't help ourselves. It's in our blood."

His eyes sparked with humor. "You know what pirates say about the ladies, don't you?"

She shook her head.

Taylor lifted his arm in a fist pump. "Death to the ladies!"

Harper burst out laughing, delighted that he'd remembered her telling him about her childhood rallying call. "You already kiss like a pirate."

He narrowed his eyes, warming to the game. "And just how does a pirate kiss?"

Harper thought to herself this was their first private joke. "He thrusts and parries."

Taylor kissed her swift and hard, proving the point, then released her as quickly. "Now ye saucy wench, stand aside. It's time to get this old sow out to sea."

Harper stood by the railing, out of the way, and watched as he moved deftly across the deck to the pilothouse back to the side of the boat to shove off. She couldn't ignore how his muscles strained at the task and how beads of sweat formed at his brow.

Taylor fired the boat's diesel engines and the growling noise filled the air along with the cries of seagulls and the strong stench of diesel fuel. He hurried to the pilothouse, grabbed the wheel, and began talking on the marine radio. Slowly he maneuvered the *Miss Jenny* away from the dock.

She thought he looked so handsome standing wide legged at the wheel, his gaze on the water, a man born to captain a ship. Harper recalled her ancestor and thought, *I know how Claire felt when she met the Gentleman Pirate.*

The great engine rumbled beneath them, and a few gulls cried and swooped in the late-afternoon sky as they pushed away from the dock. Taylor slipped his arm around her shoulder as they passed the long line of houses bordering Jeremy Creek. They stood side by side, faces to the sea, as he motored through the ribbon of racing water bordered by a maze of endless, bright green marshland. Harper thought that she'd remember this moment, standing at the wheel of a shrimp trawler, Taylor's arm around her, for as long as she lived. She'd tell her grandchildren about it. Then she smiled. No, she amended, she'd write about it. Document this moment on paper to read over and over. She felt the words bubbling at her heart.

When at last the vista opened to the Atlantic Ocean, Taylor released her and put one hand on the throttle. "Hold on, girl."

The engines roared to life and the boat vibrated beneath her feet. The water churned into white-caps, and Harper laughed out loud for the pure joy of it. She felt the power of the engines racing through her body as she hurried back out onto the deck to clutch the railing. The wind coursed over her, lifting her hair from her shoulders, spraying droplets of cool water on her face. The big trawler was pushing hard through the chop, and above, the nets hanging on the outriggers were creaking as loud as the seagulls overhead. Taylor called out for her, and turning her head his way, she saw him point to the water just beside the boat. She followed his direction and looked over the side.

"Oh, look!" She laughed again. A dolphin was racing alongside, riding in the wake. Her sleek gray body arched in and out of the whitecaps with obvious joy. Harper's heart lurched as she thought of Delphine and wondered if that sweet dolphin she'd come to love would ever again enjoy living in the wild.

Harper clung to the railing and watched the dolphin until it swam off, disappearing. Soon after, Taylor lowered the speed and allowed the boat to cruise at a crawl. He came to her side and slipped an arm around her waist.

"Like it?"

She lifted her face to him. "Love it."

"Thought you might. Hoped you would."

"I have to admit, I had no idea it was so beautiful. The lowcountry shows off her best side from the water."

"That's how people first saw this land. Farther up there"—he pointed inland—"is the great Santee River, the birthplace of the plantations."

"Do they still grow cotton there?"

Taylor barked out a laugh. "Why do people think the only crop on the plantations in the South was cotton?"

"Because we all saw *Gone with the Wind.*"

"Truth is, it was rice that built the plantation economy in these parts. Yellow gold, they called it. That and the know-how and strong backs of the slaves. Our swampy, semitropical landscape was perfect for it. The slaves from the Sierra Leone area not only knew how to grow rice, they brought their culture with them."

"The Gullah-Geechee culture."

"Right. A lot of what we think of today as lowcountry culture can trace its roots to the Gullah." He pointed out over the wetlands that bordered the land. "Once upon a time, more than one hundred and fifty thousand acres were planted with rice. Imagine it."

As she looked out over the vast wetlands, Harper tried to imagine how hard a life the slaves must have endured in those swamps, fighting snakes, alligators, and disease all while laboring under that scorching sun and humidity. She thought, too, of the manacles that she'd found in the garden.

"I can't." She turned to him. "Did your ancestors plant rice?"

Taylor shook his head. "We weren't planters. When the McClellans look out at the wetlands, we don't see rice." He smiled wryly. "We see shrimp."

"Aren't shrimp bottom dwellers?" she teased.

"They are," he replied with equanimity. "But the estuaries"—a gleam was in his eyes—"girl, this is our nursery for shrimp. *That's* where our crop grows."

"You, Taylor McClellan, are the 'son of a son of a sailor.' "

He laughed, and his eyes revealed his appreciation that she knew the lyrics of a favorite Jimmy Buffett song. "I'm the son of a son of a *shrimper*," he corrected. "Speaking of shrimp, I hope you're hungry."

"I'm starved."

"Great. I've packed lots of food."

"Packed? We aren't going to catch our own shrimp? We're on a shrimp boat!"

He looked at her with doubt. "Do you have a clue how hard it is to trawl for shrimp? It's damn hard. You need muscle and experience and a whole lot of patience. Your hands would be raw and you'd smell like a fish house when you were done. We could've done that, but I didn't think it would make for a very romantic evening."

"At least take me for a tour of the boat."

"All right, then. For starters, it's called a trawler."

Taylor took Harper on a tour of the trawler. He explained how they lowered the nets on the outriggers on either side of the boat like butterfly wings. He showed her how to tie the thick rope knot that bound the nets against hundreds of pounds of shrimp. How the nets dragged the ocean floor, tickling the shrimp up into them.

"I can't explain what it's like to pull in the nets dripping from the sea, let it hang over the deck then untie that knot and see the explosion of shrimp burst. But if you like, I'll show it to you someday. When you're dressed for it."

"You promise?"

He bent to kiss her nose. His eyes crinkled with pleasure. "Yep."

"I'm going to hold you to it."

He grin widened. "I'm counting on it." Then he released her and went to the pilothouse, returning with a folding table in his arms. "Tonight, we'll have to settle for local shrimp that's already been caught, headed, peeled, and cooked."

"I'll have you know that I know how to peel shrimp," she said in mock defense. "Lucille taught me when I was little. She always made us girls peel. With those red plastic-knife things. I'm pretty fast. Though I never took the heads off."

Taylor showed her a flicking motion with his thumbs and forefingers. "It's easy. You just twist the heads off, like this."

Harper grimaced. "I'll skip that part, thank you very much."

"Novice."

"Stubborn," she corrected.

She smiled at the banter as she took the blue-and-white-checked tablecloth from the basket and spread it over the table. "You have no idea how rare it is where I come from to even know where shrimp come from, much less how to peel a shrimp. We buy them all cleaned and wrapped up in paper at the grocery store or fish market."

"Imported shrimp, probably." He scowled.

"Probably." She laid out the napkins and tableware. "I know the difference. What's that saying? 'Friends don't let friends eat imported shrimp'?"

He was impressed she knew that expression, smiling with approval. "Right."

Harper opened up thick wedges of cheese; he uncorked a bottle of chilled white wine. The sunset brought a change in temperature that chased off the heat of the day. A sudden breeze ruffled the tablecloth, and Harper lurched for the heavy plastic cups, just catching them before they blew overboard. They laughed as he poured the wine. Soon all was ready, and they each took a chair at the small makeshift table across from each other. The air was fresh and breezy, the sea was calm, and the sun was lowering into a dusky sky.

Sliding back into her chair, she angled it so she could see his face and the glorious sunset behind him. The night was becoming as wildly exotic as a bird-of-paradise flower. The vibrant oranges, magenta, purples, and gold filled the sky as the sun slowly lowered. Balmy breezes swirled softly against her bare arms and legs. Harper tasted the sweet chill of the white wine on her lips and thought, *This is heaven.*

As they feasted on a bounty of cold local shrimp and crab, seasoned artichoke hearts, heirloom tomatoes with basil, and crusty French bread and cheese, the flavor of salt hung in the air. Taylor lit hurricane lamps that flickered in the twilight like early stars. Harper swirled the wine in her glass and recollected how she'd been on luxury yachts many times in her young life, gone on cruises with her mother across the globe where gourmet meals and expensive wines were lavishly served. Yet sitting on the deck of the *Miss Jenny* with no one else on board but her and Taylor, the great green nets swinging in tempo with the rocking boat, the vibrant sun lowering in unparalleled grandeur across an infinite horizon where sea met sky, she couldn't remember ever experiencing a more perfect evening on the water.

She glanced at Taylor and saw that he was watching the sky as well. In the dusk, backlit by the magenta sky, his silhouette was etched in her mind—her memory.

"This is," she said softly, "the most romantic dinner date I've ever been on."

"That's good news." Taylor grabbed the bottle. "More wine?"

"Love some." He filled her glass, then set the bottle down and reached over to the cooler to grab a bottle of water for himself.

"You aren't drinking?"

"I'm driving." He nodded toward the wheelhouse.

"Ah, of course."

"But generally, I don't drink much anymore. Sure I have a drink now and then. But not much. Anymore, that is."

"Did you used to drink a lot?"

"Oh, yeah."

"What changed?"

Taylor paused to consider. "PTSD and drinking are a bad combination."

In the flickering light of candles she could see his face set in somber thought and felt him closing himself off.

"Nature is the great healer. Surely all this"—her arm swept out indicating the view—"must be a salve on your wounds."

Taylor stared out at the landscape, and she knew him well enough by now to know he was working something out in his head. She gave him a wide berth to do so, staying silent and staring out at the water until Taylor began to speak.

"When I return home, this place and all its history swallows me. This geography lives in my soul. My ancestors came here by the sea. My family's survival depended on the bounty of the ocean, the wetlands, and these winding creeks. Our stories, myths, food, culture . . ." He paused. "It's all here. I don't know if it's because of our history that we have this love affair with the land and waters that surround us, or if it's just part of our DNA. Either way, this water is our mother's milk. Our history races in our blood with salt water. It's what makes us who we are. It also binds us. I feel a responsibility not only to my family, but to this boat, these waters. This *place*. I don't know if we can separate one from the other."

"Is that a bad thing?"

"No. Yes." He shook his head. "It makes it difficult to stay and impossible to leave."

As Harper listened to the stirring timbre in his voice and watched his eyes, the same gray-green color of the sea he loved, she was transfixed. "I understand your love of history and your feeling bound to it. I grew up schooled in the illustrious history of the James family in England. I can name each of the dozens of stiff-faced ancestors in portraits that line the halls of Greenfields Park."

"It must give you a strong sense of belonging."

"Obligation."

"That's not the same thing, is it?"

She shook her head. "You know what I think?"

Taylor shook his head.

"I think you have a hard time leaving this place because in your heart you know *this* is your home."

Taylor didn't respond but his green eyes flickered.

"I *long* for a home. Growing up, I was moved from house to house but never felt I belonged in any of them. I always felt like a visitor." She shivered. "I can't recall even once when my mother wrapped me in her arms to hug me when I returned home from school. Or comforted me in my bed when I cried."

Taylor reached out to place his hand over hers on the table.

"You must think me terribly spoiled. Having lived in so many houses and still searching for a home."

"Not at all. It's not the house that makes a home. It's the people."

"Yes." She gained heart that he understood. "Exactly. I had this big, gaping hole in my chest. And though I love the lowcountry, it was Mamaw and my sisters that filled me with a sense of belonging." Harper smiled. "And to be fair, my Granny James always made me feel loved at home at Greenfields Park. My grandmothers have been the guiding lights in my life. I'm lucky to have them." She smiled shyly. "And now you."

Taylor moved to slip one arm around her waist. With his other he reached out to take her glass and downed the remainder of her wine and set it on the table.

Harper stared into his eyes and saw in his unwavering gaze that the rush of feelings she was experiencing—the undeniable attraction, the unexplained, spontaneous connection—he felt, too.

Suddenly he released her and rose from the table to walk across the deck into the pilothouse.

Harper sat motionless in her chair and stared after him. The evening breeze cooled her fevered skin. She blinked in confusion. What had just happened to cause him to leave her? she wondered in a daze. What had she said? Was she too personal? Too forward or too fast?

A moment later Taylor emerged from the pilot-house carrying a large blanket in his arms. He stopped in an open space on the deck and shook open the blanket. It ruffled in the air like a flag before he lowered and spread it out on the deck. Then he walked directly to her side and faced her. His expression was tender, filled with love. He held out his hand.

Harper put her small hand in his, and immediately his long fingers tightened around them. One firm pull and she was in his arms, her breasts crushed against his chest. She caught the scents of the sea and Taylor's skin, a sweetness that had deep, strong notes. They drew closer to one another, desire welling. She leaned into him, and tilting her head, she felt his mouth on hers. She felt the moisture of his tongue and his desire strengthen. His hands raked her body, moving up her back and then to her breasts. She moaned deep in her throat and pressed harder against him, her leg riding up his.

His hand slid up to cup her head and she felt their breaths mingle as he moved away from her. He kissed her forehead, her eyes, both cheeks softly, as the sky dissolved into night. This time when he released his hold on her, he took her hand and brought it to his lips. His eyes gleamed with invitation over her knuckles. Looking in his eyes, she knew what he was asking.

There was no decision to make tonight. Harper had made this decision weeks ago when she'd opened the front door of Sea Breeze and first saw his face. She would not second-guess herself, question her decision, or ponder consequences. Tonight she would abandon her rational self and give herself up to the moment. *To Taylor.* She had never before experienced this type of connection with someone. She would not let it go without experiencing it fully.

Harper's gaze kindled, and taking his hand, she kissed each of his fingers.

Taylor led her to the center of the deck, and together they slid to the blanket. The stars above shone their silvery light as they undressed, giving their bare skins an unearthly glow. He kissed every inch of her, and closing her eyes, she heard the lapping of the sea against the boat.

When at last he entered her, her hips swayed beneath him on the gently rolling deck. She clung tight to his back and buried her face against his moist neck. Harper lifted her head and cried out to the vast sea and sky.

Later, when they lay entwined in each other's arms, Harper looked over the dark sea and saw a fiery harvest moon rising, bathing them in her golden light.

Chapter Thirteen

Early the next morning, Carson woke with a dull, throbbing ache blooming in her abdomen. Waking further, she turned from her side flat onto her back. She'd been in an odd position, she told herself. Backaches were common in pregnancy. Her fingers gently stroked her belly, willing the cramps to go away.

The ache persisted, not allowing sleep to return. Reluctantly Carson pushed back the coverlet and walked through the silent hall to the kitchen. She'd read somewhere that warm milk helped one to sleep, and it had to be good for the baby. Carson poured milk into a mug and slid it into the microwave, careful to step out of the way before turning it on. One of the articles she'd read advised against standing in front of a microwave. She'd been reading so many books and articles and online posts about pregnancy lately. If she was going to do this, she was going to do it right.

As she leaned against the counter, watching the numbers on the microwave's timer click down, the dull ache suddenly sharpened to a pain that doubled her over. A short cry escaped her lips.

This isn't good, she thought in a panic. *This can't be normal.* With another sharp pain she felt a trickle of blood between her legs.

"No, no, no," she cried as she hurried, crouched like a turtle, to the bathroom, feeling her hopes drain away with the blood running down her legs.

Mamaw was no stranger to hospitals. She sat by the window quietly doing needlepoint to keep her mind and hands busy while waiting. Across from her, Harper sat in an uncomfortable metal chair. Dora had needed to stay with Nate, so Harper and Mamaw had driven a weeping, frantic Carson to the hospital. The hospital emergency room was crowded with over a dozen people all wearing the same anxious expressions as they waited for word from a doctor about a loved one.

Thankfully, Mamaw and Harper didn't have to wait long. A petite doctor dressed in scrubs with her brown hair pulled back in a ponytail came out from the double doors.

"Mrs. Muir?"

"I'm here!" Mamaw rose to greet the physician.

Harper drew near to hear the report.

"I'm Dr. Carr. Unfortunately, Carson had a miscarriage. But all things considered, she's doing well."

"Can we see her?" Mamaw asked.

"Not yet. She's undergoing a D and C. With rest, she should recover completely. Again, I'm sorry about the baby."

After the doctor left, Mamaw went to the window to stare out at the cityscape of Charleston.

She'd spent all of her eighty years here. So many good days. So many bad. She thought back to the several miscarriages that she'd endured. The frightening gush of blood, the overwhelming sense of loss, the feeling of failure and futility. Poor Carson, she thought, her heart aching. It had been so difficult for her granddaughter to commit. A few weeks ago Carson might have viewed the miscarriage as a relief. But now, the loss of her baby would be devastating.

Mamaw knew that time would heal her hurt, as she knew that there was nothing she could do to alleviate the heartbreak now but to be there for her, to hold her hand. She would wait until she could see Carson. She would remain at her side.

She'd lost her baby.

Carson lay on her back, staring out the window of the sterile hospital room, not quite able to accept her new reality. She'd only just gotten used to the idea of being a mother. To trust her instincts and let nature take its course. Was this nature taking its course? Or was she the butt of some great cosmic joke?

She put her hands on her abdomen and let her fingers delicately tap on her tender belly. Only yesterday she had had a baby in there. Now she felt a great emptiness. A great sadness. She shivered in her thin hospital gown and reached down to grab the blanket she'd kicked off earlier.

Bending, she felt a sharp pain in her abdomen and gasped with the effort.

A nurse walking in caught the movement and hurried to her side. "Let me help you." She guided Carson back against her pillows. "No sit-ups quite yet," the nurse joked.

"I'm just trying to reach the blanket."

The nurse covered Carson with the blanket, then quickly added a fresh bag of fluid to her IV. "You're dehydrated. Have to keep up your fluids."

Carson almost smiled, remembering Mamaw's constant admonition to the girls to always stay hydrated and moisturize.

"Are you up to a visitor?"

"Who?"

"A young man. Blake Legare."

"Blake is here?"

"Poor fellow, he's been out there wringing his hands ever since you came in. He your boyfriend?"

"Yes." Carson paused, confused. "Or, he was."

"If you don't want to see him, I'll send him packing."

"Wait." Carson's heart ached to see Blake. To share this incomprehensibly sad moment with the only other person who felt the same pain and loss. "Please, send him in."

A short while later there was a knock on her hospital door and it opened.

An exceedingly disheveled Blake stood hesitantly gripping the door. His eyes were rimmed red and his dark hair stood awry as if he'd been raking his fingers through it.

"Carson . . ."

She opened her arms to him.

The following morning, Harper lay on her stomach across her bed, feet kicking the air, staring at her phone. It had been two days since her night with Taylor. Forty-eight hours of waiting for the phone to ring or a text message to chime in. Nothing. She knew because she checked her phone a hundred times a day.

She'd tried to work on her book but was too distracted. Frustrated, she climbed from the bed and walked through Sea Breeze, looking for Carson. She found her on the porch, sitting in the shade, reading a magazine with her feet up on the ottoman. She was dressed in a loose, long dress in a blue island print, and her long, black hair was wound in a braid that fell over her shoulder.

"Good morning." Harper leaned over to place a kiss on Carson's cheek.

Carson frowned. "What's so good about it?"

Harper's stomach twisted in sympathy for her sister as she slid down onto one of the big wicker chairs in the shade beside her. "Aw, honey. Bad night?"

"I have a backache and cramps. Yeah, it's been a bad night."

Harper didn't reply. Carson had been prickly since she'd returned from the hospital. The women at Sea Breeze had decided to give her time to work through the depression that was natural after a miscarriage.

Harper patted her hand. "Anything I can do? Get for you?"

Carson shook her head and closed her magazine. "I'm sorry. I'm just hot and achy and I can't even go in the water. I'm feeling bitchy but I shouldn't take it out on you."

"Aw, go ahead. I can handle it. And you have good reason to feel sad. If it's any consolation, I'm grumpy myself."

"What's the matter? You were all smiles the other day. You went on and on how wonderful your date with Taylor was. The boat, the moonlight . . . what happened?"

"*Nothing* happened," Harper replied with frustration, lifting her legs to the ottoman with a flop. "He didn't call."

Carson turned her head sharply. "He didn't call? Not once?"

"Nope."

"Did you two . . . ?"

"Yep."

Carson bridled. "That's shabby. But I don't understand. I thought you two were like long-lost lovers or something."

"Apparently it was all one-sided." Harper shook

her head and looked off. "Forget it. You have enough on your mind right now. I don't need to bore you with tales of my love life."

"Please do. Anything's better than sitting here feeling sorry for myself."

Taking heart, Harper sat up, tucking her legs up on the ottoman as she turned to face her sister. "I've had a one-night stand before. But this didn't feel like that. I know he felt something for me." Her shoulders slumped. "Or I thought he did. I'm hurt. Bewildered. So why wouldn't he call me?"

Carson removed her sunglasses and leaned closer to Harper. "Honey, do you know Taylor had PTSD?"

"He told me. So?"

"That could be why he's not calling you. Avoidance is classic." Carson tilted her head in thought. "I thought he'd overcome it, but . . . maybe not."

Carson had named Harper's biggest fear. She licked her lips. "Do you know how bad it was for him?"

Carson shook her head. "We didn't talk about it. We really don't know each other that well. He's definitely on guard, and getting words out of him sometimes feels like pulling teeth. But, he seems solid. The dolphins are good judges of character, better than humans. And they love him. But"— she sighed—"some guys never really get over it." She put her sunglasses back on and picked up her magazine. "I hate to say it, but maybe you're better off that he didn't call."

Harper murmured, "Why do you say that?"

"Because, honey, are you sure *you* can deal with his problems if he still has PTSD?"

Harper drew back. Carson was firing with both barrels, her depression making her caustic, which was unlike her. She was usually so positive about life.

"Look, Harper, be realistic," Carson continued in a big-sister, know-it-all tone of voice. "You're going back to New York. What did you really think was going to happen?"

Harper picked at her nail and shrugged. "Maybe he'd come with me."

Carson snorted. "Girl, you don't know nothin' about a lowcountry boy."

"And you do?" Harper rejoined angrily.

Carson leaned back against the cushion and did not answer.

"What are you going to do about Blake?"

Carson skipped a beat as her bravado fizzled. "I don't know," she said in a small voice, and then flippantly, "I don't even know what I'm going to do about little ol' me."

"How is little ol' you?" Harper asked gently.

"I feel like I'm floating through life. Aimlessly."

"You just had a miscarriage."

"Yeah, I know. But . . ." Carson tossed the

magazine onto the table. "It's more than that. I didn't just lose a baby. I lost *me*."

Harper tilted her head. "How so?"

"Do you believe in dreams?"

"I *have* dreams."

"No, that's not what I meant. Do you believe they have meaning? Messages?"

"You mean, like Jungian interpretation?"

"I guess." Carson's shrug implied she didn't know who Jung was.

"It's complicated. I've read a lot about dream interpretation, and basically I believe we get messages from our subconscious in our dreams. That our dreams help us work out the problems we're wrestling with. We're tapping into another part of ourselves."

Carson hesitated, then took a short breath. "Yeah, but . . I think I got a message from some other source. I don't think it was me."

"In a dream?"

"Yes. When I was under anesthesia. That was the first time. I've been having the same dream ever since."

Harper felt a tingling of interest. "There's a school that believes dreams act as a means of transferring messages from the subconscious or even the gods. What's your dream about?"

"An animal."

"What kind of animal?"

Carson looked away. "A shark."

Harper was stunned. She would have bet money Carson was going to say a dolphin. "A *shark?*"

"Yes."

Harper searched Carson's face and saw that she was in utter earnest. "I'm listening."

"When I was still under anesthesia," Carson began with a shaky voice, "I felt like I was floating underwater. I had this like . . . dream. In it, I was searching for Delphine, but she wasn't anywhere to be found. I swam and swam, calling for her. I felt so sad. So lonely. Then I saw a dorsal fin and my heart leaped because I thought it was her. But the closer I got I grew afraid. Cold. I was so cold. . . . It was the shark. The same shark I met in the water last May."

She shivered at the memory. "I tried to get away, but you know how it is in dreams when you try to move but you can't? The water was like sludge. I couldn't escape it. The shark came very close to me, so close I could stare into those dark, soulless eyes. I couldn't look away. My heart was pounding and I was back in May, looking at my own death.

"Only this time, staring into the eyes, I stopped being afraid. I kept staring into its eyes and then . . . I became the shark." She looked up at Harper to gauge her reaction. "Then I woke up."

Harper didn't speak for a moment. "Wow."

"Yeah. Right?" Carson's voice was so low Harper could hardly hear her. "I know there's a message in there somewhere, but nothing is clicking."

Harper pulled out her phone and began doing a search. After a few minutes she looked up. "Have you ever heard of animal totems?"

"No."

"There are ancient myths that speak to our natural connection to animals. We have to be attuned to the animals, respect them, and by doing so we learn to communicate with them." Harper checked to make sure Carson was following her. Her sister sat straight, eyes wide with attention. Harper was hitting a chord. "So, according to this, a totem is an animal that is a messenger for you. We can have many messengers in our lifetime, and if we're open, we can learn from them." She read further in silence. "According to this, your encounter with the shark was not coincidental. It touched a primal part of your heart and soul."

"Sure did. Fear."

"And it sounds like it stirred up some long-dormant feelings. Here." Harper handed Carson the phone. "I looked up shark totems. Check it out and see what you think."

Carson took the phone and bent over it, shading the screen so she could read. A minute later it vibrated. "It's Taylor ringing in."

Harper sat bolt upright.

"Take it." Carson handed the phone back to her. Harper took it, mouthing *Thank you*. She watched Carson swoop to her feet and hurry toward the door, no doubt to look up shark totems. Harper put the phone to her ear. "Hello?"

"Hey, it's me." Taylor's voice was animated. "Can I take you to dinner tonight?"

Harper held back her answer, letting the silence stretch out between them to inform him that she was piqued.

"Are you sure you want to see me again?" she said flatly.

"Why do you ask that? Of course I do."

"You didn't call me for two days."

After a silence he said in a lower tone, "I know. I'm sorry. I want to explain about that."

"I'm listening."

She heard Taylor let out a long sigh. "It's really something I'd rather explain in person, Harper. Come on, let me take you to dinner tonight so we can talk."

"Fine," Harper said in her best impression of her ice-queen mother. "But don't think this gets you off the hook."

"Seven o'clock?"

"Fine," she repeated.

"See you then."

Then she promptly hung up, smiling a bit in spite of herself.

At six thirty that evening Harper shut down her computer, pleased with the day's work. Her book was almost finished. Every morning she couldn't wait to get back to the manuscript. All the hard work was done, the book's climax had been completed, leaving only the resolution, which felt as if she were riding a sled down a steep hill, speeding toward the finish line.

Looking at her watch, she saw that she was running out of time to get ready for her dinner with Taylor. She couldn't deny that the snub of his not calling after they'd made love still stung. Several times this afternoon she'd thought of calling him back and canceling. Let him wait a few days to see how it felt. But if she was being honest with herself, she missed him. She wanted to see him. Hopefully her cold response on the phone earlier had been enough to let him know she wasn't pleased with his lack of manners.

She went in the bathroom to wash her face, apply moisturizer, and run a brush through her hair. Tucking it behind her ears, she stared at her face. It was her usual, familiar face . . . but different. She'd gained a few pounds since she'd arrived at Sea Breeze, mostly muscle from running and gardening. Her face had lost its gauntness. Leaning closer to the mirror, she could see the faint smattering of freckles over the bridge of her nose and cheekbones. Despite her maniacal application of sunscreen and wearing of hats, her fair skin freckled. Yet she preferred the healthy-looking, soft glow of color to her normally alabaster skin. Her red hair had blond streaks from the sun and had grown from its chin-length, sharply contoured blunt cut to fall loosely to her shoulders. Harper applied lip gloss and turned away from the mirror. This was her, she thought—au naturel. And that was enough.

Taylor rang the doorbell at Sea Breeze precisely at seven o'clock. They decided to stay local and eat sushi at Bushido restaurant on the Isle of Palms. The thick tension floating between them had each behaving in an exceedingly polite manner. More so than on their first date. The mood was decidedly uncomfortable. Before climbing into the truck, Taylor took her hand to stop her.

"Can we talk now?" Taylor asked, breaking the uncomfortable silence.

"If you wish." Harper was being curt but she couldn't help herself. She was hurt and angry and, yes, pissed off.

"Let's take a walk on the beach," Taylor suggested.

September was just around the corner, and Harper noticed small changes on the beach. The sun was setting earlier. Already the sky had shifted from blue to the mystical blend of periwinkle and lavender that preceded a sunset. The white-tipped ocean was iridescent as it reflected the silvery violet.

A sprinkling of color was returning to the

dunes as the wildflowers opened up to the cooling temperatures. She spied the first spires of golden-rod, sea oxeye, and her favorite, yellow prim-rose. She spied a large cluster of shorebirds in the distance, early birds in the migration south along the Atlantic Flyway. Soon the monarch butterflies would be passing through. Harper had always left the lowcountry for home in the North by this late in the season. She was pleased that this year, for the first time, she'd see the subtle changes of autumn at the beach.

They walked side by side, not holding hands, close to the shoreline. Harper usually ran on the beach in the morning, when the sand was wiped smooth by the outgoing tide. Now the beach was covered with footprints and the occasional litter from thoughtless visitors.

Taylor removed his sunglasses and stuck them into his shirt pocket. "Do you mind if I smoke?"

"Go ahead. But I really do hope you'll quit someday. Those things will kill you."

His lips curved slightly as he put a cigarette into his mouth. "Glad you care."

She stopped and waited while his large hands cupped the cigarette and he lit it, then took a long drag.

Walking again, he turned his head, his gaze steady. "I'm sorry I didn't call."

She looked away, thinking, *Too little, too late.* "I'm sorry, too."

"Will you give me a chance to explain?"

He'd heard her tone and knew she was putting up walls. She looked at him, walking erect, but his eyes spoke of the turmoil he was in.

She swept a lock of hair from her face, already damp from the humidity. "All right."

"I didn't call because after you left I went into my shell. It's what I do when I need to decompress. It's a survival pattern. I call it turtling. I tuck in and get quiet. It's different from relaxing. It's kind of zoning out." He took another drag on the cigarette. "See, when I didn't call, it's not because you didn't matter to me. It's because you matter so much."

Harper didn't understand just yet, but felt a quickening of hope.

"There are a lot of symptoms with PTSD. You know about the anxiety, hypervigilance, depression. For me, the worst was sleeping." He laughed shortly. "That's a gross understatement. We all have problems with falling asleep, or waking up in the middle of the night and not being able to go back to sleep. But I had nightmares." He rubbed his jaw, collecting his thoughts. "Bad. Worse, they were so damn real. When I was dreaming, I was *there,* reliving the experience. When that happens, your whole body reacts, your heart starts pumping and your blood races. I was trained to fight, and if someone woke me up while I was in one of those dreams, I'd go right into fight mode. I'd grab my gun and search the room." Taylor raked his hair, visibly shaken. "Hell, I wasn't even awake. I could have killed someone."

Harper remained silent, listening.

"When I first got home from war, I didn't leave the house. I kept away from crowds, shopping centers, anywhere people gathered. I was always on high alert. I had a girlfriend back then. We'd dated in college. Real nice girl. She wrote to me while I was away. But when I came back, she couldn't deal with me. She said I'd changed. She tried, but . . ." He shrugged. "We broke up."

Harper conjured up this pretty woman holding his hand, her photograph in his wallet. Someone he'd wanted to marry, perhaps. Harper couldn't help the flare of jealousy. "Did you see her when you returned home this time?"

Taylor shook his head. "She's married now. Wouldn't be right. And I've moved on."

As quickly as Harper had conjured up the woman, she disappeared into the ether. "What turned things around for you?"

"Thor." He smiled.

"Thor . . ."

"He's more than a dog. He was my salvation. We were together twenty-four/seven. Thor sleeps beside my bed, and if I go into REM and start having a nightmare, he wakes me up. When I open my eyes and see him, I know I'm okay."

"Do you still have nightmares?"

Taylor stopped walking and turned to face her. "Not in a long time. Like I said, I'm feeling good. I go out and leave him at home all the time. But . . ." Taylor looked at the sea again, his mouth pinched. After a moment he looked back at her, holding her gaze. "Harper, I worry that it might come back. I'm afraid, if we're sleeping together, I might have a nightmare and hurt *you.* I couldn't bear that."

Harper caught her breath, understanding. Harper knew that his not calling her the past few days, his "turtling," was not about his *not* thinking of her. Quite the contrary, he was only thinking of her.

"I'm glad you told me this." Harper reached out to take his hand. "I just wish you'd have told me right away." She laughed shortly. "Texted me, at least."

Taylor played with her fingers. "It's hard to explain all that in a text."

"The closer we get, the more we have to trust each other."

He looked up from their joined hands. "So, I take it by that that you'll see me again?"

A smile twitched at her lips. "Oh, yes."

The tension fled from his face and he smiled. He began walking again, but Harper pulled at his arm, stopping him. "Don't be shy about asking for your space when you need it, Taylor. Take all the time and space you need. Just tell me. Okay?"

Taylor's eyes kindled. "I don't want any space between us now." He leaned toward her, sliding his arms around her, and pulled her closer.

Later they ate dinner at Bushido as planned. It was a favorite among locals and tourists alike, the subtly Asian atmosphere sleek and inviting. Once they were seated, the waitress promptly came to take their drink order.

"I'll have a mango martini."

Taylor looked at the waitress. "A mango martini and a pale ale."

The waitress quickly returned with their drinks and stood poised for their order. "Do you need more time?"

Harper looked at Taylor with one brow raised. From his wry grin, she knew he'd caught the double entendre.

"Yes, please," he told the waitress.

Harper took a long sip of her martini, enjoying the chilled sweetness.

Taylor leaned across so his face was close to Harper's. He couldn't withhold the wide grin that spread across his face. "I got the job!"

Harper was taken aback. "My God, that was fast. Congratulations!"

"You're looking at Boeing's new project manager. I start training in three weeks."

Harper clapped her hands together in delight. "I'm so proud of you."

Taylor took a pull from his beer, then shook his head as though he still couldn't believe the news. "You know, two years ago, I didn't think I had a future. It's one of the symptoms of PTSD. I know that now, but back then I was deep in the dark. I didn't expect to have a career, marriage, children. A normal life. So now, to get this great job, to have you by my side . . ." He shook his head again. "I feel on top of the world." He raised his bottle of beer. "Here's to the future!"

Harper raised her glass and they clinked. In her mind she wondered, *What future?* She sipped the martini, then set the glass on the small square napkin. "So"—she looked into his eyes— "you'll be here in Charleston."

"Right."

"But I'll be in New York."

Taylor's arm froze midair. He drank from his glass, then set it on the table. "Is that definite?"

"I don't have any other plans."

"You're moving back in with your mother?" His tone reflected his disbelief.

"No," she replied in a rush. "But I'm moving back to New York. Probably."

"Why New York?"

"New York is still the heart of the publishing industry in this country. It's where the jobs are. But if not New York, it'll be London."

Taylor's eyes widened. "As in London, England?"

"Of course London, England. There are serious publishing jobs there. My grandparents live not far from the city. It makes sense."

"Aren't there jobs you could get here?"

"Maybe. But far fewer opportunities. Smaller companies. Anyway, why would I do that?"

Taylor leaned back in his chair and spread out his hands. "I would have thought that was obvious."

Harper bent her head. Her toes curled in her shoes.

"What about everything you said about loving this place?" Taylor's tone had suddenly gone dull. "Feeling at home here?"

"It's all very good to feel at home here. Unfortunately, the place I call home is being sold, and there's that business of having to get a job and finding a place to live." She said softly, "You could come to New York with me."

"What? I just got this job. And it's exactly what I was looking for!"

"So, it's me that has to relocate."

He looked broadsided. "Whoa, are we really having this discussion? Already?"

Harper let her fingers run down the stem of her glass, trying to hold her tongue. Taylor had made his decision, found a job, and his path was paved. He was assuming that she'd simply follow suit, only he'd ignored the possibility that she'd be applying for a job outside of Charleston.

And wasn't she being just as overbearing with Taylor? She'd blithely been assuming that he'd consider a move to New York with her. But he'd been ambitious and beaten her to the punch by landing a great job in Charleston. Meanwhile, here it was already the end of August and she had yet to lift one finger to prepare for the fall.

"Yes, we're having this discussion," she replied evenly. "If you want any input into whether I go or stay."

"It's simple. Stay."

"Oh, Taylor . . ."

Their eyes met and they both looked away.

Harper drained her martini glass. "We could have a long-distance relationship," suggested Harper, breaking the silence. "I could fly in on weekends or sometimes you could come to New York."

"My schedule is going to be crazy during training—day shifts, night shifts, weekends. It'll be hard enough trying to find time to be together if you were living here in town. But out of town?" He shook his head. "Forget it. It wouldn't work.'"

"I see. So it's okay for me to move or fly back and forth. But not you."

"I didn't say that."

The tang of mango lingered on Harper's tongue as she considered his words. He was holding his ground. Harper knew that if she were more like her mother, she would finish her drink, smile, thank him politely for dinner, and walk out of the restaurant and out of his life. Nothing or no one stood in Georgiana James's way.

But she wasn't like her mother. Nor was she like her father, who couldn't commit. She didn't have any role models to follow in this decision. It was hers alone to make.

The waitress came to take their orders. Harper picked up her menu and scanned it. Her appetite was gone. She ordered a roll of sushi to be polite and another martini. Taylor ordered the nigiri dinner and another beer.

The waitress took the menus and left them in tense silence.

Taylor's brows knit and he searched Harper's face. Then he reached out to take her hand in his. "I don't want to argue. Let's table this discussion until you get a job. One that you love and are excited about. It's not fair for me to put any pressure on you."

She felt a rush of relief. "I have so much I'm figuring out now. I've got to be realistic and accept things the way they are rather than the way I wish they'd be."

"I know."

She took a deep breath, trying to hold herself together and not cry. "I don't know if I can stay here."

He nodded soberly. "I know."

Chapter Fourteen

The next day Taylor began painting the cottage, and Harper dove into her job search in earnest. She wasn't sorry to have a reason not to be around Taylor at the moment. They'd finished their dinner last night in mostly strained, sad silence, each aware of the ticking clock that hung over them. They ended the night with a tender kiss on Sea Breeze's front porch, but Harper knew they both needed some space to figure things out.

Meanwhile, Dora was in stride with her job at the dress shop, and Nate had settled into his new school. Mamaw had at last begun to sort through her belongings, starting with her clothing. Filled black plastic bags began piling up in her room. Only Carson remained in a funk behind her closed door. Still, Sea Breeze appeared relatively calm.

Until Devlin called with the news that he'd scheduled a showing of the house.

There followed a flurry of cleaning and polishing. Harper raked and weeded the gardens. Taylor's father came to help with the painting. Everyone chipped in, working hard, each holding at bay the heartbreak that this showing implied. By Labor Day, Sea Breeze had never looked better. On the afternoon of the showing, they cleared out of the house, each to a separate destination.

It was, Harper thought, a sobering hint of the exodus to come.

Carson was on her way to the coffee shop. All she wanted from life right now was a nice cup of iced chai latte in an air-conditioned room. She drove her car down the business section of Middle Street. She loved these few blocks of shabby-chic restaurants and shops crowded together, each with its own quirky look. There was nothing main-stream about it, not a chain store in sight.

Only 10:00 a.m., and the lunch crowd hadn't yet descended. This used to be a sleepy town of locals. Now it was getting so crowded with guests and tourists in the summer that some of the charm had fallen off into the vortex of tourist trap.

Carson never entered Cafe Medley without thinking of Blake and their first coffee here. Here, he'd forgiven her for lying to him about Delphine. She had serious thinking to do about that man. She placed her order and waited, crossing her arms and brooding.

She had known from the start that Blake Legare would be trouble. He wasn't even her type. Not LA cool or movie-star sexy or model gorgeous. He wasn't in the film business at all. Or wealthy. She'd fallen in love with a federal employee who worked long hours for low pay because he loved what he did. A simple man with simple tastes and strong convictions. He loved the low-country, his family, his dog, dolphins—and her.

Yes, he loved her. And that frightened her.

"Carson?"

She startled at hearing Blake's voice just while she was thinking of him. She jerked her head around to see him standing in front of her, a large, steaming mug in his hand. Blake wore his usual baggy khaki shorts and a faded brown polo shirt, the collar not fully turned out. She half smiled, knowing he didn't notice such things.

"What are you doing here?" she asked.

The server handed her the cup of chai. She started walking toward a table, Blake following her. She was vaguely annoyed. She'd wanted to be alone, to think. Lately, it seemed every time she turned around, he was there.

She took a seat at the tiny table. "Shouldn't you be at work?"

"I am. I'm responding to a dolphin stranding. We're shorthanded and I took the call. Glad I did." His eyes sparked as he pulled out a chair.

They sat across from each other at the small bistro table. Blake leaned forward, his gaze searching her face. "How are you?"

Carson looked at her mug, despondent. "I'm fine."

"What's wrong?" he asked, concerned.

"Blake, nothing's wrong. Stop asking me that."

"I'm just worried about you."

"Stop hovering!"

He sat back against his chair with a hurt expression. "I'm not hovering. I just walked in for a cup of coffee and here you are."

"Yes, you are hovering. You've been stopping by the house all hours of the day and night, always checking on me, always asking me how I am."

He looked stricken. "You just lost the baby. Our baby. I care!" he added with heat. "Isn't that what a boyfriend is supposed to do?"

She didn't reply.

After a long, pained pause Blake's face fell. "Oh. I see. We're there again. You don't want a boyfriend."

She stared at her hands, clenched tight around the frosted glass.

Blake gave a short groan. He leaned far back, tilting the chair on its hind legs, and, turning his head, stared out the window, his face set.

Carson's heart ached for him. The part that loved him.

Blake put his hands on the table and looked at her. His tone was cool. "I don't want to talk about this now."

She looked at her mug. "I don't, either. But we need to." She glanced up quickly and saw his face. His head was bent and he was staring intently at his cup. "Blake, I don't want to be this woman who always hurts you." She tried desperately to find words to make him believe the last thing she wanted to do was hurt him again. "That's not who I am. But that's what keeps happening, over and over."

He was still staring at his coffee. "Yeah, it does."

"I care for you. Maybe even love you."

Blake glanced up at her, his dark eyes shining. "You're going through a lot now." He spoke quickly, as though trying to convince her. "I get that. But you don't have to keep pushing me away. You keep doing that and you keep coming back. You don't have to go through this alone."

"Yes, I *do*." She looked at him, her eyes pleading him to understand. In a small pause she gathered her thoughts. She looked out the window as she spoke. "Having a baby was always some-thing I thought I'd do someday. In the future. Then I got pregnant and all these hormones started racing through my body. Suddenly I had all these new feelings bubbling up from somewhere deep inside. Feelings I'd never had before. I was a sea of maternal instincts. I *wanted* the baby." She paused and glanced at him. "And then, the baby was gone."

Carson had to take a breath to still the trembling of her voice. This was hard to talk about with-out crying.

"But the problem is, the hormones are still raging. I feel emotional, weepy, sad, angry . . . and sometimes almost relieved."

She wiped her eyes with her fingers. Blake handed her a paper napkin, which she promptly used to blow her nose. When she spoke again, her voice was low and controlled.

"Somewhere in all that mire is the me I used to be. Someone strong. Confident. Someone I liked. Someone not like *this*." She swept her hand beside her body.

"You're still the same person."

"No, I'm *not*," she said with heat.

Blake fell silent.

"I need to find that person again. And I need to do that alone."

"Why alone? That's always been your MO when things got tough. You turn tail and run. Don't do it, Carson. Not just to me, but to yourself."

Carson shoved away her mug. "I had this experience. It was under anesthesia and like a dream. Later I had the same dream over and over. It was freaking me out. I talked to Harper and she asked me if I'd ever heard of spiritual totems." Carson smirked and lifted one shoulder in a halfhearted shrug. "Me, right? As if. But then she showed me something online about animal totems and we looked up shark." Carson blew out a plume of air. "It was weird. Suddenly, it all made sense."

"What made sense?"

"According to the book, when one gets a message from the shark, it represents survival. The shark is a master of survival. Those given a shark totem live their lives attuned to their primal instinct. That's when it clicked."

She leaned forward. "The night before Lucille died, she told me to trust my instincts. Lucille knew me better than anyone and she told me the same thing! After she died, I went with my instinct about the baby. To protect that life." Carson's voice wobbled and she saw Blake's eyes fill with tears. "That was why I decided to keep the baby. I was following my instincts."

He nodded, his lips tight, unable to speak. He reached out to grasp her hand on the table. In that moment, they shared the grief of their lost child.

She released his hand with a gentle pat, then sat back, gathering her emotions. Her mind was clear but her heart was heavy. "The book went on. Those with a shark totem are always moving forward. To be motionless is to sink. To die. I've thought about this a lot since the miscarriage. We both know I've been floating around without forward motion for a long time. I think that was the message of the shark. I need to get swimming again. Or I'm going under."

"I won't let you go under. I'm here for you."

She closed her eyes, pained by his constant attempts at rescue. She knew he'd never let her swim alone. He'd always be there to hold her tight. If she allowed that, she'd be trapped, and like a shark held over on its back, she'd be unable to move forward.

"Blake, I'm asking you to back off for a while."

He expelled a loud frustrated breath.

"Just for a little while. I need to find myself again, to get back to the water. And I need to do this on my own."

"So you *are* breaking up with me. Again."

"No, I'm not breaking up with you. I'm taking a time-out."

Blake pushed back his chair to rise and it made a loud scraping sound, almost tipping over. His face was stoic but hard, and his eyes reflected his hurt. "Yeah. Sure. No problem." He lifted his hands in the universal *I'm done* manner.

He turned to leave, walked a few steps, then spun on his heel and headed back to the table. Carson crouched in her chair, knowing a hurt was coming.

Blake bent low and spoke in a low voice hot with emotion. "But you know what? You weren't the only one who was hurt. I lost a baby, too."

Their gazes locked, each pained and unyielding. Then he turned and left the coffee shop without another glance.

Mamaw sat in the shade of Girard's back porch. From where she sat, she had a lovely view of the

Sea Breeze dock. The house peeked out from behind heavy palm fronds. She sighed heavily.

Girard put his hand over hers on her lap. "Penny for your thoughts."

She smiled wearily. "I need far more than a penny, I'm afraid." She looked at his face, so handsome and kind, and smiled reassuringly. "I'm all right. I was just thinking how my dear Sea Breeze lies just beyond, out of my reach. Rather poignant, under the circumstances."

"Marietta, you've known this day was coming. You've planned for it."

"No, that's just the problem. I didn't plan. That was my failing. I should have been more mindful when I was younger. Edward and I both should have. Money slipped through my fingers without thought for the future. I suppose I always thought that Edward would provide for me. And he did, generously," she hurried to add. She didn't want to put the blame on her dear dead husband's shoulders. "I gave far too much to my son, Parker, for far too long. And, I'm afraid, Edward and I didn't anticipate the rise in costs to maintain Sea Breeze."

"You can't blame yourself for that. No one foresaw the rise in insurance and taxes. You aren't the only one selling."

"I know, I know," she murmured, but her heart was still heavy. "I've gone through all of these rationalizations. But I still feel like a failure."

"There's no good looking for someone or something to blame. Life is not that simple."

"My parents left me with a tidy sum and Edward's parents did as well. They gave us Sea Breeze. What am I leaving my girls? Nothing. Nothing to help them get a start in life." Her voice trembled. "My summer girls. Winter is coming and I've let my girls down."

"You have to be gentler on yourself," he said consolingly. "You and I, we've reached what they call the golden age."

Mamaw huffed. "My gold seems a bit tarnished."

"Nonsense. You're well prepared for the next step, despite your worry. You've made arrangements, you're selling your house. You aren't a burden to your granddaughters. You should be proud of that fact."

Mamaw didn't reply.

"The fact is, at our age, it isn't wise to live alone. Marietta, this is the time in our lives when we have to take stock of our strengths and accept our limitations."

"You're not selling."

"Not yet. Though I admit, I'm wrestling with the same chestnut you are." He let his gaze roam his property. "What am I going to do with this place? It's a lot to take care of. My children rarely visit anymore. And I confess, I've been lonely." He patted her hand. "I might very well join you at that retirement community."

Marietta straightened. "Really?"

He smiled and nudged her knee with his. "We could be quite the item."

She laughed and coyly slapped his hand.

Later that afternoon the ladies were all restless as they waited around Sea Breeze in agonized suspense after the showing.

They didn't have to wait long.

A long, black BMW pulled into Sea Breeze. It circled the great oak and came to a stop.

"That's Devlin," Harper said to Mamaw, peering out the front window.

Harper watched anxiously as Mamaw set aside her needlepoint with studied calm and slowly rose from the upholstered chair. She smoothed out her coral-colored tunic top and brought her hand to her hair to push back a few stray wisps.

She opened the front door and Devlin walked in. He looked polished in his work clothes—pressed khaki pants and an ironed yellow polo shirt almost the same color as his hair. He was carrying a slim black leather briefcase.

"Good afternoon, Mrs. Muir." He flashed her his megawatt smile that made his blue eyes shine against his dark tan.

Harper cocked her head. Devlin usually called Mamaw *Miss Marietta* now that his relationship with Dora was cemented. Not *Mamaw* yet, but certainly no longer *Mrs. Muir.* That he was calling her by her formal name now implied this was not a personal call.

"Harper," he said, acknowledging her. "Good to see you."

"Do you want me to leave?"

"No, stay," Mamaw replied. "I have no secrets. Devlin, please take a seat."

"Thank you." Devlin followed Mamaw back into the living room and took the designated chair. Mamaw resumed her seat. He put the briefcase on the small table between them and laid his hand over it and leaned forward to Mamaw. "I've got good news."

"Oh?" More concern than joy was in Mamaw's voice.

"I've an offer on the house."

"Already?" Harper exclaimed.

"I told you it would go fast." Devlin opened the briefcase and pulled out a thick folder. He handed Mamaw the contract.

Mamaw reached for her reading glasses and, after slipping them in place, took the contract and began reading. Looking up, she said, "It's not near a full-price offer."

Devlin replied levelly, "That's to be expected. It's a reasonable offer and they fully expect a counter. What makes it interesting is that it's all cash. They flew in this weekend just to see the house and made an offer the same day they saw it. This is an eager prospect."

Mamaw searched the papers again. "What about my other stipulations?"

"They've agreed to all of them. You can set the move-out date."

Mamaw leaned back in her chair and removed her glasses. She looked at Harper for support, but Harper shook her head and threw up her hands in a helpless gesture, unable to offer any. She was on tenterhooks.

Mamaw looked again at Devlin. "What do you advise?"

"As your Realtor or as your friend?"

"Both."

"As your Realtor, I'd say make a counteroffer. This couple wants the house. They've been looking for a historic house like this for years. We could go back and forth and close on this deal quickly."

Harper tightened her lips as her heart sank.

"As your friend, I'd tell you to wait for a full offer. I haven't heard from some of the other parties I've contacted yet. Miss Marietta, there isn't another property like yours on the market. Places with the location, charm, and the history of Sea Breeze are as rare as hen's teeth. I swear, it's my favorite house on the island. And you're not in any hurry." He leaned back in his chair and rocked. "You have three days to respond to this offer. Take them. It will buy you time."

Harper excused herself as Mamaw and Devlin

began to talk strategy. She walked at a studied pace out of the living room. Once she closed the door, she began calling her sisters in a loud, panicked voice. Nate came running from the kitchen, a peanut-butter sandwich in his hands.

"What's the matter?" he said, eyes wide.

"Nothing, baby," Harper hurried to reassure him. "Where's your mama?"

"Out on the dock. With Aunt Carson."

Harper took off on a sprint through the kitchen, out the back door across the porch, past the pool and the mastlike flagpole to the dock. The late-afternoon sun was peeking out from dark clouds that were racing to the sea. Her feet pounded on the wood dock as she raced to its end. She found her sisters sitting in the shade of the covered dock, legs stretched out on the wood benches and drinking iced tea. Carson was dressed in her ubiquitous bikini, Dora in a more modest one-piece swimsuit and cover-up. They had stopped talking and were watching with expectant expressions as Harper ran toward them.

As she drew near, Dora called out, "Where's the fire?"

Harper could feel her face flaming from the run. She put her hand to her heart as she caught her breath.

Dora handed her a glass. "Take a sip, darlin', before you expire."

Harper drank thirstily and wiped her mouth in a

not very ladylike swipe before handing the glass back.

"Mamaw's selling Sea Breeze," she blurted.

Carson leaned back against the deck wall. "Is that all? We know that."

"No, I mean now. Devlin's here. He brought an offer."

Carson shot straight up again. "Shit. So soon?"

"Devlin's here?" asked Dora. "Where?"

"He's sitting in the living room with Mamaw. I knew something was up when I saw him roll in all polished like a peacock carrying a briefcase."

"That's not nice." Dora scowled at the unkind description. "Devlin's not the enemy here. Mamaw engaged him to sell the house. He's just doing his job." She sniffed and added haughtily, "And I think he looks quite handsome when he cleans up."

"Sorry. I like Dev, you know that," Harper said, chastened. "I'm shooting the messenger."

Carson demanded, "Is Mamaw going to accept it?"

"I don't think so. It's not a full offer, thank God. Devlin advised her to sit on it."

"That's a relief," Carson said.

"Not really," Dora said. "They'll counter. Another, better offer will come in. An offer she can't refuse."

"She's right," said Harper. "This couple flew in just to see the house. Devlin said they've been waiting for the right property to come up and really want it." She slumped onto the bench beside Carson and put her hands to her cheeks, feeling suddenly faint. "I think this might really be happening. Sea Breeze is about to be sold."

She looked into Dora's and Carson's eyes and saw the same shock and pain and roiling regret that she felt in her own body. For several minutes no one could speak, each lost in her own thoughts. They all knew that this day was coming. But like the storm rumbling in from the distance, it was always something they'd pushed off and said they'd deal with when it arrived.

And now it had.

"Sea Breeze . . . gone?" Carson said slowly, each word dropping in the air like a stone. "I can't believe it. This is the only house I've ever really loved. The one constant in my life. No matter where I might travel, no matter how long I might be away, I always knew Sea Breeze was here waiting for me. It was my safe haven. I can't believe it won't be here."

"It's been my touchstone going through this divorce," Dora said.

"Sea Breeze isn't really going to be gone," Harper said. "It's still going to be here. Just for another family. Not for us."

But her words held no comfort. She looked back at the house and tried to imagine anyone else but the Muirs living in it.

"I've always been really proud that this house was ours," Dora said. "I'm enough of a house snob to admit it. I mean, Sea Breeze is more than just a house. It's a true relic of Sullivan's Island's past."

"This place has been our lifeboat," said Carson. "The three of us have been floundering all summer. What would we have done without coming here?" She brought her long legs up to the bench and wrapped her arms around them. Harper recognized the gesture. Carson had done it since she was a little girl whenever she felt scared or vulnerable. "And what are we going to do now?"

"Do you think Mamaw has enough money to hold on to the house and let us rent it?" Carson asked. "She's had the house for a long time. I don't know how much her monthly payments are, but they've got to be less than if she bought it today. Think of how much the value went up. Maybe we could pool our money together and pay rent?"

"Honey, the house has been remortgaged up the wazoo," Dora reminded her. "She needed the money for Daddy. Otherwise she would have tried to work something out. Besides, Carson, you don't have any money saved, and even if I threw in all I get for my portion of the house—if it ever sells—it's a drop in the bucket. And even if we could afford to rent it, we couldn't afford the taxes."

"Mamaw always said buying the puppy was the cheapest part of the deal," said Carson. "We should still run the numbers. Mamaw would help us in any way she can. You know she would."

"I don't know if I should tell you this," Dora said with hesitation. "I almost didn't get Nate into that school. Cal said he didn't have the money for the deposit. And I didn't have anything set aside." She paused. "Mamaw didn't have the cash, so she sold her diamond earrings. The chandelier ones. She did it to make the deposit for Nate." Dora saw the shock on her sisters' faces. "I hated for her to do that," she rushed to add. "Papa Edward gave those earrings to her. But I don't know what I'd have done if she hadn't. I had to tell you, so you know how tight money is for her. She really doesn't have much left to help us with."

"She told us that when she told us she had to sell the house," Carson said. "I guess I never really understood the extent of it."

"We can't be asking her for any more help. Not ever." Harper looked pointedly at Dora and Carson.

"I'll pay her back when I sell the house," Dora said softly.

Carson looked back at the house with dejection. "I don't know what I was thinking. There's no way we could afford to rent this place."

Harper leaned back against the dock railing and reflected on what the sale of Sea Breeze would mean for her sisters. For them, Sea Breeze represented solidarity, safety, and security. Financially, both Carson and Dora were on a slippery slope. Dora at least was settled with the cottage and her job, and they all knew she and Devlin were going to get married someday. Carson was more iffy. No job, no apartment, no money set aside. She was in the most precarious position of the three women.

Harper looked out at the Cove as she had done so many times over this summer. Her gaze wandered across the familiar winding creek with its racing current, the bright green grass of the wetlands that was teeming with life and mystery. She breathed deeply, tasting salt in the air and feeling the balmy ocean breeze play with her hair. Off in the distance she heard the swell of a chorus of insects. August began the season of migration, of heavy coming and going in the lowcountry. September was a time of change and transition. Whoever said there was no change of seasons in the lowcountry didn't know how to open their eyes and observe the myriad miracles that happened every season along the coast.

She'd prowled every square foot of this island both alone and on scavenging hunts with Carson. The beaches, the historic forts and monuments, the mysterious wetlands. The wind gusted, rippling the water. Harper sucked in her breath.

In truth Harper felt more at home at Sea Breeze

than she did in any of the other houses she'd lived and grown up in. This *place* had set deep roots in her heart. Her biorhythms were linked to the tides. Sea Breeze was not for her some way station, a place to rest and refuel before moving on.

Yes, Carson had lived here as a little girl. Yes, Dora had grown up in the South. But Muir blood coursed through Harper's veins, too. She belonged here every bit as much as her sisters did. The waters of the Cove had baptized her a lowcountry girl.

And she was in love with a lowcountry boy.

Carson had been right, she realized with a short, abrupt laugh. There was no way she was ever going to get Taylor to pack up and leave for New York. He'd gone through too much soul-searching to ever leave the lowcountry again. And, she realized, so had she.

Harper felt her shoulders lower and a small smile of knowing ease across her face as everything fell into place in her heart. She'd spent the summer paying attention to all things great and small, seeking solitude for reflection, preparing herself for the change she could feel was coming. For months she didn't know what she was waiting for but persevered with patience and faith. Then, when she'd met Taylor, she'd thought that he was her answer. And he was, in part. But not all. Not nearly all.

Taylor had said that a house didn't make a home. It was the people. He was so right. Dora and Carson and, of course, Mamaw were the foundation that made Sea Breeze the home she'd been searching for.

Yet even her sisters were not the key to her answer.

It was so deceptively simple she had to laugh at herself for taking so long to come to it. Like Dorothy, she'd had the answer all along. The magic of the ruby slippers lay inside herself. She'd discovered her own strengths and talents. She embraced that she was a writer, whether or not she ever sold a book.

Through it all, Sea Breeze had been her sanctuary. This place—the smells, the tastes, the weather, the wildlife—was where she belonged. Sea Breeze was her home.

Harper felt a rush of excitement as she reached out and took Dora's hand in one of hers and Carson's in the other and squeezed. They looked at her, eyes wide at her impulsive gesture. They could sense something was up, in that way people can when some decision of import has been made.

"I know what to do." Harper turned to look into Carson's eyes, then Dora's, then squeezed their hands again. "I'm going to buy Sea Breeze."

Chapter Fifteen

Harper paused at the entry of Mamaw's bedroom and peeked in.

Mamaw was sitting on an oversize, plump chintz-upholstered chair, her feet resting on the matching ottoman. Her head was bent over a book and she was deep in her story.

Harper turned to her sisters, standing beside her. Their faces were flushed with excitement. "Wait here. I want to talk to Mamaw alone first."

Dora and Carson grumbled but complied.

Harper knocked lightly on the door. "Am I interrupting?"

Mamaw looked up from her book. "Goodness, no. Come in, Harper," she called, reaching out her hand in welcome. "I had to retreat from the porch. The heat is beastly today. But mind you, I'm not complaining. The Atlantic is quiet with nary a whisper of a hurricane. Like everyone else in the lowcountry, I'm grateful for small blessings." She adjusted her legs to make room for Harper and closed her book.

Harper closed the door behind her, then crossed the soft carpet to sit on the ottoman beside Mamaw's legs.

"What can I help you with, dear? You look troubled."

Harper leaned forward. "I'm going to ask you something, and please, I want you to be perfectly honest with me."

"Oh, goodness, this sounds serious," Mamaw said in jest.

"It is."

Mamaw sensed Harper's mood and all the joviality left her face. Her blue eyes shone with alertness. "All right. I'm all ears."

"Mamaw . . ." Harper found her mouth was dry. She licked her lips and began again in earnest. "I'd like to buy Sea Breeze. Is it too late?"

Mamaw's mouth slipped open in a gasp. For a moment she was speechless. Then she reached out to take Harper's hands in hers. "Thank God!"

Mamaw, Carson, and Dora were overjoyed at the possibility of Harper's keeping Sea Breeze in the family. Mamaw patted Harper's hand and assured her that she'd sharpen her pencil and give her the "family discount." They'd laughed over that one and knew that she'd be calling her banker and lawyer for more realistic arrangements. Harper insisted that the sales price take into consideration what Mamaw would need to pay off the mortgages and the bills and still leave enough for her to live comfortably.

While the family was talking, Harper retreated to do serious planning. She had a great deal to both understand and undertake to make the purchase happen. After resting all summer she felt the old surge of energy return. Her brain was clicking on all cylinders. Harper was ashamed at how little she understood about her trust fund, much less how to get the money out of it. She'd been lax on the details concerning her wealth, blithely cashing without question the checks that came to her. *Lazy* was a better word. *Time to put your big-girl panties on,* she told herself. Her first task was her most fearsome: facing her mother. Georgiana was the gatekeeper of Harper's inheritance.

Harper sat at her desk and did some research on trust funds in general. Then she assembled her checks and tried to figure out the sums. When she was finished, she realized just how lax she'd been. She'd been spending money freely all summer, without serious thought to what would happen when her bank account went dry. There was nothing left but to face the music. She sat at the edge of her bed and, trying to feel like her mother's daughter and not her assistant, dialed her number on the phone.

"Georgiana James."

"Hello, Mother. It's me, Harper."

"Yes?" Her tone was curt, indicating she was annoyed with Harper either for taking so long to respond to her offer, or for not returning sooner to New York, or both.

"How are you?"

"Well enough. I've only just returned from the Hamptons. Traffic was beastly." She skipped a beat. "I rather thought I'd see you here when I returned."

"Yes, well . . . I'm afraid I've made other plans."

"Dear God, Harper. We aren't going to thrash this out again, are we?"

"No, Mother, there's nothing to thrash out."

"Good. Because I've some news. An editorial position has opened up. It's in nonfiction, but it's acquisitions, and it's only a matter of time till we move you over to fiction."

"I appreciate the offer, but I'm afraid I can't accept. I've decided to look for a position here in Charleston."

The line was silent for a moment. "You *surely* can't mean you plan to stay there? Permanently?"

"I'm very happy here. And I've met someone." She paused. "Mummy, I'm in love."

"You're in love?"

Harper heard her mother laugh, and none too kindly. "With who, pray tell?"

Harper would not allow her mother to trivialize her relationship with Taylor. She answered the question seriously. "His name is Taylor McClellan. I met him this summer. He's wonderful. I hope you'll like him because I love him."

"I see. What does he do?"

"He is a project manager. For Boeing. The aeronautics company."

"Who is his family?"

"The McClellans are an old family. From McClellanville." Harper deliberately dropped the connection to a historical family that had a town in their name. That, she knew, would impress her mother.

"So he's a southerner?" Her distaste was obvious.

"Yes. Mother, you don't know anything about the South."

"I married a southern man."

Harper simmered.

"Tell me about his family."

"They're good people."

"Yes, but what do they do?"

"They're shrimpers."

"What does that mean, 'they're shrimpers'?"

"His father owns a trawler and catches shrimp for the market."

"Do they own a fleet?"

"Oh, for heaven's sake, Mother, no, they don't own a fleet. They own one boat. The *Miss Jenny.* Named after his mother. She is a schoolteacher. He has a brother but he's still in high school. Let's give him a few years to see what he does with his life," she added with sarcasm. "Honestly, Mother, what does that matter? I love Taylor and he loves me. Aren't you happy for me?"

"I'll be happy once I hear you tell me what you are doing for yourself. I didn't raise you to be a housewife. I've spent a fortune on your first-rate education. You are poised to be an important editor. If you love each other, he will understand that and wait while you get your career back on line. Perhaps he could even follow you to New York. At some point in the future. If he wishes."

"We discussed that," Harper offered. "We decided that wasn't for us. You see, with appreciation for your offer, I don't want to return to New York. In fact . . ." Harper took a breath. "There is something important I want to talk to you about. I need your advice."

". . . Go on."

"It's about my trust fund. I've never inquired before, but is there some way that I could possibly get all of the money from my trust fund at once?"

"Absolutely not." Then Georgiana asked suspiciously, "Why do you want it now? What's so urgent?"

"I want to buy a piece of property."

"A piece of property?" Georgiana sounded flabbergasted. "Where? Not in South Carolina?"

"Yes, of course in South Carolina. On Sullivan's Island." Harper loaded her mental cannon and fired. "I want to buy Sea Breeze."

There was a long silence on the phone.

"Hello?" Harper asked into the quiet.

Georgiana's voice was low and lethal. "Did Marietta put you up to this?"

"What? No! Of course not. I told you she was

selling the house last May. That was why she wanted all of us to come for the summer. To spend time together again before it was sold."

"I see what's happening. God, that woman is unfathomable! Marietta Muir smiles so sweetly and acts so friendly with her southern-belle charms, but don't you trust her. She's a spider spinning a web. She used her guile to manipulate your father, and now she's doing the same with you. It's so obvious it's laughable. You must see that's why she invited you to Sea Breeze in the first place. She wanted you to buy it! To save her from financial ruin."

"She didn't—"

"Did she tell you that the Muirs are descended from pirates? Believe it. They'll rob you blind if you let them."

"You forget that Muir blood runs in my veins, too."

"And it's rearing its ugly head now."

"Listen to yourself! What nineteenth-century books have you been reading about the South? I mean, really! Pirates and southern belles? Do you even know how crazy you sound?"

Harper stood and walked to the window. She opened the shutter and stared out at the Cove. The bucolic scene, the dock, palmettos, and racing water, pressed a delete button in her mind. She felt her anger leave her body as easily as it had come on.

"Mother, listen to me," Harper began in a calmer tone. "Mamaw has plans to move to a retirement home. The house is on the market. In fact, an offer has already come in. Mamaw doesn't need me to buy her house. I *want* to buy it, and if I don't move quickly, I'll lose the opportunity. Mother, can't you understand? I love it here. I love this house, the island, the lowcountry. It was my idea to buy Sea Breeze. It's the family house and I am a family member. Why shouldn't I buy it?"

"Because I forbid it. I will not sit idly back and allow you to throw away your inheritance. Or your life."

"It's my life, Mother. And my inheritance."

"It's always been like this after you spent time at Sea Breeze. Even when you were a child. You'd get these crazy ideas in your head, and when you came home, you were insufferably rude and selfish."

"Hardly rudeness, Mother. More speaking my own mind. When I'm at Sea Breeze, I have the freedom to make my own decisions, not have them made for me. If I didn't speak my mind or argue, as you put it, when I lived in New York, it wasn't because I was happy or content. It was because I always gave in to *you!*"

"I see," she said frostily.

"I'm not that little girl anymore. I make my own decisions now."

"Really? You have no idea of what Machiavellian

scheming Marietta Muir is capable of. Her son was cut from the same cloth."

Harper's voice was laced with anger. "Her son was my father. He has a name, Mother. Parker."

"Defensive now, are we? Well, *Parker* seduced and married me because he wanted me to publish his novel. He chose the wrong victim. I cast him out quicker than the ink dried on our wedding license. After you were born, I never got a farthing from him. He left me with *nothing*."

"Thank you," Harper said, deeply hurt.

"Harper, you know I didn't mean it in that way." Georgiana sounded instantly contrite. "You're my daughter. I care about you. That's why when I hear you talking about throwing your life away, I get frantic."

"It's my life. I'm twenty-eight years old. I called to ask you for your help. Not your permission."

After another long silence punctuated with puffs on her cigarette, Georgiana spoke again, now calmly. "You're twenty-eight years old. That's the salient point."

Harper tensed again. Her mother's calm voice was her most deadly. "What do you mean?"

"You say you're not a child?" Georgiana laughed bitterly. "You've blithely collected your income from the trust fund all these years like it fell from the sky. If you did ever bother to inquire, you'd have realized that your trust fund was set up with ironclad clauses. You can't touch the principal until you're thirty. Even if I wanted to, which I do not, there's absolutely nothing I could do to get you your money early. You must wait until you are thirty."

Harper slumped back down on the bed. She couldn't get her hands on her money for two more years. Her hopes of buying Sea Breeze were dashed.

"Will this young man of yours wait until you're thirty?"

"He doesn't care about the money," Harper said lifelessly. "He doesn't even know about it."

"Your grandmother Muir certainly does."

Harper didn't respond.

"Darling, I'm on your side. I know they've put a lot of pressure on you. You have a good heart and you've been made to feel somehow responsible to save the family house. But that most certainly is not your responsibility."

"What about Greenfields Park? Is that my responsibility?"

"You stand to inherit Greenfields Park. No one is asking you to rescue it."

"Aren't you?"

"Don't be ridiculous." Georgiana's tone changed, became more distracted. "My car is here. Harper, I don't have time to belabor this. I'm already quite late for a meeting."

"We need to finish this."

"We are finished. Your new job is here waiting

for you, but it won't wait for long. You know how busy things get here in the fall. Horses at the gate." Georgiana waited for a response. When she didn't get one, she asked tersely, "Are you still there?"

"I'm here."

"You'll feel better when you're back in New York. Get the southern miasma out of your brain. You know I'm right."

"I don't know that."

"Enough. I don't have any more time to argue this. If you do not come home immediately, not only will you not get the principal from your trust fund, but I will make certain you no longer receive your income from it. Do you understand?"

Harper did not respond.

"Let me rephrase it in terms even a child can understand. You will return to New York, immediately, or I will cut you off. From everything. Do you love this boy enough to give it all up?"

Harper sat stunned. She knew that her mother was the executor of her trust fund, but she didn't know that Georgiana could do that. Once again her mother had turned the tables. She demanded that Harper be the good little girl, the obedient daughter, and do as she was told. To do this meant not only giving up the dream of buying Sea Breeze, but relinquishing the possibility of moving to the lowcountry. She would lose Taylor.

"Do you hear me?" Georgiana asked sharply.

"Perfectly clear."

"Good. Call with your flight reservations and I'll have a car pick you up. Come home, Harper, where you belong."

Harper stood quietly and felt an odd calm. She did not feel the anger or timid remorse she'd felt after a tirade of her mother's that she had in the past. It was more the way one felt when something turned out exactly as one expected.

Her gaze swept over her bedroom, the one Mamaw had created just for her to make her feel she had her own space at Sea Breeze. To feel special . . . to feel loved. Each appointment—from the muted colors, the schoolroom desk she'd used as a child, to the books—was selected especially for her. Then she let her gaze travel out the plantation shutters to the Cove beyond. It flowed on, steadily and strong. Her talisman against evil.

"Are you there?"

She heard her mother's terse, impatient voice and knew Georgiana would never change. There would always be an issue, an appointment, a book, a lover, something that would take precedence over Harper. She knew that if there ever was to be a change in her life, it had to begin with her.

"Yes, I'm here. I am right where I belong. I'm sorry to disappoint you, Mother, but as I said, I won't be returning to New York. Really must go. Ta!"

With one movement of her thumb, a fraction of an inch, Harper disconnected. "Enough," she said, repeating her mother's words.

Stepping out into the hall, Harper heard the murmur of voices and clinking dishes in the kitchen. Needing her sisters now, she followed the sound but hesitated at the door when she heard her name mentioned. She peeked in to see her sisters at the sink, washing dishes. She ducked back to listen.

She heard Carson's voice. "Sure I'm glad she's buying Sea Breeze. Of course. Only . . . let's face it. Being invited back as a guest isn't the same."

"The same as what?" Dora said over the sound of running water in the sink. "You're a guest now."

"Yes and no. It's Mamaw's house. We're all on equal footing. What will it be when Harper buys it?"

"It will be Harper's house."

"Exactly."

"Don't tell me you're mad at Harper because she is getting the house?"

"Not mad. Jealous," Carson confessed.

"I am, too. I wish I could buy it. Who wouldn't want to live here? But it is what it is."

"I wish I had the James money bankrolling me."

"Hey, Devlin is bankrolling me!" Dora said with a laugh. "What's your point?"

"He is not. You're paying rent on the cottage."

"Not enough. . . . You're splitting hairs. Look, it's the luck of the draw at birth. The flip of a coin."

"Harper got heads and I got a kick in the tails."

Dora laughed. "Good one."

"I wasn't being funny."

"Cheer up. We've been very lucky to be able to come here all these years. It's more than a lot of people get. We have to count our blessings, not our losses. Trust me, I've learned this summer that life is a lot more fun when you see the glass half-full."

"I just wish Mamaw could have left the house to all of us. So it could all be the same as it always was."

"But she can't. We've known that all summer. Did you come up with the money to buy Sea Breeze? No. Did I? No. Harper did. And lucky us! At least we'll still be able to visit."

"Will we? It'll be where she lives full-time. Someday she'll be married, have a husband and kids here. She won't want us crashing in all the time."

"Honey, Harper'll put out the welcome mat. But be realistic, Carson," Dora added with a hint of frustration. "Of course you won't be able to just drop in unannounced and expect to stay for a couple of months like you did with Mamaw. Sorry, precious, but those days are over."

"Shut up."

There was some movement, the sound of cabinets opening and closing. Harper peeked in to see Carson putting dried dishes back into the cabinets. Dora was scrubbing one of the new stainless-steel pots that Harper had just purchased. When Carson turned back, Harper ducked behind the door.

"Now I know why she bought all these pots and pans," Carson said begrudgingly.

"Stop it," Dora scolded.

Harper heard the sound of water being turned off.

Dora continued, "We all know you've felt a special ownership over this place all your life. Think about it a minute. You lived with Mamaw as a little girl and came out here all the time. Harper and I just visited in the summer. You have the biggest bedroom, and you know I was jealous of that."

Harper heard Carson's short chuckle.

"Naturally," Dora went on, "I thought I should get the best room because I was the oldest. But I didn't. Mamaw sat me down and told me flat out that it was your room and I simply had to live with that fact. And I did. So did Harper." Dora's voice changed to almost pleading. "Carson, now *you* have to live with the fact that Harper will buy this house and will, in effect, have a bigger room. But trust me, you will always feel ownership of the house because your memories are rooted here. Nothing can change that. And don't you think I'm doing the happy dance because I know Nate can keep coming here? And someday you can bring your children here?"

Harper heard a pot fall in the sink.

"Oh, Carson, I'm sorry," Dora blurted out. "I didn't think."

"It's okay," Carson said, but she sounded as if she were breaking into tears. "It's just . . . I did see this place as my home. The problem is, I still do." She sniffed. "Being invited back somehow isn't enough when you don't have a home of your own."

"Aw, honey." Again Harper heard movement and guessed they were hugging. "I know how you feel. Being homeless sucks."

Carson made a noise that was a cross between a choked cry and a laugh. "Just what Harper needs. *Another* house."

Dora laughed at that. "Yeah . . ."

Harper's temper flared as the arrows of their words struck true. It was one thing to be reamed out by her mother for her wanting to buy Sea Breeze. It was another to be attacked by her sister for trying to save the place. On top of the phone call, the hurt felt so unfair, so unjust! Her already short fuse had burned to the quick. Harper blew into the room and stood before her sisters, her hands on her hips and her eyes sparking flames.

Dora and Carson stared back, their eyes wide with the surprise at just being busted.

"I've got news for you, Carson," Harper cried out, pointing her finger at her sister. "You don't have to worry about my getting *another* house. Or any house, for that matter. I just had it out with my mother. The Ice Queen. I tried to get my inheritance money so I could buy Sea Breeze. Something I was doing for *us*. But not only didn't I get the money, I'm getting cut out of my inheritance if I don't go home pronto. So guess what? You got your wish. I'm leaving! Just like you."

Harper could feel her face heating up, sure that it was as red as her hair. She pushed on, shouting now, letting all her pent-up frustration burst out like a volcano. "I'm *not* buying Sea Breeze. Sea Breeze will be sold to strangers. Are you happy now?" She turned on her heel and stormed out of the room. She passed Mamaw, who stood at the entry, one hand on the frame, her face ashen.

Harper slammed the front door as she left the house. Her feet pounded on the wood stairs as she fled down them, and then across the gravel driveway to the street. Why did they always see her as the lucky one? Because of money? Didn't they know yet that she was just as adrift, just as vulnerable, as they were?

Her hurt felt as if it were burning a hole in her heart, and tears were streaming down her face, causing her to gasp as she pumped her arms, faster and faster, farther from Sea Breeze. Yet no matter how far or fast she walked, she knew she couldn't outpace the hurt, the regret, and, too, the fear that was nipping at her heels.

Mamaw stood at the entrance to the kitchen staring at the shocked faces of Carson and Dora. They stood silently, looking contrite.

Although Mamaw had not heard all they had said, she'd heard enough. She looked into Carson's eyes. "Shame on you."

Then Mamaw slowly turned and left.

Chapter Sixteen

Harper pumped her fists as she ran full out along the beach. The tide was going out and her heels dug deep imprints into the sand. She ran until she couldn't run any farther, almost clear to Breach Inlet. Panting, she walked higher up to the dunes and stretched her tired legs in front of her on the warm sand.

She'd run hard, putting distance between herself and the pain she'd felt at Carson's snarky comments. They were nasty and unfair and had hurt her already tender feelings. But the running had taken the sting out of the words, and sitting here, winded and her fury spent, Harper had calmed enough to see Carson's venom for what it was—hurt, jealousy, and fear. All emotions she understood.

Squeezing her fingers in the warm sand, Harper wondered if the words burned more because they came from Carson. She was usually upbeat and genuine. Caring. Harper had always admired Carson, looked up to her, from the first moment they met.

She recalled the first time she'd seen Carson when Harper had arrived at Sea Breeze. Harper was six years old, like a tiny doll, small and delicate and all fancy dressed in a smocked dress and anklets that had frilly lace trim, with a big bow in her red and gold hair. In contrast, Carson was wearing a sand-crusted swimsuit and torn cutoff jean shorts. She was as brown as a berry, barefoot, and her wild, dark hair was salt dried and sticking out in angles.

Harper loved Carson on the spot. She looked wild and confident, everything Harper wanted to be. What her heroines looked like in her imagination. Carson had taken Harper's hand in a protective manner and led the way to the library, where Mamaw had created a bedroom for Harper. The moment Harper had walked in and seen all the books, she broke into her first smile.

Their friendship had blossomed slowly over that summer. Looking back, Harper saw that it was fate that she'd arrived that particular summer when Dora was letting go of Carson's hand. In doing so, Dora was letting go of her childhood—games and make-believe—and welcoming all the drama associated with teen years. Harper had arrived just in time to fill the void that Dora had left.

In fact, because of all the adventure books she'd read, Harper was better at their games of imagination than even Dora. Oh, the make-believe she and Carson had played! *Tom Sawyer* and *Huck Finn* had them floating down the creek looking for Injun Joe. *Treasure Island* and Mamaw's stories of their illustrious ancestor the Gentleman Pirate sent them hunting for buried treasure year after year. *Tuck Everlasting* had them convinced they'd find the pool of immortality. And *Peter Pan* was the ultimate adventure for young girls living on an island who loved pirates, mermaids, and fairies.

Looking back, Harper could see how Carson had helped her blossom at Sea Breeze. Every summer Harper would arrive looking like a prim schoolgirl on a class trip. Within a few days of her arrival on Sullivan's Island it was as if she'd removed her timid, submissive self with her fancy clothing and allowed herself to be the bright, inquisitive, adventurous girl lurking inside. She and Carson were inseparable. Their hearts beat with the pulse of the tides.

Then the inevitable happened. Carson, too, grew

older and put away her childhood games. The final summer that they'd spent together was mostly whiled away on the beach. At sixteen Carson was consumed by surfing, and eleven-year-old Harper tagged along to sit under an umbrella and read. The next year Mamaw wrote to Harper that Carson wouldn't be coming to Sea Breeze. She'd decided to stay in Los Angeles and get a summer job. Although the invitation remained open for Harper, she didn't want to spend the summer alone. Her mother had just purchased the house in the Hamptons, and Harper elected to spend the summer there instead. And that had been that.

Carson didn't see Harper again until years later at Dora's wedding. They'd both privately groaned at having to wear the pink, frothy gowns but dutifully did their duty. The next time they saw each other was a year later under sadder circum-stances. Carson had been too distraught at their father's funeral to share much with her sisters. And soon after, they came together again for Granddad Edward's funeral. All the joy at Sea Breeze seemed to have been shrouded with sadness.

That was the last time all three sisters had been together at Sea Breeze until this summer. Yet, this summer had proved that time and distance couldn't break the bond they shared. Harper could get mad at her sisters, disagree with their choices, distance herself from them, but they were always with her. They were her blood. Her family.

Now it was time for them to close ranks.

Harper rose and slapped the sand from her damp legs. She slowly stretched while looking out at the serene sea, the waves rolling gently to shore, one after the other. Not many days were left for any of them at Sea Breeze, she realized. Not with the offer to buy hanging over their heads. She didn't want to spend her final days here fighting. They were all on shaky ground now. Hot-tempered and spike-tongued. She didn't want one more moment of anger between them.

Harper knew what she had to do. Turning toward Sea Breeze, she took off on a run.

Carson sat on the dock with her feet dangling in the water, staring idly out at the racing current. She felt like a piece of the driftwood floating by, aimless and of no value. Her left hand clutched a small brown paper bag. Inside was a small bottle of tequila that she'd hidden away when the sisters and Mamaw had all taken the pledge to ban alcohol from Sea Breeze at the beginning of the summer.

Mamaw's words stung. *Shame on you.* Carson felt them deeply because she knew she deserved them. She *was* ashamed.

Carson knew in her heart that Harper's motives to buy Sea Breeze were genuine and selfless, like the woman herself. Harper was amazingly generous, more so than anyone else Carson had ever met. It was not because Harper had money. Carson knew plenty of people who had gobs of dough but held on to it with a miserly fist, always suspicious that someone might be trying to take advantage of them or steal it. They were not nice people to be around. Harper was that rare person who didn't act as if she had money or prestige. If she had any fears or suspicions, they were that people liked her only because of her money, rather than for herself.

Carson put her hands to her face. She was most ashamed because she knew this was Harper's most vulnerable point, her soft underbelly, and she'd targeted it with her barbs.

She was so good at hurting people. After Blake had left her at the coffee shop, she'd wandered around alone for a few hours, in a daze of depression. Blake's parting words resounded in her brain. *You weren't the only one to lose a baby.* Carson squeezed her eyes tight.

Why did she always feel everything was her fault? she wondered. Why couldn't Blake see she wasn't ready to let him or anyone else in that close? She'd lived a life of taking care of herself, taking care of her father. Of trusting her instincts.

What if she was kidding herself? she thought dismally. What if she didn't have good instincts? Look where they'd gotten her so far. She was a complete and utter failure at everything she'd ever tried. Jobs, sports, relationships . . . Even Delphine. The one living creature she'd ever truly bonded with, loved, trusted. Look what had happened to her. All because the dolphin had made the mistake of loving her. What was wrong with her? she agonized. Other people were getting on with their careers, were married, even had babies. Her sisters . . . especially her sisters. Dora had fallen in love, discovered a new talent, was moving on to her new place. Harper and Taylor were building a future. Once again, she was odd man out. It was fun when she had work and could jet out to some exotic film location. Even if she didn't have someone in her life, she'd had her career. Something to call her own.

What did she have now? She grimaced and put her hands to her face. Nothing. Blake deserved better. She couldn't be with anyone now. She just wanted to be alone. To think.

And to drink.

God help her. Her thirst for alcohol was so strong her body ached and her throat burned for it. She turned her head and looked at the bottle of tequila nestled in the brown bag, thought of all it promised: forgetting, numbness, immunity. Carson smacked her dry lips. She could almost taste it.

She wasn't an alcoholic, her brain was screaming at her. She hadn't had a drink in months. The original bet with her sisters was that she wouldn't drink for a week. She'd proved she wasn't an alcoholic, hadn't she? What was she so afraid of? All she had to do was open the bag, pull out the bottle, unscrew the cap, and take a little sip. Just one sip. To prove she could screw the top back on.

Even in her weak-willed state, Carson could hear the rationalizations of an addict.

The sound of feet running up the narrow wood dock pulled her face from her hands. Carson wiped her eyes and looked over her shoulder to see Harper trotting toward her, a sheen of perspiration on her brow.

Carson felt a rush of love as she rose up and ran to meet her sister at the upper dock. They wrapped arms around each other in a tight hug. Carson felt the moisture on Harper's body and smelled the tangy scent of sweat.

"I'm so ashamed," Carson cried in her sister's arms. "I'm so sorry."

"No, no, it's okay. I overreacted." Harper was crying, too.

"I didn't mean the things I said. They were vile and mean. Ugly."

"Yeah." Harper hiccuped.

Carson laughed and pulled away. "You don't have to agree with me."

Harper saw her sister's red-rimmed eyes. "Just saying . . ."

"You're all sweaty."

"I know. I've been running."

"Let's sit down and put our feet in the water. Cool down."

Carson led the way to the lower dock, a favorite spot of theirs to talk. She discreetly pushed the brown bag with the tequila out of the way.

They sat at the edge of the dock and slipped their legs into the water the way they always did when they came to the lower dock. Harper leaned back on her arms and let the refreshing breeze wash over her.

"I really am sorry," Carson said. "I'm being an idiot. It's just . . . I'm struggling. I feel lost and I just can't pull it together. I know I can get short-tempered and mean when I'm depressed. I'm really sorry I took it out on you. You didn't deserve that. You were trying to help."

Harper bent to let her hands slide in the water. "You always have a problem with my family's money."

"You know it's really all about my own insecurities that I have none."

Harper drew back and wiped her hands on her blouse. "Well, now I don't, either. So can you just quit it?"

"You really don't?"

"If I stay here, my mother is cutting off my income from the trust fund."

"Can she do that?"

"She's the executor."

Carson looked at her. "How much money are we talking about?"

Harper shrugged. "Enough that I don't have to worry."

Carson sighed. "Must be nice."

"Carson . . ."

"Sorry, but really, from where I come from, that sounds pretty good."

"I would give every penny of my trust fund to buy Sea Breeze. I don't care about the money."

Carson snorted. "Only people with lots of money can say that."

"Can I say something and not get you mad?"

Carson looked at her warily. "What?"

"Get a friggin' job! You're always bellyaching about not having money. Go get some!"

"I've tried!" Carson shouted back. "No one's hiring me."

"Maybe not here. You're a stills photographer for film and television. One of the best. You're not going to find a job like that here. Go back to LA and start pounding the pavement. Something will turn up."

Carson shook her head. "I don't think so."

"Why not?" Harper asked, exasperated.

Carson looked at her feet as they kicked the water. "I burned my bridges. I was careless and thoughtless with my career."

"Is that when you were drinking?" Harper asked softly.

Carson groaned and kicked harder in the water. "Yeah. There's a rule on set. You can get drunk on your own time, but not on the production's time. I screwed up my job. Slept with the director. Lord, I was really on a binge. Word got out and now no one will hire me."

Harper looked at her sister's averted face. Carson appeared downcast, with her long, dark hair in a flyaway knot at her neck. "Carson, you haven't had a drink in a long time. It's been three months."

Carson nodded, watching her feet swish the water.

"So . . . why are you drinking now?"

Carson swung her head to stare, wide-eyed, at her sister.

"Granny James didn't raise me stupid," Harper said, slipping into colloquial. She pointed. "Did you think I wouldn't see that brown bag? You are so busted."

Carson swallowed hard, her face pained. "I didn't drink any."

Harper made a disbelieving face.

"Really, I didn't. But I was close." Carson groaned loudly. "I want it so bad."

"It's not going to help. You know that. If you drink that now, you'll only feel worse about yourself."

"I couldn't feel worse about myself. It'll make me feel better. At least numb."

Harper heard the low, growling tone of depression in her sister's voice.

"Carson, how can I help?"

"You can't. Nobody can."

Carson was staring pensively at the Cove.

"What about Blake?"

"I broke up with Blake."

"Again?" cried Harper, her heart falling. "But you love him."

"I know," Carson said miserably.

"Why?" Harper whined.

"I'm all mixed up now!" Carson blurted. "The baby's gone. My career's gone. Soon Sea Breeze will be gone. Everything I love is going away."

"Seems to me like now's the time you need to hold on to Blake the most."

Carson pulled her legs out of the water and brought them close to her chest, wrapping her arms around her long legs. "I'm a hot mess. He's better off without me."

"No . . ."

"Really. It's that totem thing, remember? The shark?"

"I wouldn't make my life decisions based on that."

"That's what I'm supposed to do. According to the book. And my gut. You see"—Carson, eyes intent, turned to face Harper—"it's like the me I used to be is gone." Carson waved her hand out to the sea. Her voice cracked. "And she took my courage, my self-esteem, and my heart with her."

Harper leaned closer to place a consoling hand on her sister's shoulder. To show in a small way that her sister wasn't alone.

"I have to find her again," Carson said shakily. She sniffed and shook her hands in front of her, similar to the way Nate did when he was nervous. "And," she said in a normal voice, "that I have to do by myself. No one can help me do that. Can you understand what I'm saying?"

Harper thought about how she'd done the same thing for herself this summer at Sea Breeze. She'd isolated herself, given herself time and quiet to search inward for her strengths, her passions. To find herself.

"Yes," she said with heart. "I know exactly what you're saying." She held her breath. Harper hadn't planned on sharing her secret with anyone other than Taylor, but she knew now why Taylor had said writing could be a gift. "This summer I did just what you're describing. And . . ." Harper licked her lips. "I started writing."

Carson wiped her eyes, then turned her head to stare at Harper. "Writing?" Carson's eyes narrowed with suspicion. "Writing what?"

"A book."

Carson's eyes widened. "I knew it!" She pointed. "Your fingers were always tapping at something. I had a bet with Dora you were writing a book. I said it was a tell-all. Dora thinks you're writing a historical about the Gentleman Pirate. So what is it?"

Harper smiled devilishly. "You win."

Carson gasped. "Shit!"

"You can't tell anyone. You promise?"

"I promise. But why not? You should be proud."

"With Daddy's history, I'm not ready to tell anyone. Least of all my mother. It's a big secret." Harper paused. "But I'll show it to you."

Carson went very still. "Me? Why me?"

"You're my heroine. Don't you know that yet? Carson, you've always been the hero in all my stories."

Carson's face crumpled as she leaned closer to give her sister a clumsy hug.

"Come on." Harper disentangled herself and pulled her sister to a stand. "Let's go get it. Oh." Harper pointed to the dock. "And bring that bag with you."

In Harper's room Carson flopped on the bed and kicked her legs in the air with excitement. "I feel like it's Christmas and I'm getting the best present."

Harper grimaced as she went to the desk. "Well, we'll see how you feel after you've read it."

She unlocked the bottom drawer of her desk and pulled out a large manuscript. The pages were dog-eared but she carried it to Carson as if it were a bar of gold bullion. It was, in fact, a treasure beyond price. A part of her soul lay embedded in these pages. These words were like a written confession of her deepest, darkest secrets. And now she was exposing them to another's eyes.

Carson rose to a sitting position, her face apprehensive as Harper drew near with the manuscript.

"First, you have to make a trade. The bottle of booze for the book."

"Right." Carson leaned over on the mattress to fetch the brown paper bag. She handed it to Harper. "Go ahead and throw it out."

"I will."

Carson waited in anticipation.

Harper's hands grew clammy. "Don't show it to anyone else. Promise?"

"I promised already."

"Say it!"

"I promise," Carson said solemnly.

Harper took a breath, then reached out and handed over the book. It felt as if Carson were prying the book from her fingers.

Carson wiped her palms on her shorts, then smoothed the top page with her palm as she looked at it. She looked up with wonder. "You called it . . ."

Harper put her finger to her sister's lips. "You promised—don't tell anyone!"

It was late. After midnight. Carson slipped from the house to the garage. Her hands were shaking as she fired up the big engine of the Blue Bomber. She was frightened of what she was going to do. What she knew she must do.

Harper's book was a revelation. Though it was a novel and the characters had made-up names, they were thinly veiled. Anyone knowing the family would be able to identify which sister was which in the book.

Carson clutched the wheel tight as tears filled her eyes. Was that how Harper really saw me? she wondered. Callie, the character in the book, was strong and fearless. Devoted to the sea and her family, and to one beguiling dolphin in particular. This woman was a heroine by anyone's measures. *Can that be me?*

More tears, she thought with annoyance as she swept them from her cheeks. What kind of a heroine was weeping all evening? Yet, it was as though the tears were washing away the film of self-doubt that had plagued her. Tonight she'd almost fallen into a pit of despair and self-destruction. Harper—and her book—had led her from the brink. But no one could save her but herself.

She had to be the heroine in her own story.

Carson took a deep, calming breath and shifted the gears. She backed out of the garage, then drove with purpose north on Middle Street. A few minutes later she parked near Dunleavy's Pub. Cars were still parked in the slots, but she found one nearby. The laughter on the street was louder and brassier, a sign of late-night drinkers. She reached the dark green pub at the corner, past the picnic tables, and peered in the windows. It was near closing time, but a handful of people were still there, mostly in their twenties and thirties. The late crowd.

Taking a breath, she pushed open the door. Immediately she smelled the freshly popped popcorn and recalled the days it was her job to make it. She stood at the door of the popular watering hole and glanced quickly around the room. Old beer cans and license plates from across the country decorated the walls, along with photographs of local sports teams and signed photographs of a few famous greats. A soft buzz filled the room. The television over the bar had a baseball game playing.

Ashley, a fellow waitress when Carson worked here, smiled, drawing near, carrying a tray of dirty glasses back to the sink. "Hey, girl. Long time no see!"

"You took the night shift."

Ashley shook her blond head. She looked tired after a long night. "No, filling in. Hey, great to see you." She smiled wearily and, her arms loaded, hurried on to the kitchen.

Carson's gaze moved directly to the bar, the crown jewel of the pub, which dominated the back wall. Behind the bar, in his usual spot, the bartender stood facing the room, polishing a glass.

Carson walked straight to the bar, grabbed hold of the polished wood, and leaned forward, her gaze squarely on Bill. He was the bar's owner and manager and had been her boss when she was a waitress here. He was an old friend of Mamaw's, which had helped her get the job. Bill had also fired Carson for stealing a bottle of liquor.

Bill, a big man, had a long, drooping face that spoke of how he'd seen it all and suffered no fools. He had spotted her the moment she'd entered the room. His habit was to immediately check out anyone who walked through his door. His gaze had followed her as she walked across the room, and he studied her as she stood before him.

"Carson." He nodded in greeting. He set down the glass and towel, then walked to stand across from her. "How can I help you?"

Carson gathered her courage. "Do you remember how you told me you'd be my sponsor for AA?"

His expression shifted. "I do."

"I'm asking you to be my sponsor."

Chapter Seventeen

The following day, Harper didn't see the shops she passed along Highway 17 or the gated communities nor the long stretch of longleaf pines in the Marion National Forest. As she drove north to McClellanville, her mind was going full speed, caught up in a maelstrom of emotions and thoughts. She'd left Carson in her room alone. She couldn't bear to stay there while her sister read her book. It was too personal.

Harper squeezed her hands on the steering wheel and thought again of her advice to Carson—*now's the time you need to hold on to Blake.* It was high time she took her own advice.

The light turned red and Harper brought the Jeep to a stop, shifting the gears easily. She remembered her terror when she'd purchased the Jeep and realized it was manual transmission. Immediately she'd panicked. Why hadn't she believed she could do it?

As soon as she asked the question, she knew the answer. Fear. Fear of failure. Fear of not being perfect. Fear was at the root of her problems. The bedrock of her timidity.

The light turned green and Harper took off again. She was driving through a remote section of the vast Francis Marion Forest. As the miles passed beneath her humming wheels, her anger percolated. What kind of a sick mother would threaten to cut her child off? she wondered. Mamaw never cut off Parker, not even at his worst. Wasn't that the unconditional love a mother was supposed to feel for her child? Did unconditional love even exist, or was it just another fairy tale?

She'd read books on family dynamics ad nauseam. She couldn't even count the books she'd read about mother-daughter relationships. A lot of them waxed poetic about a mother's unconditional love. A love that knew no bounds. She'd never forget what Erich Fromm wrote. How a mother's love *need not be acquired, it need not be deserved.*

"Right," she muttered bitterly, never having felt that innocent, peaceful assurance of her mother's love.

Cutting the cord between her and her mother hadn't been as difficult as she'd thought it would be. She'd always envisioned that someday she'd go off on her own, but she saw now that was another fairy tale. For far too long it'd been so easy to accept the money handed to her, to live in a gilded cage. Like the child her mother had called her.

At last she came to the blinking light that signaled Pinckney Street. Harper had plugged Taylor's address—which she'd found easily enough, after a quick Google search—into her phone's GPS. She'd never have remembered this turn without it. Flicking her signal, she turned off the highway toward McClellanville, remembering the long and foliage-tunneled road toward the sea.

She drove through the few blocks of town, then turned on Oak Street and stopped at a driveway bordered by a clump of tall, leggy shrubs. She checked the address. This was it. The dirt drive was bordered by enormous live oaks dripping moss. Peeking out from the foliage sat a charming, if modest, white clapboard house with black shutters and a bright, cherry-red, sloping tin roof. Harper thought it was a vision from a classic southern painting. Two gable dormers adorned either side of the roof, and a wraparound porch embraced the house like loving arms. Jeremy Creek glistened in the sunlight behind the house.

She pulled into Taylor's driveway and spotted Thor lying on the porch. Immediately he raised his head. Harper turned off the ignition, aware the big dog was watching her every move. When she stepped out of the car, Thor immediately barked low and came trotting off the porch and across the yard, his dark eyes trained on her.

"Hey, Thor." She stuck out her hand toward him.

Thor sniffed her hand, then nudged his head against her leg for a more vigorous rub. He began whining gently, then barking excitedly, his tail wagging. Harper was giddy to be welcomed so warmly.

"Thor, back," Taylor called from the porch.

The dog responded immediately to the sharp command and backed off.

Taylor leaned over the railing and grinned with obvious pleasure at seeing her. He immediately hustled down the stairs and jogged toward her.

She saw in his expression all that she needed to know. Harper took off at a run toward him, arms out. She ran into his arms and he lifted her in the air and twirled her around. When he set her down, his face drew near to hers and their heated breaths mingled, his lips against hers.

"You're here." He buried his hands in her hair and bent to kiss her. He kissed her cheeks, her hair, her eyes, her ears, nibbling softly, then finally her lips.

Harper broke from the kiss and looked up at him, eyes shining. "I'm home."

Once again Harper was on board the *Miss Jenny*. She and Taylor had spent the last hour below-decks in the stateroom, taking their time making love. While the boat gently rocked, Harper felt treasured in his strong arms, safe. He whispered her name over and over like a litany of prayer, and she responded with sighs. She wanted it to go on forever.

Afterward he held her close. She felt the stubble

of his chin against her tender cheek and his breath at her ear.

"So, what did you want to talk about?" Taylor asked.

Harper felt her chest constrict, not wanting the seductive, peaceful mood that always fell over her and Taylor on board the *Miss Jenny* to be destroyed.

Taylor, sensing her swift change of mood, moved over her body to face her on the narrow bed. His gaze was searching. "Are you all right?"

"No. Not really."

"What's happened?" He was suddenly alert.

"I've so much to tell you, I don't know where to begin."

"My daddy always said begin at the beginning."

She laughed lightly. "Then I guess it all began the moment I decided to buy Sea Breeze."

She told it all. She released the entire story in a gush of words, like a floodgate opened, sparing him no details from the moment Devlin arrived at Sea Breeze with the offer on the house, to joining her sisters on the dock, to her decision to buy the house, to Mamaw's delighted reaction and Georgiana's vitriolic one, ending with her threat to cut off Harper's inheritance if she didn't comply with Georgiana's demands.

Taylor turned to lie on his back and laced his hands behind his head. "So, I guess you're not an heiress any longer."

"Sadly, no. I'm broke."

"Well, kiddo"—he slapped her bottom teasingly —"nice knowing you."

She threw a pillow at his face. His hand whipped up to catch it first. He spun around and tackled her back on the bed, pinning her under his arms.

Harper and Taylor burst out laughing. He kissed her lips soundly, then pulled Harper up to his chest so she could snuggle against him. Once settled, Taylor took her hand in his and played with her fingers.

"I'm glad you came to me. I want you to always feel you can."

"I do. I will."

A smile played at his lips. "You really told your mother you were going to stay here? Look for a job in Charleston?"

"Yes."

She felt his chest rise and fall. "Good."

"But I have to be realistic. I'm not kidding when I said I'm broke. I've been spending recklessly all summer and my checking account is low."

"Hey, if what you paid me is causing you trouble, you can have it back."

"You don't take money from damsels in distress?"

"No, ma'am."

She reached up to pat his cheek. "My hero," she said teasingly.

"I'm not joking. I don't need your money. I never will."

"I'll be okay." She patted his chest. "It's just that I'd always depended on the check from my trust fund. The money was always there. I never questioned it. But now that my mother is cutting me off, I've woken up to the fact that I have no safety cushion."

"You have me."

She heard the words. Was comforted by them. "Yes, but I don't want to fall back on depending on someone to take care of me. Not that I don't appreciate it," she hurriedly added. "It's more that I want a measure of independence. At long last. I don't even have a job."

"Yet."

"Let's be serious. How long will it take me to get one? Carson's been searching all summer for something in her field and hasn't found anything. I'm an editor. There aren't that many positions open in my field. Add to that, I'll have to move from Sea Breeze soon."

"Those are just excuses. Not reasons for leaving."

"They're not excuses. They're fact." She played with the hairs on his chest. "I've been thinking . . . I may have to go back to New York." She felt his breathing stop. "Just long enough to save some money," she rushed to add. "And apply for a job here. I need to buy some time."

"No," he said firmly. "If you go back, even for a day, your mother will get her claws into you and keep you there. She'll never let you come back."

"She won't do anything of the sort."

"You won't come back. You'll get involved in your job. Maybe you'll meet someone new."

"It won't be like that."

"Are you willing to take the chance?"

A labored sigh was her answer.

"Don't leave, Harper." Taylor held her tight, his eyes pleading, his voice husky. "Stay."

"Taylor . . ."

Taylor shifted to sit in front of her. He pulled her upright as well. She quickly brought the sheet up to cover her nakedness. Across from her, Taylor's bare shoulders and chest were as broad and imposing as a mountain.

"Please. Look at me."

When she dragged her gaze to his, they connected.

His sea-green eyes were turbulent with emotion. "I know fear. All too well. I faced life and death over and over. People claim that's courage. But that was the easy part compared to what I had to face when I came home. I learned that real courage is facing your fears. It takes guts to face and defeat your fear—or be defeated by it." He put his hands along her cheeks, holding her head so she couldn't look away. "Harper, I know what you're afraid of. What you're afraid to admit. You want to be a writer, don't you?"

She stared into Taylor's eyes. Her answer was welling up inside her. One that, until now, she'd been led to believe was trivial, unrealistic, and, worse, self-destructive. One she'd kept hidden.

"Yes."

"Then write."

Harper's heart was in her throat. "I've been writing. All summer."

"Exactly." He half smiled. "I seem to recall you saying that your writing was better here than anywhere else."

"True." Tears threatened. "I feel safe here."

His gaze rekindled. "I promise you, with me, you have nothing to fear. Not ever."

She pulled back, tucking the sheet higher up over her breasts. "You're asking me to put all my trust in you. To risk everything, my job, my inheritance, to stay here with you. Tell me, Taylor, why I should do that?"

Two deep furrows lined his brows as he looked steadily into her eyes. "Because I love you."

She felt her breath leave her. He'd said the words. Spoke aloud the one reason that could keep her here.

He stared back at her, his eyes vulnerable, waiting.

"I love you, too."

Taylor's eyes filled with resolution. He reached

up to gently wipe the tears from her face. "I know this is fast. Maybe crazy. We've only known each other a few weeks. But it feels like I've known you forever." He looked at her fingers entwined with his and released a quick smile. "You were right. I confess. I knew the moment I first set eyes on you that you were the one for me. It just took my jaded heart a while to admit it." He looked up at her. "I'm not as brave as you."

His words washed over her like a summer storm, rinsing away her fears, her doubts. In that moment Harper realized that there was indeed such a thing as unconditional love. A love that knew no bounds and was never ending, because that was how she felt for Taylor.

"I don't have a lot of money. I'm just starting a new job. I don't even have a ring. All that will come later. We have time to work out the details. I just don't want to lose you. It doesn't matter to me if your mother cuts you off. All I want is *you*."

Harper looked into his eyes and thought how no one had ever told her this before. Someone had always wanted something from her. Her wealth, her connections. This man wanted nothing except her.

He took her hand and she held her breath. "Harper Muir-James from New York, I offer you everything I have or will ever have. I offer you everything I am and will ever be. Will you marry me?"

They'd only known each other a little while. Already they were committing to marriage? It was crazy, illogical, irrational. Harper still had to get a job. She had nothing to fall back on if times got tough. And they would.

And yet . . . she couldn't shake the certain knowledge that Taylor was the one for her. That what she felt for him was real.

Harper's answer came not from her head, where she usually took time to carefully consider and research her thoughts and decisions. This time, her answer came straight from her heart.

"Yes, Taylor McClellan from McClellanville, I will marry you."

The following morning Harper and Taylor said a drawn-out good-bye, foreheads pressed together as they soaked up the early-morning light, and she drove back to Sea Breeze feeling as if she were floating on a cloud of joy. She was a different person driving south on this long stretch of road than she had been driving north the day before. Crossing the Isle of Palms connector, she was soaring over the vast wetlands headed straight for the sea. At its peak she glimpsed the vast Atlantic Ocean, sparkling blue in the radiant sun, and to her right the wide swath of the magnificent Intracoastal Waterway. Harper laughed out loud for the joy of it and opened her window wide to let the last warm breezes of summer blow in. Fall was coming. Already the tips of the grasses were golden, hinting at the change of seasons.

Change. The word gave her pause.

What changes she'd experienced in the past summer season! She'd arrived here in late May when the grasses were greening, that lovely spring color waving in a soft breeze. In so many ways she'd been as naive and green as the grass itself, sprouting up unawares. Over the summer she'd grown like the sea grass, tougher, rounded. Now, with the approach of summer's end and the beginning of fall, she felt ripe with love, ready to burst forth with color.

She passed the road where, if she turned and drove the three blocks toward the water, she'd arrive at what would soon be Dora's new home. Harper chuckled. Now *there* was a story of change. Dora had found not only herself this summer, but a life and a love she deserved.

Harper's gaze landed on her cell phone, maddeningly silent from its perch on her dashboard. She let out a little sigh despite all of the happy feelings roiling inside her. She had tried calling Georgiana several times first thing this morning, convinced that a mother's excitement over her daughter's engagement—even an impromptu one—would override their earlier clash. But her mother hadn't picked up the calls. Harper had finally dashed off an e-mail with the news, but still her phone didn't ring.

Harper wound her way off Middle Street to the road that led to Sea Breeze. She passed the tall hedge of green and entered the familiar circular drive. She felt as she often did when she faced the raised house with the gabled roof sitting in the shade of the giant oak: that Sea Breeze was waiting for her, arms open in welcome.

Her news was bursting at her lips. She hurried up the stairs and pushed open the front door. "Hello!" she shouted. She dropped her purse on the front-hall table. The painting of the *Miss Jenny* on the wall caught her eye and she smiled again. "Hello!" she called, entering the kitchen. "Where is everyone!"

Carson burst into the kitchen from the porch. She was wearing a skimpy bikini and her damp hair was slicked back in a loose braid. "You're back!" She looked over her shoulder to be sure no one was behind her. Then she ran to Harper, eyes blazing, and engulfed her in a bear hug. "It was wonderful! I couldn't put it down."

Harper's breath was taken away. "My book? Really?"

"Loved, loved, loved it. Especially the part—"

Dora came in behind Carson in a sleek, black one-piece suit. They looked as if they'd been in the pool. She looked at Harper with a mother's stern gaze. "You didn't come home last night."

"I've got some news!" Harper blurted out.

Unable to hold in her announcement a second longer, she shouted, "I'm engaged!"

After a second's stunned silence, Dora and Carson squealed in unison. In a rush the three sisters were hugging and jumping up and down with more squeals.

Mamaw walked into the room. Never one to be left out, she asked imperiously, "What in heaven's name is going on?"

Harper broke off from her sisters to run to Mamaw and envelop her in a hug. "I'm engaged!"

Mamaw was taken aback. The woman rarely sputtered. "Engaged? To Taylor?"

"Of course to Taylor." Harper laughed. "Oh, Mamaw, is it even possible to be so happy?"

"Sweet child, I'm so delighted for you." Flustered, Mamaw pointedly looked at Harper's left hand.

Harper caught the gesture and grasped her ringless hand in the other. "I don't have a ring." She put on a brave smile. "The proposal caught us both by surprise. I couldn't care less if he ever gives me one. I love him and he loves me and that's all that matters."

"True." Mamaw's voice wavered and she took Harper's hands in hers and squeezed gently. "You've only known him for a short while. Are you sure?"

"Yes," Harper replied with conviction. "We both know it's been quick, but sometimes you just know. Mamaw, he loves me for me. Just me. I've waited to hear those words my whole life. He's the one, Mamaw."

"Then he deserves you, my child," Mamaw said with feeling.

Harper basked in the glow of her grandmother's approval.

"A wedding!" Dora exclaimed. "At last! Have you set a date?"

"Oh, God, no. We didn't talk about that yet."

"You have to set a date," Dora told her urgently. "Charleston is a popular destination-wedding location now. Venues are booked way in advance. We'll have to start looking immediately."

"Hold your horses, Vera Wang," Carson chided Dora. "She just got engaged. Let the poor girl celebrate at least a day before we strap her to the wedding harness."

"I don't even know if I'm having a formal wedding," Harper said. "All that's a ways off."

"Of course you'll have a wedding," Mamaw declared.

"My mother won't come. And she certainly won't pay for a wedding."

"Why wouldn't she? You're her only daughter," Mamaw said.

"We had a terrible row. I tried to call her several times this morning. It went to voice mail each time. I followed up with an e-mail, but she still hasn't called me back." Harper shrugged. "I don't expect she will. My mother has the ability to slam an iron door down around herself, cutting a person out. It's a power move. I've seen her do this many times not to recognize it when it happens."

"That's cold," Carson said. "Give her time. I mean, her only child is engaged."

"We don't need Georgiana James to have a wedding," Mamaw said haughtily. "But we're getting ahead of ourselves. First, I must throw you a small dinner party to celebrate your engagement. It is time we met Taylor's parents."

"We need a good party at Sea Breeze," Dora said. "It might be the last party we have here. So let's do it proper."

In a rush of enthusiasm the women began spouting out ideas for the party, one after the other. As the mood shot skyward, their discussion was interrupted by the sound of the front doorbell.

"I'll get it. That must be Blake. Don't look at me like that," Carson warned her sisters, rolling her eyes. "He's just coming by to report on Delphine." She turned and hurried away to answer the door. A few moments later she returned carrying a piece of yellow paper with a bemused expression. "Harper, you got a telegram. I didn't even know people still sent telegrams."

Harper couldn't imagine who would send a telegram these days instead of an e-mail. She hurried to take the telegram, and with Carson looking over her shoulder ripped open the envelope.

Harper had to read the telegram twice, and it still didn't make sense.

"Who is it from?" Carson sidled closer.

"My grandmother in England. Granny James."

"Her?" Mamaw came near. "Whatever does she have to say that merits a telegram?"

Harper lifted the piece of paper and read it aloud: " 'Arriving Charleston Wednesday four p.m. Stop. Please collect me. Stop.' "

There was a moment's stunned silence.

Mamaw stood straight, her hands folded in front of her, her brows knitted in thought.

Dora spoke first. "Wednesday . . . as in the day after tomorrow?"

"I assume," Harper replied.

Dora tilted her head and made a face as if she had a bug in her ear. "You mean your grandmother is showing up here, all the way from England, just like that? Without calling you first?"

"Where is she staying?" Carson wanted to know.

"In a hotel, I suppose," Harper said.

"Absolutely not!" At the sound of Mamaw's voice the three young women swung their heads toward her. Her voice was stern with authority. "Harper, if your grandmother is flying all the way from Europe for a visit, she is most welcome to stay here at Sea Breeze. To do otherwise wouldn't be hospitable. Even," she said archly, "if she has the bad manners to show up on our doorstep uninvited."

Harper felt the sting of the insult and felt she had to defend her other grandmother. Granny James was nothing like Georgiana and was one of the only people in Harper's lonely childhood who'd made her feel loved. "I'm sure she didn't mean to impose. That wouldn't be like Granny James at all. She'll have already made reservations somewhere." Harper stared at the telegram in her hand. "Still, it's so unlike her. I can't imagine why she is coming like this, in such a rush, and without so much as a phone call."

"Can you not?" Mamaw asked.

"She's about as subtle as a Mack truck," said Dora. "Your granny's coming to check out your young man."

"But I only just got engaged. How would she know?" As soon as the words were out, Harper knew the answer. She looked into Mamaw's knowing glance. Georgiana would have called her mother in a great show of hysterics after listening to Harper's voice mail, no doubt telling her all sorts of horrible stories of Harper's downfall. She could only imagine the colorful adjectives used.

"Mummy . . ."

"Quite so," Mamaw said succinctly. "This has Georgiana's name written all over it."

"She must've painted a pretty horrid picture to get Granny James to hop a plane and come rushing to see me. She's nearly eighty, after all."

Mamaw sniffed. "That hardly makes her a dinosaur."

"That's not what I meant," Harper hastened to reply. "But she broke her leg last spring. She'd only act like this in an emergency."

"Naturally your grandmother would see your throwing away your fortune to rush off and get married to someone you hardly know as an emergency," Mamaw confirmed.

Dora snickered. "Well, when you put it like that . . ."

"You're right." Mamaw smiled wryly. "When you put it like that, I find your grandmother's actions admirable. She had to see the situation for herself. She wouldn't want you forewarned, either, for fear you might run off." Mamaw paused, then added begrudgingly, "I would do the same myself."

Harper felt a well of emotion for both her grandmothers. "She *is* rather like you, strong, refined, educated." Harper grinned. "Opinionated."

"This ought to be good," Carson said. "The dueling grandmas."

Dora giggled and began humming the tune "Dueling Banjos."

"Enough of this lollygagging." Mamaw crisply clapped her hands. "If we have a guest arriving in a little over forty-eight hours and a dinner party to plan, we have more work to do than I can shake a stick at."

"Where will we put her?" asked Dora.

"I could give her my room," Harper suggested.

"Heavens, no," Mamaw said. "I won't feel comfortable sharing a bathroom with someone I've never met."

"Do you want one of us to give up a room?" Dora asked. "Anyone but Nate, of course," she added hastily. "We all remember how easy it is to move him."

"There's no need for anyone to give up a room. The cottage should do nicely. It's freshly painted and Mrs. James will be much more comfortable with a space of her own."

"Mamaw, it's virtually empty," said Carson. "All that's in there is the iron bed and the desk. We've given everything else away to charity."

"Not everything," Dora said. "The hooked rugs are just out being cleaned. They're due back tomorrow."

"That still leaves the entire living room."

"And curtains and dishes. . . ."

Mamaw held up her hands. "Girls, we can do this. Taylor and his father did a beautiful job and the walls are dry. I have furniture in storage. All we have to do is shop for a few items. I've never known you girls to be shy about shopping. Dora, you have the most wonderful eye for decorating, and Harper, just look at how you fixed up the kitchen in short order. Carson, you can keep these two in line so they don't go too crazy.

How hard can it be for three talented, energetic women to fill a small cottage?"

"We need to go simple and clean," said Dora, warming to the idea. "Lots of white with bursts of blue here and there. It's the end of summer. There are lots of summer things on sale."

"But, Mamaw," said Harper, "I can't pull out my checkbook. Those days are over for me."

"No worries," Mamaw replied breezily. "It won't be much if we're careful. Bare necessities. Spartan, eh?"

"Think Santorini," said Harper. "Granny James loves Greece."

Dora clapped her hands excitedly. "I've helped Devlin stage a few houses for sale, and honestly, girls, Mamaw's right. We don't need that much. In fact, the less clutter the better. We need to make a list of only what we absolutely need."

"Hold that thought," Harper exclaimed, getting caught in the enthusiasm. "I'll get a paper and pen."

"Let's move this conversation to the cottage," Mamaw said, upbeat. "I swanny, I can't think on my feet anymore. And I always do better with a cup of coffee."

Chapter Eighteen

Wednesday afternoon, Harper stood at the security gate of Charleston International Airport clutching her raffia purse, which held a bottle of cool water, searching the faces of the line of bedraggled-looking people walking through the exit. Some walked with heads bent, arms pumping with determination. Others strolled lazily, dragging carry-on luggage behind them. A lucky few were met with high-pitched greetings and kisses from loved ones.

While she waited, Harper felt a wave of guilt wash over her as she realized she hadn't seen Granny James for over two years. Harper used to travel to England to see her grandparents every year, usually over spring break. As she grew to be an adult, her mother bought the house in the Hamptons, and Granny James began flying over to the States to spend several weeks in sunshine. She loved the warm air and sea. For the past few years, however, Papa James's health had been poor, and Granny chose not to leave him.

Harper frowned, worried how her grandmother had managed to fly all this way with a broken leg. What was Georgiana thinking to encourage Granny to make such a trip? Harper kept her eyes peeled for a wheelchair.

A minute later Harper spied striding toward her an older, handsome woman of average height and chin-length auburn hair, stylishly, if conservatively, dressed in a well-tailored navy suit with crisp white piping and sizable pearls. She still had beautiful legs, yet on her feet were thickly soled navy shoes, what Granny referred to as "sensible" shoes. A testament to Granny's no-nonsense approach to life. Her arms were burdened with a floral-patterned bag, which undoubtedly held her knitting, and an enormous black leather purse.

"Granny James!" Harper called, waving her hand.

The woman paused, catching Harper's wave, and her stern expression lifted to reveal an astonishing smile of relief and joy. "Dear girl!" Granny James feebly tried to lift one arm burdened with a heavy bag, continuing at a determined pace through the passage, past the exit guard, directly into Harper's waiting embrace. She dropped her parcels and wrapped her arms around her granddaughter. For several minutes, time stopped as Harper was engulfed in the familiar, loving scent and feel of Granny James.

After the embrace Granny pulled back and gripped Harper's shoulders. Standing eye to eye, Harper studied her grandmother—her hair swept to the side in soft waves, a red much deeper than Harper's softer color. Granny's pale blue eyes under finely arched brows were searching Harper now like an acetylene torch.

"You look well enough," Granny James said in way of a verdict.

Harper laughed. "Of course I'm well. In fact, I'm better than I've ever been. How are you?"

Granny James dropped her arms and straightened. "As well as can be expected after a hellish journey crammed into a tin box in the air. I flew coach," she added with distaste. "I couldn't get first class at such short notice."

Harper laughed. Same old Granny. Picking up her grandmother's parcels, Harper moved several feet to where rocking chairs faced the plate-glass windows. It made for a pretty waiting spot with a southern motif.

"I . . . I'm confused"—Harper looked at Granny's legs—"I expected you to come out in a wheelchair or something."

"A wheelchair!" Granny James sounded insulted.

"Yes. Your leg . . ."

"What about my leg?"

"Didn't you break your leg?"

"Whatever are you talking about?"

"Mummy told me at the beginning of summer that you couldn't come to the Hamptons this year because you'd had a bad fall and broken your leg. She very much wanted me to fly to England to be your nurse."

The puzzled expression on Granny James's

face shifted to one of resigned understanding. "Your mother told you I broke my leg?" It was more a statement of fact than a question. Granny James shook her head with exasperation. "I did no such thing. I broke my toe! She made a tempest in a teapot. As usual."

"Your toe . . . ," Harper repeated slowly as understanding dawned. Her mother had manipulated the truth to get Harper to go to England rather than South Carolina.

Granny James's face softened with affection. "So you expected to see me pushed in a wheelchair?"

"At the very least hobbling on crutches."

"Poor dear, you must have been worried."

"More than worried. I couldn't imagine why you flew here in such haste."

"I think, perhaps, you can."

Harper waited.

"Your mother called me. She was very upset." Granny James hesitated. "Dear girl, I'm just going to come straight out with it. Are you getting married?"

Harper smiled. "I am. Someday. For now we're engaged."

Granny James was taken aback. All pretense fled. "Then it's true."

"What else did Mummy tell you?"

"Oh, she was in a state, I can tell you. She said how you're throwing away your inheritance.

Cutting yourself off from the family. All to marry some . . . fisherman? Your mother made it sound like you've been trapped by some kind of cult!"

Harper burst out laughing. "A cult?" Then, seeing how upset her grandmother was, Harper realized Granny was exhausted and worried. Harper shouldn't respond flippantly. "Granny, there is a lot to discuss and you're tired. Let's get you to Sea Breeze and we'll thrash it all out."

"I'm staying at the Charleston Place hotel. I have my reservation number in my bag."

"Oh, we wouldn't dream of you staying at a hotel. You're to stay at Sea Breeze. It's all arranged."

"I wouldn't dream of the inconvenience."

"It's no inconvenience. We've got your room all ready for you. Besides, it's too far to go back and forth from the city way out to Sullivan's Island."

"I thought perhaps you could stay at the hotel with me. I reserved you a room as well. Honestly, you're the only one I've come to see. I don't see much point in mingling with the others."

"With the natives, you mean?" Harper grinned crookedly. "Meeting Taylor and Mamaw and my sisters is exactly why I want you at Sea Breeze. To form your own opinions. Granny, I want you to see me in my element. I need you on my side."

"Darling girl, I am already on your side."

Harper leaned forward to kiss her cheek. "Trust me, you'll be much happier at Sea Breeze."

Granny James looked resigned to the idea, if not entirely convinced. "If you insist," she said through pinched lips.

"I do. Thank you." Then, trying not to sound worried, Harper asked, "How long are you staying?"

Granny James straightened her shoulders and delivered a no-nonsense look that would have sent her staff scurrying if they'd seen it. "As long as it takes."

Harper had borrowed Carson's vintage Cadillac to pick Granny James up from the airport, as it required less of a climb to get in than Harper's Jeep. Granny's blue eyes sparkled when she saw the baby-blue convertible with the great fins rising like a phoenix. Harper had cleaned out the empty water bottles, the coating of sand and trash, and given the car an inside-and-out cleaning. Harper was fastidious about such things and, she acknowledged, a little obsessive-compulsive, especially when compared to her sister.

Granny James let her hand graze along the high tail fins. "Vintage. Very nice. This car has style."

Harper grinned and opened Granny's door. All Harper's efforts had been worthwhile.

The sun shone in a cloudless sky as they crossed the wetlands leading to Sullivan's Island. All chatter ceased as Granny James stared out her window in silence. Harper smiled, understanding full well the awe and wonder Granny was experiencing. Harper felt it every time she crossed on the narrow road. Once on Sullivan's Island, they turned onto Middle Street. Harper slowed down and drove past the charming restaurants, the art gallery, the park, the fire station. The steeple of Stella Maris Catholic Church rose up in view. The lovely church, a favorite of local artists, was set back from the road amid palm trees and flowers. At nearby Fort Moultrie a few people were milling about. Harper briefly told her grandmother the long history of the fort in the Revolutionary War, the Civil War, and World War II. Granny James took everything in with silence, but Harper knew she was listening from the watchful look in her eyes. At last Harper turned off Middle and headed down small-town roads toward the back of the island. Moments later she was turning past the tall row of hedges into the circular drive of Sea Breeze.

Granny James leaned forward in her seat, eyes sharp and her hands tightening on her purse. Harper circled the great oak tree to park directly in front of the house.

"Here we are!"

Granny James pushed open the door and slowly, stiffly, climbed from the car.

Harper ran around the hood to assist. "Let me help."

"I'm all right." Granny brushed away Harper's hand. "I'm just stiff from the long flight."

In the bright sunlight Harper could see the new, deep lines that coursed a path in her grandmother's face.

"My suitcase is in the boot." Granny James looked at the long flight of stairs to the front door. "Can someone help us? It's very heavy."

"I've got it." Harper opened the trunk and, with a soft grunt, hoisted the big suitcase to the ground. She saw the surprise on her grandmother's face that she could lift it with such ease. "Lifting forty-pound bags of soil and compost all summer does wonders for the muscles."

Granny James looked confused.

"I've been gardening. . . . No worries about the stairs." Harper began dragging the suitcase toward the cottage. "You're staying here. In the cottage. It's quite nice and will give you some privacy."

En route to the cottage the front door of the main house opened. Mamaw, Dora, and Carson stepped out onto the porch, all smiles and welcome.

"Hello there!" Mamaw crooned. "Welcome to Sea Breeze."

Granny James turned her head in acknowledgment but, Harper noticed, did not smile.

"I'll just leave the suitcase on the cottage porch. Let's go up and say hello."

Granny James made the climb, clinging to her

large purse as though someone would snatch it from her.

At the top of the stairs Mamaw, standing tall and refreshed, stepped forward, hand outstretched. "I'm so glad to meet you at last. I'm Marietta."

"Imogene." Granny James accepted the hand with a stiff smile. "I do hope I'm not imposing. I had reservations at a very nice hotel but Harper insisted."

"Of course. You're family, after all. Harper has told us so much about you. These are my other granddaughters." Mamaw stepped aside and gestured. "Dora, the eldest. And Carson. Harper's sisters."

The sisters stepped forward with southern hospitality, smiling and warmly shaking Granny James's extended hand.

"You're all half sisters, isn't that right?"

Mamaw raised her brow. Harper knew she despised the term *half sister.* "Yes. My son, Parker, is their father."

"Yes, but they have different mothers—all three?"

Mamaw bristled at the implied criticism. Dora and Carson exchanged a wary glance.

"That's right." Mamaw's pithy tone went tit-for-tat. "But we don't refer to them as half sisters. It's the parents who gave up halfway. My girls never give up." Mamaw smiled warmly at each of the three young women. "Sisters are sisters. *My* summer girls," she added territorially. She lifted her chin with the air of someone who had just won the first round. "Let's go indoors. It's a bit hot out here."

The house smelled of lemon polish and soap, testament to the preparations they'd made for this visit. The mood was formal as the three women each found a seat on the antique furniture in the living room. The pale blue grass-cloth paper on the walls, the delicate side tables, and gilt-framed paintings, mostly of scenes of the lowcountry, made for an elegant yet still beachy room that Harper was proud of.

"Early-American furniture?" Granny James's eyes swept over the highboy. "Eighteenth-century, I suppose?"

"Yes." Mamaw's eyes brightened. She loved to talk furniture. "That highboy is Chippendale. When my husband, Edward, retired, we moved from our house in Charleston to the island. It broke my heart to deaccess so much of my furniture. I only kept the family pieces, and even of those I selected only my favorites for this house. I keep the rest in storage off island. Away from hurricanes."

Granny James sniffed as though smelling mold. "Yes, keeping furniture would be a worry living on an island. With all this humidity and sun. Good furniture, that is. Our family heirlooms date back much earlier, of course. Was it difficult giving up your home in Charleston to move to this . . . quaint little island?"

Mamaw sat straighter and smiled stiffly. "Quaint, perhaps, but utterly perfect for our needs. We were ready to downsize from our large house at his retirement. Edward and I loved this house and the island. This is a family house. We spent our summers here, you see." Her gaze fell on Harper. "With the girls." Mamaw's face grew solemn. "What proved difficult was Edward's passing after only a year."

"You've lived here alone? All those years?"

"Yes. With Lucille. My maid and companion. Lucille passed this summer, sadly. And now that I've reached the ripe old age of eighty, I'm afraid, even though I love it, the house is proving to be too much."

"Too big? Really? Why, it's a very sweet house. Cozy. I should think it'd be perfect."

Mamaw drew herself up. "You have no idea of the maintenance a house of any size demands on an island."

Granny James was listening intently. "I heard you were selling Sea Breeze."

Mamaw's expression shifted to curiosity at the comment as Dora and Carson bustled into the room carrying trays of tea and cookies. The scent of Darjeeling, which Harper had informed them was Granny's favorite, filled the air as Dora poured.

Harper was relieved to see her grandmother accept the tea with relish. She shifted on the silk sofa, her teacup balanced expertly in her hands, and sipped.

Granny James made a face. "Oh, this tea isn't hot. Did you steep the tea in the harbor, like the colonists?" She laughed as though it were a joke, but set her cup and saucer on the table and coupled her hands stiffly in her lap.

Harper cringed. Mamaw's face was granite. Carson and Dora silently simmered. It was getting warmer in here, Harper thought. Though the air conditioner was on, Mamaw never kept the house cooler than seventy-two. Mamaw was wearing her usual linen tunic, this one a pale blue that brought out the brilliant blue of her eyes. Dora looked cool in a Lily Pulitzer sundress, as did Carson in her long white caftan. Harper wore her green sundress and pearls. In contrast, Granny James appeared to be sweltering in her dark suit, but Harper knew her grandmother would expire before she would remove her jacket.

Mamaw was launching into the plans she'd made for Granny James's visit. Trips to Charleston to tour the old houses, perhaps a stop at the plantation houses. Harper saw her grandmother's face grow still and her eyes glaze.

"You might wish to freshen up," Mamaw continued. "We've prepared a lovely dinner. We serve at six."

Granny James slowly rose to her feet, dragging her enormous purse with her. "I'm afraid I won't be joining you for dinner. I'm very tired. Jet lag and all. If you don't mind, I'd very much like to retire to my room." She sighed. "Or cottage."

Mamaw's smile slipped. But she rallied and pulled her smile back into place as she rose to a stand. "Why, of course. You must be exhausted from your long journey. It's not like the old days before the airlines cut costs and provided a good meal and special accommodations for the elderly. And you do look warm. We don't wear dark colors on the island." She looked to Harper. "Be a dear and see your grandmother to the cottage and help her feel at home. There's a small kitchen there," Mamaw explained to Granny James. "We stocked it with cereal and tea and nibbles. In case you get hungry later. But do let us know if you need anything."

Mamaw clasped her hands in front of her, her duty as hostess complete.

Granny James slipped off her navy-blue jacket the moment she entered the cottage, then reached up to pat her hair. Draping the jacket over the nubby white sofa, she walked around the sparsely furnished, freshly painted white room, taking in the brilliant Jonathan Green painting on the wall, the raffia-covered coffee table, the sea-grass rugs, and the long white cotton curtains at the windows. Harper followed her into the bedroom. Harper had left the windows open and the pale blue linen curtains ruffled on a breeze. Here, too, the walls were white and the linens a matching pale blue.

"I feel like I'm in Santorini," Granny James said with a slight smile.

"That's what I was hoping you'd feel."

Granny James stretched out her arms and, bending over, tested out the mattress.

"Brand-new," Harper assured her. "Everything is new. This was Lucille's cottage. We stripped it and freshened it up. You're the first guest."

"I should hope so. I understand the woman died in here."

Harper sighed. "Mamaw's tried very hard to make you feel comfortable. Sea Breeze is very dear to her."

"Yes, she seems a proud person." Granny took off her sapphire earrings. "With very little to be proud about."

Harper shook her head. "I'll get your suitcase."

When she returned to the bedroom, her grandmother had slipped off her shoes and was standing at the window, staring out. Without the boxy jacket, in her knit shell, Harper saw that her grandmother had kept her slim, curvaceous figure.

"Not Santorini," Granny James said wistfully. "This cottage takes me back to Cornwall. My family had a cottage there once, overlooking the sea. A cottage very much like this one." She sighed. "I was very young. I loved it there."

Harper dragged the large black suitcase to the center of the room. "You brought enough for a long stay."

Granny turned from the window. "I didn't know what to pack. I planned for every contingency."

"A swimsuit and shorts would have been enough for Sea Breeze."

"Yes, I see that now." Granny walked to the bed and sat down, sinking into the down coverlet. "Harper, dear. Please sit down."

Harper went to sit in the small antique lady's chair beside the bed.

"This engagement of yours"—Granny James got right to the point—"it feels rushed. I've not yet met the man. Or his family."

"I know it seems like that. It all happened so fast." Harper laughed. "We're kind of in shock ourselves. But it just felt right."

"But marriage, Harper . . . it's too important a decision not to take seriously."

"Granny James"—Harper sat straighter—"we're not rushing into marriage. We haven't even set a date. I have to find a job, a place to live. Taylor is just beginning his new job. We both know that we have a lot to get settled before we get married." She looked into Granny's eyes. "I assure you, we are taking it seriously."

Granny James studied Harper's face, considering,

then sighed. "Very well. That's enough for tonight. We can talk more tomorrow. Just you and I." Granny put her hand to her mouth to stifle a yawn. "I'm completely knackered. And"—she dropped her hand—"I have no intention of being a tourist."

Summarily dismissed, Harper went to her grandmother and chastely kissed her cheek. Even under the best of circumstances, Granny James rarely gave out kisses or hugs. Unlike Mamaw, who made stepping into her arms so easy.

"Good night." Granny James's face softened and she let her hand linger on Harper's arm. "It really is good to see you again, my dear. I've missed you."

Harper smiled at the tender expression. "I've missed you, too. Good night."

She closed the door behind her when she left.

Chapter Nineteen

Harper woke the next morning and hurried to the kitchen to prepare Granny James's breakfast. She was stirring a pot on the stove when Mamaw walked in, breezy and sweet scented in a tangerine top and khaki pants.

"Smells good. What is it you're cooking?" She looked in the pot. "Grits?"

"I thought Granny would enjoy it. Being a southern dish and all."

"How long does Imogene intend to sleep, do you think?" Mamaw asked, her disapproval thinly veiled. She laid out on a tray her usual morning meal of coffee thick with cream, a biscuit, and cut fruit.

"She's usually an early riser," Harper replied somewhat defensively. "England is five hours ahead of us, so she went to bed last night at what was past midnight for her. Plus, I think she's been very worried about me. Probably hasn't slept well for days."

"That might excuse her rude retreat last night."

Harper rolled her eyes.

"Whatever was she worried about?"

Harper twisted her lips. "My mother called her and filled her head with stories about how I was running off to get married."

Mamaw made a soft harrumph. "I thought as much. And I assume Georgiana told her, with relish, that you'd wanted to buy Sea Breeze?"

"Yes. Afraid so."

"Horrible woman. So now your grandmother is here to rescue you, I suppose?" It was more of a statement of fact than a question.

Harper kept her eyes on the melon she was slicing into small pieces.

"I wonder if she'll be up for a tour of Charleston today?"

"No," Harper answered quickly. "I mean, let's give her a day or so to relax. Remember, you always say it takes three days to acclimate to island time."

Mamaw stilled her hands and asked, concerned, "How long does she intend to stay?"

Harper shrugged. "I don't know. A few days, at least."

"I've heard of European visitors staying for months. Fish and visitors . . ."

"Oh, I shouldn't think it will be long." Harper stirred the pot faster, thinking of Granny's enormous suitcase filled with clothes. "After all, we won't be here ourselves in a month."

Mamaw looked at her tray. "I suppose not," she said flatly.

Harper didn't want to dwell on the unpleasant inevitable. "I'd better make up a tray for Granny. Go check on her."

A knock on the front door was followed by a woman's voice calling out, "Halloo!"

"In here, Granny James!"

Harper hurried into the front hall to greet her grandmother. She was dressed more casually than she'd been yesterday, in a pleated gray linen skirt that fell to her calves, a crisp white linen shirt that, being linen, was forgivably wrinkled, and espadrilles. Her hair was brushed back from her face and she looked rested, younger today, though still pale and eyes rimmed red.

"How are you feeling? Truthfully?"

"Perfectly well. A bit stiff, but a good walk on

the beach should cure that. I am parched, however. I drank all the bottled water but was a bit afraid to drink from the tap. In this jungle."

"You won't get sick. And there's a filter on the kitchen tap. In the meantime, come into the kitchen. I've made you breakfast."

Stepping into the kitchen, Harper saw that Mamaw had already fled the room. Sighing, she knew she'd have to deal somehow with the friction between the two women. She poured her grandmother a large glass of water and a cup of tea with milk and handed them to her.

Granny James looked at the tea. "Did you make it?"

"Yes."

"The water came to a roiling boil?"

"Yes. And I warmed the pot."

Granny James tasted the tea. "Much better. These Yanks still haven't mastered how to make a decent cup of tea."

"That should handle the liquids. I've cut up some fruit. And I've made you something special."

"You're cooking now?"

Harper laughed. Her grandmother had often remarked affectionately on Harper's general ineptitude in the kitchen. "Hardly cooking. Though I am trying."

"What is that you've made? *Porridge?*" Granny James asked in horror.

Harper laughed. "No, it's grits. Stone-ground

and cooked with milk and butter and cheese. It's a southern classic."

Granny James made a face. "Grits? Isn't that what they fed the slaves?"

"I have no idea. I thought you'd like to try something different. If not"—Harper indicated the tin of bakery goods—"there are biscuits and scones."

Granny James looked idly around the kitchen, then made a beeline for the wide swath of windows. She stared out at the Cove, her face still and watchful.

Harper came to join her at the windows. "It's magnificent, isn't it?"

Granny James stepped back and took a sip from her teacup. "It's a prettyish bit of river, I suppose."

"It's not a river. There are lots of winding creeks in these wetlands. But that out there is part of the Cove. A heavenly body of water that connects to the great Intracoastal Waterway. You could go from Florida to New England and never go out into the ocean."

"Really?" Granny James appeared interested.

"Do you want to go out and take a look?"

Granny James gave a long-suffering sigh. "I suppose I might as well." She walked out on the porch carrying her teacup, her gaze glued to the winding creek that snaked through the waving green grass, sparkling in the morning sun.

"Good morning, Imogene," Mamaw called out.

She was sitting at the black wicker table eating breakfast from her tray. A newspaper was spread out.

Granny James turned and, surprised to see Mamaw on the porch, walked to the table, a stiff smile on her face.

"How did you sleep?" Mamaw asked politely.

"Oh, the usual way. Eyes closed. Rhythmic breathing."

"Please. Come join me." Mamaw offered a chair. "I always eat breakfast out here early in the morning before the heat descends. Harper, be a dear and fetch your grandmother's tray, will you?"

Harper knew a bolt of fear at the prospect of leaving the two women alone, even for a moment. She didn't expect a catfight . . . not exactly.

She hurried to the kitchen for the tray. Carson was inside, picking at a scone with two fingers.

"Please come join us on the porch," Harper begged. "I could use the help. I feel like I'm commandeering the *Titanic* through the icebergs."

"Not me." Carson backed away. "No offense, but your grandmother is one frosty woman." She made as if to shudder with cold.

"She's not that bad. Normally. Last night she was tired."

Carson made a face of doubt. "What's her excuse for this morning?"

"Okay, so it takes a while for her to thaw. Please?"

"Can't. I've got a meeting with Blake at NOAA. Must rush."

Harper reached for the tray but hesitated. "Blake?"

"Don't get your antennas up." Then Carson's eyes sparked. "We're planning Delphine's release."

Harper released the tray and hurried to hug Carson. She knew how much Delphine's release meant to her sister and to Blake. To all of them. "I'm so happy for you. Oh, this is such good news. When?"

"Soon." Carson's eyes were bright. "Blake and I both want this release to go smoothly, and we're getting together to work out the details. It forces us to work together, and I'd like us to remain friends. And speaking of together"—Carson tilted her head toward the back porch and drew back—"if I were you, I'd get back out there ASAP."

Harper blew out a plume of air and picked up the tray. When she returned to the porch, she found both women reading the newspaper in silence. "Here we are," she called out cheerily. She laid the tray on the table. "I've brought you a pair of sunglasses." She handed them to Granny James. "It can get bright out here."

"You've always been a thoughtful girl." Granny James slipped on the black sunglasses.

"Yes, she has," Mamaw confirmed. "Southern girls are raised to know their manners."

"But Harper comes from good British stock.

For the English, good manners come as naturally as the air we breathe." Granny fanned herself with the newspaper. "It's positively Congo-like out here." She looked at her grits with distaste, then took a hesitant bite. "Oh, my, dear . . . quite lovely," she said, clearly swallowing with effort and then moving to the less offending fruit.

The three women sat in silence for a few moments. "That's a lovely garden," Granny James finally remarked, looking out across the yard. "Would you show it to me?"

Harper beamed with pride. "It's the garden I mentioned yesterday, Granny James. I planted it."

"Really?" Granny James said with disbelief.

"I'm becoming quite skilled in all the domestic arts," Harper replied smugly.

"In the South, all properly brought up young ladies are skilled in the domestic arts," Mamaw added.

"In the James family, young women also learn the domestic arts." Granny James smiled thinly. "So that we can direct the staff." She turned to Harper. "Come, my dear. Show me this pretty little patch you call your garden." Granny James rose to her feet.

Harper knew her grandmother wanted to steer her toward a private moment away from Mamaw. As they strolled through the garden, Harper began what she knew would be a long conversation. She explained how she and Dora had started the small garden, digging out the tough weeds under the relentless sun and discovering the slave manacles.

"You mean to say you dug the dirt yourself? Without help from a gardener?"

Harper laughed. "You're looking at the gardener," she claimed with pride. "I planted each and every one of those flowers, each rose-bush, each herb. I hover over them like they're my children. I'm much more proud of this garden because I did the work myself, rather than if I'd just told a gardener what to do. Oh." She stopped herself. "Sorry, Granny. Your garden is so large. I couldn't . . . I didn't mean to offend."

"No, of course not," Granny James replied wryly.

"I do so enjoy it. Getting my hands in the soil, making something my own. Who knew? Me?"

Her grandmother removed her sunglasses and studied Harper's face, then replied thoughtfully, "Yes, you."

Harper enjoyed the expression on her grand-mother's face. As if she were seeing Harper for the first time, or at least the woman she had become. She felt different inside and liked to think that difference showed on the outside as well.

"Do be careful though, dear." Granny James slipped her sunglasses back on. "You're getting freckled. Now, let's sit a moment. Over by the water, shall we? In the shade."

From the garden they walked down the slope to the shade of the covered dock. The tide was high and racing, glistening in the sun. The lower dock creaked against the ropes as the water lapped its sides. Overhead a fleet of gray pelicans flew past, wings outstretched. Somewhere in the water, Harper heard the plop of a large fish jumping.

Granny James stared out a while, her eyes gleaming with appreciation. Then she turned to Harper, her expression serious, yet tender. "Tell me all."

Harper regaled her grandmother with stories of this incredible summer. How Carson had met the dolphin Delphine, how they'd befriended her, how this beguiling dolphin brought them all joy and laughter when they needed it most. And the sad consequences of her accident. How Harper had gotten to know her sisters again, her nephew. How the ocean and the beaches, the palmettos and pluff mud, the sounds and scents of the lowcountry, had seduced her. She spoke of meeting Taylor, how it had felt like a thunderbolt, the kind she'd read about in all her books. She also told of the many hours she'd spent staring out at this very same view, pondering who she was and what she wanted out of life.

"Sea Breeze was my sanctuary. Where I discovered myself."

"You obviously love it here. And"—Granny James sighed—"I can see why. It is beautiful.

Bucolic. But let's get to the heart of it, shall we? As lovely as it all is, I didn't travel all the way from England for the view."

"I don't know what Mummy told you, but first, you need to know that I'm well, clear thinking, and happier than I've ever been before in my life."

"I can see that." Granny James paused. "Am I to assume it's all this fresh air? Or is it because of this young man you've fallen in love with?"

Harper grinned and impulsively hugged her grandmother. Granny James felt stiff and unrelenting, but Harper knew that her grandmother felt a deep affection for her, even if she couldn't always express it with words or physical gestures.

"I'm so happy." Harper pulled back. "His name is Taylor. Taylor McClellan. He served in the Marine Corps. Now he's in business. He's not a fisherman, though his father used to catch shrimp. He's brave and kind and compassionate and smart. I love him, Granny. I truly love him."

"Yes, but does he deserve you?"

"Do I deserve him is the real question."

"I'm quite serious."

"I know you are. You'll just have to meet him. Make your own judgment."

"I intend to. That's why I'm here." Granny James reached out to place her hand over Harper's. "Darling, will you listen to my opinion?"

"Of course."

"And if I don't like him?"

"I hope you will. But"—Harper withdrew her hand—"if you don't, I'll marry him anyway."

Granny studied Harper's face for a moment, looked off at the water, then turned back, her face resolute. "About your trust fund," she said, shifting gears. "Tell me about that debacle. Why did you ask your mother if you could access your funds immediately?"

"I wanted to buy Sea Breeze."

"That's what your mother said." Granny nodded in self-satisfaction.

Harper released a labored sigh. "Why don't you begin by telling me exactly what Mummy told you?"

"Well"—Granny James slightly lifted her shoulders—"I guess I have to go back to last May. Georgiana called me after a row she'd had with you. She was very upset that you up and quit your job at the publishing house. Really, dear," Granny scolded, "to quit your job without notice."

Harper simmered. "Go on."

"She was very upset that you'd refused to return to New York or even go to England to see me. I tried to calm her. I reminded her that you were not a child, after all. You're a grown woman capable of making your own decisions."

"Thank you."

Granny James gave Harper a pointed look.

"Though I admit, I would have appreciated a phone call from you this summer."

"You're right," Harper apologized. "I was selfish and rude. I'm sorry."

Granny James accepted the apology with a wave of her hand. "Anyway, summer passed, and then just this week Georgiana called again to tell me that not only were you staying here, but that your grandmother, Marietta Muir, was manipulating you to get your trust fund early so you could buy her house and help her financially. Georgiana made all sorts of slurs and comparisons to your father. Not at all kind, I'm afraid, and I won't insult you by repeating them."

"It's all ridiculous!" Harper said, steaming. "Nothing could be farther from the truth."

"Why don't you tell me your side of this sordid story."

"First of all, Mummy treated me horribly at the publishing house. I won't go into my personal relationship, or lack of one, with her. We've been through that before. God knows how many times I've cried at your knee about it."

"Yes, dear," Granny James said in a softer tone, and reached out to touch Harper's hand. "Your mother can be harsh."

Harper released an unladylike snort. "She can be cruel. And an utter bitch of a boss. You'd expect her to be at least professional, but she treated me as her lackey, not her editorial assistant. It was embarrassing. She refused to promote me. I honestly believe she enjoys keeping me under her thumb. Last May we had words." Harper didn't add that the argument was about Granny James, how Georgiana had demanded Harper fly to England to be her nurse. "She told me my job was to do what she said, period." Harper shrugged. "That was the last straw. I quit. You must believe me. It was all between her and me and had nothing to do with Mamaw."

"Except that you happened to be at Sea Breeze when all this transpired."

"I came here for Mamaw's eightieth birthday party. Initially it was only supposed to be for a few days, but then she invited all of us girls to spend an entire last summer together at Sea Breeze. Like we did as children. Call it serendipity, but it just worked out that we could. You should know that Mamaw informed us from the start that she was putting the house on the market at the end of summer. That was why this summer was so important. To all of us. Mamaw does *not* need my money, nor does she need me to buy her home. In fact, she has two offers on the table at this very moment to buy it."

"I see," Granny James said doubtfully.

"It's true. Oh, Granny, what can I tell you? I love it here. I belong here." Harper waved an arm out toward the Cove. "Sea Breeze is a wonderful place and I *wanted* to buy it. I wanted to live here forever. I still do," she added wistfully. "It feels like home."

"And Greenfields Park? Don't you have affection for that place? Don't you feel it is your home?"

This was tender territory, and Harper didn't want to upset her grandmother. "Yes, of course I do. I have strong feelings for Greenfields Park because it's where you and Granddad live. Where I spent so much time growing up. But . . ." Harper looked at her grandmother, gauging her reaction.

Granny James sat as still as a cat but her eyes were watching Harper intently. "But . . ."

"But I don't feel like it's my home." Harper could only offer the truth.

"I see," Granny James said stoically. She looked at her hands.

There was a silent stretch. Harper heard the mournful creaking of wood as the dock moved with the tide, stretching tight the rope that bound it.

Granny James lifted her head and appeared ready for battle. "So you asked your mother for access to your trust fund."

"Right. A purchase offer for Sea Breeze arrived. I panicked. I'd run out of time. I had to buy now or lose Sea Breeze forever. The trust fund was my idea. You have to believe me. I wasn't asking for anything that wasn't mine. So, I gathered my courage, swallowed my pride, and called my mother."

"Why her? Why not me?"

"Because she is the executor of my trust fund. I asked her if I could get the principal of my trust fund early so that I could buy the house." Harper paused, feeling the bitterness well up inside her again at her mother's reaction. "I was naive to ask her for help. I don't know why I thought she'd respond as a mother. Concerned. Wanting me to be happy. You'd think I'd have learned by now."

Granny James didn't respond.

"You know what happened next. What always happens with Mummy when she doesn't get her way. She ranted and railed against me, Mamaw, and my father, and the whole Muir lineage. It was terrible. She threatened to cut me off if I didn't return to New York immediately. You know her well enough to know that she'd do it, too. I was distraught. Confused. I'm ashamed to admit I was a breath away from being the meek daughter and returning home at her command. As I always have. As she expected."

Granny James tilted her head, her eyes bright. "But you didn't."

"No." Harper smiled a bit, embarrassed. "I told her to take her money and shove it."

Granny James raised her brow.

"Then I got in my car and drove straight to see Taylor. It was instinctive. I knew I wanted to be with him. That I'd be safe with him." Harper paused and said with tenderness, "That's when he asked me to marry him."

"Now we're at the part that concerns me most."

"My getting married?"

"Of course. You're my only granddaughter." Granny shifted her weight, frowning. "Georgiana told me that this man is, to put it mildly, a gold digger."

Harper felt her blood begin to boil anew. "Is that all?" She smirked. "He wasn't giving me drugs, too?"

"Don't mock me. I've just flown thousands of miles across the ocean to—"

"To save me."

"Quite frankly, yes."

Harper saw that love in her grandmother's eyes and lowered her shoulders. "I love you, but I don't need saving."

Her grandmother sighed heavily. "I love you, too, dear. But the rest remains to be seen."

"Oh, please . . ." Harper put her face in her hands with a dramatic moan.

"Tell me. Does your young man, this Taylor McClellan"—Granny waited till Harper dropped her hands and was paying attention—"does he know about your trust fund?"

"Yes."

Granny James looked like the cat who ate the canary. "I see."

"I told him that I lost it when I decided to stay here. That I gave it all up."

"But you haven't lost it. You'll inherit when you turn thirty."

"I know that. Mummy told me. But Taylor does not."

"Ah."

"He asked a penniless, homeless girl to marry him." Harper's eyes suddenly filled with tears. "Oh, Granny, I've waited my whole life for this man. Someone who loved *me*." Harper brought her fist to her heart. "Without my bloody fortune."

"But you've only just met him."

"But we've had a connection since the moment we met."

"Oh, Harper . . ."

"Such things do happen, Granny," Harper insisted stubbornly.

A winsome smile spread across Granny's face, one laced with memory. "I know. But marriage is not to be taken lightly. One mustn't confuse love and lust with commitment. Love is a sprint. Marriage is a marathon. An endurance race, if you will."

"I know all that, Granny, I've dated many men."

"Please, spare me the details."

Harper laughed.

"But what about Howard Salisbury?" Granny James asked in the tone of a last-ditch effort. "He's such a nice young man. So handsome. And a peer! He's quite taken with you, asks after you all the time. I thought you two were quite an item."

"Howard is in love with Greenfields Park, not me."

Granny James frowned. "Don't be so sure. The Salisburys are a fine family."

"And so are the McClellans. Granny, I've always known I would marry for love. That I wouldn't settle." Harper patted her grandmother's hand in a manner that indicated the conversation was ending. "Why don't you wait to meet him and form your own opinion?"

"Indeed. I'd like to meet this young man."

"Super. Because he's coming for dinner tonight."

Chapter Twenty

It was a night for surprises.

Mamaw was dressed to the nines, as Edward had liked to say whenever she stepped out of her dressing room in a new gown and paraded for him like a runway model. It was a silly game, but one they'd both enjoyed.

She let her palm rest against the waist of the raspberry-colored silk gown that, like all her other gowns, held her so tight she could barely breathe. She inhaled, feeling the constricting cloth against her belly. Why did everything she ate seem to go directly to her belly?

She released her breath and let her gaze survey her sage-green dining room. A satisfied smile eased across her face. At least here everything was perfect. She'd outdone herself tonight. The long Sheraton table was draped with her finest Belgian linen. She'd polished her silver until it shone under the crystal chandelier like fallen stars. Penta, roses, and other flowers from Harper's garden were in low vases trimmed with leathery, dark Magnolia leaves. From the kitchen she heard the clatter of dishes as the caterer prepared their meal.

She rested her hands on the back of a Chippendale chair as memories of other dinner parties flitted through her mind. Back in the day, at her great house on East Bay, her parties were legendary in Charleston. She was reputed to be a favorite hostess south of Broad. She felt a flush of pleasure at the memory.

Far fewer parties had been held here at Sea Breeze. Her life had changed dramatically after Edward died. Goodness, she could count on one hand the number of parties she'd thrown here. The last was the previous May, when her granddaughters arrived to celebrate her eightieth birthday. She chuckled, remembering. What a night that had been! The laughter and secrets had flowed with the brut rose champagne.

Yes, she loved parties. Loved an excuse to throw one. She had to seize this moment while Sea Breeze was still in her hands for one last hurrah. Harper wanted to introduce her young man to her grandmother. And, she thought with a smile, she wanted to take this opportunity to introduce a gentleman friend of her own . . . Girard.

She glanced at her watch. He would be arriving soon. Straightening, she walked through the living room, smiling at her granddaughters, Taylor, Devlin, and Imogene as she passed to the foyer. There she stood by the front door, hidden from view, and waited, gathering her thoughts. It was perfectly normal for her to invite a dear friend to the dinner party, she told herself. Nothing to feel nervous about. Yet, pressing her palm flat against her jittery stomach, she felt just that. Like a young girl on her first date. The girls had all met Girard before, of course. But this was the first time she was bringing him into their home as an invited guest. The invitation implied more than neighborliness. She only hoped Dora would keep her tongue.

The doorbell rang, startling her. Taking a calming breath, Mamaw opened the door. The sight of Girard had her releasing the breath in a sigh. He looked especially handsome tonight, even debonair in his navy jacket and red tie. His blue eyes shone with warmth against his dark tan.

"Marietta," he said, handing her a bouquet of

roses and freesia. The scent rose up, heady and sweet. "You look beautiful tonight."

"Thank you, Girard. Please come in," she said nervously, and stepped aside.

Girard waited in the foyer until she closed the door. "It's been a very long time since I've been inside Sea Breeze. I've stared at the back of the house from my dock for years. I'd forgotten how charming this house is." He winked at her. "Like its mistress."

Mamaw felt a brush creeping up her neck. "You silly coot. Come, let me introduce you to my family. Before you turn my head."

When she stepped into the living room with Girard by her side, all talking ceased as heads turned their way. The girls stared back with obvious curiosity and surprise. Mamaw noticed Imogene's brow rise with interest as she sipped her drink.

"You remember Girard Bellows?" she asked the girls. "Our neighbor."

"Oh, you mean . . ." Dora, on the direct line of a freezing glare by Mamaw, cut her comment short. She'd been about to call him by Nate's nickname from earlier that summer, *Old Man Bellows*. Dora held out her hand and smoothly shifted to "You're the kind man who helped Nate with his fishing."

"How is that young man?" Girard asked.

"Very well, thank you. You'll see him at dinner."

"Good."

Carson and Devlin stepped up for an introduction, both on their best behavior. After a few polite queries, they stepped aside for Taylor and Harper.

"The guests of honor," Mamaw announced, ushering them closer. "Girard, my granddaughter, Harper, and her fiancé, Taylor." The word *fiancé* slipped easily from her lips, feeling right. She noticed, however, that Imogene stiffened slightly with disapproval at hearing the introduction.

Finally, Mamaw drew Girard toward Imogene, standing alone a few feet away, clutching her drink with both hands. Imogene was wrapped in a cocoon of midnight-blue silk that accentuated her well-kept figure. The diamonds in her ears and on her wrist shone like stars. Or small planets, Mamaw thought with distaste. Imogene looked up as they approached, her gaze settling on Girard.

"Imogene, I'd like you to meet my friend Girard Bellows."

Imogene smiled then, quite coquettishly. "The neighbor," she said. "But I do not detect a southern accent."

"Guilty as charged," Girard replied. "I'm from the North. Connecticut."

"Really?" Imogene said, her gaze appraising. "Charming."

A waitress in black pants and white shirt stepped closer to Mamaw. "There's a question for you in the kitchen."

"Thank you." She turned to Girard. "Excuse me a moment. Will you freshen Imogene's drink?"

While the final preparations for dinner were being readied, Granny James guided Taylor to the back porch, away from curious ears, for a private discussion. On this lovely night the humidity was low, the moon was high, and Imogene thought, glancing around the porch, that Marietta had been wise enough to set out those Tahitian-looking candles that kept the mosquitoes at bay.

Imogene sipped her vodka martini and studied the man standing across from her. He was handsome, to be sure. A tall, strapping young man who would turn any girl's head. He was neatly dressed in tan pants, an ironed shirt, and a navy-blue jacket. Though not well tailored, she noticed. Unquestionably off-the-rack. Unlike Dora's young man, who looked quite smart in his nicely tailored jacket and silk polo shirt. Still, that was hardly a condemnation of Taylor. And unlike the haircut on Dora's man, Taylor's head was shorn as a sheep.

She'd picked up a few details more important than his style of dress. He certainly wasn't skilled at making idle conversation, but then neither was Harper. But like Harper, he seemed to be bright enough—sharp minded and quick-witted. Imogene prided herself on being skilled at wheedling out important information from unsuspecting guests —their family ties, connections, and address (always a clue to status). Taylor was unabashedly open about all these things. There were no surprises.

Sadly, she thought as she took a bracing sip of her martini, he was just as Georgiana described. The son of a fisherman, a soldier . . . or rather, a Marine. He'd corrected her on that distinction. He had little money, lived with his parents, and was all around not a suitable candidate for her granddaughter. Though overall he seemed to be a nice young man.

A waitress with lavender hair came out on the porch to announce that dinner would be served in ten minutes' time.

Best to get started, then, Imogene thought with a sigh. She took a final swallow of her drink and handed the young woman her empty glass. The woman's arm was covered with tattoos. When she left, Imogene sniffed derisively, "I don't know how they can hire a woman with purple hair and tattoos to serve dinner. It's absolutely off-putting."

Taylor half smiled. "I don't think that will have any effect on her performance."

"Rather a bold comment, coming from an officer."

"How so?"

"I understand that tattoos are not permitted among officers in the military."

"In some branches of the service, that's true. But the lady in question is not in the military."

"Do you have a tattoo?"

"I do not."

Granny James nodded yes, as though proving her point. "Neither are you in service any longer."

"No, ma'am."

"We British always admire a man's sense of duty. The Prince of Wales served in the military service. As well as Prince Harry. If I'd had a son, I'd like to think he, too, would have done his duty." She paused. "I don't mean to be a nosey parker, but now, what is it you do?"

Though her tone was mildly insulting, intended to be, he answered with a composure that impressed her despite her best intentions. "I'm a project manager."

"Yes, but what does that mean, exactly?"

"I manage men."

Granny James narrowed her eyes. "Ah, like you did in the military, I suppose?"

"Yes."

"And do you enjoy this line of work?"

"I do."

"I imagine you're good at it." She thought he would be. His natural reticence and his strong-minded answers would serve well as a leader of men. He didn't prattle, a trait she found annoying in men. Every word he said was meant to be heard. "Do you also manage women well?"

"There are women who will work under me, yes."

"I meant in your private life."

He laughed at that and shifted his weight. "I don't think of it that way."

"What way would you think of it?"

His smile fell. "I don't think of it at all. I don't try to *manage* women."

"And yet"—Granny James arched a brow—"you seem to be managing my granddaughter quite well."

Taylor's brows furrowed in anger. Granny James licked her lips, glad to see that she'd at last gotten a rise out of him.

"If you think that I am managing Harper, then you don't know your granddaughter very well."

"Oh, I think I know her far better than you," she replied haughtily, then elucidated, "Harper is a people pleaser. She gives of herself, especially to those she loves."

Taylor crossed his arms and looked at Imogene steadily.

"My daughter, Harper's mother, I'm ashamed to say, is a narcissist. Her love of self and her career is paramount. She has little room for others in her life. Never has had, even as a child. Not even for her own child. She has railroaded that girl to fit her own mold since the day she was born. She used Harper's gentle, willing nature against her."

"*Abused,* don't you mean?"

Granny James scoffed. "Please. It was not all *that* unfortunate. She lived a life of privilege. Was well cared for. She was never abused."

"Neglect can be worse than physical abuse."

Granny James felt a shaft of shame shoot through her heart. "That's not true."

"It is true. As Harper would say, look it up."

Imogene was shaken and griped her fingers together. "Even if it is true, for all her selfish motives, Georgiana wants the best for her daughter. Harper has had every advantage. My husband and I, too, have seen to it that she will want for nothing."

"Perhaps nothing material. Things that money can buy. If you're referring to her trust fund, you do know that Harper already rejected that?"

"To marry you."

After a challenging silence, Taylor said, "Even before she agreed to one day be my wife, Harper chose her own path. It just happened to be the opposite of what her mother wanted for her."

"Her mother is a very strong, determined person. Rather, I think, like you." Imogene paused for effect. "You must know Harper has always let herself be controlled by Georgiana's will."

"Yes."

"Are you sure she's not doing the same with you?"

Taylor's face went very still, and Imogene knew her words had hit their mark. He paused, put his hands on his hips, and looked at his feet. When he lifted his head to speak, his words were measured. "I admit, I was worried about that."

Granny James appreciated his honesty. It surprised her, as few things did any longer.

Taylor narrowed his eyes as he looked at her. "The difference is, I love her."

He, too, hit his mark. "I believe you," Granny James said softly.

Taylor's face softened.

"However"—Granny James looked him squarely in the eye—"if you truly love her, you'll let her go. Harper has a brilliant mind. With her education, her connections, her experience and talent, she can rise to the top of her career. Yet you would keep her here? A big fish in a small pond?"

Taylor shifted his weight and clasped his hands behind his back. When a smile cracked his stern expression, Granny James was taken aback.

"I wonder how well you know Harper, after all. Not Harper the child, but the woman she is today. She is not one to be pushed around. That was at the crux of her argument with her mother. Georgiana ordered her to come back to New York. And Harper said no."

"And you told her to stay. And she said yes."

Taylor rubbed his jaw and laughed lightly. "She's not some trained animal who responds to *come* and *stay*. Give her some credit. She knows

402

her own mind. She came to the decision to stay here all on her own."

Imogene shrugged in the Gallic manner that implied *we'll see.*

"Mrs. James, are you aware that she doesn't want to be an editor?"

Imogene's eyes widened with surprise. "What?"

As though on cue, Harper came out on the porch, her face aglow with happiness. She wore a soft, strapless blush gown that swirled around her slender legs as she made her way across the porch to their sides.

"There you are!" she sang out, immediately linking arms with Taylor. Looking from Imogene to Taylor, she said, "Oh, my, such serious faces. Granny, are you giving my fiancé the third degree? Nails pulled out? Waterboarding? I should warn you, Taylor's a Marine. He's trained to withstand such treatment."

Taylor laughed and patted her hand on his arm. "Nothing I can't handle."

Granny James looked at Taylor shrewdly and said with a smile to reassure her granddaughter, "He handled himself quite well."

"We should go. We don't want to hold up dinner." Harper reached up on tiptoe to lightly kiss Taylor. "We're the guests of honor."

This was her favorite time of a dinner party, Mamaw thought satisfactorily as the catering staff cleared away the last of the plates. When the push of the meal was finished, the dishes were cleared away, and her guests were sated with good food and good wine. Many toasts had been offered tonight, and the conversation had been lively. Now they were ready to settle into brandy or coffee.

Mamaw leaned back in her chair and let her gaze wander from face to face. Girard, Dora, Nate, Taylor, Harper, Carson, Devlin. All of them dear. Her gaze fell on Imogene. Well, almost all, she amended. She wanted to always remember this night, like a photograph that she could bring out from time to time when the girls were gone and she was alone at the retirement home. Her girls were radiant tonight. Her summer girls, she thought with a smile. The dears were thoughtful and had all worn the pearls that she had given them the night of her party when they'd arrived at Sea Breeze in May.

Harper was wearing the triple-strand necklace of gleaming ivory pearls with the ruby-and-diamond clasp. They showed off her creamy complexion perfectly and punctuated the striking red color of her hair. The showy choker made Harper look like a queen tonight, as well she should on this occasion. Tonight was her night. Her face shone with joy and confidence. Mamaw had never before seen her so lovely.

Dora looked chic with her blond hair wound in

a French twist and the boat neck of her gorgeous scarlet dress. A perfect accompaniment to the opera-length strand of pearls that dripped down her voluptuous body. Marietta had worn that impressive strand at her wedding and had a special fondness for it. Thirty-six inches of perfectly matched pearls. Over the summer, Dora had gained a luster that was a match for them.

Mamaw's gaze rested last on Carson. She looked stunning in her burnished-gold dress that clung to her athletic body and contrasted dramatically with her deep tan. Carson was wearing the magnificent baroque-shaped South Seas black pearls that only a woman with a dramatic flair could carry off. Yet tonight, unlike her sisters, Carson behaved less like an exotic flower and more like a wallflower. She was present for the dinner, responded to questions, and laughed at the appropriate times. Yet her usual sharp humor and joie de vivre were gone. She'd refrained from drinking, but she'd spent most of dinner staring at the wineglasses. It worried Mamaw.

Her attention was brought back to her guests by a gasp of indignation from Imogene. Mamaw cringed. That woman had been nothing short of annoying all evening. Imogene had flirted shamelessly with Girard throughout dinner. Mamaw wouldn't be surprised if the brazen hussy had played footsie with him under the table.

Imogene drew herself up in her chair and glared

at Devlin across the table. "What do you mean, the monarchy has no relevance today? I'll have you know England has had a monarchy long before your country had a democracy, and we're doing quite well, thank you very much. We may be a small country but we have a proud history. The queen is beloved by her people."

Devlin shook his head with a laugh that rumbled low in his chest. "Hell, that's one mare that should be put out to pasture. When's she going to give her boy a chance? She's holding on to that scepter like a terrier with a bone."

Mamaw covered her laugh with a napkin. Not that she agreed with Devlin. She was fond of Queen Elizabeth, a contemporary. But Devlin was being a bit of a devil tonight, and didn't he know it. He was deliberately playing the good-ol'-boy card, dropping old southern expressions and exaggerating mannerisms, just to rile Imogene.

Imogene lifted her chin with hauteur. "Let me stop you before you mix any more metaphors. You Americans certainly know how to brutalize the English language."

Devlin guffawed, but others at the table took offense and began grumbling in dissent.

"I don't mean to be rude," Imogene said.

"Of course you do," Mamaw replied with a short laugh.

The two grandmothers' gazes clashed.

Carson leaned over to whisper to Harper,

pretending she was keeping score on a napkin. "Mamaw, four . . . Granny, three."

"If you'll excuse me"—Imogene lifted her napkin from her lap—"I've had a perfectly lovely evening. And this wasn't it."

Everyone at the table stopped speaking as Imogene walked out of the room in the manner of the queen they were just discussing.

Mamaw leaned over to Girard but said loud enough for all to hear, "That woman thinks the sun comes up just to hear her crow."

Nate, who had sat beside his mother and behaved like a perfect gentleman throughout the meal, saw his chance for an escape. "Can I go, too?"

"Yes, you may," Dora told him. "Thank you for being such a gentleman."

Harper rose to her feet and skewered Devlin with a glare. "I'm glad *someone* at this table was a gentleman."

"Oh, come on, Harper," Devlin said good-naturedly. "She was grilling us all night. I only gave back a little of what she was dishing out."

"Harper's right. She's a guest in this house, Devlin," Dora scolded.

"What does that make me?"

Dora caught Devlin's eye and tried to stop her smile. "Family."

Devlin sat back in his chair, eyes gleaming.

Harper looked to Mamaw. Her grandmother

sat erect in her chair across the table, eyes bright, deliberately silent.

Harper leaned close to Taylor at her right to whisper in his ear, "I'll be right back. I want to check on her."

"You sure you'll be all right? Want me to come with you?" She'd sensed a tension in him tonight, ever since his conversation with Granny James. During dinner she'd seen him glance at her grandmother a few times, as if he were scoping out the enemy.

"Heavens, no. I'll be right back." Setting her napkin on the table, Harper hurried to the kitchen after her grandmother.

The caterers were almost finished packing up the food and washing the dishes. The two women and one man, all dressed in black pants and white shirts, moved about the kitchen with focused intent, eager to finish the gig and get out as soon as they could. Granny James was standing at the counter, pouring herself a liberal glass of red wine. Seeing Harper, she reached for a clean glass and lifted it in the air, asking whether Harper would like one.

Harper nodded.

Granny filled the second glass, handed it to Harper, then reached for her own and lifted it high in the air. "That, my dear, is the big question of life. Do you see the glass half empty or half full?"

"Granny, what went on in there?" Harper demanded, feeling her temper spike.

Granny James glanced at the catering staff busy in the room. "Come outside a moment, dear. I could use some fresh air."

Harper glanced anxiously back toward the dining room, where the hum of voices could be heard. Reluctantly she followed her grandmother to the back porch. She didn't want to be rude and leave the party but needed a few words with her grandmother. Outside, the night was not much cooler.

"Granny, are you angry or upset?"

"Neither, darling. I just wanted a break."

"A break? From the performance you gave in there? I've never seen you act like that."

"Like what?" Granny took a sip of her wine.

"Like a bad stereotype of an upper-class British snob."

Granny laughed, almost spilling her wine. "Me, a stereotype? That's rich. What about that Devil fellow?"

"His name is Devlin."

"That man is going to marry your sister? Why, he's a . . . a redback."

Harper had to laugh. "You mean a *redneck.*"

"Either way." Granny waved her glass in the air.

"Granny, he was just playing with you." Harper sighed. "You made it so easy."

Granny James sipped her wine, then said in a

superior tone, "I was just playing with them."

"Were you just playing with Old Man Bellows, as well?" Harper asked smartly.

A sly smile crossed Granny James's lips. "You mean Girard?" she purred, exaggerating for a moment Mamaw's southern inflection.

"You know very well I mean Girard. You weren't exactly subtle with your flirting, Granny. I thought Mamaw was going to bust a gut."

Granny James laughed and smiled like the cat that ate the canary. "Yes, she was, wasn't she?"

"I suppose that was deliberate, too?"

"Of course. She can be so smug. It wasn't exactly work, though." Granny swirled her wine. "That Girard is certainly a handsome man."

Harper laughed at her grandmother's antics, even while trying to keep her features stern. She threw up her hands in frustration as she laughed. Suddenly her laughter shifted to tears.

Granny James set her wineglass down and placed her hands on Harper's arms. "What's the matter, darling?"

"You're what's the matter!" Harper dropped her hands, pouting like the little girl she didn't want to be seen as. Especially not tonight. Especially not in front of her grandmother. "I was so glad that you were here with me to share my engagement. But I'm afraid you've gone and ruined everything."

"I am sorry that you're hurt," Granny James

410

said gently, letting her hand rub Harper's arm consolingly. "And perhaps I did go too far." She paused and let her hands drop. "But I am not sorry that I gave your young man the grill, as you put it." She paused to pat her hair smooth. "You should know," she said, "he passed with flying colors."

Harper's head shot up. "He did?"

Granny James smiled. "I was hard on him. Asked the tough questions. That is my duty as your grandmother, after all."

"And?"

"He's a fine young man. Proud, confident. There's something about his presence that demands respect. Most of all, I believe he loves you very much. If he is your choice, my dear, I believe he deserves you. You have my blessing."

"Oh, Granny." Harper impulsively hugged her.

"My," Granny said, flustered by the hug, "you certainly have become quite affectionate."

"I have." Harper hiccuped, trying not to cry. "I'm a girl in love. And I love you, too."

Granny put her hand on Harper's cheek. "And I love you. Now let's return to the table before we get too maudlin, shall we? I promise to be on my best behavior. See?" Granny drained the rest of her wineglass. "The lion has turned into the lamb."

All chatter at the table stopped when Harper and Granny James strolled back into the dining room carrying a tray of champagne glasses, chocolates,

411

Marcona almonds, and a bottle of champagne. Harper and Granny James were all smiles.

At the table, Mamaw and Girard exchanged a glance. She looked around the table to see the others with equally puzzled expressions at the obvious change of mood. Still, she felt a huge relief that a peace had obviously been made.

"More champagne?" Mamaw said. "Dear me, I don't think I can drink any more."

"Just one more toast!" Granny James exclaimed, handing the bottle to Taylor. "Dear boy, do you think you could do the honors?" She arched her brow teasingly. "You certainly seem strong enough." As Taylor easily popped off the cork, Granny James exclaimed, "Delightful sound! My favorite."

Devlin winked at Dora.

Imogene began walking from person to person, gaily filling glasses with champagne.

"We've heard many toasts for the happy couple tonight," she began when she had finished making her rounds. She cast a pointed look at Devlin. "Some more colorful than others."

Devlin had the grace to laugh, and the ice was broken.

"But I've yet to make a toast."

Mamaw leaned forward in her seat. She saw Carson and Dora exchange a quick glance of worry.

Imogene paused a moment to smile dotingly on

Harper. "Harper is my only grandchild. I am not as fortunate as Marietta to have three such lovely granddaughters. So you'll forgive me, I hope, if I've been, shall we say, inquisitive?"

"The Grand Inquisition is more like it," Mamaw murmured.

A soft, if surprised, laughter of acknowledgment followed at the table. Relieved at the note of humor in Imogene's voice, Mamaw joined in.

"The news of the engagement was a surprise, as you can imagine," Imogene continued in a more serious tone. "Engaged! I hadn't even heard Harper mention the name Taylor McClellan. So I packed my bag and crossed the pond to see for myself if my only granddaughter's future was in safe hands." Imogene turned to Taylor.

Taylor looked back at her, sitting erect in his chair, shoulders back, poised like a cat about to pounce, Mamaw thought. If he had a tail, it'd be whipping back and forth.

"We had a little chat, Taylor and I." Imogene smiled warmly. "And indeed, her future is in good hands. Good, loving"—Granny smirked—"*strong* hands."

Taylor's shoulders visibly relaxed. He ventured a slight smile and turned to Harper, sitting beside him, for verification. Harper smiled knowingly and placed her hand over his.

"Taylor, speaking for Jeffrey and I, we welcome you to the family. A toast!" Imogene raised her glass higher. She was smiling now, whereas earlier she'd frowned. Radiant with joy. "To Harper and Taylor."

"Harper and Taylor," everyone at the table joined in, glasses raised.

The whole table dissolved into laughter as they touched their glasses together in celebration. Mamaw, amazed, puffed out the breath she'd been holding. She'd never forget the sound of the joyous peals of mirth blending with the clinking of crystal.

Girard moved closer, his wineglass held between him and Mamaw. She turned her head, her face inches from his. So much drama tonight, she thought, she'd practically ignored the poor man. Yet he'd handled it all with his usual grace and charm.

"Marietta," he said in a low voice so only she could hear him. He raised his glass. "To us."

Mamaw raised an eyebrow at him teasingly. "Don't you mean to you and Imogene?"

Girard let out a belly laugh. "No." His eyes flashed. "I most certainly do not."

Mamaw's heart skipped as she lifted her glass and, staring into his eyes, took a sip. Never, she thought, had champagne tasted so sweet.

Chapter Twenty-One

"Don't leave yet!" Harper called out to everyone. "I have one more surprise."

Devlin was half-risen from his chair, his napkin on the table. Others were following suit, but everyone sat back down at Harper's words, exchanging glances of anticipation.

Harper rose from her chair as the others returned to theirs. Then she took off down the hall at a fast clip.

Imogene returned to her chair to sit. She and Mamaw exchanged polite smiles.

Mamaw leaned closer to ask her, "Do you know what this is about?"

"Not a clue. I seem to be getting all the news secondhand."

During the wait, no one ventured to start conversation.

Devlin coughed and reached for the water.

Carson drummed her fingers on the table.

Dora reached for another chocolate.

Taylor looked down the hall for Harper. When he spotted her, her arms loaded with bundled paper, he leaped to his feet and went to her. Taylor lifted the burden from her arms and followed her into the dining room.

"Where do you want them?"

"You can set them right here." She tapped the table.

Piles of papers were bundled together with red ribbon. Taylor set them in two tall stacks, the focus of everyone's attention.

"Whatever is this?" Mamaw's eyes gleamed with anticipation.

Harper turned to Taylor, the only one who knew what was up. He asked, "Are you ready?"

"Ready as I'll ever be." Harper turned to the family, who were watching her expectantly.

"Don't keep us waiting." Dora leaned forward. "It's already late."

Harper cleared her throat and clasped her hands tightly. "Someone very wise once told me"—she looked at Taylor—"that sharing one's writing is to give a gift. Because you're giving a piece of your soul. Everyone here has given me gifts, none more precious than your love. This"— she placed her hand on a stack of manuscripts— "is my gift to you."

Harper looked at each face in the room, capturing the moment. "I've written a book."

There was a collective gasp.

"I knew it!" Dora turned to Carson. "I told you so! Didn't I?"

Carson smiled smugly. "I've already read it."

"What?" Dora said, immediately deflated.

Harper looked at Granny James. Her eyes were alert beneath raised brows. Clearly she had not seen this coming. She cast a questioning glance at Taylor. He met her gaze with an *I told you so* grin.

Mamaw was shocked. Harper thought she looked as if she'd just seen a ghost.

"Do you want me to pass them out?" Taylor asked in a low voice.

Harper licked her lips, feeling parched, and nodded. She grabbed two off the top of the stack and went directly to Mamaw.

"I told you I'd let you read it someday," Harper said quietly.

Mamaw slowly took the manuscript in her hands. They were trembling.

Harper moved on to personally deliver a manuscript to Granny James.

"Is this what you've been up to? Your newfound passion?" Granny James gently teased.

"Yes." Harper looked into her eyes without guile.

Granny James accepted the manuscript solemnly, letting her fingers stroke the top. "I'm impressed. Profoundly so."

"I don't know how good it is"—Harper backtracked, walking quickly to Taylor's side—"but it's finished. Beginning, middle, and end."

Taylor reached out and slipped his arm around her protectively.

Mamaw held the manuscript in her hands and stared at Harper. She looked as if she'd suddenly aged. Her face was pale and her blue eyes were dull, clouded by memories. Harper knew she was thinking of her son, their father, Parker. Harper looked at Carson and Dora, but they, too, had their gazes set on Mamaw.

Mamaw put the manuscript on the table and with two fingertips delicately untied the red ribbon.

Granny James rose, the manuscript clutched to her chest. "I'm going to say good night. It was a lovely evening. A fine celebration. Thank you all. But"—she gave a quick smile, her eyes on her granddaughter—"I've got some reading to do."

Mamaw looked up, oblivious to Granny James's departure. Her eyes were round with stunned surprise. "Harper! The title!"

Harper released a short laugh. "What else could I call it?"

Mamaw's lips trembled as a million memories flitted across her face. *"The Summer Girls."*

Later that evening, after the party had disbanded and the attendees had all found their way to their beds, Carson slipped to the kitchen for a cup of tea. The undercabinet lights dimly lit the room and guided her path in the dark hall. Entering, she was surprised to find Mamaw there, standing by the teakettle as it simmered on the flame.

"You're still up?"

"Of course," Mamaw said. "I doubt anyone is sleeping. We're all reading."

Carson crossed the room to fetch a cup

from the cabinet. "Where are you in the book?"

"Not far. I'm savoring every word. I'm at the part where you and Harper are playing pirates, climbing the hill at Fort Moultrie. I never knew you entered those dark dungeons. I'd have forbidden it."

Carson set her cup on the counter beside Mamaw's cup. "That's why we didn't tell you."

The water came to a boil, sending the teakettle whistling. Mamaw lifted the kettle from the heat while Carson selected a tea bag from the open box of chamomile tea on the counter. Mamaw filled the cups with steaming water. Instantly the sweet scent of the tea filled the room.

"She's really exceptional." Mamaw set the kettle back on the stove.

"Yes, she is."

"I was terrified to begin. Afraid I wouldn't like it."

"Me, too. What a relief, huh?"

Mamaw laughed shortly. "Yes."

Carson grabbed two spoons from the drawer, then pulled honey out from the lazy Susan. She carefully scooped a teaspoonful of honey from the jar and transferred it to her steaming cup, then passed the honey to Mamaw.

"So, it looks like someone in the family got Daddy's gene for writing."

Mamaw's spoon made soft clinking noises as she stirred. "So it seems."

"Dear Daddy. I got his gene for alcoholism. Gee, thanks, Dad."

Mamaw set the teaspoon down on the counter, moving it slightly to set it straight. "Are you all right with all of this fuss over Harper?"

"Yes," Carson replied honestly and without hesitation. "I'm happy for her. It's her turn."

"But it does shine a light on your own darkness. Is that it?"

"I guess so." Carson lifted her teacup with two hands, relishing the warmth that seeped into her palms.

"My dear"—Mamaw set down her cup—"confide in your old grandmother."

Carson sighed. "I'm always talking about my problems. I'm tired of listening to myself."

"I'm not the least tired."

Carson cast a grateful smile Mamaw's way. "It's just . . ."

"Just what?"

"I was sitting at the table tonight, looking around at all the happy faces. Harper and Taylor, Dora and Devlin. Even you and Girard!"

Mamaw lifted a corner of her mouth ruefully. "All couples."

"Yeah. And then there's me. Poor Carson. All alone. Again."

"That was your choice."

"I know, I know. . . ." Carson sighed heavily. "I'm so good at messing up my life."

"You're also good at living life to the fullest. My darling, you cannot live fully and not sometimes get hurt. Your capacity for love equals your capacity for pain."

"That's why I don't want a relationship. It hurts too much. I hurt them too much." Carson shook her head decisively. "It's not worth it."

"Then what is your choice? To armor yourself against love? To lock yourself indoors?" Mamaw reached out to place her hand on Carson's arm. "Carson, that isn't *you*."

"Maybe it should be."

Mamaw picked up her cup and, closing her eyes, took a bracing sip. When she set the cup down, she crossed her arms in front of her. "Remember back to last May. When that shark frightened you. You were terrified to go back into the water. Do you remember how miserable you were? You felt cut off from what gave you the most joy. But then you found Delphine. Her greatest lesson to you was to remind you how to live in the present. To laugh. To dive headfirst into the water without fear."

"And she got hurt."

"*And* she got well."

Carson frowned and looked at her tea.

"In all my years I've made many plans." Mamaw laughed at herself. "As you know. I've learned that my priorities often shift as time goes by, and I have to adjust my plans accordingly."

She shook her head with both resignation and humor. "Life is full of surprises. And timing . . . people always underestimate how important good timing is."

She paused and gazed off a moment. In the dim light, with her wistful expression, Carson caught a glimpse of how Mamaw must have looked when she was a young woman making those plans. Her profile so elegant. Her expression so full of intelligence and purpose and personality. Carson saw her father's profile. Her own profile.

Mamaw turned back with a wry smile. "Allow me to share this one piece of advice. Welcome change. Accept the good and the bad. Your triumphs and your mistakes. There will be plenty of both in your life, I assure you. It's all part of the process. The secret to happiness is to embrace the humility to accept what comes and the courage to continue on your life's path with an open heart."

Carson leaned against the counter and thought of the shark again. "Moving forward."

"Yes, dear." Mamaw leaned forward to place a gentle kiss on Carson's forehead. Then Mamaw straightened and took hold of her cup of tea. "I think we've had enough conversation for one night. I'm taking my hot tea and saying good night." She wagged her brows. "I'm off to read."

Later, Carson lay on her bed, her hands behind her head and ankles crossed, staring up at the elaborately framed portrait of her ancestor Claire Muir.

Mamaw had hung the portrait in Carson's bedroom when she was an adolescent in her ugly-duckling stage. She'd desperately wanted to be the blond-haired, fair-skinned southern belle her sister Dora was. Mamaw had told Carson the fabled story of how Claire had brazenly broken with her family to marry the famous Gentleman Pirate. Their love story was legendary. Since then, whenever Carson had felt insecure or troubled, she'd gazed at the portrait of the beautiful woman with the raven hair and brilliant blue eyes and found solace, clarity, and inspiration.

As Carson stared at the portrait now, she wondered how Claire had acquired her fierce courage and independence. Carson brought to mind Mamaw's words: *The secret to happiness is to embrace the humility to accept what comes and the courage to continue on your life's path with an open heart.*

"Grandmother Claire," Carson whispered, "give me strength."

Carson pulled herself into a sitting position and sat cross-legged on her bed. In AA she had learned that she had to examine her past mistakes. To ask for forgiveness for these errors. She lifted her phone and in her contacts found the number she was looking for. After punching the CALL button, she took a deep breath.

A man's voice answered, "Hello?"

For a moment, Carson froze. Then she blurted out, "Hello. Is this Jason Kowalski?"

"Yes." The voice sounded impatient, as though he'd regretted answering the phone. "Who's this?"

"This is Carson Muir. I hope I'm not bothering you."

"Carson Muir?" The question in his tone indicated he didn't remember who she was.

"Yes. I was the stills photographer on your film *Aimless.* You fired me."

There was a pause, then a wary ". . . Oh, yes."

"I won't take much of your time. You see, I joined AA recently, and part of the program is for me to make amends. I'm calling to apologize to you for getting drunk during the shooting of your film. I know I caused delays. It was unprofessional and I'm very sorry." She took a breath. "That's all. Thank you for listening."

"Wait. You said you joined AA?"

Carson hesitated. "Yes."

"How long has it been since you've had a drink?"

"Three months."

"Good start."

"Thanks."

He coughed. "I'm in AA myself."

"Oh?" She held her breath.

After a pause, Mr. Kowalski cleared his throat. "Listen, you do good work. When you're sober," he qualified. "If you're interested, I might have a job for you."

Chapter Twenty-Two

Morning came softly to Sea Breeze. The women slept in, all thoroughly tuckered out from the events of the previous evening.

Harper rose slowly, yawning loudly as she squinted against the sunlight, bright and piercing, pushing through the seams of the closed shutters. It was a late-morning sun, Harper thought, but for the first time in months she didn't feel the urge to leap out of bed.

She would not run today, she decided. She'd had too much to drink last night, too much excitement, and, she recalled, stretching luxuriously like a sated kitten, too much kissing. Harper rubbed her face with her palms, yawned again, and rose slowly. The room spun a bit so she sat on the edge of her bed, waiting for equilibrium.

"Water," she murmured through parched lips. "I need lots and lots of water."

She rose and went to her desk to finish off a half-empty glass of water. Her mouth moistened, she opened the sliding door that separated her room from Mamaw's, heading for the kitchen.

She stopped suddenly, seeing Mamaw sitting in her bed.

"Oh, excuse me!" Harper exclaimed, embarrassed for having invaded her grandmother's privacy. Ever since Mamaw had transformed her sitting room into a private bedroom for Harper, she'd been exceedingly careful not to invade Mamaw's space. Harper usually left her room early in the morning through her door to the porch, and even then she often found Mamaw already making coffee in the kitchen. It was highly unusual for Mamaw to be in bed so late.

Harper began to duck out of the room, closing the sliding door.

"Wait, Harper!"

Harper stilled.

"I've been waiting for you to wake up. Come here, child." Mamaw held out her arms.

Harper smiled and scrambled to the large four-poster bed. She crawled across the bed to cuddle against Mamaw's chest as she had as a little girl. Soon she was enveloped in Mamaw's arms, inhaling her signature scent. "I didn't mean to wake you."

"You didn't. I read till very late. Then slept like Rip Van Winkle. I had the best dreams." Mamaw bent her head to kiss the top of Harper's head. "All of my summer girls."

Harper had promised herself she wouldn't ask, but she couldn't stop herself. She tilted her head up to meet Mamaw's gaze. "Did you like it?"

Mamaw's smile was like the sun coming out, resplendent and inspiring. "Oh, very much. I loved it."

Harper blew out the puff of air that she'd been holding and beamed. Mamaw's opinion meant the world to her. "I want to thank you."

"Me? Whatever for?"

"For encouraging me. For believing in me when I didn't believe in myself."

"Oh, my dear . . ."

"I was very worried about you."

"Worried about me? But why?"

"You looked unsettled last night when I gave you my book."

Mamaw's expression shifted from confused to knowing. "I admit, I knew a moment of sadness. Not because you wrote your book," she hurried to assure Harper, "but because for all his dreams, Parker never could manage to do that." Mamaw paused and said softly, "I would have liked to see him finish his book. Maybe not publish it, but at least to have had the satisfaction of seeing his project through to completion. To write *The End,* as it were. But I suppose that was his weakness. And it is rather sad, isn't it?"

Harper nodded against her grandmother's chest. "Maybe not his weakness," she mused after a short while. "Maybe his fear. After so many years spent talking the book up, claiming to be writing, taking your money . . . he set the bar pretty high. He boasted he was writing the Great American Novel, after all." Harper laughed sadly. "Who can live up to those expectations? I suspect he figured he'd rather fail by not finishing than finish and have his book fail. Because that would have meant the end of his dream. He was afraid that he'd never had the talent after all. I know that fear. It takes a lot of courage to see the book through. And even more to let someone else read it."

"You're a brave girl."

"I don't know about that. I was shaking in my boots last night. Daddy's reputation preceded me."

Mamaw sighed sadly. "Oh, Harper. Don't be ashamed of him."

"No, not ashamed," she hurried to answer. "But, all my life I lived with his name being the source of jokes in my family. So to tell my mother, or, by association, Granny James, that I was writing a book . . . I shudder to even think of what they might have said. I had to keep it a secret from them, and eventually it became so I couldn't talk to anyone about it. Not even you, Mamaw. At least not until I knew I could finish it. Given Daddy's history, I had to accomplish that much." Harper nestled closer to her grandmother.

"I had no idea."

"You couldn't have. I didn't tell you." Harper paused as Taylor's face came to mind. "I couldn't have done it without Taylor. He helped me to overcome my fears."

"He is a courageous man. A warrior."

"Yes, but I don't mean that kind of courage. He risked his own skin in battle and was injured." Harper looked up at Mamaw's face. "But he says that was the easy part." She laughed at seeing Mamaw's surprised expression. That had been her own reaction when Taylor had told her that. "Taylor taught me that real courage is belief in yourself. To face and defeat your fear, or be defeated by it."

Mamaw stilled and looked out the window. She said softly, "I understand that kind of courage."

"I know you do," Harper replied, thinking of all Mamaw's losses. To lose someone you love, especially your own child, Harper imagined, required great courage.

"You know," Mamaw said, "the word *courage* comes from the French root *coeur*, which means 'heart.' You, Harper, have great heart."

"Whatever happened to his book?" she asked suddenly. "Is it upstairs in the attic? In one of those boxes?"

Mamaw shook her head. "He destroyed it," she said sadly. "Parker destroyed everything he ever wrote. Even his letters. There's nothing left."

"That's tragic." Harper felt the loss deeply. "And selfish. I would have loved to read his writings."

"Perhaps it was selfish. I read some of his early

work. Let's just say Parker did not respond well to criticism. And, perhaps, having failed, he didn't want his work to be criticized posthumously." Harper felt her grandmother's shoulders shrug under her head. "It was his choice. But"—Mamaw stroked Harper's hair—"his spirit is alive in you. And I know that he would be very proud of you. As am I."

Harper's heart swelled. "And I am proud that I'm like him."

"Yes"—Mamaw sighed—"except, my dear"—she kissed Harper's head again—"*you* have a gift that was missing in your father. Determination."

Mamaw fanned her face as she sat in her favorite place in the shade under the black-and-white awning of her back porch. It was late afternoon, yet waves of shimmering heat still hovered over the water. Lord, she wasn't complaining, she thought. It was September and the weather in the tropics was calm without a threat in sight. She'd take the heat any day over a storm front. Still, she thought, reaching for her glass of iced tea, this summer was ranking as one of the South's ten hottest on record, all those just since 1998. That, and the increasing number of manatees she was seeing in the Cove, convinced her the earth's climate was changing.

"Lord, Lord, Lord, it's hot," she said again, then took a sip of tea, smacking her lips. That was good, she thought. Setting the glass on the table, she surveyed the playing cards laid out before her in a game of solitaire. Despite the heat, she was most comfortable out here in the shade where the occasional breeze brought relief. She couldn't bear to be cooped up indoors like a hen in a henhouse.

"Halloo! Marietta!"

She turned her head to see a woman walking around the side of the house. She squinted to be sure she was seeing straight. Yes, it was Imogene, but for a moment she thought it might be one of the girls. Imogene was wearing gray jogging pants with a racing stripe down the sides and a thin running shirt, the kind that Harper wore. Under her floppy hat, her black sunglasses were large and her face was pink. That woman looked rode hard and put up wet.

"It's beastly hot today," Imogene exclaimed as she drew near.

Marietta removed her sunglasses and asked with veiled criticism, "You were running? In this weather?"

"No." Imogene's tone implied she was not that silly. "Walking." She was breathing heavily from exertion. "I've been walking for hours. I just love the beach," she said with vigor. "And," she begrudgingly acknowledged, "this is a particularly lovely stretch of sand. Crikey! I almost fainted when a cargo ship passed."

Marietta reached for a fresh glass on the tray and poured tea from the thermos she kept nearby. She handed it to Imogene. "You look parched."

"What is it?"

"Iced tea."

"Oh, perfect. Thank you." Imogene took a big swallow and scrunched her face. "It's so sweet!"

"Of course it is. It's sweet tea. That's how we drink it here."

"Do you have any unsweetened tea?"

"No. Not made. Would you care for some water instead?"

"Don't trouble yourself." Imogene sighed with resignation, then took another swallow. She licked her lips and looked at the glass with curiosity. "What's in this? It's actually rather good."

Marietta smiled and reached for her own glass. "I made it myself from an old family recipe. It's as sweet as a baby's kiss."

Imogene set the glass down on the table along with her beach bag. Marietta watched with shock as Imogene began stripping off her damp shirt and pants. Underneath, she was wearing a swimsuit. The modest navy one-piece suit nonetheless revealed her slim figure. She was small boned, like Harper, and fit for a woman her age. Imogene was fit for a woman of any age, she thought with chagrin. Marietta smoothed her tunic self-consciously, glad Girard wasn't here to witness the spectacle.

"I'm going for a quick dip to cool off." Imogene strolled down the steps to the lower deck. She stood at the edge of the pool, arched her arms over her head, and with a buoyant spring dove into the water. Marietta knew a moment of envy watching Imogene stroke across the length of the pool with vigor. Back and forth she swam, kicking her legs, clearly enjoying herself. When she was done, she emerged from the pool as sleek as a seal.

"Bless her heart," Marietta murmured, and took another long swallow of tea.

"That's much better," Imogene exclaimed when she returned to the shade of the upper deck. She slicked back her auburn hair from her face, then grabbed a beach towel from her bag. After shaking off the sand from it, she rubbed her body vigorously. Wrapping the towel around her shoulders, she took a seat beside Marietta.

"May I?" Imogene lifted the thermos.

"Help yourself." With a smile playing at her lips Marietta watched her pour another glass of tea. "Swim much, do you?"

"Every day. In the season, that is. I try to get to Georgiana's house in the Hamptons in the spring when it's still nasty in England. The water there is still nippy, but I grew up spending summers at my family's summer house in Cornwall, so I'm accustomed to a bracing dip in icy water." Imogene looked to the pool. "Your pool water feels rather like a bathtub. Not very refreshing."

That woman could start an argument in an empty room, Marietta thought. She answered cordially, "Here, the sun is a natural pool heater. I like it warm."

"Hmmm." Imogene settled into her chair. "Where is everyone?"

"Out."

"Harper, too?" She sipped her tea.

Marietta's sunglasses hid her roll of the eyes. "Yes, Harper, too. She went with Dora to help hang curtains in her new house. She'll be moving in next week. The first to go." She gave a long sigh. "And Carson is taking water samples from the Cove in preparation for Delphine's release."

"Delphine, that's the dolphin she befriended. The one that was injured?"

"Glad to see you're getting your stories straight."

"Well, there are so many." Imogene sipped her tea.

"We are nothing if not interesting. And we're all aflutter for the dolphin's release, coming up any day now. Maybe you'll *still* be here to witness it with us."

"Perhaps." Then, as if a veil were removed, Imogene's face drooped. She shook her head slowly. "I don't know how much longer I dare stay. I'm afraid I must leave soon. Jeffrey doesn't do well when I am gone."

Mamaw was alert to the change in tone. "Is your husband ill?"

"Not in the usual sense. He has Alzheimer's."

"Oh, I am sorry," Mamaw said sincerely.

"Yes, well . . ." Imogene's face reflected a troubled heart. She placed her sunglasses on, then just as quickly took them off again. "He's had the diagnosis for several years. We've managed through the early stages well enough. He was forgetful, occasionally would mix up dates. That sort of thing. Then, two years ago, things took a turn. Now he's confused, he can't complete tasks, he wanders with a dazed look in his eyes." She brought her hand to her forehead. "He can't read," she said emotionally. "It's heartbreaking to watch. Jeffrey had a brilliant mind and was an avid reader. Books were his life. Now"—Imogene sighed and dropped her arm—"he forgets what he's read. Reads the same book over and over without, I fear, comprehending. Even his speech . . ."

Mamaw thought that Imogene was beginning to slur her speech.

Imogene continued, leaning closer. "He repeats things. Or blurts out the strangest comments. Travel is out of the question. He gets lost at Greenfields Park. He could never navigate a strange area. And, he gets far too agitated away from home." She paused, collecting herself. "Forgive me. I don't know what's come over me.

Must be the heat. I didn't mean to go on and on."

"Don't apologize," Marietta said, feeling expansive. "Sometimes we need to let our thoughts out or it feels like we'll burst."

"It does, doesn't it. I haven't been out much lately. Jeffrey and all."

"It must be very difficult."

"It is." Imogene sniffed. "Jeffrey was always my rock. And now . . ."

"I do understand." Marietta felt a bit teary herself. "Edward and I had such plans for when he retired. And then he passed. Heart attack."

"I don't know which is harder to bear. A quick death or watching one dwindle."

Marietta took a long drink of her tea, reflecting on that point. "I really don't know. Do you have help?"

Imogene nodded. "I have a nurse come by daily. And someone stays with him when I'm away, of course. But it's not the same as when I'm there. I calm him. As much as I'd like to stay, I must return."

"Of course." Mamaw patted Imogene's hand comfortingly.

"I had dreams that Harper would return with me." Imogene's smile was wistful. "It would have been comforting to have her with me now. It gets quite lonely rattling around alone in that big house. I'd hoped she'd eventually take over the estate. I wanted her to love Greenfields Park like she does Sea Breeze. But I think we both know the answer to that, don't we?" Imogene took another long sip of tea.

Marietta followed suit, sipping her tea and reserving comment.

"Selfish of me, I realize that now," Imogene continued. "She's her own person. Capable of making her own decisions. For me to force the responsibilities of Greenfields Park on her by virtue of guilt would be to take advantage of her willing nature. I wouldn't want to do that to her." Imogene brought her hand to her heart and her voice cracked. "I love Harper far too much to burden her in that way."

Marietta felt her heart soften toward the woman and refreshed both of their glasses.

"This tea is growing on me with every sip. It has a bit of kick. What exactly is your secret ingredient?"

Marietta smiled mischievously. "Rum."

"I knew there was something about it I liked." Imogene laughed, then hiccuped. "Goodness, I'm feeling a bit tipsy."

"I'm afraid we're both stewed."

Imogene looked at Marietta and smiled ruefully. "You know, when I came here, I was prepared to dislike you. I thought you were trying to unload your burden of your house on Harper's shoulders."

"Like you."

Imogene shrugged and wagged a finger, the

alcohol clearly taking effect. "I wasn't going to let you get away with that." She shrugged again. "I see now that I was mistaken. Harper's made her choice. She wants to live here."

"What will become of Greenfields Park?"

"The writing is on the wall. Like you, Marietta, I've come to the realization that I can no longer manage it." Imogene put her face in her palm. "As I must face the decision that I can no longer manage Jeffrey at home." She dropped her palm. "When I get back, I shall have to find a suitable facility for him." She was having a difficult time with her sibilant consonants. "And once I do . . ." She paused. "I guess I'll have to find a place for myself as well. It's time for me to move on." She made a sailing motion with her hand.

Marietta laughed and raised her glass. "Here's to the future."

The two women clinked glasses.

Marietta asked the question that had been niggling at her since Imogene's arrival. "What about your daughter? Doesn't she want the estate?"

"Georgiana? Good God, no. The last thing she wants is to be burdened by the responsibilities of Greenfields Park. Georgiana is all about her career."

"Isn't there some uncle or nephew?"

"To do what?"

"To take over. You know. Inherit."

Imogene tilted her head in thought. "Are you under the impression that Greenfields Park is a family estate? Generations of Jameses and all that?"

"Well, isn't it?"

Imogene laughed, high and trill. Mamaw couldn't help but laugh with her.

"No, not atall," she said with affection, "Jeffrey and I bought the estate. And now"—Imogene raised her hands—"we'll sell it." She leaned forward and waved Marietta closer as one telling a secret. "For a tidy profit, too." Nodding, Imogene leaned back in her seat. "I'll be glad to be rid of it. I want to travel."

"Do you?" Marietta leaned forward. "So do I!"

"Bora-Bora," they said in unison.

Both women smiled and again clinked their glasses together.

Imogene smiled. "I think we're going to be great friends."

"I do, too. We're a lot alike in some ways. We're both from another era," Marietta said pensively.

"So true. These young women don't want to be saddled with large estates that demand all their time and attention. Besides, who can afford to maintain them?"

"Exactly."

"Life seemed simpler when we were young," Imogene said. "Though I admit, I've relaxed since I've been here. There's something sultry and seductive about this place."

"It's the magic of the lowcountry. And the rum," Marietta added conspiratorially.

Both women laughed.

Imogene picked up Marietta's fan. "May I?"

"Please." Marietta gestured.

Imogene began fanning lazily. "You know, it's a wonderful thing you've done for your granddaughters. Bringing them all here to spend this time together. I can see how close they are. They're really quite devoted to one another."

Marietta's breath caught at the power of that statement. "You can't know what that means to me to hear you say that. I was acting purely on instinct. The girls had drifted so far apart. Not only in geography, but in their communication with one another. They'd become little more than strangers."

"It happens in families. More often than not."

"Then it's up to us to fix that. I've been accused of being controlling, of being a manipulator . . . more often by Harper, I might add. Truth be told, I didn't know what I was doing. But I had to do something. Felt it in every fiber of my being. Sea Breeze had to be sold. I couldn't change that. But even if my girls didn't have Sea Breeze, I wanted them to have each other."

"You're a wonderful grandmother." Imogene hiccuped.

Marietta removed her sunglasses and dabbed at her eyes with a paper napkin. "But I was not a wonderful mother. You met my son, Parker, didn't you?"

"Once. They were married and divorced so fast, you know. A handsome man."

"He was, wasn't he?" Mamaw felt a twinge in her heart. "I mollycoddled him. The doctors today have a fancy new term for mothers like me. *Enablers.*"

Imogene scoffed and waved her hand dismissively. "Bollocks! Don't they just love to blame the mother. They said that about me, too. With Georgiana."

"Really?"

"Indeed they did. Enable? Pshaw." Imogene again waved her hand. "I'm ashamed to admit, I hardly knew what the girl was doing most of the time."

Marietta burst out laughing, then covered her mouth. "Sorry."

"But it was the way we were raised. Children were seen and not heard, eh? I had a nanny for Georgiana, as Georgiana had for Harper. Of course," Imogene said defensively, "I oversaw all things that concerned my daughter. Directly."

"Well, you're a wonderful grandmother, too." Marietta again patted Imogene's hand.

"I am," Imogene staunchly agreed. "Harper is so easy to love."

Marietta returned a watery smile. "She is."

"What's going to happen to them, do you think? Harper and Taylor. Can he provide for her?"

"I believe he can. Not, perhaps, in the style she was raised, but comfortably. And more important, happily."

"She truly loves this place, doesn't she?" Imogene's gaze traveled across the Cove, then to the house. "This Sea Breeze."

"Yes, she does."

"And it's a family home? Generations and all?" Imogene asked, referring to the question Marietta had asked earlier.

"Yes. Ask me sometime to tell you the story of the founding member of our family in Charleston."

"The pirate, you mean?"

Marietta laughed lightly and wagged her brows. "Indeed."

Imogene laughed, fanning herself rapidly.

They fell into a comfortable silence, each lost in her own thoughts.

"Have you sold the house?"

Marietta shook her head. "Not yet. We're in negotiations. In all honesty I'm dragging my feet. Devlin tells me sooner or later I have to bite the bullet and just accept an offer. They're all what he refers to as 'good.' "

"Dora's Devlin? *He's* your real estate agent?"

"Yes."

"Good God, Marietta, you're putting your fortune in the hands of that redback?"

Marietta's laugh was hearty. "Don't let his good-ol'-boy mannerisms fool you. That boy is as sly as a fox in the henhouse when it comes to business."

Imogene shifted the towel on her shoulders and didn't appear convinced. "So, the house is still for sale?"

Marietta had been bringing her glass to her mouth, but her hand stilled midair because of something in the way Imogene had asked that question.

Imogene removed her sunglasses and gave Marietta a look laden with import.

Marietta lowered the glass and straightened in her chair. "It is."

"I see." Imogene folded the fan in her hand with a snap. "Don't sell it."

"Oh? And why not?"

"I'd like to buy it. Or rather, Harper will buy it."

"Harper?"

"Eventually. I have to work out a few details yet. I will consult with my lawyers when I get back to England. But if this is what my granddaughter wants, enough that she is willing to throw away her fortune if she can't have it, then I will move a few mountains to make it happen."

Mamaw drew a deep breath, a small flutter of

hope in her chest. "But, Imogene, are you sure you want to sell Greenfields Park? To help Harper buy Sea Breeze?"

"Don't be balmy. I don't need to sell Greenfields Park. Let's just say that Harper will be borrowing the money from me until she's thirty. She can repay me when she comes into her trust fund."

"I thought . . ." Marietta paused, confused. "I thought Georgiana said she would stop Harper from inheriting."

"Oh, please," Imogene said with exaggeration. "You don't think for a moment I'd allow Georgiana to be the executor of Harper's trust fund?"

"That's what she told Harper."

"Of course it is. Georgiana always manipulates the truth to suit her. But it is not true. I am the executor, and not only will Harper inherit her fortune at thirty, she will continue to receive her monthly payments until that time. Georgiana has nothing whatsoever to do with it."

Marietta burst out laughing and grabbed her glass and raised it. "Brava, Imogene!"

Imogene met her glass and they clinked a third time.

While Marietta refilled their glasses, Imogene looked at the cards spread out on the table. "Playing solitaire, I see?"

Marietta handed Imogene the glass filled to the brim. "Yes. It's my state of affairs lately."

"Girard doesn't play cards?"

"No, not really. Poker with the boys from time to time. That's not my game." Marietta looked slyly at Imogene and reached for the cards. "Do you play cards?"

"I adore cards."

Marietta's heart beat faster. She began to shuffle. "What's your game?"

"Cribbage. Do you know it?"

"No, sorry."

"How about gin rummy? That's a popular American game, I believe."

Marietta grinned from ear to ear, and her opinion of Imogene reached new heights. "I do indeed. Care for a game?"

Imogene moved her chair closer to the table. "Deal."

Chapter Twenty-Three

Carson stood at the end of the boat ramp that slanted down into the Cove. For the past several days Sea Breeze had been a beehive of activity. Everyone was busy, buzzing around in individual circles as the summer was coming to an end. Carson had spent her days preparing for Delphine's release. Dora was driving back and forth from Summerville, packing up boxes for her move to the cottage. Harper and Granny

James were spending mornings together walking the beach and talking, and afternoons in consultation with lawyers and financial advisers both in the United States and abroad. In the evenings, however, Granny James and Mamaw sat together on the back porch, heads together in conversation as they played cards.

Not until the end of the week did one event bring all of them together. To no one's surprise the agent of their gathering was Delphine.

NOAA had decided to release Delphine today at this boat landing on Sullivan's Island. Carson looked up at the sky. It was a good day for a release, the sky being overcast with a brisk breeze, but no sign of rain.

Looking out across the expanse of water she loved, Carson could detect early signs of summer's end. The thick patches of sea grass were tipped in gold, and she felt deep in her bones the subtle shift in the air that signaled change.

Closer in, the wind was blowing the flags on the pole: the stars and stripes of the American flag and the blue crescent moon and palmetto of the South Carolina flag. She'd always thought it was the prettiest of the state flags. Despite her having spent a large chunk of her life in California, seeing it meant home. Farther down the boat ramp she spied the metal signs alerting visitors and fisher-men: WARNING DO NOT FEED WILD DOLPHINS! Signs that Blake and his team at

NOAA had put up. There were also a few fishing-line disposal bins.

One thing was for sure, she thought, looking out over the Cove where dozens of dolphins roamed. She'd never feed a wild dolphin or any wild animal again.

The water rippled in the wind and lifted wisps of her hair. Lifting her chin, she felt hope. Soon Delphine would again be swimming free in the Cove. Today was a celebration. It was also Carson's greatest test. She'd promised to stay away from Delphine. To never again call her to the dock with thumping the wood or a whistle. Or to feed her or swim with her or in any way engage her.

Carson pinched her lips in worry. Could she look in Delphine's warm eyes and not respond? Carson didn't know if she was that strong.

Which was one more reason why she'd taken the job in Los Angeles from Mr. Kowalski.

She hadn't yet told Blake. The right moment hadn't come up. In the past few weeks they'd reached more or less a platonic relationship while they'd worked together on the release. Yet every time they were together, they both knew that they were holding back a tidal wave of emotions. She just had to get past the release, she'd decided. Then she'd tell him.

She felt a light touch on her elbow. Turning, she saw Nate standing beside her, his eyes wide with wonder beneath his shock of blond hair. Her heart went out to her nephew. She knew that he was every bit as much affected by Delphine's accident as she was. And every bit as happy at her return.

"Nate"—she bent to his level—"are you excited?"

"When is she going to be here?"

"Soon. I just heard from Blake. Delphine arrived at the airport safely and they're on their way."

Nate rose up on his tiptoes and shook his hands, a sign of his excitement. "Aunt Carson," Nate said in a high voice, "my mama and I, and Devlin, too, we went kayaking"—he took a breath—"and saw so many dolphins. There were mamas and babies. It looked to me like they were training their babies how to fish."

"No doubt they were." Carson was delighted with his story and that he was so animated telling it. "Did they come near you?"

Nate nodded, eyes wide. "The little babies did. I think they were curious about us. But the mamas wouldn't let them near our kayaks. They just steered them clear away."

"Yep. That sounds right."

"I didn't touch them," Nate added with great import. "But they looked in my eyes and I looked right back at them. They *saw* me, Aunt Carson. I know it."

"I know they did, too. And I'm proud of you." She meant it. Her heart bloomed with love for the boy. Whether or not she ever had her own child, this boy would always be close to her heart. "Let's go tell the others that Delphine is on her way."

She and Nate walked to join the others, standing in a cluster near the dock entrance. Dora was telling her own version of the kayak trip to Granny James and Mamaw.

"Those little baby dolphins were the sweetest things, weren't they, Dev?"

"Yep. We picked up some shrimp from the dock later on and steamed 'em up and ate them straight from the shells." Devlin turned to Granny James. "Now that's what I call a perfect lowcountry summer day. I'll have to cook up a batch for you before you leave. With my special hot sauce." A mischievous twinkle was in his eyes.

"Dear man, you are a rhinestone in the rough," Granny James quipped, and he guffawed.

Carson stepped forward. "I just got word from Blake." She held up her phone.

Immediately all talking ceased and eyes were on her.

Nate heard the name Blake and came trotting over. "What? Are they here?" His hands shook wildly.

"Just about."

Looking up to the road, Carson saw the bright yellow Penske truck reaching the boat ramp. She felt her heart rate zoom and was overwhelmed with the desire to see Delphine. "Here they are!"

Everyone moved to the side as the truck turned, then began backing down the ramp, high beeps periodically piercing the silence. Finally the brake lights flickered and the engine went dead. The truck doors opened and she recognized Eric and Justin as they climbed out, wearing brown NOAA T-shirts over shorts. Blake was among them.

Blake strode toward her and the family waiting in silence. Carson thought how she'd always recognize his walk—slope shouldered, lanky, arms swinging. She straightened and brushed her hair from her face as he drew near. She knew that expression. He wasn't here to celebrate. This was serious business for him, and his focus was on Delphine.

"Okay, gang," Blake said. "Big day, right? How you doin', pal?" he asked Nate with a smile.

"Good." Nate's eyes were bright.

"You all have your assignments. Any questions? Taylor, Dev, I need you up in the truck. All we're going to do is to take hold of her in the wet transport, lift her, and put her in the sling. But she's heavy. We need all hands on deck. The rest of you, why don't you stand over there." Blake pointed to a dock that stretched out in the water. "We'll be carrying her past that dock, so you'll have a good view from there."

The group of women turned to walk off to the dock, as instructed. Dora hurried to hustle Nate away as the men retreated toward the back of the truck. Suddenly Blake turned around and walked back to Carson's side. His face softened and he reached out to touch her shoulder in reassurance. "I know you'll do great. Delphine looks real good." His eyes brightened. "She's going to be fine."

Carson met his reassuring gaze and felt her frustration melt away. "Thanks." Such a simple word to convey so much feeling.

"Okay, then." He dropped his hand. She heard the business back in his voice. "You're the water girl. The bucket is in the truck. Fill it with seawater and keep pouring it over her. We want to get her acclimated. And"—he smiled crookedly —"I know she'll want to see you."

Carson's heart filled with gratitude at his understanding of how worried she was about Delphine. He always surprised her in this way, always had her feelings in the forefront of his mind. She followed him back to the truck, focused now on the task on hand.

Blake climbed up the truck to join the other men. Carson grabbed the bucket and ran to the water to fill it and lug it back to the truck. She climbed up on the truck and moved closer to the box. A blue tarp lined the box, and over that was the sling that would carry the dolphin into the water. Leaning forward, she stopped short, overwhelmed at seeing Delphine again. She let her gaze travel over the sleek dolphin's body. The wounds from the fishing line had healed, but she could still see the multiple scars crisscrossing her beautiful gray body. Carson's eyes roved over the tip of the dorsal fin that had been lopped off by the line, the partially missing tail fluke where the shark had bitten it off. And smiling, Carson saw the dime-size hole in her right tail fluke, the one that helped identify Delphine as part of the Cove's community. Delphine lay calm, motionless, her nearly closed eyes mere slits in her head.

Blake moved aside so Carson could get closer. Pushing between him and Taylor, Carson gently poured the Cove's water over Delphine. Carson knew the moment Delphine recognized her. Her eye opened from a slit to wide and eager.

Blake tapped Carson's shoulder and she stepped aside to allow Blake back into his position at the side of the box. Time was of the essence. As she hurried off to get more water, inside the truck the men followed Blake's orders to grab the poles of the sling. Two women she'd met in the planning stages, Dr. Pat Fair of NOAA and Dr. Karen Spencer, the veterinarian, stepped forward to help. With a chorus of grunts, they all hoisted the dolphin from her wet transport berth.

"Careful now," Blake shouted as they prepared to lower her from the truck. Taylor and Eric, both big men, jumped down from the truck to grab the front handles of the sling.

Once they had Delphine out of the truck, they slowly carried her to the end of the ramp, where the water lapped up, and gently set her down. Carson ran to the plastic bucket and poured more water over Delphine, while Dr. Spencer monitored her temperature and heart rate. Blake and Dr. Fair attached a small transmitter to her dorsal fin. Dr. Fair explained how the transmitter could pick up her location from up to two miles away to help them determine how she was doing. The transmitter would fall off in less than two months.

Throughout, Carson continued to pour water from the Cove over Delphine. All the while the dolphin kept her gaze on Carson.

"She's stayed amazingly calm through all this," Dr. Fair noted. "Some of them get jumpy and anxious. Their heart rates accelerate."

Eric agreed. "She's one remarkable dolphin."

Blake caught Carson's eye and winked. They both knew Delphine was calm because of her presence.

"Let someone else get the water," Blake called out to Carson. "Stay close to Delphine so she can see you. We want to keep her calm as we move her out."

Carson promptly handed Taylor the bucket and hurried back to sit beside Delphine's head. "I'm here," she crooned, bending closer.

Delphine went still and her beautiful almond eyes gazed at her trustingly. Carson's immediate reaction was to pet her, but she stopped her hand midair. She glanced at Blake. His dark eyes were watching her. When their gazes met, he nodded, signaling her to go ahead.

For the first time in weeks, Carson felt Delphine's wet, rubbery skin under her palm. She gently stroked Delphine's head as Taylor poured water over her gleaming gray body.

"Feel the water of the Cove," Carson said softly to Delphine. "Smell the pluff mud. Hear the sounds of the birds. You're home again."

"Ready?" Blake called out.

Carson joined Blake, Devlin, and Taylor in wrapping their arms around the sleek body and slowly lifting Delphine from the sling. The ramp dropped off slowly and soon they were walking in the sandy, squishy mud of the Cove. The water was warm this late in the season, refreshing as it swirled around them. They had a ways to walk to clear the grass and the dock. Once buoyant, the dolphin felt light in Carson's arms, and she felt they were more guiding Delphine to a safe release spot than lifting her. As she walked, Carson felt Delphine's eyes on her and turned her head to meet that deep, dark gaze.

"Thank you." Carson gently stroked the dolphin's head. "Thank you for teaching me how to live." Tears streamed down her face. "Thank you for saving my life. Thank you for being my friend. Thank you."

"Okay, this is good," Blake called out when they'd passed the dock.

They stopped moving, still holding the dolphin loosely in the water. Wind splashed droplets of water on their faces. Carson remembered the day they'd carried Delphine out from the Cove. The wind had raged that morning, an angry sea pushing waves into her face, over Delphine's blowhole. This gentle spray was so different, Carson thought. Refreshing. Welcoming. This morning she shed tears of joy.

Blake called out, "On the count of three, release. Ready?"

Carson bent closer to Delphine, holding her near. She stared at the dolphin's face, her sweet, perpetual smile, committing each feature to memory. It was a bittersweet moment having to let go.

"One," called Blake. "Two."

"Good-bye," Carson whispered.

"Three."

Sequentially, they released their hold on the dolphin and stepped back, Carson last. Delphine floated in the water between them for a moment. Then, like a shot, she swam off.

Everyone cheered. From behind her, she heard Nate shouting, "Good-bye, Delphine!" Carson stared out, following Delphine's path. She was heading in the right direction, into the heart of the Cove. Then, suddenly, the dolphin turned around.

Carson saw her arching in the water, speeding back toward them. Toward her.

"Oh, no . . ."

Carson shared a quick glance of worry with Blake. They both knew that if Delphine did not swim off, if she lingered with the humans, she could be deemed nonreleasable.

Everyone on the team had silenced, watching to see what the dolphin would do.

"Don't come back," Carson murmured, hands pressed together as in prayer. "Swim away."

The dolphin swam to within fifteen feet of them, then veered off to swim in a small circle. Twice she circled. Carson watched with the others as Delphine dove back under the water. Her tail fluke waved in the air before disappearing.

"Did that dolphin just wave good-bye?" said Dr. Spencer with disbelief.

Dr. Fair smiled. "Never underestimate a dolphin."

They all continued watching to see where she'd resurface. Holding a collective breath.

"There!" Blake shouted. "At two o'clock."

In the distance, they saw Delphine leaping in the air, a spray of gray against the sky, before she disappeared again.

After a collective sigh everyone laughed, hugged, and patted backs, delighted with the successful release of another dolphin to the wild. Everyone began walking slowly back to the ramp.

Except Carson.

She stood alone, waist deep in the warm water, staring out after Delphine. She felt a hole in her heart. Letting go was harder than she'd thought it would be. She stood quietly while inside her emotions roiled, seeking one more glimpse of glistening dorsal fin arching over the dark seawater. But she saw nothing. The current ran strong, creating ripples in the water. But Delphine was gone.

"Carson?"

Carson swung around to find Blake standing beside her in the water. She studied his face, long and slender, the thick, dark brows over eyes the color of chocolate, which were searching her face with worry. Blake had come back for her. Of course he had. . . .

Carson would later blame it on the high emotions of the day, the highs and lows she'd endured the past few weeks. But seeing Delphine this morning, watching her swim off to join her family, to live her life fully, as she was meant to, brought Carson to the brink. The tide of tears that she'd been holding in erupted like a dam bursting. Carson fell into Blake's arms and released great heaving sobs and torrents of tears. Blake tightened his strong arms around her and held her close.

She heard his voice by her ear. "I know . . . it's okay." Blake held her close, bringing his lips to her forehead. "I'm here."

"I know you are," she choked out, lifting her

arms around his neck. "You're always here for me."

"Baby"—he held her tighter—"don't you know I always will be?"

She pulled away and wiped her eyes. He looked tired, his dark hair damp and askew. She saw worry etched in his brow. Love shining in his eyes. A single drop of water hung from his impossibly long lashes.

She reached up to wipe the water from his face. "I love you."

Blake's eyes flared. "I love you."

In a swoop of passion he lowered his face and kissed her. A long, unrelenting kiss that was filled with yearning and desire. One that forgave the past and promised a bright future. Carson stood waist deep in the water in Blake's arms and kissed him with all her heart, not caring who saw.

When he loosened his arms and the water flowed in the space between them, he glanced over his shoulder. People clustered at the shore, waiting for them. "We have an audience." He chuckled low.

"Let them watch." Carson stepped back and washed her face with water. "They think I'm crazy already."

"Maybe not crazy."

She slanted a look his way, daring him to continue.

"Unique. And mine."

"I'll take that."

Blake held out his hand.

Carson took it but stayed still, holding him back as he began to walk. He turned to her, his expression quizzical.

"There's something else I'd like to talk to you about. Alone."

"Sure." Again he searched her face. Then turning, he guided her through the thick, sucking pluff mud back to the ramp, where the truck was already loaded and locked and the engine was running.

Blake said farewell to his team while Carson hugged the family and told them they'd meet them at the house later. Alone, she and Blake walked to a bench along the waterway. They swept away a layer of sand and dirt and sat side by side, holding hands.

"We have our best chats on park benches," she told him.

"Except Hobbs should be here."

"How is the old dog?"

"He misses you."

"Tell him I'm getting him a big ol' chew toy."

Carson looked at their joined hands and composed herself. Then, placing her free hand on top of their joined ones, she looked up to meet his expectant gaze.

"I got a job offer."

His gaze sharpened.

"As a stills photographer for a film. In LA."

Blake went very still but his face reflected shock and confusion and, she hated to see, worry.

"But you just said . . ."

"That I love you. I do."

"Then why are you running away again?"

"I'm not running away. Not this time. I'm going *toward* something." Carson reached up to stroke away a fallen curl from his forehead. "You."

His brow was troubled. "I don't understand."

"Blake . . ." She paused, then looked into his eyes. "I'm not going to take the job. I'll be honest. When I woke up this morning, I thought I would be telling you that I was. You know I've been floundering. The miscarriage was only part of it. I've been adrift all summer. When I got the job, I was thrilled. Relieved. It's been a long time since I had any work in my field. I thought I *had* to take this job. I need it, God knows. Not only because of the money. But to rebuild my reputation. My career. My self-esteem."

"But you're not taking it?"

"No. I don't want to be alone. I'm not afraid anymore."

"What about that thing about needing to swim alone? The shark?"

"When I released Delphine, it was like once again she chased the shark away." It was one of those things Carson understood instinctively but found hard to put to words. "Today, out in the

Cove," she tried to explain, "when Delphine looked at me, I didn't see forgiveness. For her, the past was already forgotten. Delphine lives in the moment. All I saw in her eyes was love. Acceptance. And joy. She was so happy to be back home. She showed me what release meant. Watching her, I felt a release from my past. My fears."

Blake was listening, not interrupting her.

Carson smiled. "I don't want to push you away anymore. I want to stay here. With you. Where I belong."

Blake exhaled a long plume of air. He looked at her hand and played with her fingers, deep in thought. After a bit, he turned his head and looked at her. "I am glad that you got the job offer. A film. That's big."

"Yes."

"I'm proud of you."

"Thank you. I'll find something else." She smirked. "Someday."

Blake lifted his arm to lay it over her shoulder and draw her closer to his chest. "You should take the film offer."

"What? But I thought you'd be happy I'm staying."

"Of course I am. I want you to stay. But you've earned that job offer. And I think you're right. You should take it for all the reasons you listed. But . . ." he looked at her. "How long this time?"

Carson sat straight, staring back at him in earnest. "Not long. Maybe four months."

"You will come back? In four months."

She took a breath, not quite believing where this conversation was heading. "Yes. I promise. I'll rent a place by the month. Nothing permanent. Then I'll hop on a plane and come right back home. To you. If you'll wait." She paused. "Are you sure you'll wait?"

"I'll wait." A smile was in his voice even as he sighed deeply.

Carson closed her eyes. "Thank you."

"If . . ."

Her eyes flashed open and she looked at him under a raised brow. "If what?"

"If you'll marry me when you return."

"Marry you!" she exclaimed. She hadn't seen this coming. "Are you kidding?"

"Nope. I figure this is my best chance for you to say yes."

Carson stared back at him, momentarily stunned. The past summer flashed in her mind. Months of connection, of healing, and of release. Throughout the turbulent days Blake had weathered the storms, never wavering, steadfast in his love for her. This was love one could build a future on.

Her lips curved and she shrugged. "You might be right. I'd better say yes."

Blake's eyes widened as he broke into smile. "You said yes?"

"I said yes."

Blake swooped to kiss her again, sealing the promise.

She snuggled deeper in his arms, listened to his heartbeat as they held each other tight, neither wanting to let go.

Chapter Twenty-Four

"Well, that's it!" Mamaw exclaimed, clasping her hands together. "Sea Breeze is now officially yours."

Harper's chest constricted as she looked at her signature on the deed. There, on the bottom of the real estate deed, was her name written in her tight vertical script: Harper Muir-James. She'd done it. Or rather, Granny James had done it. With some careful manipulating and planning, she'd managed for Harper to buy Sea Breeze. It felt unreal. As if she were floating in some dream and someone would soon wake her up.

But it was real, she thought with amazement as she looked around in a daze at the smiling faces sitting around the long, polished dining-room table at Sea Breeze. So many people were impacted by this one decision. Taylor, of course. Carson and Blake. Dora and Devlin.

Most of all, her grandmothers. Mamaw and Granny James. She stood between them and looked from one to the other. How lucky she was to have these two remarkable women as role models in her life.

This was a shared joy. Everyone was smiling. Harper brought a trembling hand to her mouth. With one signature she'd succeeded in bringing joy to all the people she loved most in the world.

Taylor came to her side, put his hands on her shoulders, and bent to kiss her mouth. His lips were warm and firm. Possessive. "Congratulations, honey. I know this was important to you."

She looked in his eyes with a wry smile. "I know you'd be just as happy living on the *Miss Jenny.*"

"Oh, I reckon I could get used to Sea Breeze. After we're married."

The resounding sound of a champagne cork's popping drew everyone's attention.

"This is cause for celebration!" Devlin called out as he filled the glasses on the tray. The bubbles rose in the flutes and overflowed the rims.

"Good man," Granny James exclaimed.

"Careful, Dev," Dora cried, rushing to assist.

"There's plenty more where that came from," Devlin said, chuckling.

"What are you so happy about?" Carson teased him. "You lost your commission."

"You kidding?" He handed her a glass. "I live for days like this. I just gained some great new neighbors!"

Dora stepped forward to pass the tray of

champagne glasses. Taylor grabbed two and handed Harper a glass. They raised their glasses and shared a look of promise. Before she sipped, Harper caught a glimpse of Mamaw and Granny James, standing together by the silk-lined window. Mamaw was in a brilliant blue dress that matched the unmistakable blue color of her eyes. Granny James was wearing her navy suit with the crisp piping. They looked quite smart together. Quite conspiratorial, Harper thought happily as she watched them raise their glasses to each other in a silent toast, clink glasses, and, smiling, sip the champagne.

She brought her champagne flute to her lips, felt the bubbles tickle her nose, smelled the sweet, yeasty scent of it. The scent of joy and grace and celebration.

She looked at the man standing beside her, broad shouldered and as solid as the granite of his features. Her future husband. Taylor would, she knew, always stand at her side, fixed and unyielding in his love for her, in his protection of her and the children that she hoped would come. She smiled, observing his tanned skin, his pelt of brown hair, longer now and streaked by the sun. He was her lowcountry man, as much a part of this place she now called home as the salt of the air, the pungent scent of the pluff mud, the shrimp that he fished, the traditions, the values. He was her home.

As were her sisters, she thought, looking at the smiling faces of Carson and Dora.

Harper took a deep breath. She was the mistress of Sea Breeze now. She would tend the house with a loving hand, protect it from the storms that would come, plant seeds there, and watch them grow. Sea Breeze would always be a haven for her family. She would keep the light burning, as Mamaw had before her.

As she raised her glass, the room silenced. All eyes fell on her. This was her moment. "To family." Harper's voice rang clear. "To Sea Breeze."

After everyone drank the wine, Harper looked at her watch. "We need to hurry, Granny James, or you'll miss your plane!"

With the usual commotion of hugs and fare-wells, Granny James, Mamaw, and Harper hurried out to the front of the house, where a hired car was waiting with the engine running.

Granny James clasped her hands and blinked rapidly, seemingly reluctant to go. She looked at the cottage with yearning. "I should make a final walk through the cottage to make sure I have everything."

"You've already checked it twice." Mamaw linked arms with her. "If you've forgotten anything, I'll mail it to you."

"No, don't trouble yourself. I'll come back for it." Granny James gave a quick smile.

"Please do." Mamaw gave her a kiss on the

cheek, then released her arm and turned back to the house, giving Granny James and Harper a moment of privacy.

"I can never thank you enough," Harper told her, "for all you did."

"No thanks necessary. I did it simply because I love you."

"I wish my mother felt the same way."

Granny James looked into Harper's eyes with sincerity. "Georgiana does love you, as difficult as it might be to believe sometimes."

"I don't think she'll ever forgive me for buying Sea Breeze. Or you, for that matter."

Granny James released a short laugh. "Of course she will. Who else does she have to call and natter?"

"Or that I've written a novel. Do you think I should send it to her? Along with my wedding invitation?"

Granny James feigned a scolding glance. "One at a time, darling. Rome wasn't built in a day." She leaned forward to place a kiss on Harper's cheek. "I'll call her. Explain how things are. I'm her mother. I still hold some sway. Even over Georgiana."

"I'll miss you, Granny James."

"And I you." She cast a final sweeping gaze around the property. "And I shall miss Sea Breeze."

"Come back soon."

"I intend to!" Granny James said with her usual spirit. "With that strapping young man you're going to marry, I expect there will be great-grandbabies coming."

"Granny . . ." Harper laughed.

"I'm serious! I'm not getting any younger." She clapped her hands. "Chop chop!"

The following morning Harper rose from her bed and tiptoed to the sliding door that divided her room from Mamaw's. The door rattled along the frame as she pushed it open.

Mamaw was wide-awake, propped up against pillows in her enormous four-poster bed. "There you are! I was just thinking of you."

Harper felt a flutter of happiness as she scurried across the room to join her grandmother in the four-poster. Soon she was leaning against the pillows beside Mamaw. She kicked her legs under the blanket, stretching them out. This was the second time in as many weeks they'd had a private tête-à-tête. She hoped there would be many more.

Harper closed her eyes and was enveloped in a scent of exotic woods and spices, slightly oriental. "Mmm," she sighed. "I love your perfume. I always think of this as your scent. I tried it on me." She scrunched her nose. "It didn't smell at all good. It smells yummy on Carson." She sighed. "Of course."

Mamaw laughed. "Why *of course?*"

"Because she's so much like you. She's tall, beautiful . . ."

"You're every bit as beautiful. You have your own unique beauty. As does Dora. It's rather like perfume, you see. Each of you has your own distinct scent. Quality perfumes never compete."

"I don't have my own scent."

"Then let's find you one. I should think"— Mamaw tapped her cheek—"you would do well with Joy. Another French perfume, *very* good. It's sweeter, more floral, but with very deep base notes. And very fussy about who can wear it."

Harper's thoughts moved back to Carson. "She's really going to Los Angeles?"

"Yes," Mamaw said brightly without a hint of worry. "She's moving forward. This is a good thing, Harper. She has to see this cycle through. To come full circle. As you did."

"Me?" Harper asked, surprised by the comment.

"Yes. You found yourself this summer. You've written a book!"

"I have," Harper said with self-satisfaction.

"What are your plans for it?"

"First I'm going to get an agent. I know several good ones that I like very much. I'm sure they'll at least give it a read. And, hopefully, it will sell."

"Oh, it will," Mamaw said with certainty. "It's very good."

"You're my grandmother. Of course you love it."

"Not true! I wasn't a fan of your father's book. I suppose you think that's wicked for his mother to say?"

Harper shook her head. "No. Just an honest critique."

"Your book is wonderful. It will sell. You'll see. I'm never wrong about such things. And Dora is well on her way. I like Devlin. He's ever so much better than Calhoun Tucker. That man's not worth the salt in his bread."

"And Carson?"

Mamaw thought for a moment. "Carson will do just fine."

"Will she come back?"

"I hope so," Mamaw said pensively. Then she smiled. "I believe so. This is her home."

"And it's yours." Harper turned her head to look at Mamaw against the pillows. "It will always be yours. My buying Sea Breeze changes nothing."

"Why, it changes everything! This will be a family house again, with young children running through the rooms, as it was meant to be. It's time for the old to move on. To make way for the young."

Harper sat up on the bed to face Mamaw. This was too important for idle chatter. "You're not leaving Sea Breeze," she said firmly. "This is your home."

"I appreciate you saying that, but I really should give you and Taylor your space. You don't want an old woman hanging around."

"Don't be silly. Of course we do. Mamaw, you *are* Sea Breeze. Don't you know that?"

Mamaw's eyes moistened and her lips trembled with emotion. She looked at her hands in her lap. The large mine-cut diamond that had been her engagement ring shone against her pale skin. "I've made plans. . . ."

"Change them. Aren't you the one that's always telling us to welcome change? You only planned to move because you couldn't maintain Sea Breeze any longer. You don't have to. I'm here. And after we're married, Taylor will live here. Sea Breeze is in good hands. You have nothing to worry about any longer. Stay here, Mamaw. With us. Where you belong."

Her eyes were as bright as a bird's. "If I did, I can't stay in this room. It's the master bedroom. Where you and your husband should sleep."

"It will always be your room."

Mamaw shook her head firmly. "No. Not any longer. I would feel uncomfortable in here, especially after you're married. And"—a gleam of amusement brightened her blue eyes—"I've always thought your room would make the best nursery."

Harper smiled at the thought. A nursery . . . "But, Mamaw—"

"No argument about this. I'm quite firm. But . . ."

Harper leaned forward.

"Since you want me to stay, I confess, I would be very happy to. To stay at Sea Breeze would be such a comfort." A glint of coquettishness sparked in Mamaw's eyes. "And it would keep me close to Girard."

"Mamaw . . ."

"Perhaps I can suggest a compromise. I could move into the cottage."

Harper hadn't considered this possibility. In her mind, Mamaw was always ensconced in the main house. Her house. The cottage had belonged to Lucille, and Harper had assumed she would keep using it for visitors. Yet, she thought, that arrangement had a certain serendipity.

"Are you sure? I don't want you to feel you have to move out of the house."

"Quite sure. I've always doted on that cottage. Living there, I will have some degree of privacy. As will you."

"We will be nearby. And you'll join us for dinners."

"Some dinners," Mamaw replied sagely. She smiled, and her expression was contemplative.

"Then it's settled."

"If you insist." Mamaw smiled. "Now"—she clapped her hands together—"I have something I want to give you." She looked down at her hands. "I know that you love this ring." She indicated the diamond on her hand. "It's been in the family for generations. It's believed to be the ring that the Gentleman Pirate, your ancestor, gave to Claire. It's as pure a diamond as you'll ever find. Flawless." She smiled warmly at Harper. "Like you."

Mamaw slipped the ring from her finger. "Back when I'd asked all you girls to choose something you loved from Sea Breeze, I recall that this was all you wanted. As you don't have an engagement ring . . . here." She placed the ring in Harper's palm. "I want you to have it."

Harper gasped. "I couldn't. I have Sea Breeze."

"You saved Sea Breeze for all of us."

"It wouldn't be fair to the others."

"For once, Harper, think of yourself." Mamaw slipped the ring onto Harper's bare finger. The faceted diamond sparkled in the morning light.

"Do you like it?"

Harper gazed at her hand. "Oh, yes."

"Then it's yours, dear girl. With my love."

"Thank you." Harper almost squealed, flopping back against the pillows and staring at the ring on her hand with glee.

Mamaw sat back against the pillows and said with satisfaction, "No thanks necessary. Imogene and I had already discussed this."

Harper made a face and turned her head on the pillow to look at Mamaw. "Granny James will be cheesed off that you're moving into the cottage. She loves that cottage. She'll fight you for it."

Mamaw's laugh was a pure thing, as full of light and mystery as the prisms of color dancing on the walls from the diamond. "I'm counting on it!"

Chapter Twenty-Five

Carson's bags were by the front door. Beside them sat a few more boxes of Dora's belongings, ready to be carted off to her new house. It was a time of leave-takings. But tonight the women of Sea Breeze were having a farewell dinner. No boys allowed.

Mamaw strolled through the house, flicking on lights, watching the golden light spill out onto the polished floors and cast shadows on the walls. In her mind she heard the voices of the past. So many years spent in this dear house. So many memories. She meandered through the rooms, letting her fingers glide over furniture, her gaze catching a favorite painting, lampshade, figurine, as she made her way to the back porch.

She expected to find the girls sitting on the black wicker chairs, sipping drinks and chatting like magpies. They never seemed to have a shortage of things to talk about, she thought with a chuckle. Stepping out on the porch, she paused, hand on the door. Candles were glowing on the table but no one was there. Now where did they get off to?

The sound of high-pitched laughter caught her attention. Looking past the porch down to the dock, she spied the shadowy figures of three women clustered there. Laughing and talking, free as you please. Smiling, Mamaw moved to stand at the edge of the porch to watch them.

Her summer girls, she thought, her chest expanding.

Little did they know that she'd been watching them carefully all summer, as she had every summer since they were young girls. This summer especially. She watched as the women ventured out to the lower deck and slid their coltish legs into the water. Mamaw didn't know what they talked about. She didn't need to. It was enough for her to know that they shared their problems and struggles, their hopes and dreams, with each other, together under the southern stars.

Ah, girls, she thought, bringing her hand to her face. Could they ever possibly know how the sound of their laughter brought her such joy?

She used to think of her summer girls on the beach, holding hands together as they ran into the surf. Now when she thought of them together, she'd always think of them sitting on the dock, shoulder to shoulder, staring out at the Cove. As they were tonight.

Mamaw felt her heart expand to take in the panorama of another glorious sunset. Were there sunsets better anywhere else in the world? she wondered. She didn't think so. A sunset in the lowcountry was moody and sultry. The reds tinged the sky like blood after the day's battle. The golds were transcendent, settling over the horizon like hems of the angels. Some said the colors were surreal because of the gas from the detritus in the marshes. Mamaw didn't believe that. Each time she saw one, she felt it was a gift from God to his favorite children. Those he blessed to live in this paradise. The sight had the power to fill her entire soul with shimmering light and fill her with hope.

As the sky deepened, the creek wound its way through the shadowy cordgrass like a translucent snake, sleek and seductive, and full of mystery. She sniffed the air, stirred by the pungent scent of salt, fish, and that mineral-tinged, soul-sucking pluff mud.

Lifting her face to the sunset, Mamaw said a prayer of thanks as the earth hushed around her at this twilight benediction.

"Thank you, Lord, for allowing me to live another day." Then she smiled with introspection. "Another summer."

For indeed, this summer had ended. But there was no sadness here. It was the beginning of a new era. Mamaw clasped her hands together before her. There would be joy in this house again. Weddings and baptisms. Birthdays and anniversaries. And, she knew, too, funerals. She took comfort in knowing that her memory would live long and as teeming with life as these winding creeks in the minds and hearts of Dora, Carson, and Harper. Her family, she knew, was the greatest treasure she could leave behind.

But today was for the living!

Loud laughter and squeals brought her attention back to the dock. She squinted in the dimming light. The three women were scuttling down to the lower dock, laughing. Eudora, Carson, and Harper. For all his capricious ideas, Parker had been wise to name his daughters after great literary figures. It gave them each something to live up to. And in her book, her granddaughters were her heroines. She'd never known women with more heart. Or who understood more fully where their home was.

She watched as they stood together at the edge of the dock, holding hands, a lowcountry sunset before them. Mamaw's breath held, knowing she'd keep this image in her heart forever. Then, with a joyous shout, the girls leaped together into the Cove.

Mama's laughter joined theirs to be carried off on a breeze and join the universe.

"We did it, Lucille. Our summer's work is done."

Suddenly she felt young again, free of her burdens. Like the young girl she once was who

Acknowledgments

At the close of the Lowcountry Summer trilogy, I thank again Dr. Pat Fair at NOAA for her continued mentorship on all things related to the Atlantic bottlenose dolphin. Thanks, too, for reading the manuscript for accuracy, for brainstorming possibilities, and especially for the incredible experience of monitoring the health of the Charleston resident dolphins. That final scene with Delphine was inspired by that glorious release into the Charleston estuarine waters.

Heartfelt thanks to my wonderful home team: Angela May, Kathie Bennett, Buzzy Porter, and Lisa Minnick for your unflagging support. And to my sisters: Marguerite Martino for talking through characters, James Cryns and Marjory Wentworth for guiding the poem, and Ruth Cryns for being the Thelma to my Louise. Love and thanks to the Gems for their inspiration: Leah Greenberg, Linda Plunkett, Emily Abedon, and Susan Romaine.

A special thanks to everyone at the South Carolina Aquarium. Your staunch support is always deeply appreciated. And especially for the glorious launch party for this book. I can't thank you enough.

Thanks as well as to all my friends and to the

beloved dolphins at the Dolphin Research Center, Florida—especially Tursi, Jax, and Rainbow, my inspirations. I'm proud to be associated with you.

I'm fortunate to have the brilliant support of the fabulous team at Gallery Books: Lauren McKenna, Louise Burke, Jennifer Bergstrom, Jen Long, Liz Psaltis, Jean Anne Rose, Elana Cohen, Diana Velazquez, and everyone who supported this trilogy. A special thanks to my agents at Trident Media Group: the incomparable Kimberly Whalen and Robert Gottlieb, Sylvie Rosokoff, Adrienne Lombardo, Laura Paverman, and Tara Carberry. And to Joseph Veltre at Gersh.

A special nod of thanks to Judy Fairchild at Dewees Island, Shane and Morgan Ziegler at Barrier Island Eco Tours, and Amy Sottile at Wild Dunes.

As always, I close with thanks to Markus. Keep the light on.

Readers Group Guide

The
Summer's
End

MARY ALICE MONROE

Introduction

In *The Summer's End*, the third installment in Mary Alice Monroe's Lowcountry Summer trilogy, a remarkable summer is coming to an end and the women of Sea Breeze struggle with impending decisions. Harper blossoms over the summer in the natural rhythms of the island, quietly exploring secret ambitions. When an unlikely stranger knocks on her door, she opens to the possibility of love and searches deep to find the strength to decide her own life's course. Dora struggles to find the balance between her newfound independence, her son's needs, and the attentions of one very dedicated suitor; and Carson is faced with a tragedy that threatens to upend everything she's worked hard to achieve. The summer girls are adrift but Mamaw, usually their guiding force, mourns the loss of her dear, longtime friend Lucille.

Looming over them is the impending sale of the beloved Muir family home. The "Summer Girls" are poised for leaving. As the season changes, the sisters draw on the wisdom of their grandmothers, their abiding love for one another—and some much-needed inspiration from a beguiling dolphin—to weather the shifting tides. Together they embrace how lives can change over one magical summer.

Discussion Questions

1. The book opens with the ladies of Sea Breeze mourning the loss of Lucille, whose presence is felt throughout the book despite her literal absence. How does the loss of Lucille lead the ladies to the next step in their lives?

2. Harper's core issue is her relationship with her mother, Georgiana James. Her mother is controlling over Harper's career and her personal life. Harper questions the existence of a mother's "unconditional love." What are your thoughts about Georgiana's mothering? Is there any justification for her behavior? Do you believe in unconditional love?

3. While in the attic, Harper finds the trunk Mamaw gave to her and her sisters to store their treasures at the end of their childhood summers. Do you think the girls have changed much over the years? If you were to go through a box of treasures from your past, what might you find?

4. "What a wonderful book!" (p. 169) is how Mamaw responded when young Harper presented her with a story she'd written and

illustrated herself. Why do you think that positive reinforcement was not enough for Harper to overcome Georgiana's criticism of her daughter's writing?

5. Harper claims that Carson is jealous of her family wealth. Do you think that is all there is to it? Does Harper do anything to invite Carson's jealousy? There is often wealth disparity in families. Discuss possible ways for families to adjust.

6. Harper and Taylor decide to get engaged after only a few weeks together. Are you surprised at the speed of this decision? Do you know of anyone who married quickly? What do you think it is about Harper and Taylor that instantly drew them together? Do you believe in love at first sight?

7. Carson agrees to take the film job in California at Blake's urging, and promises to return. Theirs has been a turbulent relationship. Do you agree with that decision? Do you think Carson is equipped for this new phase of her life? Are you optimistic about her future well-being or their relationship?

8. Compare and contrast Mamaw, from the South, and Granny James, from England, and their reactions to Harper's engagement. Do

you agree with their responses? Why or why not? Finally, at the book's end was there a "winner" to the tally of arguments, as Carson quipped?

9. Mamaw tells Carson, "The secret to happiness is to embrace the humility to accept what comes and the courage to continue on your life's path with an open heart." Compare this with what Carson told Blake, ". . . when Delphine looked at me, I didn't see forgiveness. For her, the past was already forgotten. Delphine lives in the moment. All I saw in her eyes was love. Acceptance. And joy. She was so happy to be back home. She showed me what release meant."

10. Discuss who changes the most from the beginning to the end of the trilogy—*The Summer Girls*, *The Summer Wind*, and *The Summer's End*. Who has made the toughest decisions? Which character did you relate to the most and why? Where do you see these characters in a few years?

11. Throughout the trilogy the reader has journeyed with the dolphin Delphine, through connection, injury and healing, and finally release. Discuss how the story of the dolphin parallels the three novels in the trilogy.

12. While cleaning Lucille's cottage, medicine bottles were collected in a box to take to the pharmacy for disposal. Blake had told Carson how damaging it was to the local water quality for people to toss their unused medicines into the toilet. The medicine is not completely filtered out in the water filtration plant. This pollution is one of the reasons dolphins are getting sick in the wild. Discuss where you can safely take unused medicine in your community.

13. Discuss how dolphins are a sentinel species. As mammals, they are our siblings in the sea. What does it mean to the human population if dolphins are getting sick?

Center Point Large Print
600 Brooks Road / PO Box 1
Thorndike, ME 04986-0001 USA

(207) 568-3717

US & Canada:
1 800 929-9108
www.centerpointlargeprint.com